PRAISE FOR JENN LEES' ARLAN'S PLEDGE SERIES

'Incorporating rich Scottish lore in a fantastical land, the story of Arlan and Rhiannon comes alive in a fast-paced tale of love and fate. Full of twists and turns, nothing is as it seems as we pass through the portal into the world of Dál Cruinne. The magic, captivating and bold, swept me away into this world of mages and dragons. But the real magic is between the star-crossed lovers. I was completely enthralled by this masterfully written story.'

SL Dooley, *author of bestselling Portal Slayer series and the award winning duology The Summertime Circus (Bookfest 2023 Christian Fantasy) and The Cold Moon Carnival (Bookfest 2024) (Anatolian Press).*

'Everything about this novel is captivating, from the world-building all the way to the enticingly romantic love story that readers feel is unfolding directly in front of them...This novel makes readers want to hold on to the world and clutch every page until the end, simply because it's that good'. **Austen Grace** *InD'tale Magazine*

'Lees, a masterful storyteller, wove her own peculiar magic through a rich brocade of description and imagination to create believable reality drawn from the misty past of the Scottish Highlands.' *Fantasy Author* **Elizabeth Klein.**

'The Crossing (re-released as *Of Myths and Portals*) is an exciting story that mixes authentic historical aspects with those of an amazingly created magical world. The level of world-building that Jenn Lees has put into her world is comparable to many fantasy classics.' **Tawny Moliner** *Reedsy Reviewer.*

'Arlan's Pledge, Jenn Lees weaves two worlds and many characters into this uniquely Celtic portal fantasy.' *Lorehaven Magazine*

The Crossing: Arlan's Pledge Book One (manuscript) achieved Finalist in 2021 OZMA Fantasy Fiction Awards CIBAs (Chanticleer International Book Awards). Manuscript republished as *Of Myths and Portals: Arlan's Pledge Book One* (2024).

Of Myths and Portals

Arlan's Pledge

BOOK ONE

JENN LEES

OF MYTHS AND PORTALS

ARLAN'S PLEDGE BOOK ONE

Cover by Fiona Jayde Media

www.fionajaydemedia.com

Map by J I Rogers, Mythspinner Studios

www.mythspinnerstudios.com

Previously published as:

To our youngest daughter, Emma.
Of all my imaginings and creations, you are one most wonderful.

May you be a strong warrior in the fight,
Your hall ring with songs of triumph,
And on the gentle breeze
May you hear the voice of Love unseen.

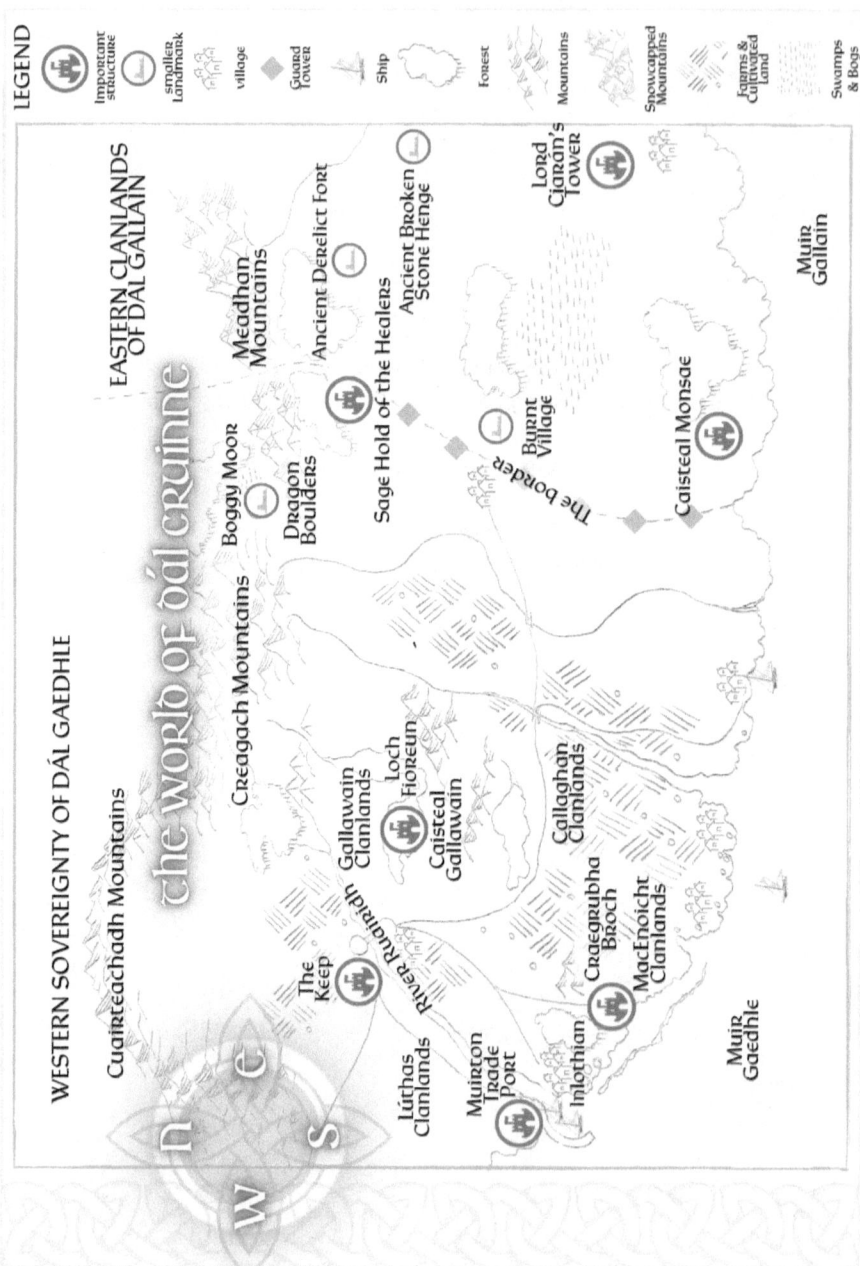

the world of Dál Cruinne

WESTERN SOVEREIGNTY OF DÁL GAEDHLE

EASTERN CLANLANDS
OF DÁL GALLAIN

Cuairteáchadh Mountains

Creagach Mountains

Meadhan
Mountains

Boggy Moor

Dragon
Boulders

Ancient Derelict Fort

Sage Hold of the Healers

Ancient Broken
Stone Henge

Lord
Ciarán's
Tower

The border

Burnt
Village

Muir
Gallain

Caisteal Monsae

Loch
Fioreun

Gallawain
Clanlands

Caisteal
Gallawain

Callaghan
Clanlands

The
Keep

River Ruaidhri

Craegrubha
Broch

MacEnoicht
Clanlands

Lúthas
Clanlands

Muirton
Trade
Port

Inlorthian

Muir
Gaedhle

N
E
S
W

LEGEND

🏰	Important structure
🏠	smaller Landmark
🏘️	Village
♦	Guard Tower
⛵	Ship
🌳	Forest
⛰️	Mountains
🏔️	Snowcapped Mountains
	Farms & Cultivated Land
	Swamps & Bogs

CONTENTS

Both clan chief and king gone mad with power's greed.
Mages with ambition'd magic consumed.
Once formidable, wild, and free
Dragon beasts now bent to the will of men.
Dál Cruinne in devastation wrought—
The world unmade.
Henceforth, our chronology by these historic events
Marked, measured, and maintained.
Let each year proclaim a span of time
Stretching forth from our decimation.
Never may the ways of men return to such disgrace and ignominy.

Declaration of the Sàsaichean, Sage Council,
Post Dragon Wars Year 0

PROLOGUE

Let it be known, in this the third year of my reign as Àrd Rìgh of the Sovereignty of Dál Gaedhle, the four disgraced clan lords now proven to conspire against my rule, be stripped of lands, titles and inheritances, rights and fealty owed, and hitherto be banished from Dál Gaedhle, never to show their faces nor cross our borders on pain of death.

SIGNED BY DONNACH FINNBAR MACENOICHT
ÀRD RÌGH OF THE SOVEREIGNTY OF DÁL GAEDHLE
6053 POST DRAGON WARS

The World of Dál Cruinne
Post Dragon Wars Year 6053
The Border between the Western Sovereignty of Dál Gaedhle and the Eastern Clanlands of Dál Gallain

Now he was free.

Ciarán rode past the derelict border-fort tower where Dál Gaedhle became Dál Gallain. The wooden wall, long rotted, stretched between squat rough-cut sandstone fortifications dotted along the borderline for the length of the land. If his gaze could reach its end, he would spy the Muir Gallain, the great sea of the south. The guards who had travelled with him stayed back, their mounts tossing manes and jangling tack. The horses reflected their riders' wishes to be away, no doubt. Aye, eager to leave but requiring certainty of his departure.

Ciarán's mount slowed and picked his way through the broken cut stone and rubble strewn across the path between two ivy-covered fort towers as the rumble of hooves receded behind him.

Good. Donnach MacEnoicht's obedient escorts had done their high king's bidding and turned for home.

The warrior-clansman escort had returned to him his sheathed sword, its baldric's smooth leather belt wrapped round it tight, addressing him only as Ciarán Gallawain.

Ciarán ground his teeth. Never again would a soul address him by his clan chief title of *lord*. Neither would he feel beneath his fingertips the patterned surface of his highly decorated chieftain's belt about his waist. The weight of his sword, Dearg, now pressed down on his back. That insipid àrd rìgh could choke on his mercy, for it only displayed his weakness.

Aye, one day my sword will draw blood and redden the ground at Donnach's feet.

Ciarán kicked his horse to a gallop. He could not hasten from the border fast enough. Huffing, he pushed further southeast, urging his horse on, leaving Dál Gaedhle... and Alana... well behind.

He swallowed hard against the thickness that threatened to line his throat. Best to leave those thoughts alone. *What's done is...*

Grey clouds churned beneath the sun, and the day dulled around him. His legs were heavy from this past week's ride, as if rocks filled his muscles. Cold rain beat hard on his forehead, running over his jaw and trickling down his chest beneath his fine wool shirt. Weak sunlight angled through the tree foliage, edging the leaves of the forest in silver. Dense undergrowth slowed his pace and encroached on the road now turning into a goat-track.

Narrowing his eyes and sharpening his focus in the dimming surrounds, he dismounted and led his steed at a walk, swiping branches to the side to clear a path. Sprays of water droplets wet his breeches and soaked his plaid. The cold seeped through chilling his skin and burrowing deeper. He must rid himself of the cloth, though he was loath to—the last remnant of his connection to any clan. Even so, some in the east might recognise the tartan of a noble clan of the west.

He could take no chances.

A dim glow showed through the thicket like a beacon. He headed for it, leading his horse through the edge of the forest, which stood like a wall around a small dwelling in the middle of a clearing covered in night. Light shone in the window of the wattle-and-daube cottage—the home of a commoner, and a poor one at that—and smoke rose from its primitive stone chimney. He tied his mount to a nearby post and stood at the wooden door above which hung clumps of rowan, ash and heather—and a shrivelled raven's foot.

He grunted and lifted his baldric from his shoulder and strapped the belt around his waist. His blade must be ever ready.

He raised a fist to the door. It swung open, his knuckles hitting air. A hag with long silver hair matted to knots and hanging over humped shoulders, stood in the doorway. Her face, as crinkled as summer-dried fruit, opened to a toothless maw. Her breath wafted to him—vomit, rotted meat and the reeking pile of excrement at the bottom of the long-drop of The Keep on a sweltering day. His throat tightened, threatening a gag, but he swallowed against it.

"Come, young man, ye have wandered far." The crone's head bobbed her welcome.

He lowered his fist slowly. The crone seemed harmless enough, and with no other dwellings nearby—and the gnawing in his belly—he stepped in. A fire filled the hearth, its heat bathing his face and raising vapour from his clothing.

Her withered fingers drew the length of plaid from his shoulders. Strands of his long hair dragged with the woollen cloth, flicking his cheek. "Ye have the fair hair of a noble clan, young man."

Ciarán stiffened. "Ye are bold, old woman." Taking a step back, he drew his sword, its ring filling the tiny dwelling.

"I meant nae harm, my lord." She dipped a shaky bow then lifted her head, her gnarled hands caressing his tartan clasped to her breast and her eyes glimmered. "Just wishing to show kindness to a weary traveller, is all."

The woman stood by the rough-hewn wooden table sitting in the centre of the room, illuminated by squat candles placed on any available flat surface, their melted wax leaving deformed sculptures in their path. Far, indeed, were the comforts of a caisteal. Yet warmth seeped through his damp clothing, chasing away the chill. A pot bubbled over the coals, the aroma more palatable than the woman's breath.

Her gaze followed his. "Ye will be hungry, my lord."

She draped his plaid over the chair nearest the hearth, then ladled broth into a wooden bowl and placed it on the table. His stomach growled.

Ciarán re-sheathed his sword and approached the chair, never lifting his gaze from the old crone. She was familiar. Not in physique, but in spirit.

I... have... known this *before.*

Ciarán sat on the creaking chair and, steadying himself, poked the contents of the bowl with a wooden spoon. Sparse chunks of meat floated in the thin brown liquid.

He ate, the gamey flavour of rabbit scarce throughout the soup, and let his gaze wander the one-roomed dwelling. Herbs hung to dry above the grey stone fireplace. Cooking pots of assorted sizes sat stacked on the hearth and next to them, a neat pile of firewood.

"Ye should go further east tomorrow when ye resume your travel, my Lord Ciarán Gallawain."

He stopped the spoon inches from his mouth, sloshing out the contents with a jerking halt.

By the antlers of Cernunnos! His plan of wandering through the land incognito was now impossible if even *this* isolated old hag had recognised him. He returned the spoon to the soup and scooped once more, narrowing his eyelids.

But how does she know?

The woman stood with her green eyes fixed on his, and the back of his neck prickled.

"Ye must go to where ye find the ends of the world." A tremor to her tilted head accompanied the instructions. "That is the way to the one who truly possesses the power." Crinkled hands rested on the tabletop; on their backs thin translucent skin revealed a river delta of veins. "Ye will receive more than you first perceive, for ye have tae trust *Cumhachd adhar.*"

Ciarán's brow tightened. The hag had spoken the old tongue, and he had heard the name—a long time ago. *The Power of the Air.*

He tightened his grip on the spoon, digging the handle into his palm as his heart leaped within his chest. He required power to gain what, in truth, belonged to him.

He lifted his chin. *I, Ciarán Gallawain, was born to rule.*

His wet-nurse had spoken often of his destiny. He saw it now, as vivid to him as his present surroundings—she stood by the great fireplace in the caisteal of his birth, chanting to herself and pricking his finger then flicking his blood into the hissing flames.

Bile rose in the back of his mouth and burned. For he was now a wandering exile and coming second to Donnach MacEnoicht in *Töireadh*—the Quest for the High Kingship—had thwarted all. A dull, thick sensation returned to his belly, like a pot of stew set on low coals, brewing slow and long since losing his love, his quest and his dignity. The grumble in his gut had been an intimate friend for three years, and now he would name it—resentment, and he would suppress it no longer.

His life had changed indeed. He must start from naught wherever he landed, and much hard work lay ahead.

"I have a word for you, Lord Ciarán Gallawain."

His vision refocused and the woman's gnarled hands came back into view, the river delta melting to smooth youthful skin.

His gaze rose to hers. She stood taller, a whispering caress of cloth slipping over skin accompanied her patched garment's slide to the floor. Transformed, a shining mane of golden curls cascaded across smooth skin, pouring over perfect breasts on its path to curved hips.

Ciarán gasped. *A mage disguised as a crone—that explains all.*

The sudden appearance of her home, her knowledge of him, and her enigmatic advice.

The mage raised slender youthful arms above her head and the hearth's blaze lit the room in an orange glow. She lifted her hands higher, as if in supplication, while candles blazed as bright as lightning. A stunning younger version of those green eyes locked with his, and he sat, unable to move.

"When sunlight bids farewell to day
Or with morning tide enlightens,
A crossing to other worlds at bay
With magicked power opens.
Then shuts the gates for those to stay
Until the orb-illumined run
Its courses of the worlds then done.
Where light caresses land as one
There, travellers' journeys fill their sum."

The air rang with her rich voice, her tone holding the glimmer of a chant, verging on a wail.

Ciarán's thundering pulse joined the candled-lightning of the room and his breathing staggered with a heaviness pressing on his shoulders, as if the eyes of the universe weighted their stare upon him.

The mage's arms slowly lowered, her youthful form retained, and her lips curving.

She spoke a riddle. A conundrum. A challenge... A command.

Power lay behind it, whatever it may be. And this striking beauty before him a messenger only.

He shook the weight from his shoulders and, rising to his full height, stepped to the mage, his face now inches from her delicate lips and her apple-scented breath invading his own.

"Where is this place? I will find it." He blinked at the earnestness of his own voice.

"Not one but many, my Lord Ciarán."

His breath caught. Here was his new start. His chance to begin afresh.

But to have it—a chance I must take.

"So be it." A heat ignited within him, as sparks ran to his fists and swirled in his mind. "Tell your master I wish to enjoin my goals with his."

"Nae, my Lord Ciarán Gallawain, for ye yourself shall inform him."

ONE

—·—

The lines of the endless knot represent time and eternity,
Weaving around, over, and under.
Such as the lives of those with whom we pass through time.

SAGE GLIOCAS
(2870-2962 POST DRAGON WARS)

Our World, 2016
Perth, Scotland

My life had changed.

I was at work, placing newly delivered novels into their assigned positions on the Top Ten Best Sellers stand, my thoughts wandering. The Last Chance Bookshop—aptly named by Mr Watson, my elderly boss who maintained it to be the last opportunity to purchase a book before leaving Perth, the Gateway to the Highlands—was quite a come down from the Main Library of Edinburgh University. Budget cuts had come, along with a last-in-first-out policy, losing me my dream job and giving me little choice if I wanted a position involving books.

For me, it was rent money and food on my table, and possibly my last chance at stable employment as the state of the UK economy remained tight. Mr Watson was great, but my love of all things library now had to wait until... who knows when. I was wandering, with failure hovering over my shoulder, living a second-rate life, and just like most times of uncertainty, with aspirations on hold, my insecurities clambered for attention.

But I yearned for that instance in life—the critical moment—that would tell me who I was. Who I really am in this big world.

Man, I was in my twenties already! You'd think I'd know by now.

"Rhiannon, I must leave a tad early." Mr Watson's salt-and-pepper moustache danced above his lips. His coat hung over his arm held against a stout midriff. "You don't mind manning the shop on your own after lunch, do you?"

"Of course not, Mr Watson." I smiled at my boss, warmth welling within at his willingness to take me on—and his trust in me.

"See you tomorrow, then." He turned on his heels and left the shop.

The opening and closing of the Last Chance Book Shop's door were like parentheses to the blaring horns and revving double-decker bus engines of the High Street. Diesel fumes wafted in through the dull glare.

"Excuse me," a feminine voice huffed behind me. "I'm after a romance."

I turned to the woman. She wore a cream tailored suit and immaculate make-up. My teeth tugged at my inner cheek, and I flinched a little at the pinch.

If only I could master the art of makeup.

"Of course." I strode the short distance to the far end of the store, passing through the scent of freshly printed books, a thrill tingling my spine. The customer followed, her high heels clicking on the vinyl floor. We passed shelves chock-full of paperbacks, front covers facing us, eager to please and be the novel to stand out amongst the rest and win the prize of being her choice.

"Here's one by a Scottish author. It's set in the times when the Romans were conquering Britain and tried to subdue the Picts and Celts who lived in the north." I pulled the book from the shelf, its smooth cover cool under my fingertips, then held it out for the customer's perusal, my heart drumming in my chest. "A Celtic clan war chief falls for a..."

The young woman stared at the novel's front cover, her nose crinkling, and her tongue protruding from flawless painted lips. Her shoulders shook, and her face erupted with laughter.

"You're kidding, right?" An immaculately plucked eyebrow rose.

My fingers froze around the paperback. I forced my arms to move and replaced the book on the wooden shelf, then guided the woman to the Top Ten Best Sellers stand near the front of the shop where a romance novel sat at the number three position, gleaming under the fluorescent lighting. I lifted the book from the display, my fingers grasping the cover comprising a barely clad muscular male torso. The woman's eyes lit up and she bought the novel, then swiftly left, closing the door behind her.

The doorbell *pinged* with her exit, echoing in the empty shop. I brushed down my plain grey skirt and checked my blouse. The top button kept coming open unbidden.

Stupid button!

I grabbed a strand of my hair—loose from its tie again—and twirled it around my index finger. Why did I never look neat and immaculate, like the woman who'd just left the shop?

Her impression of me hung like a fog, poking me with misty fingers. She was the third person to show an aversion to this book.

"Hmph!" I marched back to the shelf, grabbed the book, and stomped to the front of the shop. "Well, it's pay week, and a love story set when the Celts kept the Romans at bay would be on *my* to read list!" My voice bounced off the counter as I shoved the book underneath.

I stormed back to the bookcase and bumped a thriller onto the shelf, then slammed a non-fiction self-help into its neighbour. I grabbed yet another novel with a cover of a half-naked man and *thunked* it face down. Thudding books on wooden shelves echoing in the quiet shop formed sound exclamation marks that hung in the air around me.

I shut the shop for a late lunch, then strode along Perth's High Street. The sun warmed my head as I hurried along to the South Inch to eat my sandwich in the parklands. I bet the strands of hair escaping from my hair-tie stuck out as a frizz, but the sunshine was worth it. The South Inch, a beautiful expanse of green dotted with garden beds and playgrounds mirroring the North Inch on the opposite side of Perth, ran alongside the River Tay.

Today I needed green. It always soothed me.

Because it just happened again.

My throat felt as if it was falling into my stomach. Always did after a person's negative reaction to a comment I'd made. Someone like *that* lady customer. It'd always been like this.

"Why do I bother being so enthusiastic about things when people look at me as if I'm... odd?" It seemed, once more, my likes and preferences were in the minority. The small minority.

"Why is nobody interested in the things I'm interested in?" My comments grew louder, my pace matching in momentum. "Or *anything* I'm drawn to?"

I screwed my mouth to the side.

Maybe they're right.

I *hmphed,* but it choked off.

I reached the Inch, and slowed my pace, walking the path snaking through and passing the rhododendrons growing in the beds at the edge of the swathe of green. They were in flower, and their purple blooms caught my eye—and mocked me. According to Mum, my mauve eyes were like the actress Elizabeth Somebody-or-Other's. *Another* thing about me that was different.

Mum had always maintained I was too self-conscious. *Hmm.*

For a moment I was back in primary school when the boys joined in with the mean girls' mocking rhyme, their chanting ringing in my ears as I folded in on myself and hugged tight.

"Rhiannon with the purple eyes,
Looks right through you to the skies.
Where o where has she been?
She thinks she is a royal queen."

I chewed my lip. Thankfully, I hadn't done that for a while: stared into space watching people who weren't there, doing things in places I'd never been.

Mum used to say I would go off in my *own wee world* and she would shake me out of *staring into nothing.* In my teens, I'd discovered they were *visions.* Well, that's what an old aunt from the Highlands had said. Not to me. I'd been eaves dropping on a conversation she'd had with Mum about the *second sight*. Then I'd done a little googling of my own.

I'd never told Mum.

Or anyone else.

My eyes pricked with tears, so I shook my head and focused back on the Inch.

The park was quiet today. Not far ahead of me walked a man, the only other person on this side of the green. He walked slightly stooped and carried a bundle of books and papers under one arm. His tweed jacket had leather patches on the elbows like a previous professor of mine had worn. He'd tied his long white hair behind in a ponytail. He must've been a pretty cool old guy.

He passed one of the public seats and his pace slowed. Then he stumbled, dropping his books and papers, the breeze picking up loose pages and spreading them across the grass toward the nearest seat. He staggered, jolting, and headed face first onto the hard asphalt path.

I ran the few paces to reach him just as his hand extended to brace himself and prevent a face-plant. I grabbed his arm and pulled him upright. He regained his balance, but his eyes were wide, and his breath rapid.

"You okay?" I asked, trying not to sound puffed after my brief exertion.

He peered at me, his eyes growing even wider, with his crinkled expression tight around his mouth as he focused on my face. His arm was thin beneath my grasp and he straightened with a lot of effort.

"Let's get you on this seat over here." I led him to the wooden park bench nearby and sat him down.

He still made hard work of his breathing, but he didn't take his eyes off me. A waft of muted spices filtered from him, overpowering the sharp mustiness of his tweed jacket.

"I'll call an ambulance." I dug into my pocket for my phone.

He placed a cool hand on mine. "No, young lady." His voice was surprisingly deep and resonant. "I shall be well in but a moment. No need to call a heal—*ambulance*." He pronounced the word with care. He spoke in strongly accented English. *Maybe he's Welsh.*

"I'll sit with you until you're better." I kept my hand in the crook of his arm.

It had been ages since I'd sat beside a person so much older than myself. I chuckled inwardly. Here I was thinking I'd have a quiet lunch. In an odd sort of way, his presence had a calming effect on me. My inner churns about myself were settling.

The wind tugged at my hair. "Oh, your books. I'll get them."

I ran after the papers that had scattered and stuck on a nearby rosebush at the edge of a garden bed, which was an explosion of yellow and orange. On my way back to the old man, I collected the books, keeping an eye on him. He now sat tall, his gaze on me, and his face filled with a kindly expression. He breathed easier now. Pulling a handkerchief from his waistcoat pocket, he wiped his mouth. He was clean shaven and quite dignified looking from this angle, and probably would've had some important position in a university somewhere. Despite almost falling head first, his composure had quickly returned. The breeze ruffled the papers I held, but the whirlwind of emotions that had swirled in me on my way to the Inch had blown away.

"Are you feeling better?" I asked, handing him his books and papers.

"Ah, perhaps." He placed the books beside him.

The one sitting on top of the bundle had a shiny dust jacket. On the cover, a circular broach inlaid with bronze swirled round and around. Dogs, similar to Scottish deer hounds, intertwined their legs within the circles. The symmetry and craftsmanship were perfect. It was a book on Celtic art, and I let go a slow sigh.

The Celts *really* understood beauty. Maybe he lectured on Celtic subjects and I could learn something from him.

"Perhaps I'd better stay until you're fully okay." I sat beside the books. "You're interested in Celtic art?"

"Oh, aye." His voice held a gentle edge as he spoke through a couple of breaths.

If only my attempts at drawing knots came anywhere near such intricacy as that on the cover of the book resting between us on the bench seat. My early circular knotwork doodles were in my secret scrapbook. I'd shown them to Michelle Stone in high school when, on that rare occasion I'd had a friend to stay, she'd slept over. I suppressed a cringe. *Fool!* After that, the popular girls had laughed at me—laughed at everything Michelle had pretended to enjoy while staying that night at our place.

I swallowed the hard lump in my throat.

I hadn't touched my drawings since.

"My name is Eif... er... Evan." His voice brushed away my recollections of the past. Definitely a Welsh-sounding accent—he'd said *Evan* the way they do.

"I'm Rhiannon. Are you a professor?"

"Nae. But some say I am learned. And maybe even wise." His smile crinkled his face further, and he let out a breathy, staggered chuckle.

So, possibly the only *other* person in the world who held Celtic knotwork in fascination was an unwell old man. *Argh.*

"You're a good lass. I'm sure your parents are proud of you."

I fiddled with my bag resting in my lap as a tightness flashed across my chest. "My parents are no longer living."

"Ah, so sorry to hear that. Your man would be proud, then."

My man? I gave a snort, covering my mouth with my hand. *If only.*

Well, there was George. He seemed to think I was okay. He'd been around since university and I had to admit he was a good friend, but that was all. My guts niggled. George's understanding of the relationship wasn't too clear.

The breeze blew through my silence, brushing stray strands of hair across my face. The old man focused his warm gaze on me, as he breathed calmly. He inclined his head, waiting for me to respond.

"There's sort of someone..." Why had I said that? But then my shoulders eased. It wasn't often I had someone around who *actually* listened to me.

"Ye hesitate. He is not...?" Tough white eyebrows rose slowly.

I skewed my mouth to the side. "No. He isn't."

"Be not in a hurry." His voice was stronger now that he'd regained his breath. Like a boom muffled. As though if he let it go, it would be commanding. "It is best to know yourself before ye seek to know another."

Know myself?

Who am *I, anyway?*

"We are all in the process of becoming who we are." He patted my hand then gathered his books and papers.

I blinked. *Did he just...?*

"I am well now." He rose from the park bench.

"Are you sure?" I stood with him. "But you've only just got your breath back."

"Aye. Many thanks for your assistance. It was not what I expected of this world"—he coughed over his words— "part of the country." He looked me in the eye, then smiled and marched away, his books tucked under his arm and a spring in his step.

I parked my car at the front of my cottage in the small village of Abernethy and stepped out, inhaling the cool country air. A faint scent of lanolin wafted over to me from the sheep in the field across the road, their bodies now small, spindly, and white without their wool. The farmer must've shorn them today. On the slope of the hill opposite, the trees wore leaves turning russet orange and at its peak, the Iron Age Fortification's earthworks were now a silhouette with the sun's descent dimming the evening sky.

I walked up my flagstone path; echinacea, dahlias and the last of the pinks edged the way to my door. I rummaged in my bag for the door key, my calves brushing the lavender, its calming aroma pervading the final paces of my journey. I sniffed and filled my head with its scent.

I rented a cute cottage, with white-washed stone, a grey slate roof, and large double-glazed windows. I'd often sit at my two-seater kitchen table and gaze up at the remains of the Iron Age Fort's earthworks, and my insides would tingle. That had been the tipping point. Why I took on the lease.

Plenty of space surrounded the cottage with the field at the back, and a run-down animal shelter sitting by the far fence, so neighbours weren't on the doorstep. Quiet and private, except for the guy who lived in the semi-detached on the left and shouted at his wife. I huffed. He still objected to where I placed my rubbish bin. But I had no other option. *That* argument continued to linger. For the sake of his wife, who'd probably get it in the neck if I argued with the man, I held my peace.

I stepped through the door and over the pile of bills lying on the doormat. This renovated estate worker's cottage was compact and bijou, to say the least. I immediately entered my kitchenette. It had only enough bench space for the usual appliances, then three paces in, and a person was through to the main room.

I dropped onto the beat-up couch in the living room and groaned. It was grey, along with the rug on the floor and the open stone fireplace. The cottage had come furnished, and the landlady's tastes were eclectic. A busy pattern covered the wallpaper, and none of the pieces of furniture matched. A large flat-screen television hung on the main wall, covering most of the brown and yellow paisley.

Thankfully.

The couch had a dent in the seat from the posterior of a previous tenant, I suppose. No visitors had graced my humble abode. I preferred it that way. People only laughed at me anyway.

No people, no laughter. No...

Pursing my lips and blowing out to ease my tightening chest, I raised my hand to twiddle a lock of hair.

My phone rang and the living room's brown and yellow came back into a bleary focus. I wiped my eyes with the back of my hand then found my phone at the bottom of my bag. It was George, and I slid to answer.

"We still on for tomorrow?" George's enthusiastic-as-ever tones blared out from my phone.

"Ah, that's *this* Saturday?" My gut tightened.

"Yes. I'll catch the last train from Oxford tonight." George's refined accent came through. "Got the last tweaks of the proposal for my research on the migration of the Gaelic language through the lands of the ancient Picts to finish first. I'll be in Perth early morning. Don't worry, I'll make my way out to you. Can't wait to see your place for real. I looked it up on Google Maps. I'd love to stick around for the entire weekend."

"Okay." I fought to keep my inflection steady. "We can work on my Goidelic."

That'll be the most interesting thing to happen this weekend.

"Ha! You need all the help you can get. Your accent when you speak that ancient language is atrocious."

"I don't understand how you know what a dead language sounds like," I said, shaking my head at all historical linguists.

"Scholars say it's very akin to the Gaelic, and—"

"Oh, don't get started on my Gaelic!" I laughed.

I had to admit, I always had fun with George. We enjoyed the same things. I frowned at myself. Then my cheeks heated. How stupid of me to have my earlier hissy-fit while on the Inch.

Grow up, girl.

"How about we go to the Celtic Festival?" George's voice lightened.

"Celtic Festival! Where?"

"On the grounds of a stately home near Inverness. Well, a castle, actually—"

"Inverness is only a two-hour drive from here. We're going! I'll book the tickets on-line. I'll pick you up from the station and we'll go from there." My right leg jiggled with anticipation.

"Great. Will we dress-the-part?"

"Do you mean wear fancy-dress?" My jiggling leg stilled.

"Not fancy-dress. A costume."

I groaned, unable to hold it back.

"Oh, go on." George spoke over the end of my groan. "It'll be fun. I can be a Celtic warrior, and you can be a Celtic princess."

"Princess! No way. I'll be a warrior if I'm anything at all."

"Ha! I should have known. You've definitely gained confidence since you've started martial art classes. Tomorrow, then."

Two

— · —

Never force love, for it may not come.
Once upon ye, it steps forth from naught, encircling your heart.
Ye must resist not and hold fast.
Loose not your hold
Or lose the chance.

VISIONS AND SAYINGS OF THE BLIND LADY SAGE

Our World, 2016
Inverness, Scotland

George had offered to park my car, as the nearest space was miles away in some field.

I let him.

I strolled through the crowd on the grounds of the Scottish Highland Estate. Marquees edged the large green, now a mock battlefield. I let out a chuckle. Later there'd be a *mock* battle between people dead-serious about re-enactments. My grin lingered. Perhaps, if I had a weapon, I'd even join them.

Ahead, flying from the tall posts of the tents, colourful slim flags snapped in the breeze under a watery sky. I wandered past the refreshment stalls, the aroma of roasted nuts and fried chips filled the air and the scent of a honey-sweet delight wafted past my nose. A stall sold mead, and people drank from pottery mugs. Further on, a slow turning spit ensured the gentle cooking of a whole pig. The barbeque aroma blowing on the breeze hit my nostrils and my mouth watered of its own volition.

Celtic warriors, and Celtic princesses wearing flowing gowns edged in gold embroidery, wandered past me. The costumes were inventive and ingenious. Leather armour sat over quilted gambesons, with re-enactment swords sitting on belted hips. Wow, some swords even looked real. Other costumes were outright bought from fancy-dress shops, with modern synthetic materials and machine sewn embroidery.

I tucked my shoulder bag into my side, bulky from the items for my outfit.

9

"You've got to go through with it, Rhiannon." George spoke right into my ear and his hand pressed into the small of my back.

I jumped. "Boy, you can disappear in a crowd! Don't do that to me again."

George's mouth pulled upward in his usual cheesy-grin, and he reached out to take my hand.

I grasped my bag tight with both hands and squeezed out a smile. "Give me some time. I scoured my wardrobe for a costume, but I need more. You go get changed and I'll find the rest of my outfit."

"Okay." George blinked a few times behind his gold-rimmed glasses, then his shoulders drooped a little as he turned toward the public amenities.

Good. Now I could start my quest. I strode through the crowd, heading to the stalls at the forest's edge where enormous trunks of ancient trees skirted the far end of the field.

I rubbed my hands together. "Weapons. I need weapons."

"Up by the far tree, lass." A tall man dressed as a warrior in dark trousers and a leather vest turned to me, his long hair gathered in a ponytail and his beard plaited at his chin. "What are ye after?"

"Oh, I'll know it when I see it. Thank you." I flashed a smile and walked on.

Better stop thinking out loud.

I passed a few Druids as I wandered to the artisans' stalls right at the edge of the forest where warriors and goddesses perused the handiwork on display. Racks of garments stood beside leather belts, bags, and leather armour embossed with exquisite patterns. Jewellery stalls had items made of various metals, featuring intricate interwoven designs of dogs, horses, birds, and humans. I released a sigh through a smile. It probably sounded dreamy, but I didn't care. I was in my version of heaven.

Stall holders joked with bright-faced customers. I strolled through their laughter and cheery banter, the tension in my shoulders easing at the lack of hard-sell.

At a weapons stall, I picked up a knife. Swirls of metal symbolising a dragon's head and its elongated wings, with its legs interwoven with another's, decorated the handle. The two beasts danced around where the wielder would grasp. I couldn't tear my eyes from the work. The skill involved in its crafting was a gift.

A stocky man wearing a leather apron stood behind the stall, his gaze fixed on me. He grinned at me as I handled the weapon. My expression must've been enough praise for this metal-artisan.

Swords rested in a rack next to the table display, their tapered edges blunt on each side. Double-sided broadswords, I guessed. Horses galloped on the handle of one, their long legs entwined and manes flying. These wild and muscular creatures wrapped themselves around the handle and each other, their brassy bodies standing out from the dull silver metal of the rest of the sword and galloping straight into my heart.

"How much are the swords?" I asked the man in the leather apron.

"Aye, well that one is my best piece of work, ye ken?" He scratched his whiskered face and pointed to the sword now in my grasp. "It's one hundred and fifty quid."

10

I gulped. The weight of the sword handle pressed into my palm as my fingers traced the embossed forms of beasts encircling it. I just couldn't let go.

"Here. My holiday in Ireland will have to wait." I paid with my credit card, then strapped on the sheathed sword and strolled amongst the nearby stalls.

The sword handle jostled at my waist. I shrugged, my chest buzzing and my mouth tight in an irrepressible grin despite the scabbard tip touching the ground with every step.

A few paces along, leather shields leaned against a stall table. Four horses pranced on their hind legs, embossed in each quadrant of a shield, pawing at the air. Interwoven lines, travelling over and under each other, divided them. My breath escaped me.

So beautiful.

I grimaced at the thought of the cost, but bought it, ignoring my own budgeting advice.

I slung the shield on one arm and held the sword handle with my other hand to keep the scabbard point from digging into the ground, and walked back to the main green. Examining those stalls again, I found the one I had in mind. If I were to dress-the-part, as George put it, I'd do it well.

No one's going to laugh at me today.

Scrunching my jeans and jumper into my shoulder bag, I emerged from the portable toilet by the tree line, dressed in my costume. *Phew!* Changing in there had been a tight squeeze. The knitted metal thread of the fake chain maille top sat cool against my skin. I adjusted the green plaid wrapped around my hips and admired my old brown knee-high boots. *Hmm.* Not bad for a last minute scrounge through my wardrobe. I examined my *pièce de résistance*: the fake tattoo of the tree of life on my bare midriff. I couldn't repress the tug at the corners of my mouth as warmth spread throughout my body.

"I look okay," I whispered to myself.

I searched for George. Near the mock battlefield, warriors warmed up with fake broadswords, and adjusted shield straps. Around the marquee area, Celtic princesses sipped mead and chatted to those not so enthusiastic about fighting but who wore weapons and bared their muscles anyway. George had blended into the crowd once more, so I walked back to the edge of the forest, rested my shield against my leg, and stayed put. Surely, George would reappear soon.

I hadn't waited long when a movement caught the corner of my vision, so I turned. A tall man strode out from the forest further along, with his bearing right toward me. He had long, flowing jet-black hair, so black it shone with a blueness, and he wore a kilt of forest-green tartan, in the paler colours of the older dyes. Two large sword handles protruded above his massive shoulders. Thick sword belts on which the swords hung, crisscrossed over his chest, and were the only covering for his well-toned upper body.

A typical gym junkie—he must've spent hours in one. Or in a dojo, for he moved with a grace of a fighter. Tattoos covered his left arm, all Celtic in design.

"Wow." I breathed out the word.

This guy had gone all out. His costume looked authentic, right down to the scar on his left eyebrow. He looked like he knew how to use those swords, too. The young warrior walked toward me, smiling.

I looked over my shoulder—only trees behind. I turned back.

What? He's smiling at *me*?

He'd moved even closer now and I glanced at the intricate knotwork on his arm. Why was he still advancing? His gaze locked with mine, sending my pulse rate up a notch. Did he want to speak to me? I gave a slight shrug. Perhaps he thought my outfit was okay.

He slowed his pace. His eyes caught my attention—sky blue with flecks of navy, and a navy ring encircled his irises.

Fascinating.

But now he was right there, in my personal space. The place reserved for close friends—usually allowed only by invitation. My back stiffened and my neck heated, and he seemed oblivious to my unease. Still smiling. Still approaching like we were old friends.

Umm... this is uncomfortable. I really didn't recognise him.

I opened my mouth to speak, but nothing came out. I tried to take a step back, but my feet wouldn't budge. He moved to stand toe-to-toe with me, his intense, spicy scent pervading the air around me. I should've protested, but his soft smile reached his eyes. I shook myself. I ought to say something.

"What *are* you doing?" My speech wavered.

"Do ye not know me, *a ghràidh chridhe*?" He spoke with a kind, deep, and very masculine voice. "Do ye no' remember I said I would come back for ye?"

Shivers travelled across my exposed skin. His accent had the lilt of those who speak the Gaelic. Like a Highlander from the Isles; not exactly, but it had the same breathy *sing-song* nature to it. Definitely a Gaelic speaker, and with my poor knowledge of the language, I interpreted his non-English words.

Love of my heart.

My own heart skipped a beat. "I'm sorry, sir, but I don't know you."

"Aye. Too soon then. Ye have nae met me yet, my love." His mouth broadened in a wide grin, and smile-lines fanned from the corners of his eyes.

Oh, no. My knees went to jelly, threatening to give way. He spoke to me like... like I'd always imagined a man who loved me would.

He placed his warm arm around my waist, tugging me against him. I blinked. Was this actually happening? *Oh, man.* I swallowed, unable to stop myself from taking in every part of him within my sight. Strands of his loose, long hair escaped over his shoulder and fell forward across his smooth pale skin. With his other hand he cupped my head, its heat burning me. I let out a silent gasp.

The man leaned in, his chin dipping and his thick black lashes lowering over those unusual blue eyes. He placed his lips on mine.

It was... nice.

His lips were gentle and his kiss pure, and I melted against his body's heat.

"Rhiannon?" George's pitch rose until it strangled his voice. Right in my ear.

The warrior broke off his caress and I took a step back, releasing my grip on the leather sword belts criss-crossing his bare chest—*when had I grabbed those?* —and breaking whatever connection he and I had just shared.

I looked from the man to George, and back again. Around us, Celtic princesses and Druids had paused in their perusal of the nearby stalls and now faced our way. My cheeks heated.

"What are you doing?" George held a palm to the warrior in a dismissive manner. "Move away from her, if you don't mind." George's tone was now deep and solid—not like him at all.

The young man stared at George, then took a short step back, a smile returning to his lips as he placed a gentle gaze on me, apparently not bothered by George—at all.

"Rhiannon, are you okay?" George asked.

I didn't answer. I couldn't. I could only stare at the strong jawline covered in a black two-day growth.

The man glanced in George's direction again, his eyelids narrowing and his jaw tightening for a flash, then his gaze returned to me. "Farewell, then." He turned and walked back to the forest.

I took a breath to steady myself, the warmth from the man's touch burning off slowly.

That shouldn't have happened, let alone been so good. Maybe I should've been indignant. Told him off and pushed him away.

But nope. I'd stood there inhaling his musky scent. I could've stayed forever.

"And that will be enough from you!" George yelled at the retreating man.

The dark unbound hair falling down the warrior's back, skimmed across his shoulders as he turned his head and glared at George. George stiffened beside me and took a step closer, his bright yellow tartan trousers and simple cloth shirt appearing clownish compared to the clothes of the tall dark man.

The warrior turned once again to the tree line and, not breaking his stride, continued into the forest, his kilt swinging with each step.

THREE

— • —

The World of Dál Cruinne
Post Dragon Wars Year 6083
Western Sovereignty of Dál Gaedhle
The Village Below The Keep

Arlan wandered past the spice stall, cinnamon's earthy-bark scent sticking dustily in his nose. Permanent market stalls lined the grey granite walls at the base of The Keep. In the centre of the market square, the traders from the west coast placed their carts and arranged their wares under their makeshift shelters of oiled cloth or seal hides, providing protection from the regular showers of rain. They displayed smoked meats and fish, cheeses, pickled vegetables in earthen pots, and dried fruits according to colour and size. The chatter of chickens and bleating of sheep echoed off the solid stone walls behind them.

Arlan's head throbbed, and his eyes felt as though they would burst if he gazed at the sky, his body so determined to remind him of last evening's tavern celebrations.

Arlan bumped shoulders with Bàn, who shot him a sideways glance.

"Ye are looking as I imagine you feel." Bàn cocked his head, a scar slowly distorting the dimple on his right cheek. "Too much of a victory?"

Arlan shook his head a fraction and winced, a vice clamping his skull in its imaginary grip.

"Ye have nae damaged that pretty face, either." Bàn nudged him. "It's a rare occasion that ye not only beat your opponent in the backstreet fighting pits but come from the fight yourself unscathed."

Arlan didn't reply but stopped in the centre of the market square.

A tanned, fair-haired girl in her late teens stood behind a stall and smiled in Arlan's direction. The desiccated bodies of fish, squid, and eels from the western shores of the land hung from the struts of her stall. Arlan took a step toward her cart and Bàn shook his head at him.

"She'll smell like her wares." Bàn pulled the long black braid that held Arlan's hair at his back and peeked out from under his hat, tugging Arlan's head twice and turning the vice further.

"Ow." He put his hand to his forehead, blinking while the vice slowly unscrewed. "But she's a beauty, is she no'? I need to practise my... whatever language she speaks."

"Which is?" Bàn laughed.

"We will see." Arlan clapped Bàn on the shoulder, then walked to the stall. His mouth pulled with an irrepressible grin. The younger woman swayed under his gaze and her top teeth grazed over her bottom lip. She had similar features to the Inerlothian clans who lived by his family's lands on the west coast. He spoke a few phrases in that language. She cocked her head to the side, then shrugged.

"Och well, not that coastal tongue, then."

A fair eyebrow raised above the seller's brown eyes. Arlan spoke a spiel of Nemedian. The young woman's face lit up, and the exchange began. He was rusty, but she corrected him in a polite manner. The words flowed with more ease as the moments passed. He bought a brace of dried sardines and glanced at Bàn, who leaned against a stall, his arms folded over his bare chest and his breech-covered legs crossed at the ankles. Bàn slowly shook his head and smiled from the corner of his mouth. Arlan bade the woman farewell and ambled back to him.

"Did you enjoy babbling away in a tongue I cannae get my head around, let alone my mouth?" Bàn's blue-eyed smile filled his features. "Ye've given that young lass much happiness." His gaze fell to Arlan's hand. "What did you pay for those stinking dried husks-of-excuses for fish?"

"Too much, I'm certain, but I dinnae mind, for she gave me a lesson in Nemedian."

"She's fair chuffed. She'll no' be able to wipe the beam off her face for days!" Bàn pointed his chin in the young woman's direction, then slid his gaze back to Arlan. "Gifted in languages and an expert fighter. The women adore you. *Dragon's teeth!* If I did nae love ye so much, I'd surely hate you."

Drops of cold, heavy rain hit Arlan's head. He ran with Bàn to the edge of the marketplace, bumping and jostling with the crowd of market goers hastening to shelter. Arlan stood with his back to the wall, his sword clunking on the stone behind him.

A woman with five children scampered into the shelter and stood in front of him, the odour of unwashed humans hanging around them. Gaunt, with dark circles under their eyes, their slack postures hinted at travel weariness.

The small boy of the group strained his neck, his eyes tracing Arlan from his boots to his broad-brimmed hat. The boy's eyes widened.

"What's that?" The lad reached out his hand and hovered it over the swirl of colour on Arlan's forearm.

"*Weesht.* Dinnae touch!" The woman reprimanded the lad. "Begging your pardon, lord warrior. Our apologies." She dipped her greying head at Arlan, then slapped the boy on the back of his with a weathered hand.

"Och no, 'tis fine. Here lad, take a closer look. I dinnae mind, truly." Arlan leaned down, presenting his arm covered in inked emblems to the boy. "Where are you from?" He directed his question to the woman.

"Lord warrior, we are from Leverden." Her accent confirmed her claim. "The troubles have pushed us north." The acid-fruity scent of those long hungry lingered on the air around her.

"Ye have travelled a long way." Now a daily occurrence, refugees entered the village in hope of food and shelter. Arlan's throat tightened. The trouble in the land's southeast now impinged on his once peaceful life in Dál Gaedhle. "Here." He held the brace of dried fish up to the woman. "Have some fish for your supper."

"Och, no, I cud nae." She waved her hands in front of herself and stepped back.

"I insist." Arlan held the brace closer to her. "Please, feed the children tonight."

The woman blinked. The boy turned to her and set a pleading expression on his upturned face. She glanced down at him.

"Thank you, lord warrior." She bobbed her head at Arlan and took the fish.

Arlan's mouth tugged at the corners.

The rain ceased, and the crowd dispersed and continued perusing the market. Arlan walked side by side with Bàn out of the square, leaving the chatter, animal calls, and earnest bartering behind. He approached The Keep where a ramp at a dip in its solid grey granite-base, the foundation of the fortification, was the access to this fortress. He grunted. *Fortress.* For most of his lifetime, peace had reigned due to the wise rule of the current àrd rìgh, and the townsfolk had no need to shelter within its thick bailey walls.

Arlan walked toward the iron reinforced wooden gates of the double-towered gate-house at the top of the ramp. The entire scene would be *dreich* if it weren't for the plants in flower, with pinks and reds spilling from hanging baskets, arraying colour on the walls and balconies. His heart twinged. Lady Alana had established these hanging gardens during her lifetime.

"The troubles down south aren't going away," Bàn said beside him.

Arlan's insides knotted—the hungry family in the market were proof of Bàn's statement.

"Ye'll be required to fulfil your predestined role sooner rather than later, I think." Bàn pursued the issue—again.

"Aye." Arlan ground his teeth.

"Halt! Name yourselves!" the guard yelled from the left-hand tower, his spear raised, and his long shield covering his torso.

"You must look dangerous," Bàn said from the corner of his mouth.

Arlan flicked his dark cloak aside and removed his hat.

"Oh! Lord Arlan, your pardon." The guard bowed his apology, then shouted below to the other guards.

The small gate within the gate opened with its usual creak and Arlan stepped through. He and Bàn walked across the grounds of the inner bailey toward the main fortified building of the caisteal, The Keep proper, passing armed warriors who nodded to him in respect. Rows of spears and shields leaned against the high inner bailey walls. An armourer organised weapons while another spoke to the master sword-crafter standing by his forge near the practice yard. The heat from the forge touched Arlan's face as he passed.

Arlan flung off his cloak and folded it over his arm, shaking off his subterfuge, his day's outing to the market incognito now over.

"Well?" Bàn strode forward, his eyebrows raised.

Arlan stopped walking. *So, Bàn is my conscience now?*

Bàn backtracked to where Arlan stood with his arms tense by his sides.

"Aye, I ken," Arlan growled. "Do you know what bothers me?"

"You dinnae—"

"What sears my heart like the snort of a fire breather is the fact that as the second son of the àrd rìgh, I've nae choice and I *must* do it." He huffed. "Perhaps if my father were any other man, or one with *only* the position of clan chief, I might not have to comply, and my father wouldn't force me to be battle chief of our clan. Or maybe I could forestall it and not assume the responsibility for some years. Delegate to someone more enthusiastic while I continue to enjoy myself in the ring. But as my father will busy himself here at The Keep being the àrd rìgh, I *must* take up my predetermined role."

Bàn's forehead puckered. "By my sword, Arlan, ye'll love it." His words came out in a rush. "Whether you were born to it or no'. *It is you.* You were made for it! And your fellow warriors love you. They'd fight to the death if you ordered them. *Because* you ordered them."

"I never expect—"

"Aye, and that's why they'd follow you into battle. They know you would be right there with them. In the thick of it, blow upon blow."

Arlan studied his boots. He'd trained alongside fine young warriors under the warrior sages, who'd cheered and encouraged him, slapped him on the back in camaraderie and pledged their support for him as battle chief. He didn't deserve such dedication.

He inhaled deeply to dispel the heat in his gut, but it still burned through his muscles and sinews.

Not. Fair.

"Where's ma free will in all o' this? Or has that flown off along with the dragons!" He lifted his head, narrowing his eyes for a moment, then strode on. "Privilege comes with responsibility." Arlan waggled his head from side to side in mimicry. "So my father's sage reminds me. But I'm trapped with the prospect of a future in which I have no say."

Bàn marched double-time to reach his side, spreading his hands. "I have a role to perform also, choice or nae choice, as a son of a clan chief."

Well, maybe Bàn had come to terms with it.

But why should I?

"What if I wish for the freedom to continue enjoying myself? There's more life to live. More contests to win in the arena." Arlan's insides leapt at the prospect of sword tournaments. "More drink to enjoy in the taverns. More of this beautiful world to see." He waved his hands about him. "Oh, and there are plenty of women, too. Who wants to wed some boring clan chief's daughter who is as dull as the edge of a practice sword?" His breathing came hard, heating his chest further.

A figure caught the edge of his vision. Eifion strode toward them in his advisor-sage robe of heather-mauve, his long white hair hanging about his serious expression. Eifion's lined face crinkled to excess, and his aged eyes were more weary-worn than usual.

Arlan halted. Sage Eifion would never come in person but send a messenger with a summons.

Not this time.

"Lord Arlan, your father, the àrd rìgh, wishes to hold council." Eifion's resonant voice always magnified his presence. "He will soon meet with his advisors and clan leaders in his side-chamber. I believe you should attend."

FOUR

— · —

Wise kings do not act in haste.
A considered decision is like free-flowing mead.
A hasty choice,
Vinegar wine choking the throat.

WISDOM WRITINGS ON KINGSHIP
SAGE GLIOCAS
(2870-2962 Post Dragon Wars)

Western Sovereignty of Dál Gaedhle
The Keep

"I must see my father." Bàn's hand on Arlan's shoulder gave a warm squeeze. "He'll be with the other clan chiefs meeting with the àrd rìgh. I'll see you there, sword-brother." Bàn left him at the entrance vestibule of the caisteal proper.

Arlan stepped through the open double doors of the Great Hall of The Keep. The throne of the àrd rìgh sat on its high plinth, an ornamented bronze chair overlaid in gold, made by master craftsmen three centuries ago. Even today, the metalwork reflected the beauty and strength of the animals and the power of the high king of the land. Their bodies were the frame and seat, and their heads each an arm of this grand chair. As a child, he'd traced the fine filigree lacework that wove in between the two horses, amazed at the continuity of the lines.

He sighed.

Childhood... *Happier times.*

Memories of studying under the rigorous tutelage of the warrior sages flooded his thoughts. The first time he'd held a real blade in his grip at the smithy's forge and the scent of hot metal and oil filled his nostrils. And that time he'd unseated Bàn when practicing sword play on horseback. He laughed. They were just boys then, and he'd pulled Bàn up from the dirt and chased his mount, bringing the pony back while Bàn dusted himself off.

Arlan stood tall and grinned. He'd excelled at horsemanship and fighting skills, with and without weapons, and he could never learn enough of the art and strategy of war. But he rubbed his cheek, as if a fresh slap from Kyle's bullying in the past stung there. Every time he'd shone in the skills of war, Kyle had found a well-placed comment to crumple his broadening shoulders.

"I would speak with you, little brother." Kyle's icy voice echoed up to the high ceiling, and Arlan's shoulders tightened.

He turned, regaining his focus. Kyle's grey eyes maintained their cool hooded stare as his vision ran up Arlan's body, his fair hair pulled back tight, accentuating an expression oozing disdain. If only Arlan were in the unofficial fighting pits *right now*. *His sanctuary.* Kyle never deigned to go there. The screaming, bawling crowd of sweaty, ale-reeking spectators was more welcome than Kyle's scathing commentary on his technique—or on *anything* he did.

"You will go to this meeting?" Kyle spoke into the echoing silence of the grand hall.

"Aye, Eifion suggested I go."

"He suggested *you* go?" A hint of pique edged Kyle's tone. "Did he not mention me? As heir to our clan lands, I should be the one to attend the council of the àrd rìgh on a regular basis." Kyle pursed his lips. "Come. Now."

Kyle pivoted and strode through the doors of the Great Hall, his kilt swaying with each step, and headed to the side chamber Father used for meetings.

Arlan followed, their footsteps echoing off the granite walls. Tapestries draped the walls in between the tall windows, the largest depicting a battle scene with victors sitting tall and graceful on muscled steeds, weapons held high in triumph, overshadowing men and horses wounded and limp.

Murmured voices spilled from the largest of the side-rooms that led off the Great Hall, and Arlan entered after Kyle. Faint blue smoke filtered through the warm room, filling his nostrils with its peaty scent.

Father sat on an ornately carved wooden chair at the head of the room beside a fire-grate. Sages milled in clusters amongst the gathering, with Eifion nearest Father. Around him, noble clansmen and women wearing their clan tartans, stood rosy-cheeked and attentive, with some older members resting on the bench seats against the wall.

Sunlight streamed in through the narrow windows and candles aided illumination in the dark corners. The members of the àrd rìgh's council spoke amongst themselves in hushed tones. Bàn stood next to one of the warrior sages who wore an earthy-brown plaid.

Arlan joined him. Kyle stood to the right of Father, his grey stare boring into Arlan. Arlan folded his arms over his chest and clenched his fists under his armpits.

"Dinnae let him unnerve you," Bàn whispered from the side of his mouth.

Arlan blinked his acknowledgement to Bàn and focused his attention on the head of the room.

Leuchars, the war chief, stood on the other side of Father. Massive, solid, with coppery hair, scarred arms and trunk, he was no beauty, but a keen and strategic mind made up for what he lacked in looks. He could reprimand with a stare, grind out orders all day, and punish at the merest hint of an insubordinate thought. The man was a trinity, loved and hated and respected, all in equal measure. His expression was sterner than usual.

Hmm. Never a good sign. This meeting Eifion insisted he attend was sure to *not* be easy news.

Father stood, the silver torc of the àrd rìgh nestled at his throat. Arlan lifted his chin, pride coursing through him, for all claimed him to be a younger version of this great man. Grey peppered Father's black hair, and his white beard sat below wrinkled features of late-middle age. His athletic build remained, but at this moment, his shoulders wore an uncustomary droop.

"My friends, I fear the troubles in the eastern regions of our land have finally encroached upon us. I have received information that my kinsman by marriage, the banished Ciarán Gallawain, causes this unrest. He seeks alliances with eastern clan lords. Those who do not comply, he subjugates by force, having obtained wealth, lands and warriors during his thirty years in the clan lands of Dál Gallain. The information we glean from the refugees pouring across our border causes me to believe he heads toward the sole rule of Dál Gallain, hitherto resisted by the clan chiefs of the east since the end of the Dragon Wars." Father spoke to every corner of the room.

Leuchars remained stony-faced, as did Eifion. Those present shuffled where they stood, casting worried glances at each other.

Arlan's brow tightened. He scraped at his memory for details of this cousin. None came.

"It is said Ciarán Gallawain employs the services of a mage," Father added, his expression grave.

Huffs and stifled comments came from all corners of the room.

"Aye, weel. Ye ken the mages cannae be trusted." Resentments ruffled through a white-haired clan chief's voice. "'Tis all their fault. The mages were the ones who worsened the violence of those ancient wars by bringing the beasts into the conflicts."

"Aye," a sage agreed, "the significant time of our history, of which all the counted years remind us and beseech us to never repeat."

"Reports from Leverden, near our south-eastern border, tell us there are bands of marauders attacking and burning villages and crops," Father continued. "This coincides with the most recent wave of refugees entering our city. Increasing numbers of people have fled from these bands of evildoers who associate with Ciarán Gallawain and his machinations for rule in the east. We need to address the provision of aid for those fleeing this violence near our border."

"We must ease the flow of refugees entering our lands!" The brusque statement came from a clan nobleman who wore a tartan of the clans closest to the border.

"How can we?" a clan chief asked from across the room. "We cannot refuse those in need."

"Until we are able to deal effectively with these troubles at our borders, we must increase our crop plantings to allow for the additional population," another clan leader said. She held large holdings of arable land near the eastern border, if Arlan recalled correctly. "Harvest is a few months away. It is essential we ration what food we have stored."

"We must move now and engage them in battle!" a youngish sage shouted.

Settle down, boy-sage. Arlan sent a glare in the sage's direction. *You'll not be amongst those who risk their lives in a fight.*

"We must crush this evil before it comes any closer," a senior clansman suggested.

Father lifted a staying hand, and the loud advice ceased. "Aye, it is a grave situation we face. The troubles in the south-east are decimating the lands of our distant relatives. Those clan chiefs have closer ties to their trading partners in other lands across the seas, and I believe some have sought the aid of their allies in trade."

A murmur ran throughout the room.

"We must be on our guard," he continued over the subsiding comments. "We must not allow this trouble to reach us. We will defend our lands at all costs."

"Send out our warriors to rid us of this threat at our door." The young sage spoke once more.

Blast of a dragon's roar! The boy-sage is free with his opinions.

"They're not at our door, and they may never be." Arlan's arm muscles tensed as he kept his fists under his armpits.

The room quietened and all eyes settled on him. He rolled his shoulders to relieve the tension and swallowed past a tight throat. They'd see his statement as reluctance and may interpret it as cowardice. And at any moment Kyle would decry him as spineless. Arlan's neck heated, and he braced himself for Kyle's comments to ring loud in the chamber.

But this trouble was still so far away. And if it came closer, wouldn't negotiation be foremost? Arlan narrowed his eyes and landed his vision on Leuchars. He must be loving this. Leuchars would champ at the bit for some action after years of peace.

On ye go, man.

Arlan lifted his gaze from the war chief. The advisors to the àrd rìgh still held Arlan in theirs. Dampness collected on Arlan's brow, and the room now stifled him with its heat.

Father cleared his throat. "Do you wish to comment further, Lord Arlan?"

"My àrd rìgh and father, in my opinion, we should do nothing." Arlan dropped his arms and straightened his shoulders. "I believe it's too soon to be engaging with the trouble-makers. And isn't diplomacy preferred over combat? If, indeed, we are anywhere near that."

Leuchars' copper-red hair glowed in the corner of Arlan's vision. The War Chief of Dál Gaedhle had focused his intense stare on him.

"Let them wear themselves out. Maybe their activity will dissipate." Arlan put conviction into his voice. "The cause of the unrest lies in the east, does it not? It's not ours. Leave it as such. And we need not risk warriors' lives by engaging with them."

The room stirred. Clan leaders and sages alike shuffled in their seats and mumbled into their beards. Father frowned at him, and Kyle remained silent.

"So, you advise to do nothing?" Father used his àrd rìgh's tone, ringing loud in the now quietened room. "Are you blind to our situation?"

Once more, all eyes fixed on Arlan. He swallowed.

"What I mean, Lord Àrd Rìgh, is that we should protect and defend. Provide for those in need. Not the offensive that some of your advisors are advocating." He spoke the last words through his teeth. Now his turn to glare, he bore it into the young sage who'd headed the conversation into an assault. An assault on enemies, real or otherwise.

Forcing me to open my mouth and say what I really think.

"Reconnaissance." Leuchars broke the silence.

At last, every face in the room turned away from Arlan, and advisors and clan leaders gave their attention to the war chief. Arlan released the breath he'd held.

"My Lord Àrd Rìgh, I propose a small group of warriors go to the borders and gather information, but not engage." Leuchars pointed his chin in Arlan's direction. "I suggest Lord Arlan selects a troop. He can report to this council on his return." The war chief grinned.

Father's attention returned to Arlan. "Aye. No engagement. Investigation only. A troop, not a war band. I am sure you are capable of that, Lord Arlan." He gave a slight nod. "Prepare yourself."

Arlan's fingertips tingled. It would be a mission—see the land and test a troop on something real. His insides buzzed. Bàn nudged him, showing his support. Kyle stood by Father's chair, his hooded stare focused on the floor.

Arlan bowed his acquiescence. Father or not, he could never disobey the àrd rìgh. But he didn't mind the order. For given the choice, he would have grasped the opportunity faster than the flash of a fire breather's belch.

FIVE

— · —

Be not deceived. The elemental powers of the universe are the masters. We but servants.
The magical energies they lend are consuming. The soul of the mage longs for it. Decades
of disciplined mastery lie ahead of those who would claim the title of sorcerer. For as
with papaveretum, imbibed to excess and habitually, magic will elicit an addiction of
both body and soul.

MAGE MASTER FÀISTINNAECH
(3310-3380 POST DRAGON WARS)

Dál Gallain, the Eastern Clanlands
Lord Ciarán's Tower

Bliss filled his silence.

With each inhalation, tingling spread through Drostan. From his lungs and along
every nerve, vibrations ran, sending sparks of warmth, leaving life's energy in their path.
Drostan kept his eyes closed, his inner world sharp and clear.

Moments such as now—with power surging through him—were those times when he
became truly alive.

This is why I live. Nothing else compares.

It flowed through his body in waves. It streamed through his spirit and brought
meaning to his existence. The energy of the universe... the solid immovable rock in the
centre of the whirlwind and the flood of this transitory life.

Horses' hooves clattered in the flagstone courtyard below his window in the round
tower. Drostan shuddered at the intrusion.

The clear waters of his stone divination bowl came back into view, and here he
lingered. He kept his grip on the carved stone, solid beneath his hands, and his spirit
held every tendril of energy he could grasp until forced to relinquish it. The aromas of
blended herbs that cloyed the air registered on his senses once more as with gradual
steps he released the power.

Surrendering his source, Drostan removed his hands from the cool bowl's rim, strode out of his workroom, then down the circular stone staircase of the tower, shedding the last traces of his power. He would never let his lord have a sniff of it.

Lord Ciarán Gallawain has no respect for the magic arts.

Drostan grunted. An evening by a fire and a very drunk Lord Ciarán came to mind.

A rare occasion that *was.*

And a time of revelations. Lord Ciarán had relayed to him a childhood memory of a nursemaid pricking his infant finger. A hissing fire in the great caisteal of his clan chief father, as she flicked his blood into the flames. A promise to a spirit. Lord Ciarán had shivered at the recollection.

Lord Ciarán's life reflected not an iota of that agreement.

Still, Drostan would not refuse free bed and board, and liberty to use his gift—to drink in his power on a regular basis—no matter what his lord and master thought of his lifelong gifting. Prestige belonged to the position of mage to a lord. The corner of Drostan's mouth pulled his cheek into a wry grimace.

Even if the lord barely tolerates magic and is only concerned with its uses to achieve his own agenda.

Drostan reached Lord Ciarán's private chamber in the tower, that which the lord preferred to call a library, and knocked.

"Come!" The lord's voice, muffled through the door, hid none of its edge.

Drostan opened the door, the whiff of mildew and rank cold stone assaulting his nose. The fireplace sat empty and the chill from the air in the chamber touched the bare skin of his forearms. Drostan rolled his eyes. He'd given up reminding his lord of the danger to the integrity of his study's contents if he continued without a heat source.

"Yes, yes! What is it?" Lord Ciarán sat at a large mahogany desk, a scroll in his hands. Scrolls, manuscripts, and vellum-bound tomes covered the desktop. The creaking of leather chest armour accompanied the tall, greying man straightening in his chair and lifting his gaze from the parchment over which he pored. The candlelight cast a shadow of his head of long, once fair hair against the high bookshelf behind him. Row upon row of bound knowledge in various leather covers formed a backdrop for his tall silhouette. "Well? Got something to tell? What have you observed in your wee bronze bowl?"

"Divination bowl, my lord." Drostan gritted his teeth.

An elaborate sigh filled the chamber. "Is it important? Can you not see I am busy here?"

Drostan's shoulders eased at the lack of further reprimand. "I have found a portal, my lord."

Lord Ciarán's hands ceased unrolling the scroll he held, and a grey eyebrow rose. "Go on."

"It lies not far from this side of the border."

"By the antlers of Cernunnos, that is still too far away." The library filled with Lord Ciarán's huff. "There is another matter to which I must attend."

"Aye, lord?"

"The warrior languishing in my dungeon. The one found deserting from my army after our most recent battle. The man, who, as well as functioning as mercenary, has at times"—Lord Ciarán leaned forward and lowered his voice— "performed other duties for me. I understand you knew the man in your youth."

The assassin—Vygeas. Oh, Drostan knew him. Before his training on the fair isle of Innesfarne, when playing hermit mage to his village, Drostan had gifted the man his heart's desire. Too late the fool had considered the price of magic. This peasant had been too eager to fulfil his own desires to become a warrior.

"What do you wish, lord?" He would cross paths with Vygeas again?

"I make my plans, but I require your services to fulfil them." Lord Ciarán opened his mouth as if to say more, but the clomping of boots came up the stairs and someone pounded on the door.

Lord Ciarán let an expletive fly. "What is it?"

The door creaked open and the lord's man servant entered the library with his habitual air of smugness.

"A young lad has arrived and claims he's tae be yon mage's 'prentice, mi lord." He dipped his head to Lord Ciarán and glowered at Drostan.

"Have you been expecting such a one, Drostan?" Lord Ciarán turned a querying glare to him.

"Aye, my lord." Drostan suppressed a grunt. It seemed Lord Ciarán had relegated this information to his *to-be-ignored* list. "We have spoken of it. And as I said on those occasions—"

"You have mentioned this more than once?" Lord Ciarán continued to look down his aquiline nose at Drostan.

"Aye, lord, he is a bright young acolyte who the mage masters of Innesfarne have assigned to me for instruction. I shall attend to him." He gave a short bow.

Lord Ciarán nodded a brief dismissal and Drostan left the library, taking a wide berth past the lord's man, then strode down the circular stairway.

Drostan stepped out onto the flagstone-paved courtyard where a youth stood beside a mule. The animal's head hung low, and it limped as the stable lad led it away. The young man dressed in a black mage robe held but one bag, his attire dusty, and his face lined. The journey from his place of study to this tower had been a lengthy one, and he stood with a serious expression. Drostan held out a hand to the tall youth, who nodded and grasped it with a firm grip.

He had dark brown, nearly black eyes that looked almost pupil-less, as if they could pierce a soul. His face had the angular qualities women would swoon over, with dark locks of long wavy hair framing handsome features. But the life of a mage had no place for such bonds. A serious mage, one who would aspire to attain the rank of a sorcerer, would soon discover matrimony and family could have no hold on their life. This one, Bram, had acquired the reputation of an ardent learner with much natural skill in the magical arts while studying under the mage masters.

He must accept this truth, good-looks or not, or all instruction would be futile.

"Bram," Drostan said. "Follow me. You must meet Lord Ciarán. We will attend to formalities, then I will see you to your chamber. You must need rest after your journey."

The young man followed without a word, his steps echoing in unison with Drostan's as they ascended the circular stone stairway to Lord Ciarán's library. The door had remained open, and his loud voice rang down the stairwell while he berated his man.

Drostan paused on the step. "You will become accustomed to this," he whispered to Bram. "Our lord has a severe temper. Prone to flare without notice."

Bram shrugged. "So I have heard, my master." His voice was deep for one so young, but it held a tone of respect.

Drostan's mouth tugged at the corners.

The lord's man stomped from the library, barging past Drostan and Bram, and slamming them against the wall on his way down the narrow circular stairwell, which led to the dungeon in the very foundations of the tower.

They paused on the landing outside the library.

"What!" Lord Ciarán spat, then looked up from his desk. "Oh, your junior. Come in."

"My Lord Ciarán, this is Bram, an aco—"

"Yes, yes. Welcome." Lord Ciarán's tone held no warmth of greeting. He turned to Drostan. "Let us see if you can achieve twice as much now there are two of you."

Drostan gave a brief bow. "Aye, my lord."

Lord Ciarán flicked his hand in a dismissive manner. "On you go. I have things to do, as do you. Settle your assistant in and get on with it." He strode to the doorway, ushering them out and shutting it firmly behind them.

Drostan climbed the stairs to the floor above, stepping onto the landing and through the swirling, familiar scent of herbs emitted from the workroom opposite, and showed Bram to his room.

"Tell me if there is anything you require. We shall tour the grounds once you are rested. There is an adequate herb garden beside the kitchens and the forest nearby grows many useful plants. I have much to discuss with you." He pressed his lips together, his cheeks gaining an unaccustomed warmth. "You must pardon the lord, he is..."

"An unhappy man, my master," Bram finished for him.

Drostan swallowed. Unhappy would not be the word he would apply.

"I had many a lengthy conversation with Grand Master Llew." Bram spoke as if this answered a question.

Drostan inclined his head, inviting more from his new student.

"He is a wise and learned man, Grand Master Llew." Again, it appeared as though Bram believed this comment provided enough explanation.

Drostan clasped his hands in front of him, and the young mage placed his bag by the cot, then Bram turned and set his eyes on him.

Drostan resisted the urge to take a backward step. "Of what did Grand Master Llew speak?"

Bram smiled, open and deferential, one seemingly careful not to breach a boundary. "He has known of Lord Ciarán from the time he held the position of clan chieftain in the northwest."

"Aye, go on."

"He told me of Lord Ciarán's flight here to the clan lands of the east thirty years ago, after the discovery of his plans to oust Donnach MacEnoicht, the àrd rìgh of the sovereign lands of the west."

"Also, this I know."

"But are you aware, my master, that it is said by Grand Master Llew, whose opinion I respect, that your very same Lord Ciarán then went on to meet and seal a pact with Deamhan." The lad's open expression displayed an honesty.

Drostan blinked. "The lord told me himself he was promised to the magic arts as a child, but I have sensed no spark of that nature in him. Nor a power from a touch of such a one you mentioned so freely."

Bram's cheek muscles rippled, as if he were chewing over his next words.

"Grand Master Llew wished me to know that Lord Ciarán sold his soul for power. The man now gathers an army and spreads mayhem here in the east, seeking in his own efforts to fulfil those promises pledged to him."

"My apprentice, you tell me no new thing. I am involved in this lord's plans. He is a brilliant man. And ambitious. You must deliver your next words with much caution, for I believe you have yet more to say."

The screech of an osprey flying through the trees that bordered the tower's gardens came through the window, tearing the silence of the room. But the youth spoke not a word, only pierced Drostan with his gaze.

"You are here now, and you will be part of those plans." Drostan continued to return an authoritative stare. "He is not easy to work with, for the lord can be exacting in his demands, but you will learn much."

"Aye, my master. All I say is, Grand Master Llew believes the bitter disposition of Lord Ciarán is due to dissatisfaction."

"Pardon?"

"That Lord Ciarán is displeased with the terms of the agreement and inwardly seethes, as he waits till... *the one with whom he sealed the deal...* fulfils his side of the bargain." Bram nodded, his eyes widening.

Drostan scrunched his lips. There was much to ponder in the speech of his apprentice. A great deal of which rang true. He would ensure opportunities to hear what else Grand Master Llew had said, but there were more pressing matters.

Matters associated with their current tasks assigned by their lord.

"What have you learned from the mage masters at Innesfarne in relation to dragons?"

Six

— . —

When things changed forever,
Forever changed.

VISIONS AND SAYINGS OF THE BLIND LADY SAGE

Our World, 2016
Abernethy, Scotland

My boots crunched the narrow gravel track as I trekked up the steep incline to the site of the Iron Age Fort. Breathing steadily, with my stride warming my leg muscles and stretching them comfortably, my mouth tugged with the beginnings of a smile. My determination to walk this every day since moving to my wee cottage had paid off.

I stopped at the sharp bend in the path where, down the slope on the precipitous side, I viewed my cottage. It looked closer from this angle.

I resumed my walk, with the wood of Douglas fir and beech like a wall of trees to my left, their branches overhanging the narrow path, and to my right, the steep drop down the side of the hill. The beech were shedding their summer foliage, and I kicked through the piles of fallen leaves collected on the path, flinging them into the air then watching them fall to a messier arrangement on the track.

I sniffed the forest's scents, the tang of Douglas fir invigorated me, lifting my spirits. The days were drawing in and the late afternoon air touched my exposed skin with a cool kiss.

Peace pervaded my mood today. Stillness and quiet dominated—unlike the other day when George had come to see me... *again.*

But he was a good friend, and we'd been through a lot together at university. He'd found me summer jobs, and we both had a passion for Celtic history... but not any other passion.

My jacket scrunched in my grip.

George was great, but that thing they called *chemistry*... just wasn't there.

George! I huffed. *That's my serenity shattered. Thank you. Not!*

Now, that guy at the Celtic Festival last month... My lips tightened in a grin and my heart rate went up a notch—*he* was something else. If I'd had the guts, I would've asked him for his phone number. I squashed the grin.

As usual, I hadn't had the guts.

He'd spoken—and behaved—like we were an *item*.

I sighed, my heart twinging. If only there truly was a man like *him* in my life.

No, not *like* him.

Him.

"Wake up, Rhiannon! Not possible!" My self-admonition filled the quiet woodland track.

A dark shape crossed the edge of my vision. I turned.

Leaves from the beech trees continued to fall behind me, lining the path. One or two spiralled their lazy way to earth.

Silence.

The lowering sun sent shafts of light through the branches now half-filled with leaves. No wind blew and the dappling sunshine left patchy warmth on my cheeks. *Hmm.* Must've been the shadows. I exhaled slowly, then turned back to the track and continued my hike.

George was in love with me, it was *so* obvious. And even more obvious—I could never return the feelings. It would hurt him, but I had to do it—had to tell him. I let my shoulders slump. That'd mean upsetting a nice person, and it was why I'd let it go for so long and not clarified that I could *never* be more than a friend.

The leaves rustled.

I spun.

A tall, slim youth stood behind me dressed in hunting camo top and pants. He lunged forward, seized a handful of my hair and yanked, spinning me into him. My scalp burned beneath his grip and my back thumped against his solid but bony torso. He shoved his arm over my shoulder and thrust a knife to my throat, the blade's sharp edge along my neck, right above my collarbone. My bounding pulse pushed against it with every heartbeat.

I took a deep breath and pushed out an eardrum-piercing shriek.

"Quiet, slut!" His snarl came hot in my ear. "No one's gonna hear you up here. Get over it."

His reeking breath wafting into my nose lifted my stomach, pushing acid into the back of my mouth. That blade on my throat was as frigid as the ice in my chest, like a snowflake crystal extending out its pattern as it crept through me.

But my veins heated.

How dare he!

I slipped my hands up, keeping them tight to my body, and reached for his arm that lay in front of my shoulder.

He said something, his voice rumbling through his chest pressed against my back. His words were just noise. I grabbed his forearm, jerking it and the knife away from me to my right. I quickly twisted around and dug my sharp shoulder deep into his armpit.

"Oomph!" His breath rushed out into my hair as his arm thudded against the back of my neck and sat at an awkward angle. I held on tight to his wrist, my forearms burning and fingers whitening.

He let out a sharp grunt. My arm shook with my effort, but I kept my hold tight, trying a lock to remove the weapon—a pocketknife—from his grip.

A loud cry filled the forest trail.

I focused on my attacker. He wasn't yelling.

Nor was I.

A thundering human voice surrounded me. Filled me. My ears caught the shake of the leaves in the branches above as the roaring reached the sky and returned, shuddering the earth beneath my feet.

Deep. Sharp. Bone-vibrating.

My attacker's grip eased. He wasn't looking at me. He didn't seem to notice I'd wrenched the knife from his hand. I grasped it tight and pointed it at him. But he'd fixed his stare along the woodland track. He let out a yelp and his wide-eyed gaze passed over me as though I wasn't there. He twisted away and ran down the hill.

The roaring continued behind me. I turned to face a man riding a heavy horse charging along the forest track. Blue circular patterns covered the horse's forehead. Blue body paint of some sort covered the man, and dark splatters crossed his bare skin. He tucked a long shield tight to his side and brandished a broadsword, dripping red. He headed toward me and my fleeing attacker.

What?

My mouth dried. I had to get to the wall of forest. But that'd mean running in front of this charging horse! No chance. Behind me—a sharp drop. *No choice!* I flattened my body to the ground, the drumming in my temples almost drowning out my thoughts.

I turned my head to look. With any luck, I'd be out of this animal's path. The horse's solid muscles flowed beneath a shiny black coat as its hooves pounded the earth, kicking up dirt with each hoof fall. The man's long, dark hair streamed behind him in his wake. His war cry filled the air as he pursued the lad who'd held me by force. Leaves flew from hooves, now at my eye-level, as horse and rider thundered past me.

The rider focused on my young assailant who'd disappeared into the thicket on the steep-slope side of the track and whose falling shriek now echoed in the deepening dusk.

That was my chance. I got to my feet and shot across the track, then through a tight space between the trees and crawled a short way up the hillside. I turned to view the man on the horse.

The rider spun his mount and ceased his loud cry. Then, shaking his head, trotted his horse back to where I'd been lying beside the track. He scanned his surroundings, blinking often, his brow crinkling deep, his shoulders heaving and his breath misting white with the cool of the evening.

I swallowed, then peered from behind a tree trunk. This man was a warrior, that much was for certain—by his outfit, his animal, his war cry, his bearing, and not least, the long blade he held dripping blood. And he wore blue war paint, like the warriors of ancient Britain.

He looked so... so Celtic.

His horse shook its head and whinnied, jet-black mane flying, and stomped its hooves. He patted its neck and spoke in a soothing tone, a breathy language—*maybe the Gaelic*.

The warrior kicked his horse's flanks, and it sprang into a gallop, heading back the way he'd come. I peered around the tree trunk to follow his progress. His head moved from side to side, like he looked for something. Then he stopped the horse, and it turned sharply on the narrow track. I blinked. I didn't think such a large animal could turn in such a small space.

The man urged his horse on with a cry, coming back along the track and nearing my hiding place. Again, he turned his head from one side of the track to the other, searching for something.

Hopefully, not me.

He pulled on the reins, and the horse pranced a little, then stopped and nickered, flicking its head and panting.

The man patted and smoothed its neck, shaking his head, his forehead scrunched.

Twigs and leaf litter beneath my feet gave way with a loud snap. The warrior turned sharply. I caught a glimpse of his stare directly on me as I snuck closer behind the fir tree.

Damn it.

"Trobhad!" he commanded. *Come here*—if I recalled my Gaelic correctly.

I stood immobile behind the fir tree, tucking myself tightly into the firm trunk, and held my breath.

"Trobhad boireannaich!"

I had no choice. Come here, woman, he'd said. If I didn't go to him, he'd come after me for sure. Letting out a shaky breath, I stepped from behind the tree. He removed the long shield from his arm and hooked it on his saddle. Then lowered his bloodied sword, wriggling the fingers of his free hand in a *come here* gesture. I clambered down the slippery forest hillside with care, and stood on the path in a crouch, pointing the pocketknife at him. This armed, wild-looking man had scared off my attacker, effectively saving me.

Surely, he wouldn't now hurt me?

He pointed, directing his gaze to my trembling hand gripping the knife.

I couldn't give him any excuse to attack me, so I lowered the knife. I snuck a look around for a way of escape. He blocked the way downhill, and the earthworks of the ancient fort, with a steep cliff drop on the far side of them, sat at the top. My chest constricted.

His horse pawed the track. The warrior's eyes were wide, and he exhaled hard as he patted his horse's neck again in a calming gesture. Up close, this animal was massive. Big and black with enormous hooves. One stomp would kill someone.

Yep, a war horse.

My pulse still thudded in my head, and the trembling moved to my middle. The woad-faced warrior stared at my shaking hands while he spoke to me. But I couldn't understand what he said—wasn't taking it in. His voice was gentler though, and not the screeching war cry of only moments before. I blinked, trying to absorb what I'd just seen and heard.

The trembling continued as my mind grasped just as shakily at my thoughts.

Where did he come from?

Seven

— • —

Mercy is the robe of the àrd rìgh.
An ermine collar kissing the kingly torc of judgement.

WISDOM WRITINGS ON KINGSHIP
SAGE GLIOCAS
(2870-2962 POST DRAGON WARS)

The World of Dál Cruinne
Post Dragon Wars Year 6083
Western Sovereignty of Dál Gaedhle
The Keep

Arlan drew aside the heavy curtain to his private alcove, the familiar peaty scent suffusing the air. He slumped into the wooden chair, slung a leg over one arm and let his shoulders ease. Someone cleared their throat and Arlan stiffened. Kyle sat across from him in the small nook covered in a soft glow from the fire.

"Why does the wizened old man wish to speak to us?" Kyle sent a scowl Arlan's way.

"He'll know of our kinsman, Ciarán Gallawain." Arlan leaned forward and rubbed the coarse, wiry coat of the deerhound that had followed him in and dropped to the hearthrug. "The one Father blames for the disruptions in the southeast and whose activities are the supposed cause of the influx of refugees."

Kyle remained mute, his eyes narrowing to slits.

The curtain parted, swirling the thin smoke through the small space. Arlan rose and offered his chair to Eifion. Kyle didn't move.

"My young lord princes." Eifion glanced at Kyle, nodded thanks to Arlan, then took his seat. "There is a past you should know, and your father requests I should be the teller of the tale. Thirty years ago, the personal guard of the àrd rìgh caught Ciarán Gallawain, the cousin of our late queen and your dear mother, organising a rebellion against your father, the high king."

34

Arlan lowered his gaze to the hound now asleep by the fire, his inner vision drifting. Mother holding him close in tender arms. Her face kind. Fair hair surrounded love-filled eyes. The sting on his scraped knee fresh once more. His pony hovering over him, blowing a soft nicker. Mother bent her face to his injured knee and kissed away the pain. *You must remount, my son.*

"Lord Arlan?" The sage's deep voice drew him back to the present.

Arlan dragged his gaze from the lanky grey dog on the hearth and returned his full attention to Eifion.

"Ciarán Gallawain convinced some clan nobles of the time to join him in overthrowing your father. Not content with the role of chief of Clan Gallawain, he desired to be the àrd rìgh. Along with the other clan chieftains, he had had his chance the previous year to win the high kingship in *Tòireadh.*" Eifion pursed his lips. "I believe Ciarán resented gaining second place to your father in the Quest." Eifion gave a quick shake of his head. "On passing sentence, mercy was foremost in your father's mind. His wife's kinsman was guilty of his crime, but did he deserve death?" Eifion lifted a hoary eyebrow briefly. "Your father delivered the sentence of banishment. He hoped that forgiveness and mercy would gentle a hard heart. That contemplation in exile, away from home and clan, would assist repentance." Eifion sighed. "To your father's regret, it appears not."

"Why have we not heard of this incident, and but little of our cousin?" Kyle asked. "You taught us history. Were we not to learn of this episode in our own family history, and a significant moment in our father's reign?"

Arlan hardened his stare at Kyle. "I'm certain both Eifion and Father had good reason to omit this from our lessons, Kyle."

"But why—" Kyle began.

"Your father and his clan chiefs wished to put the matter away..." Eifion's gaze rested on Kyle.

Kyle's nostrils flared. "I wish to know more details of this cousin."

"I understand you have always felt more akin to your mother's side of the family, Lord Kyle, but you would gain little more than I have revealed by examining—"

"And yet I wish to," Kyle snapped.

Eifion gave a modest bow. "It is written of him in the annals. You may search the libraries yourself, my prince."

Kyle jolted out of his seat, flipped aside the curtain to the alcove, and left. The curtain fell closed, leaving a silence only disturbed by the hound starting awake and following Kyle out, its claws clicking on the bare wooden floor.

Kyle's always so dramatic.

Arlan took his gaze from the fluttering curtain and directed it at Eifion. "Should I follow?"

Eifion sighed. "Aye. Although the archives will not inform you that Ciarán Gallawain was a privileged noble who treated many as lesser, behaved as if his needs were above his fellows, and lived believing others existed solely for his use."

Arlan didn't move. Eifion seemed to have more to say but ushered him out with a wave of his hand, so Arlan flung the curtain aside and hastened after Kyle.

The clicking of dog claws on stone flooring travelled down the long corridor that led to the library. Ahead of Arlan, Kyle commanded the hound to stay, slipped past the thick oak doors, and pushed one behind him to close it. Arlan raced to the door and braced it with his extended hand.

Kyle's eyes flashed up at him. "Oh, you wish to know the truth as well."

"I wish to know why ye were so rude to Sage Eifion." Arlan fully opened the door. "He only desires we know the truth."

"A truth I would discover for myself without the biases of that ancient."

"He is a wise—" Arlan's words stuck in his mouth, stopped by Kyle's glare.

"We shall discover together, little brother. After all, you wouldn't know your way around such a hallowed place of learning." He sniffed and strode past tall shelves of parchments, scrolls, and books covered in leather and gem encrusted metals. "While you were busy falling off your pony and hitting your fellow young warrior *lords* over the head with a wooden sword, I learned important things such as governance and history."

Arlan rolled his eyes and followed Kyle's brisk strides to the very back of the room, where scroll-filled shelves lined the walls.

"These sections are designated by their years. We require texts from thirty years past." Kyle placed his finger on his upper lip and cast his gaze over the shelf in front of him.

"May I be of assistance, young lords?" A croaky voice came from Arlan's right.

He turned to face a sage in a crumpled purple robe, peering up at him. The man started.

"Oh, my lord princes. I beg your pardon." He gave a slight bow.

"Yes." Kyle spun, and the sage flinched again. "I require access to the archives for the..." Kyle's finger tapped his upper lip. "Post Dragon Wars Years 6050 to 6053."

The sage's eyebrows rose. "That is quite a number of scrolls, my Lord Kyle. Do you seek any particular incident or occurrence of the day? Or are you wishing for a general—"

"Lord Ciarán Gallawain." Kyle pierced the sage with his stare. "I wish to peruse the record of the events surrounding his attempted rebellion against the àrd rìgh."

The sage's mouth shut slowly, his shoulders dipping in a sigh. "Very well, my young lord." He passed Arlan and reached a section halfway along the wall, pulled scrolls from a shelf and stepped to a long table near the far side wall. "I shall leave them here where ye can open them, young lord princes." He placed the scrolls on the table and walked away.

Kyle curled an eyebrow and strode to the table and grasped the first scroll. Arlan followed, took the scroll labelled *Post Dragon Wars Year 6051*, spread it wide, and read.

"Ah! This scroll is the first half of 6053, before the summer solstice." Kyle's eyes sparkled. "I was a child, and you were not even a thought."

Arlan lifted his hands from the scroll he'd spread on the large table. It curled in on itself.

"And?"

"It's the record of the rebellion attempt." Kyle didn't lift his eyes, but continued reading.

Arlan puffed, now loud in the quiet room. No light shone through the tall windows and a young sage had placed lighted candles nearby.

"And it says?" Arlan exaggerated his encouraging tone.

Kyle continued to scan the scroll, not answering.

Arlan huffed and took the last scroll from the pile: the second half of the same year. It recorded an investigation of some sort. He read further, his heart rate gradually increasing, and blinked in the poor light.

It couldn't be.

"They investigated Mother..." Arlan's mouth went dry.

"Hmm." Kyle pressed his finger to his front teeth and continued reading.

Arlan tapped his shoulder. "Kyle, they investigated Mother."

"What!" Kyle tore his attention away from his reading and snatched the scroll from Arlan's hands.

"Careful! It's fragile."

Kyle's eyes followed the lines of script as he placed the scroll on the table and rolled it out further. Arlan leaned in for a better view.

"*Wheesht.* Go away," Kyle growled. "I shall tell all once I've read."

Arlan's skin prickled.

"It appears the closeness of our mother to Lord Ciarán had brought suspicion upon her..." Kyle read more. "Close family ties... A confidant... Many hours together."

"What does *that* mean?"

"It's what it's not saying." Kyle threw a glare at him.

"What do they imply?" The skin on Arlan's arms grew cool. "How close?"

Kyle stiffened and his hands fisted as he held the scroll down and continued reading.

Arlan's neck heated, and his fists curled in solidarity with Kyle's. This possible betrayal of his parents' marriage by his mother's actions threatened to mar his tranquil childhood recollections of warmth, comfort, and security, all personified in a loving woman. The image he cherished and had clung to in his darkest moments. *Surely no?*

"And our mother's reputation?" Arlan bit on the words.

"Let me read!" Kyle spoke through gritted teeth.

Arlan speared his gaze at the ceiling, clenching and unclenching his fists, swallowing down bile for what seemed an age.

"So..." Kyle raised his grey hooded eyes to him at last. "Her honour and her loyalty were never in Father's doubt. He publicly praised her to all the clan chiefs. It is on archival and public record that Mother's allegiances and devotion were forever to Father the àrd rìgh, and to the high kingship itself."

"That is all well and good. But why did they question her at all?"

EIGHT

— · —

Choose those who fight fiercely and with skill.
May the brave be the edge to your sword.
Above all other attributes, choose warriors who hold their
lives as naught to protect their chieftain and clan lands.

ADVICE TO WAR CHIEFS
WARRIOR SAGE TAPAÌDH
(4009-4059 POST DRAGON WARS)

Western Sovereignty of Dál Gaedhle
The Keep, The Practice Yard

"I mean it." Arlan kicked the soft sand with his boot and tossed his wooden practice sword from one hand to the other. "Ye'll not come with me solely because I like you. Ye have to earn it." He grinned at Angus.

The young clansman stood opposite him, mirroring his own stance and holding a wooden broadsword. The lad had potential—the framework was up, the building work just begun...

"My lord, you smile, but I fear ye shall not treat me kindly." Angus flicked his dark blond plait over his shoulder, his brow furrowing.

Arlan landed three heavy blows, putting his full weight behind them. The younger clansman took them all. Arlan gave more. Angus staggered back, stumbled, and wobbled on his back foot, then feigned a weight-change in footing, correcting the overbalance. Soft laughter came from the edge of the practice ring. In the corner of Arlan's view, Morrigan rubbed her fair chin with a leather-gloved hand, hiding a smirk.

"You'll be next, young lady." Bàn leaned on the rail beside her.

"Why don't *you* have to try out?" Morrigan's tone held an edge, hiding none of her sense of unfairness.

"Lord Arlan and I've had our spar, sister," Bàn said. "Now *wheesht*. You're distracting your lover."

Puffing hard, Angus glanced in Morrigan's direction. Arlan stepped in with a heavy overhand within Angus' now distracted line of sight. The lad snapped up his sword and blocked Arlan's blow, then parried. Arlan brushed it away.

"Focus." Arlan hardened his voice. "If ye'll have your woman fightin' beside you, ye'll have to leave her to her own devices or ye'll no' have yoursel' to love her with!"

"So, she's coming too?"

Arlan gave Angus more blows for his cockiness, then stepped in closer, locked swords, and pushed Angus back. It could be a wee bit difficult to get into the tall man's close space and under his arcs. Angus' agility and reflexes were excellent.

He'd do. And that woman of his.

"Next!" Arlan yelled, regaining his breath.

"What?" Angus held his fighting stance. "That's it?"

"Aye, lad." Arlan tilted his head in the direction of the rail at the edge of the yard. "Dinnae spoil it. Go."

Angus trudged to the perimeter where the warriors who'd tried out stood with the others awaiting their turn. Leuchars stood behind the rail, his expression creased in its usual scowl, and his arms crossed over his chest.

"Cutting your teeth on this exercise, my lord prince?" He broke his silence and grinned suddenly.

More like a constipated grimace.

Arlan dipped his head to the war chief. In his former role of warrior sage, the man had been harsh—too harsh at times. Arlan planned to modify Leuchars' strict code for the skills required in a fighting troop. He needed the right skill-mix for this reconnaissance, and as a mostly untried group, he'd aim for camaraderie and pre-existing bonds.

A woman of slight build walked onto the sand. She held a bow and a quiver of arrows hung at her slight waist.

"An archer. *Hmm*." Arlan cocked his head to the side. "Can ye shoot while riding?"

"Aye." The young warrior's eyes lit up, then she ran to a horse by the perimeter railings and jump mounted. It gave a nicker in protest, then she rode without the use of the reins, directing the animal with her knees and shifts in her body weight.

"Kill that rail over yonder." Arlan pointed to the other side of the yard as he stepped over to stand beside Bàn, all the while keeping his eye on her.

She grew in stature on the back of the beast, their combined weight now bearing toward the empty rail on the farthest side of the practice yard. She slid three arrows from her quiver and held them in her bow hand as she notched one, drew, and aimed. *Thwack, thwack, thwack.* The rail now wore three spikes of arrows close together.

Arlan clapped. "This archer is due more credit than I thought."

"She's Erin." Bàn's voice took on soft edges. "Very nimble and also quick in hand-to-hand."

Arlan lifted his chin in question, and Bàn gave an imperceptible nod.

"Right, ye'll do," Arlan shouted to Erin, who leaned from her mount to retrieve arrows from the fence.

Erin faced Arlan, her mouth partly open, then let her gaze slip beside him to Bàn. A smiled flickered across Bàn's face.

"Muir, Douglas, and Leigh." Bàn pressed his lips together.

"Aye, definitely. What about Adele? She's a solid lass who kens how to fight. Even I'd hate to meet her in a foul mood." Arlan chuckled.

"Good choice, my lord. I'd give her my back to defend any day."

Erin dismounted and walked to the rail where the others stood. A man in a broad hat held his head low and walked onto the practice yard, his stature slighter than most and the tip of his practice sword dipped as he strode along, kicking sand with the toe of his boots on every step.

Arlan sighed. "No, Kyle."

The man raised his head, his tilting hat revealing Kyle's eyes squinted tight and lips a line.

"No, brother." Arlan spoke low and firm.

"I know you hold trials for a place in the troop you will lead." Kyle pointed the sword at Arlan. "I will try out, like any other."

Arlan's throat seemed to close, threatening to unsteady him. Kyle's harsh words of the past returned. *You're stupid. You would never attain my standard. You haven't earned the right to your actions. Incompetent at all you will attempt.* Threats from Kyle if he didn't do as he bade him battered Arlan again as he resisted the instinct to flinch. Arlan swallowed the rising bile.

"No. Brother."

"It adds to my experience as a warrior. In a troop on a mission, no less. This is an excellent opportunity. You *will* give me a trial." Kyle spoke in the tone of their youth. Insisting. Ordering.

Beside him, Bàn crossed his arms over his chest, sword resting flat against his collarbone.

Arlan couldn't voice all his reasons. Not without exposing Kyle's meanness. *That* he'd never do. One day Kyle would be a clan chief, and maybe even àrd rìgh. He needed the respect of these young clansmen. Kyle could use his menacing looks all he wished—he would *not* go with them.

Kyle stood speechless, his stare hitting Arlan like daggers.

Heat simmered in Arlan's middle.

Oh, how I'd love to pay back that abuse.

He could disarm Kyle in an instant. It would embarrass him but not humble him. Only increase the enmity that crashed in waves over Arlan's shore. Not a beneficial relationship for a clan rìgh and his battle chief.

If I must be battle chief.

Arlan turned to Bàn and beyond him, where those who'd tried out still gathered at the railing—an audience. Arlan returned his gaze to Bàn, who'd read his mind on many occasions and had witnessed the gradual deterioration in his relationship with Kyle. He'd appreciate the issue here.

Kyle must not go. He would be an easy failure, but Arlan shouldn't be the one to do it.

"My brother-prince, I've much to prepare, for we leave tomorrow." Arlan spoke to Kyle, but his vision never left Bàn. "My assistant, Lord Bàn, will gladly spar with you."

The corner of Bàn's mouth twitched, tugging the torn dimple, as he cocked one eyebrow, all out of the view of Kyle.

"Aye, my lord, it will be a pleasure." Bàn stepped forward.

Arlan exited the yard with the clunk of wooden practice swords clashing and the coinciding grunts of effort ringing in his ears.

Arlan strode across the courtyard of the inner bailey on his way to his chambers and approached the great yew tree that grew near the hall of worship. Its thick trunk proclaimed its age, and it spread shelter and shade in equal measure. It drew him, and he stood in silence beneath its leafy shade.

Tomorrow it would start—no games nor contests, but truly leading others. Not to a battle, but still a test of his leadership and judgement. He released a sigh.

"Heavy thoughts, my young lord." Eifion sat in the shade on the bench seat by the base of the noble tree, his robe wrapped around him in the chill of the late afternoon.

"You are quiet, wise sage."

Eifion approached Arlan, laying a cool hand on his forearm, the skin on the back of this hand stretching tight over tendons.

"Tomorrow you go on a journey. *Tobraichean na Beatha*, who is not far from us, go with you." His small face turned up to Arlan, crinkling with a smile.

Eifion had repeated this saying many times to Arlan. The old man kept true to the ancient faith and did not follow the many gods and goddesses of his contemporaries. He believed in the truths of the god who surrounded all and supplied every living thing with breath and very life itself. Or so they said.

Love and support lived behind those wise eyes now peering into his own. Eifion had always been there for him and listened, when, as a youth, he poured out his soul regarding Kyle's treatment. Arlan swallowed and engulfed Eifion's hand with his own sword hand.

"Thank you, Eifion. I wish the same for you." He turned to leave.

"He is jealous of you." Eifion's voice held an edge.

Arlan pivoted.

"Your brother recognises your gifting as a leader, your prowess as a warrior, and the love your fellow warriors have for you." Eifion's tone softened. "It makes him feel inadequate. Be forbearing."

"Haven't I always been?" Arlan said, voice low.

"Be more so, my Lord Arlan. Whenever there is true greatness and good, there is always the opposite. I speak not only of this land or our world, but of a trial, such as the one your brother consistently provides."

"Do you say Kyle is a bad man?" Arlan's brow tightened. "He'll become a clan chieftain and be eligible to contest for àrd rìgh in *Tòireadh* when the time comes."

Eifion stared in earnest. "Nae, Arlan, I speak of that which is within people. The propensity for evil as equal to the ability to do good. It resides within us all. Whether it is to act in a base and evil manner, or to refrain from acting responsibly and with courage when one should." Eifion's querying eyes searched his. "Are you listening?"

Arlan stilled at his question. "Aye, I heard you."

"Nae. I asked were you listening."

"You've never misguided me." Arlan held Eifion's stare. "I'll take it to heart, my sage."

"Aye, do." He nodded gently. "For it will be your greatest battle, warrior-prince."

NINE

— • —

RECONNAISSANCE TROOP

Muir: Spear. (Named 'Sleaghach') Veteran. Sharp, good for rear guard. Does not chatter idly. When the man speaks, worth the listening.
Douglas: Twin swords. Masterful fighter. Good sense of humour.
Leigh: Twin swords. Dog handler. Grumpy, dark. Prudent. Practical. Good judgement. Note to self—Listen to his advice.
Angus: Sword. Young, but has skill and determination.
Morrigan: Blade. Has won tournaments.
Bàn: Blades.
Erin: Archer. Coming on Bàn's recommendation.
Adele: Whatever she can get her hands on... Big woman. Strong fighter.
Me: Blades...

FROM THE NOTES OF ARLAN FINNBAR MACENOICHT

Western Sovereignty of Dál Gaedhle

Arlan relaxed his grip on Mengus' reins and sank deeper into the saddle, his stallion's beautiful gait giving a comfortable ride. With winter's passing and spring's hold, sowing the fields had begun early in these parts, confirming the comments from the noblewoman with lands in the east of Dál Gaedhle. Farmers had sown hoping to produce enough food for the ever-increasing refugee population. Flowering trees in the copses dotted the fields on either side of the road with pinks and golds, offsetting the rich greens, and birdsong rang from the trees.

The grandest mountains in the land, the Central Meadhan Mountain Range, lay to Arlan's left, snow-capped granite peaks sitting tall in the near distance. For some leagues, a loch sat at the base of the closest mountain, with a river flowing from it, coursing its way to the southern oceans. The River Ruairidh also ran from these mountains and flowed past The Keep. The narrow bridge spanning the river at the base of the fortress provided the only crossing between east and west. Father, as àrd rìgh, gained most of his wealth from the tax extracted from all and any who'd pass, thus making the office of high king greatly coveted.

Hmm. Ciarán Gallawain would surely seek this wealth.

The deerhounds trotted beside the horses, their breed almost the size of a small pony. They sniffed the air, eyes scouring the roadside and folded ears lifting at the slightest sounds. The youngest lagged and Arlan whistled it back into line with its pack. For aye, a pack they were when time to hunt.

Douglas' voice drifted along as he told Leigh a joke. Arlan rubbed his jaw, the bruise under his beard still tender. He'd often competed against Douglas in the ring—the official contests *and* the backstreet fighting pits. Douglas' humour would keep up morale, for they may require it on a lengthy journey.

With luck, morale would be the only issue.

Morrigan's and Angus' soft conversation caught Arlan's ears. The fine hairs of youth covered Angus' chin, yet he'd gained the love of a beautiful woman. Arlan stifled a snort. Only good fortune could assist their future. Angus, from clan lands by the coast north of his own coastal clan home, claimed no noble clan heritage. His skill and sheer determination, plus the sponsoring of a generous chieftain, had won him the tutelage of the warrior sages. His lack of wealth and station made the future of his liaison with the daughter of a clan chief almost impossible.

Bàn rode ahead, Erin next to him, his face inclining to hers, deep in conversation. His mouth angled with a slight smile while he spoke, describing something with his hands as he lightly held the reins. Erin glanced up at him often during his explanation. Her lips curved, and she ran her tongue along them, her attention fixed on Bàn. His hand actions ceased, and he looked down, his smile broadening as his gaze rested on her.

Arlan faced the way ahead, the corner of his mouth tight.

None of my troop have seen genuine conflict.

Except for Muir. He grimaced. But experience wasn't gained without opportunity. Erin had skill and confidence with her bow, and Adele, well, she towered over some men and had just as much muscle, but again, she'd seen no proper action.

Aye, this mission was a grand and much needed endeavour.

The warmth of the sun, the snort of his stallion, and the fresh air from the countryside warmed Arlan's heart—no, his very soul.

Let them ride relaxed for now. From what he'd encountered so far, the conflict was a fair distance away. Trouble could come soon enough.

But his plan remained—travel to the border area, spy out the land and the enemy, then return with their report.

Simple.

There'd be taverns to visit along the way and he'd try the local speciality of each village.

Mengus' hooves clopped out a steady rhythm as the day wore on and Arlan squinted at the sun lowering in the eastern sky. Roe deer roamed the lower grassy moors beside him, ducking in and out of the protective forest cover skirting the edges of the moors. An eagle soared above, circling on the wind, its cry reverberating through the sky.

Arlan led his troop through agricultural lands toward the village where they would stay for the night. The chatter of the villagers walking home from the fields and the percussive clang of the smithy working at his forge rose to meet them as they neared the hamlet. Chickens and children scampered away from their war horses' hooves. The malty aroma of warm beer and roasted meats wafting in their direction hit Arlan's nostrils. His stomach growled.

Douglas rode up to him. "Follow your nose, Lord Arlan."

"Aye, smell that brew. And no *lord* tonight, if you please." Arlan slapped Douglas' shoulder.

"Aye, sir." Douglas doffed his forelock, a smirk on his lips.

Arlan tucked his plain black plaid tighter into his belt—plain, for he wouldn't identify himself unlike his warriors who wore the plaid of their clans.

They haven't my concerns.

Bàn trotted his horse beside him. "I'll get lodgings."

"Aye. From the cleanest inn with the best tasting ale." Arlan's tongue tingled.

"Hmm, may not be the same place."

"Do your best."

He dismounted along with the others and walked his horse further into town while Bàn rode ahead and chose lodgings. The townsfolk smiled, nodding greetings as he passed, unperturbed by the strangers in their hamlet. The villagers' clothes were neat and clean, their faces rounded and tanned from their work outdoors, the warmer weather of spring having come earlier here.

Bàn led his horse to Arlan. "I've secured us rooms. We can stable our horses behind The Griffin's Wing." Bàn leaned in close. "The pretty serving lass assures me their ale is the best in town."

The bright-red griffin swung on its board above the wooden doorway to the two-storey stone construction of the dusky-pink local sandstone. The ostler led their animals to the stables, Muir and Leigh accompanying him. Arlan entered the inn, its interior dimly lit. A serving girl led him upstairs to three rooms, with three beds in each, the linen clean and the doors lockable.

Arlan settled his warriors in their rooms, then returned downstairs and sat at the long table nearest the large fireplace. Muir and Leigh ambled in after bedding the horses and hounds for the night. Muir tied his thinning grey hair back into a ponytail, giving a brief nod to Arlan, indicating the stable had met with his approval. His sun weathered face had browned further during these days of travel.

A man entered the inn's eating room, keeping his cloak on and hat low, and swiftly exited with two bowls of food.

Suspicious, but his intentions unclear. Arlan's brow tightened in a frown.

"A traveller like us." Bàn sat beside him, the bench seat creaking with his weight. "He, with another, obtained a room soon after I did."

The rest of his company came downstairs and sat, and they dined on a stew of meat flavoured with garlic and onion in a thick gravy, served in wooden bowls, with a rustic bread and jugs of ale refilled. They chatted with the patrons, and women surrounded Douglas. Despite his pugilist's nose and the deep scar on his left arm, making it look somewhat deformed, the man drew women like bees to mead. The women, of various ages, gazed up at him from beneath their eyelashes as he leaned against their table and told his selection of jokes. Laughter and flirtatious comments streamed from his direction.

Arlan's warriors retired one by one, leaving Bàn and himself to finish the last jug of ale. He wiped froth from his mouth with the back of his hand, moistening his beard with beer, not needing to bother with caisteal dining room etiquette. He leaned against the wall of the inn where he viewed the entrance door, the stairs to the rooms, and the archway to the kitchen.

Senior men sat beside the fire and discussed their concerns over the early planting enforced upon them by their lady laird. Farmhands played cards and gambled away their coin. Laughter blared from the booths, and a lad staggered away, swaying. The fire crackled and sparked, and its heat washed over Arlan as the chatter continued.

A wizened figure approached the hearth, his cane tapping in time with his slow step. He passed Arlan's table, the hem of his threadbare robe dragging behind him. With a harp under his arm, he pulled at the stool by the broad hearth and sat. He rested his instrument in his lap, then his fingers plucked the strings with a delicate touch, as if picking fruit from the choicest of vines. His dancing fingers hovered over soft notes, demanding a silence in the noisy tavern. The woman serving the brew placed a tankard beside him.

"What have ye for us tonight, old man?" one man sitting in the booth closest to the fire asked, then shuffled away from the hearth, either to give the ancient some room, or for a better view of the entertainment to come.

"Tonight, I have for ye all a *Dragon's Tale*." The elderly man took a long pull of his ale.

A snort arose from the table of gamblers. "An' a tale 'twill be, old uncle. None have seen such a beast, ever."

"Aye, tell us your fable," grunted another, "an' we'll decide if it's worth our coin or no."

The robed performer cleared his throat and lifted his face, ignoring all disrespect. Arlan studied him. There was a bard in this ancient one. He'd come to a ragged state, yet his music held its magic as he began his ballad, and every ear and heart seemed to turn to him.

"Beltane fires would blaze brightly that eve,
Bright as the passions of Nyer,
For his true love was to meet him, she said
This night of the raging fire.

But his mother compelled him 'Search for our sheep
For a dragon has flown them away
One by one to his lair for to eat,
This terrible Beltane day.'

'Oh mother be not daft
For no such beasts ha' been,
Since afore old Bochra and her boat
O'er the floods were seen.'

'Ye ken I saw it son
Now off ye go to look.
I fear it shall be hungry soon
And seeking meat on hoof.'

Grumbling under his breath went Nyer
But wasted all his day.
No dragon spoor, nor claw marks deep
Had lighted on his way.

Our hero turns home to Beltane fires
With quickened step to tread,
The prospect of love sparks a-flying
Ringing in his head.

Tongues of flame flicker.
Worshippers encircle the blaze.
He joins the throng with dance and song
Catching his fair maid's gaze.

They run through fields, hand in hand.
They hold, they kiss,
They laugh, they love,
Leaving a ground-scorched tryst.

As their own incendiaries subside,
A rush of wind surrounds them,
With hide-stretched dragon wings,
The dreaded beast has found them.

Reaching for his trusty blade
But too late to defend,
Shocked, Nyer sees his naked woman

Enclosed in claws ascend.

Now our man believes.
But engrained for all eternity:
A vision of his love's bare arse
As the dragon ascends with glee."

Laughter erupted and travelled through the room to where Arlan sat with Bàn. Men by the fire spat beer and slapped their knees. Women laughed, their toothy smiles splitting their faces. Bàn shook, his chuckles overtaking him.

"I expected the old man to be more sombre." Arlan's belly rocked with his own mirth.

"By my sword, that's no way to lose your woman," Bàn snorted.

Arlan nodded, unable to speak with the tightness of a stifled laugh. The guffaws and shrieks of laughter settled and the bard, now having finished his ale, placed the empty tankard on the floor. Coin, tossed by the revellers, clinked, slowly filling the empty vessel.

"We'll start early tomorrow. I'm to bed." Arlan leaned forward and lifted an eyebrow. "You and Erin are...?"

"Friends." Bàn's cheeks blossomed in a rosy hue.

"A friend who is a lady doesn't wet her lips while talking to her friend who is a man, if she wants to remain just a friend."

Bàn lifted his tankard, taking his time to drain it. He brought it to the bench with a clunk. "I dinnae need your advice when it comes to women."

"Speaking of curious creatures"—Arlan swallowed the dregs in his own tankard— "Dragons. Myth or real?"

Bàn gave him a crooked smile. "Don't discount their existence because ye've never encountered one."

Arlan snorted. "Inform me when the legend comes to life."

TEN

—·—

The one I love has cursed me,
He who suckled at my own mother's breast.
His words are sharp daggers.
His lies fly like arrows
Swiftly loosed from the bow.

POETRY OF THE WARRIOR
WARRIOR SAGE TAPHAÌDH
(4009-4059 POST DRAGON WARS)

Western Sovereignty of Dál Gaedhle

Early morning sunlight peeked over the western horizon as Arlan sat astride Mengus, his troop following, walking their mounts through the hum of the awakening town. They stayed the night in a village ten leagues further south, with contented people and a welcoming inn pouring a flavoursome beer.

Chill air touched Arlan's bare arms and torso while Mengus' body heat warmed his legs where they rested against the horse's flanks. He held the reins loosely in his gloved hand, leading his troop out of the town heading in a south-easterly direction where a track wove through a thick forest of tall straight pines interspersed with rowan bright red in berry. The tangy scent of pine wafted across their path.

Mengus snorted, blowing a mist around his muzzle. Arlan surveyed the undergrowth on either side of the track. Mengus had saved him from a *felid* several times while out riding the mountains that encircled the valley surrounding The Keep. He would always pay attention to his stallion whose nose was more sensitive than his own to wildcats. Arlan inhaled deeply, opening his nostrils to the aromas floating on the air. No scent of wildcat today.

The dogs trotted beside the horses, keeping clear of their hooves, and their ears twitching toward the woods.

Arlan glanced aside to Bàn, who gave a short nod, his mouth set. He must have sensed it too. Arlan followed Bàn's progress as he rode to Muir at the rear guard. Muir acknowledged Bàn and indicated into the woodland. They peeled off, Douglas and Adele joining them, and walked their mounts into the forest. The deerhounds followed Leigh, noses to the ground, catching every scent.

The trees creaked, and branches snapped, followed by the crash of horses through the undergrowth in the wood beside Arlan. The hounds bayed and took up the chase as Bàn and the others pursued those who'd sought cover in the trees and were now urging their horses harder through the forest.

Arlan kicked Mengus to a canter to keep up with the chase progressing through the thick foliage beside him. Morrigan, Angus, and Erin fell in behind him.

Colours of the garb of those racing through the forest flashed in between the foliage—a cloak and a broad hat—two riders only. A gap in the trees revealed them with the dogs at the heels of their mounts. The wind caught the large broad-brimmed hat worn by the rider at the rear, lifting it into the path of those who pursued and uncovering the man's fair hair.

Kyle's fair hair.

Dragon's blaze! Arlan dug his heels into Mengus' sides. *I'd rather a kick in the head from a fully shod steed.*

Kyle slowed his gelding and Bàn rode alongside and grabbed the bridle, steering it out of the forest and toward Arlan on the track. Leigh whistled the dogs into line. Kyle held his chin high and his back ramrod straight.

"Why are you here, Kyle?" Arlan allowed the hard edge in his words.

Kyle snatched the control of his horse back from Bàn. "I will join you. I desire the military exper—"

"No. You will not." Arlan pulled Mengus to a halt, stabbing the air in front of Kyle with his finger. "You and your man will return immediately."

"I am a clan prince." Kyle glared at him beneath hooded lids. "I will do as I wish."

"I'm the head of this mission and I say who rides with us." Arlan spoke through gritted teeth. If this got dangerous, the last person to ride with them would be a *clan prince.*

Brother or no!

"Oh, so you want to take up your responsibilities now? Now that it's fun? Going on a special mission. Spying out the land." Kyle's mocking voice grew louder. "Does your troop know how much you do not want to be their battle chief? Do they know how irresponsible and selfish you really are? All fun and no accountability? How you abhor your duty, have no respect for obligation, and only want the privileges and benefits? How you'll abandon your people when the danger comes?"

Kyle's words poured from his mouth and Arlan let the wave wash over him in silence. Many words. Many accusations. Kyle was desperate, but Arlan couldn't discount his speech. It had an element of truth to it.

But once Kyle had finished, it would be *his* turn.

Arlan firmed his lips and slid his gaze to the side. His troop remained in the saddle. Angus' eyes went round, Muir turned away with a look of disgust, and Morrigan examined the reins resting on her war horse's mane.

The rant ceased, and Arlan flung his right leg over his stallion's neck and jumped off. He stepped up to Kyle still on his mount, suppressing a sneer at the pony-like stature of the beast. Arlan bore his eye-level glare into Kyle.

"Giant's steps!" Arlan growled his whisper. "What are ye doing?"

"I will accompany you and your troop." Kyle's tone and thick-lidded stare never wavered.

"Does Father know where you are? He'd never allow it. How will you explain your absence?"

"He thinks I am inspecting our lands at *Creagrubha Broch*. For all he knows, I'm tucked up next to the fire in our broch's round hall or galloping my steed along the beach." Kyle lifted his chin further.

Arlan inhaled slowly then let it out, his shoulders sagging.

After their days of travel, it was too far on their journey to send Kyle back. *I'll have to endure him.*

"You'll do as I order." Arlan stifled the impulse to slap his brother's superior expression off his face. "Despite your attempt to malign me, I am still the warrior—" Arlan stopped himself. He would've said *of our family*, but Eifion's admonition to forbearance echoed loudly in his head. "On this mission, I am in charge." Arlan used the tone of command reserved for his warriors.

Kyle flinched, then fiddled with the reins. "Understood." His gaze swung to those behind Arlan.

Will the others believe Kyle's rant and accusation about me?

Bàn stood at Arlan's back. He'd never believe he'd desert them, surely? The tension in Arlan's neck eased. He trusted his troop would see Kyle's ploys for what they were—a desperate attempt to get his own way.

Arlan turned on his heel and faced Bàn, whose nostrils flared, and a loud grunt came from Muir's direction.

"Morrigan."

Her head flicked up as she snatched her gaze from her hands. "Aye, lord?"

"You will guard Lord Kyle and his man. Do *not* leave their side."

She nudged her horse toward Kyle, wrinkling her nose.

"What!" Kyle spat. "I do not need a minder."

"Aye, but ye do." He spun to face Kyle and gave him a hard stare. "Not warrior trained, you're a liability. Ye weakened my troop by following us despite not qualifying."

"I protest!"

"Protest denied," he yelled. "Now we'll *all* have to watch your back."

Eleven

— • —

*For to the mage-sorcerer, matrimony, family, and clan will
have no hold. The pledge to magic surpasses all other
allegiances.*

*MAGE MASTER FÀISTINNAECH
(3310-3380 POST DRAGON WARS)*

**Eastern Clanlands of Dál Gallain
Lord Ciarán's Tower**

Drostan leaned over the stone-carved divination bowl in his workroom chamber. Bram stood with his back against the solid wooden door, an earnest expression covering his features.

"Weave your *staying* over mine while I perform this *seeing*. I will have no intrusions." Drostan sighed. If only he could justify a permanent *staying*. Lord Ciarán's patience grew thinner by the day, and interruptions were regular.

Drostan dropped his gaze to the divination bowl and placed his palms on the rough outer edges of the carved rim. With the dish itself polished smooth, the water within provided a clear reflection. The dark green eyes and short inky hair surrounding a plain-featured face of a man past his best years stared back at him.

He inhaled deeply and steadied his mind and body, for excitement would affect the management of this task, a technique requiring much practice and a skill essential in another mission Lord Ciarán had assigned to him. Today he would choose a small subject, but eventually he would control an animal of much greater proportions.

The clear water of his divination bowl now reflected the landmass of Dál Cruinne, the traverse of power through his conduit strengthening these images.

Drostan tightened his grip on the bowl's rim and centred himself, focussing on his inner source and combining it with the energy streaming through the stone.

His body thrummed, then his soul dived in.

He travelled to mountain peaks surrounded by air as clear as crystal and found an eyrie up high. The mother eagle lifted elegantly in flight from her twigged nest. Hatchlings, uncoordinated and floppy, screeched their baby chirps.

Drostan headed to her and joined her flight path, then collided and entered the bird—to a glorious view.

Oh, to see as far and as clear as a bird of prey!

She resisted. Drostan pushed against the pull and wrested control.

He flew her to the border between Dál Gallain and Dál Gaedhle, then headed northwest. The eagle pulled back on him the further they flew from the eyrie, but he urged her on. With her sight he spied a group of horsemen about four days' ride from the abandoned border forts. He guided the eagle closer, and with his heart soaring as high as wings, he let out an eagle shriek. Then, raised on thermal winds, he circled.

Energy bathed Drostan's spirit. Magic flowed through every fibre of his being.

Now with his *seeing* task complete, he would hold this magic for as long as he was able.

He sucked more energy from each source of his conduit available to him. From the divination bowl and the walls of the tower. From flagstone in the courtyard below. From the drystone walls surrounding the fields nearby and the very rocks that lay within them. Even through the sarsens standing not far from here, which the ancients had lifted to their positions when Dál Cruinne was young.

Magical power came from the earth, deep in the centre of this world's core, the derivation of all beginnings, the foundation of all. It flowed to the surface, through bedrock and shale, through the walls of the caisteal—and him.

He would savour every moment of this force of the universe.

How it filled his empty heart—*the only equal consolation*.

Someone pressed a firm grip on his shoulder, then shook his body. Jolted, his spirit let go. The magical energy slipped through his grasping spirit fingers like smoke as an urgent disturbance wracked his body.

"Master?" Young Bram's voice laced with concern, pierced his hearing. "Master Drostan! Awake!"

Drostan returned, jerking into his body, now slumped with his face resting on the edge of the divination bowl.

The lad hovered over him; brow as furrowed as a newly ploughed field.

"Master Drostan, ye scared me so. Ye would not wake."

Drostan raised to stand but his legs, as though filled with water and not flesh, slid his body to the floor. Bram eased him down, then pulled a blanket from the short couch by the wall and placed it over him.

Drostan lay down fully, the floorboards firm against his back but his body smouldering with the residual traces of his power... the all familiar afterglow.

"Drostan, master, ye have been at the divination bowl so long..." he glanced at the workshop door. "It is now past mid-morning, and I hear Lord Ciarán stir below. He will wish a report, will he not?"

Ciarán perused the spines of his newly acquired volumes neatly displayed on a bookshelf in his library. *Dragons: Myth or Legend? The Art of Simian Empty Fist. How The Keltoi Built the World.* And his favourite: *Tobraichean na Beatha: Dead or Alive?* Ciarán's snort echoed in his quiet chamber.

Then he huffed. Of all his searching these past thirty years, scarce were the texts on portals. He jiggled his hands held behind his back, nails digging deep into palms. Employing a mage was a strategy yet to prove as fruitful as he wished.

Surely those acquainted with magic would have the nounce to find them!

He dropped his gaze to the unrolled scroll on his desk, held open thus with a smooth stone on one edge and a bronze statuette on the other.

It was one of his most antique documents—an Ionan Scroll.

He had revised the archaic tongue from yet another of his many texts. He grunted an acknowledgement at his foresight in the choice of collections.

He rubbed the back of his neck. Yet deciphering the intriguing characters had proved difficult. But what gems of knowledge he had already glimpsed! He chuckled to himself. This text had hinted the Fae were not all they purported to be. According to the lore of Dál Cruinne, the other world belonged to the Faerie folk. But if he'd interpreted correctly, the world of the Fae was a sham. A ruse to divert people from the true nature of the Faerie realm—another world altogether. And to keep the unwanted away from portals—and to all they gave access.

A substantial portion of another Ionan text, as yet undeciphered—for the language was in such an ancient form—supposedly discussed the treatment of dragons at the time immediately after the wars. It hinted that some noble-minded souls, thinking themselves righteous, had saved the surviving creatures and placed them in sanctuaries. This text held, he hoped, information of where to find them.

Further translation was required... and Drostan must do *his* part. Use his magic to discover the whereabouts of these beasts.

Where *was* that mage? He clasped his hands behind his back once more.

It was Drostan's custom to be annoying him well and truly before midday, but there had not been yet one sign of him. No disdainful looking down his nose at him. No hovering when he should get on with it. Those portals would not find themselves!

Ciarán strode out of his room and up the two flights of stairs that curved around the sandstone walls of his tower to where the mage's chamber sat at the top. The mage's workroom would be dingy, dirty, and smelly, and full of books and parchments containing spells, the macabre ingredients of which were no doubt displayed in containers sitting on a shelf within easy reach, along with the other paraphernalia relevant to his magical arts. He would find Drostan stooped over some primordial soup, with, of course, the bronze goblet in a prominent place in the workshop.

Ciarán approached and raised a hand to knock. A warmth buzzed in his clenched fist, holding it in place a hand's breadth from the aged timber. With a jerk, the buzz released.

"Hmph. Magic," he grumbled, then pounded on the wood.

Soft steps came toward the door, and it opened.

"Aye, my lord?" The mage peered out from behind a straight fringe, and the sensation that this man barely tolerated Ciarán returned.

But a good mage he was. Gifted. Talented. Highly recommended. Yes, even if he did not require a mage for certain projects, he would retain this one's services to have the appearance of the mystical.

That always helps to keep the rabble in a state of awe and fear.

"Well?" Ciarán snapped, then peered past Drostan, who immediately stepped onto the landing.

In the workroom, Drostan's apprentice busied himself with those rotted plants they picked and hung to putrefy on the rack now lowered from the ceiling. The room stank of them. The mage pulled the door closed on his view.

"With what have you found to occupy your morning, Drostan?" Ciarán folded his arms, creaking his leather armour.

"My divination bowl, my lord." The mage stood stiffly.

Ciarán snorted. "So, what has your little bronze cup been up to now?"

"It is carved of stone, my lord." The tone of the mage's words mocked patience.

Despite his young age, some had labelled this one a *sorcerer.* He maintained stone to be his power *conduit. Whatever that could mean.* It was difficult to comprehend the manner of magic in which this mage engaged. Drostan insisted touching rock of some sort was essential to his magic. Most inconvenient at times, for it meant confining the man to the caisteal.

Maybe on further occasions I could nail him to a standing stone—

"It will interest you, my lord." The mage's voice snapped Ciarán back to his stare of deep, deep green.

"Another portal?" Ciarán's heart quickened. Access to the other world was imperative for his plans, and the geographical situation of the nearest portal—so far, the only one identified—very much out-of-bounds.

"I have seen a troop making their way from the northwest, my lord."

"Not another portal then?" Ciarán's boot tap echoed up the stairwell. "Why do you tell me of this troop?"

"I suspect that amongst the group are clansmen-relatives of yours from the northwest, for they are mostly warriors of noble birth who ride. They disguise it poorly, as most wear the tartans of the Houses of Dál Gaedhle and they bear no body armour as is the custom of warriors of that sovereignty. They are young, so your cousins perhaps?"

"*My* cousins?" Ciarán's brow tightened. "My sole young cousins would be the sons of Alana and Donnach, only one of whom I have met as a snot-nosed babe." He clamped his mouth shut.

Alana had not come to mind for some years. It had taken him much time to mention her name and not grieve all over again. Twin tongues of flame erupted and licked each other, threatening to scorch his soul. He could name them both—the burn of anger and the fire of passion. He shook himself, snapping his attention to the here and now. "Tell me more. What do they look like?"

"The tallest is a massive man with black hair and rides his stallion as one. Another, much slighter, has fair hair and grey... eyes... my lord." The mage passed his gaze over him, briefly resting on his long hair, which today he wore loose, then looked him in the eye once more. "The other riders respect him, defer to him, even the tall dark-haired one who leads them. It is an interesting dynamic, my lord."

"*Interesting dynamic*—" Ciarán dragged in air between his teeth, curling his hands into fists. "So, the forays to the villages by our warriors for hire have finally got Donnach MacEnoicht's attention. *Hmm.*" Leather creaked. "And a portal?"

"No, my Lord Ciarán, it will take some time. Dál Cruinne is a large realm."

"Do not search the whole of Dál Cruinne!" He spat the words. "Find something here in Dál Gallain! I do not wish to travel far each time I require the use of a portal! Do I have to clarify every point?" Ciarán spun on his heel at the top of the stair. "Get on with it!" he tossed the command over his shoulder and strode down the steps.

So... if the two Drostan had mentioned were the sons of Alana and Donnach, it made sense one would have Ciarán's own colouring. He gave a sharp, satisfied grunt.

Had Donnach MacEnoicht ever realised this son and heir was not his own progeny?

TWELVE

— • —

Treat all persons as noble,
Down to the poorest beggar.
For we are all sons of kings.

WISDOM WRITINGS ON KINGSHIP
SAGE GLIOCAS
(2870-2962 POST DRAGON WARS)

Western Sovereignty of Dál Gaedhle
In the East

Ache settled in Arlan's thighs and back as he rode Mengus toward the small inn in the wee village.

"I've never been ahorse for an entire week afore," Angus said behind Arlan. "My legs feel like they're filled with the sand of the practice yard, lord."

"Yer heid, ye mean." Douglas spoke as he rode past Angus, then nudged his horse beside Arlan. "We have been blessed with the kind hospitality of farmers these past days, Lord Arlan. Ye paid them for their kindness, and that was well. It warmed my heart to know care for the stranger is still a code in this part of the world." He lifted his chin in the direction of the wattle-and-daub inn, its wooden lintel rotting. "But..."

The faded sign hanging above the door stated *Hound and Hare*. Two dogs fought on the street, and Leigh called their own hounds to heel and leashed them. A middle-aged man watched their approach with a squinted eye and a bland expression. His breeches showed wear at the knees and his jacket was ill-fitting.

"Aye, smiles all round, if ye please, warriors," Arlan said under his breath. Grunts acknowledged his quiet command. "And do yer best to keep it peaceful."

Arlan dismounted and stood a pace from the man who rested on the steps of the inn. The man expectorated a glob of dirty-yellow sputum at Arlan's feet.

"Friend, would ye be so kind as to show us to your stables?" Arlan glanced at the glob next to his boot.

With a silent flick of his head, the man directed them to the stables that sat past the chipped corner wall, so they led their horses to the stalls. There was room but barely enough feed for all their animals, and they tended to their mounts themselves.

"I'll stay with the horses." Muir grabbed some hay and rubbed down the rump of his war horse.

"We'll secure the lodgings." Arlan stepped to the stable door.

"And I'll remain with the horses," Muir repeated, his expression stern.

"Aye, so will Douglas and mysel'." Leigh nodded his agreement. "Dinnae like oor chances of enough cots inside, anyways."

Arlan walked with Bàn back to the inn and entered, dipping under the low front doorway and stepping straight into a woman holding a tankard out to a patron. The sharp scent of stale beer filled the small main room of the tavern and stung Arlan's nose. The woman wore a dirty apron and wisps of hair poked out from under her cloth-cap sitting askew.

"'Ow many?" she snapped, revealing a toothless mouth.

"We are eleven in number, but three will stay—" Arlan began.

"Got two rooms." Her breath, as stale as the beer scent, wafted into Arlan's face.

He stifled a gag. "I'll take them both, please. Some of my men will be with our horses in the stable."

"Tha's extra."

"Aye, we'll pay." Arlan reassured her.

"Up front. Vittles is extra, an' all."

Arlan peered into one of the assigned rooms where a double bed sat beneath a grimy window and a stub of a candle rested on a chair in a puddle of wax.

"I think the women can share this one." Arlan moved along the narrow hallway to the other room, with Bàn a step behind him. "You and I, Kyle and his man, and Angus, this one."

The windows, cloudy with grime, let in sparse light, and Arlan flicked the blankets back on the beds for inspection. Grey, unwashed sheets wafted the odour of stale sweat into his face.

"I don't like the distance between rooms." Bàn held the door handle, his mouth screwed to the side. "The women will be far from us."

"Nae choice," Arlan grunted. "I'd like to see anyone try to give Adele trouble." He poked Bàn's bare abdomen. "But you're not concerning yourself with Adele, are you?"

Bàn's cheeks pinked. "We'll see what the other clientele are like."

Kyle stood in the passage, his cheeks a deep red hue. Morrigan stood at his back, her arms folded across her chest, glaring at him.

"I would much prefer camping in the woods and taking our chances with bandits than rubbing shoulders with this rabble." Kyle dipped his head in a mock bow. "But the decision is yours, o great leader. I shall dine in our room tonight."

"This smells as sweet as a horse's fart." Douglas held a spoonful of the evening meal under his nose.

"Does nae taste much better. I'm guessing it's rodent." Angus made hard work of swallowing it.

"Now, now, lads." Bàn spoke in a low voice. "At least ye did nae have to catch it."

"Nae body caught this. It was already *deid* on the side o' a track." Douglas put the spoon into his mouth at last.

"Oh, don't be babies! It's not that bad." Adele shovelled her meal into her mouth with gusto.

Arlan swallowed the stew, then leaned back into his seat. With his shoulders to the wall and his face to the door, he scanned the inn. Deep-voiced chatter echoed off bare walls and interspersed with orders called by the tavern wench. At the wide hearth, wood smoke funnelled away from a partially blocked chimney and vented into the tavern's one and only public room, then hung in the air. At every table people sat in faded, threadbare clothes, drawing on tobacco sticks. During the constant murmur of conversation, the diners often glanced toward Arlan, then beside him at his troop, but none with welcoming smiles. Their fellow patrons avoided them, only offering glares in their direction and commenting amongst themselves. The candlelight didn't reach the dim corners.

Morrigan walked down the stairs, returning from taking bowls of stew and chunks of bread to Kyle and his manservant, shaking her head and muttering. A serving woman, rotund, middle-aged and wearing a grease-stained apron, walked by Morrigan and with dirty hands grabbed her tartan plaid draped over her shoulder, pulling it aside.

"What d'you wear under tha'?"

The chatter quietened and wolf whistles erupted from the long bench crowded with male customers. Morrigan slapped the woman's hand away and tugged her plaid back across herself, covering the leather banding around her breasts, and her fit, muscular torso.

"Show us what ye got, ladies!" The shout came from amongst the leering diners.

Arlan and Bàn rose together, Douglas cursed, and Adele placed her hand on the top of her boot, grasping the handle of her short blade hidden there.

"No, Adele," Arlan hissed, then he swore, for their broadswords were upstairs, held by Kyle's manservant for safekeeping and as a show of their intentions for a peaceful evening.

The chorus of comments ceased, and tankards clunked on wooden benches once more.

"Please sirs, did nae mean no trouble, just curious, is all. Have nae seen many women warriors afore." The serving woman performed an awkward curtsy to Morrigan—who stifled a laugh at this—then scurried along to shush the lingering murmurs of the men at the long bench.

Morrigan returned to her seat and Angus slipped his arm around her waist in a proprietary manner, sending a scowl across the room.

"By my blade, that leaves a taste in my mouth as foul as the ale they serve." Bàn spoke in low tones to Arlan.

"Aye. I think you should sleep at the door to the women's chamber tonight as a deterrent." Arlan nudged Bàn, and they both sat.

Leers faded from the faces of the patrons on the opposite side of the room.

"Do you think we can't protect ourselves?" Adele kept her voice low.

"I know you can." Arlan mirrored her quiet tones. "You know I prefer to avoid conflict. They appear unused to women warriors and their curiosity may prove to be an issue. Bàn by your door will be off-putting enough."

Adele grunted a reluctant sounding acquiescence.

Arlan leaned into the wall. Erin's gaze rose from her supper to Bàn, and he returned a look from across the table. She smiled and Bàn's dimples pitted.

After the meal, Douglas, Muir and Leigh bid Arlan and the others goodnight and left to sleep wrapped in their plaids beside the horses and hounds as planned.

"I shall go up soon after the women," Bàn whispered to Arlan. "I ken we're not welcome here, and I believe we tempt a *stramash* if we sit here much longer."

"Lord Arlan." Adele stood. "We'll be away to our beds." She turned and left.

Angus, Morrigan and Erin left the table after her. Erin reached the base of the stairs and snuck a glance at Bàn. Bàn drained his tankard.

"Ye should give them time to settle before you go up." Arlan sipped his beer; it was sour on his tongue.

"I'll lie across their doorway." Bàn burped and squinted at him. "Maybe even get some sleep."

Arlan grinned as Bàn ascended the stairs, then left the tavern's main room himself to share the upstairs chamber with Kyle, his man and Angus at the opposite end of the corridor.

Conversation and laughter from the tavern's patrons below muffled through the floorboards and kept him awake most of the night. Loud voices followed by a scuffle erupted as light from the late rising moon shone weakly through the dirty window of their room, the snores of Kyle's man gradually drowning them out.

Arlan rose early, his eyes gritty, and strode along the corridor to the women's room where the doorway sat bare. Murmurs and shuffling came from within the chamber. He knocked, and Adele invited him to enter with a note of amusement in her tone.

He pushed the door, but it stopped part way, stuck against something solid. A male voice grunted, so Arlan poked his head around the door. Behind it, Bàn lay on the floor draped in his tartan plaid, which he'd used for a blanket overnight. He lifted the length of woollen cloth to reveal Erin tucked by his side. They both stood, allowing Arlan to open the door fully.

Erin strode to her gear, with cheeks flushed and a strangled grin. Adele sat on the bed, her hand covering her mouth and shoulders shaking with mirth.

Morrigan slid by Arlan and through the door. "I'd better go tend to my charge, lord." Bàn walked past Arlan.

"Sleep well?" Arlan lifted an eyebrow.

Bàn pressed his lips together, unsuccessfully preventing a smile.

Arlan went downstairs to the tavern's one main room to breakfast on gruel and dry bread. The rest of his troop followed in dribs and drabs. They sat as a group and ate in the quiet tavern, the raucous attentions of last evening absent this morning. Muir and Leigh sat at the bench with dark circles under their eyes and Douglas had remained at the stables with their animals.

Kyle and his man approached the table with Morrigan on their heels. Kyle glared at her and huffed.

"Must I continue to have a babysitter?"

"Aye." Arlan glanced up between spoonfuls of the tasteless oats in water.

Kyle narrowed his eyes at Arlan, then sat on the far side of the table. "You slept poorly, my friends?" He directed his question to Muir. "Were you concerned for our mounts?"

"Aye, and rightly so, lord prince, for we disturbed intruders lurking near on three occasions." Muir pulled his salt-and-pepper hair back, tying it into a bun.

"Four," Leigh said dourly, plonking a crust of bread into the gruel, and dipping it up and down.

"Ye tell 'em, old Tam!" The rotund serving woman spoke to an elderly man at the table on the other side of the room, lifting her chin in their direction. The delegate from those breaking their fast on the far side of the tavern approached Arlan's table, screwing his soft cap in his hands. Arlan stood, inviting the old man to speak.

"Lord." He craned his neck to look Arlan in the eye. "We see ye are warriors."

Arlan nodded his encouragement for the man to continue.

"Ma grandson's a braw rider, ken? He snuck awa' frae the village wha' he bides. The one tha' sits batween the twa forts that used tae guard us frae the east, ken?"

"Oot with it, man!" the serving woman yelled from the other side of the room. "Yer kin's a dyin'."

The man's knuckles whitened around a hat scrunched to nothing. "Och, well, they was bein' attacked by Dál Gallain bandits, ye ken?"

Wooden eating utensils clattered on the tabletop behind Arlan. His troop gathered their gear and Muir and Leigh hurried out to ready the animals.

"What are you doing, Arlan?" Kyle stepped close to him as they walked their horses out of the ramshackle stable, holding his mount's reins in a tight grip. Morrigan had mounted already and rode her horse not far behind Kyle. War horses nickered, tack jangled and the warriors murmured gently to their mounts as they prepared to leave. "You cannot go. Did Father not say you and your troop were to observe only? No engagement." Kyle's voice held a faint tremor. "At all."

"It's a chance to eyeball the enemy. That's what we're here for, is it no'? What better way than to see them in action?" Arlan spoke low and steady. *Kyle needs to understand we are going. No argument.* "Ye could stay here and wait with Lady Morrigan, if ye wished." Arlan leaned into Kyle, raising both eyebrows. Kyle flinched, and Morrigan groaned. "But I'm uncertain if we will return this way." Arlan bore his stare into Kyle, willing him to protest further.

Kyle's nostrils flared. He cast his hooded gaze over the tavern and its occupants, who now waited outside to see Arlan and his warriors in the right direction. Kyle's throat muscles worked as he swallowed.

"I shall accompany you. To keep an eye on you, little brother. Non-engagement, remember?"

Arlan halted, Mengus' nose bumping into him, and his war horse nickered in annoyance. "If people require help, I'm no' going to stand by and watch." He pointed his finger at Kyle's face. "But you can just keep out of the way. If we must intervene, ye are to stay behind, understand? I need *warriors* if that occurs."

Kyle blinked at the implied insult, but remained silent.

Bàn ran toward them, having clarified the directions from the elderly fellow.

"The report is but an hour old. The lad says the village was aflame when he rode for help sometime before midnight." Bàn leaped onto his stallion. "If we hasten, we may catch them."

Thirteen

— • —

Stay awa frae am fuath. *For a one ha' only tae pass by their door and they git ye und drag ye in, aye? Some come back at once. Some after mony a moon. Ye'll no' be the same when ye do come back... if ye do at all.*
Old Tam.
This recounting of Dál Cruinne Lore is a typical representation of local belief held by inhabitants residing within the vicinity of portals. Am fuath *meaning the Fae.*

FROM THE JOURNAL OF CIARÁN GALLAWAIN

The Border Between Dál Gaedhle and Dál Gallain

Arlan rode hard, pushing his troop toward the Dál Gaedhle village midway between two fort ruins that sat on the borderlands. A peaceful truce had reigned for years, the original purposes of the now abandoned line of forts lost in the annals of time. Arlan grimaced. His tutors would have known, but swordplay had held more excitement than a droning history lecture.

Arlan and his troop arrived at the hush-filled village, the scent of burning wood and hot metal blowing into his face. Their mounts foamed at their bits as the descending sun touched the charred black roofs of this wee hamlet. The remains of once sturdy wooden dwellings were smouldering ruins and a smoke-haze lingered in the air. Arlan blinked away the sting from his eyes. Empty livestock pens stood with gates open, fresh corpses lay beside their dwellings, and the stench of burned flesh wafted through the air, searing Arlan's nose. Dogs lapped at pools of blood beside the slain.

"Deamhan's balls," Muir breathed.

Leigh leashed their hounds, who whined and paced. Arlan covered his mouth and nose with a handful of his dark plaid as Mengus skittered sideways and shook his head, giving a throaty neigh. Arlan turned to Erin and Morrigan, whose eyes streamed, smoke perhaps not the sole cause of their tears. His warriors held the reins of nickering, jostling mounts and patted their necks, tack jangling with the animals' discomfort.

"—*a dragon's*— Pardon, ladies." Douglas covered his nose and mouth with his plaid.

Bàn's eyes were slits above his makeshift mask.

Kyle rode up beside Arlan. "What has happened here?"

"Isn't it obvious, brother?" Arlan swallowed hard, the dryness in his mouth unassuaged. "Evil men have decimated this village!"

"That's not what I mean. You, in your usual ignorance, state the obvious. I look for the motive behind it. Why are people of Dál Gallain turning against us? We are their Dál Gaedhle cousins. We have lived in harmony these many years. Why this...?" His hand dropped limply to his side.

A thin wail caught the edges of Arlan's hearing, and he turned toward a nearby lane. He nudged Mengus forward to where a lone child stood, swaying, legs trembling and about to collapse beneath him. Adele jumped off her horse, ran to the injured child and cradled him in her solid arms. His skin was raw and black in places, his wails growing louder where her embracing arms touched red sloughed flesh. Arlan jumped off Mengus and joined Adele, leaning over her; the smell of charred flesh and the acrid scent of burnt hair rose to Arlan's nose.

His heart stuttered.

The child whimpered and shivered, his jaw chattering. Adele held him close and shushed and crooned. Arlan's breath caught. This child would certainly die, and his toughest warrior woman's gentle embrace would be this wee boy's last memory.

Moments passed and the child's wails, now piercing the air less often, grew softer. Behind Arlan, Kyle tutted, Morrigan sniffed while Douglas cursed. The others seemed to hold their breaths.

The child stilled, and Adele carried the lad to a patch of soft green away from the charred buildings and laid him on the cushion of grass, then lifted her face to Arlan, wet droplets falling from her eyes.

"We must give this poor soul—all these poor souls—a proper burial, lord."

The dull thunder of horses' hooves came from the far end of the village. Their own horses nickered, restless, and Bàn, holding his own stallion tight, grabbed Mengus' reins.

Arlan's heart seemed to tear within his chest. To only observe the troubles meant the perpetrators would flee without answering for their actions.

Not fair. Not right. Not *just*.

Nae other choice. "We must pursue," Arlan shouted, then vaulted onto Mengus.

Adele flicked tears away from her cheeks with her fingers. "But Lord—"

"We'll attend to burials another time. We must catch these *bassas*."

Adele's nostrils flared, but she remounted. They all followed him, kicking their horses to a gallop.

Ahead, the drumming of hooves faded with the attackers leaving the village on fresher mounts than theirs and charging on. Arlan strained forward in the saddle to follow their tracks, peering into the forest outside the village.

The woodland thinned and became a grassy moor edged by trees. The bandits were in the distance. Pursuing them over the moor's wide-open space would expose his own warriors. Arlan turned Mengus back into the woods and led his troop along the inner forest edge. In their confidence, or carelessness, no bandit had looked behind them as they galloped across the moor. The corner of Arlan's mouth tugged—he'd keep his warriors in the tree line.

The raiders rode to the forest directly ahead. Arlan signalled for his troop to be quiet while they walked their horses with care through the ash and alder to the other side of the moor. Arlan dismounted and his warriors did the same and, with mouths shut, they led their mounts in the direction the bandits had gone.

Smoke drifted lazily through the foliage, and the clanking of cooking pots and brash laughter filtered through the trees. The bandits must have a camp of sorts. Arlan ordered his warriors to settle in the dense, bushy growth by the forest's edge about a bow's range from the camp. He tethered Mengus to a tree close by while his warriors did the same and Leigh muzzled the dogs. Arlan squatted behind a large grey boulder and leaned back on it, Bàn joining him against the hard rock.

"We need to know how many are our foes, and what they do in their camp," Arlan whispered to his fellow warriors now squatting in front of him.

"Erin and I will go and see." Bàn signalled for Erin to join him. "It's almost dusk. We'll keep to the shadows."

Arlan nodded in reply, and Bàn and Erin crept away without another word. The cloying stench of burned flesh hung about Arlan still, permeating the cloth of his plaid, lingering in the back of his mouth, and swallowing did naught to remove it.

The troop remained quiet, listening to the activity in the bandit camp. Women's voices, shrill and tremulous, mingled with the deep loud tones of the male bandits. Morrigan's brow creased, Adele checked the handles of her blades, and Douglas and Muir tensed, their expressions hardening. Leigh clamped his hands around the alpha hound's snout, shushing them all to silence. Kyle opened his mouth as though to speak. Arlan widened his eyes, putting a finger to his lips until Kyle shut his mouth tight, teeth clunking, and scowled.

Dusk drew closer with the chirps and rustles of nocturnal forest dwellers stirring nearby, and the warriors' ears were alert and eyes sharp. Bàn and Erin slid back through the low hanging foliage.

"There's a dozen of them," Bàn whispered, crouching beside Arlan. "And half as many women and girls, most tied together in a huddle. The one who I take for the bandit leader is a hard-looking man. Scarred. Strong. They're all well-armed with broadswords and wear the leather cuirass of the east." His voice was as tight as his expression. "They dinnae wear plaid. Cannae tell their clan."

Strained female voices floated across to Arlan, echoing his childhood cries at a beating from an older, bigger Kyle. Arlan's throat constricted. "They're hurting these women." Arlan ground his teeth. "I will *not* let these bandits go unpunished while they harm those weaker than themselves."

Bàn's stare was like flint. "We must release them."

Muir brought a pot of woad from his saddlebags, and the warriors painted their faces and arms.

"We're fewer." Arlan clenched his fists—*a warrior's duty is to protect*. "We need a diversion."

"Aye," Muir said, "then we'll sneak in and free the women and—"

High-pitched screams shredded the air. Erin and Morrigan flinched, turning their faces sharply in the camp's direction. The horses nickered their unease, and Leigh shushed the hounds. Adele grasped her sword handle as they all froze in a crouch. Ropey arm muscles tensed, gripping weapons, and all nerves were as taut as a dragon's skin-stretched wing.

Arlan stood and peered over the edge of the boulder. Firelight flickered with figures passing back and forth before the glowing flames. A deep burning stirred within him. It came from his guts and stayed in his heart and fists. He faced Leigh and Muir. He needn't ask. The hard lines of Muir's expression deepened by the moment, and he never flinched. Leigh nodded, grim faced. So did Bàn. His entire troop, including Kyle, faced him with jaws set, and looks mirroring what his own heart held.

"Mount up." His whisper came out harsh. "We're meant to be no' engaging, but I cannae do naught and let *that* happen." He flicked his chin in the bandit camp's direction. "Our actions will be construed as aggression, which could lead to something bigger—but so be it."

He'd given his first real orders—his troop were now a warband. His pulse beat at a faster pace.

"Prince Kyle, ye and yoor man will remain here with Morrigan," he commanded, and Kyle's eyes narrowed. "I mean it. You stay here." Arlan maintained his stare until Kyle acknowledged him with an abrupt nod.

"You can also stay with Prince Kyle," Arlan said to Erin and Adele. "Keep a lookout for us so we may make a quick escape."

"We will not remain here!" Erin's whisper scratched at Arlan's ears, her eyes glinting in the poor light of near dusk. "Pardon, my Lord Arlan." Her tone mellowed a blade's width. "We can release the captives while you other warriors deal with these merciless monsters."

"I'm dealin' with the bandits!" The hiss of Adele's unsheathing sword wove through her words. "I'll gladly slay those child murderers."

"*No, no, no, no...*" A female voice pierced the evening air.

Arlan faced the bandit camp. Women screamed and coarse male laughter mingled with growling commands.

"Very well," he ordered. "No one be foolish."

His warriors scrambled to mount, and Erin and Adele ran through the cover of the trees toward the bandit camp. Arlan kicked Mengus to a gallop. Morrigan's and Kyle's voices—hissing and argumentative—rose from their hiding place behind the boulder.

Arlan glanced over his shoulder at the halfway mark to ensure his warriors readied their weapons. He glanced again. Kyle and his man rode at the back of the troop, trailing behind with a grim-faced Morrigan in pursuit.

Dragon's teeth! Too late to turn him back.

If Morrigan engaged, Kyle must fend for himself.

Arlan stifled a groan—*too much else to concern me now.*

They crossed the open moor in no time, the figures in the camp's firelight sharpening in definition as Arlan drew nearer. By the fire, two men leered at their companion who lay on top of a shrieking, struggling woman. Another dragged a woman by the hair to the edge of the campfire's light and threw her to the dirt, then loosened his breeches.

Arlan entered the camp, his cry growing, almost silent at first. Rising through his voice box, it boiled and throbbed until he roared. His warriors took up his war cry, their roars ringing through the trees.

The bandits occupied with the woman by the fire faced Arlan and his troop, eyes widening and leering mouths dropping open at the mounted, screaming warriors daubed in blue woad, brandishing blades and heading their way.

Ahead of Arlan, two bandits stood. One spun to face him, holding a sword in readiness, alerted by the pounding hooves of his approaching troop, no doubt. He stood his ground at Arlan's approach. Spinning Mengus at the last moment, avoiding the blade aimed for his mount, Arlan cut to the left with his sword, slicing the bandit deep across the chest. Warmth sprayed Arlan's bare skin.

The bandit's companion ran to the tethered horses, picking up sword and shield as he did.

Arlan turned Mengus and charged for others standing in a huddle mid-camp, beheading one as he rode past, his shoulder jolting with the act. Bàn sliced the one beside him. Mengus snorted then bayed a loud neigh, his hooves thudding in the dirt.

A whoosh of air brushed past Arlan as Muir's spear, *Sleaghach*, flew by and through the back of the man who ran holding up his loosened breeches.

Arlan reached the back of the camp and spun Mengus around, readying for another charge. His heart sledge-hammered his chest as his grip tightened on his blade dripping blood, and his vision now clearer than ever. He kicked Mengus forward and slashed down on a bandit wielding an axe. The axe and the man's hand dropped to the ground.

On Arlan's right, Erin burst through the foliage, Adele not far behind her, jogging in a crouch. Knife in hand, Erin scurried to the tied captives, their guard fleeing with Muir on his heels.

Off to the side of Arlan's vision, a flash of grey fur headed for the far edge of the camp to where a bandit ran, fumbling and dropping a dagger and a sack. Leigh had let the hounds go. Barks turned to shrieking growls as they pounced, knocking the man to the ground and, as a pack, they sunk their teeth in and tore at him. Fur, skin, and blood flew.

Adele grappled with a bandit while Erin cut the bonds of a girl. The air filled with the shrieks of women and horses' shrill neighs as bandits hurriedly mounted, most kicking their horses to gallop and heading away from the camp. Gruff cries from bandits and his warriors came at Arlan from all directions. He blinked, clearing the sweat from his eyes. Mengus jostled beneath him.

Arlan pulled in Mengus, turning him to head for one mounted bandit who'd remained. Hooves thudded past him. It was Bàn, headed for Erin, yelling a cry of warning. Arlan turned back to Erin. A bandit had pulled a dagger from her back. It glinted wet in the firelight as she crumpled to the ground like a discarded garment. Arlan's guts clenched and campfire smoke stung his eyes.

Bàn roared through his teeth, kicking his war horse to a gallop toward the murderer, his sword aloft. He sliced through the man's leather armour, leaving a deep red gouge in the man's ribs and shoulder. He spun his mount and sliced again; the man's head hung loosely from his neck as he dropped like a rag doll.

Arlan urged Mengus on to the mounted bandit, who now flew toward him roaring in a foreign tongue, his shield partially covering leather-plated armour of the east. Arlan's sword clashed with the charging man's blade. Metal rang and his arm shuddered. The *droch dhuine's* gaze seared him as he passed. Arlan grunted, turning Mengus tight to follow the bandit.

Bàn's horse skittered riderless in Arlan's path and for a heartbeat, he struggled to find Bàn through the mêlée and dust.

There! Over by a makeshift shelter.

Bàn embraced Erin's body, his chest slicked red with her blood.

Pounding hooves caught Arlan's hearing so he rounded Mengus. The *droch dhuine* was making another charge. Arlan squinted, now facing into the light of the setting sun. The bandit threatened Arlan with his sword and black eyes pierced him from beneath a leather helmet. The man roared.

Mengus snorted, his flanks hot beneath Arlan's thighs. He kicked hard, his war horse rearing and tearing at the air with his heavily shod hooves, then he lurched in the saddle as they galloped on. Arlan held his broadsword tighter and tucked his shield closer, a whiff of willow wood filling his nostrils, competing with the stirred dust and the metallic scent of blood.

A few paces more and his adversary would be on him. Arlan screamed his war cry.

Yelling his lungs empty.

Bawling the heated, pulse pounding ache that came from a deep place.

The forest changed.

And all went white.

Fourteen

— • —

Where were you when I established the worlds?
When I crumpled the ground like a cloth,
Pushed landmasses together with my bare hands
And formed the mountains?
Did you have being when I opened my storehouse of seas
And poured full the oceans of the worlds?

SECRET SACRED WRITINGS OF THE SAGES

Western Sovereignty of Dál Gaedhle
The Keep

The words of the scroll echoed in Eifion's mind, directing his reflections. He rested his finger on pursed lips. This text had drawn him, one he had not touched for some time. Its words were both a comfort and enigmatic. He closed the scroll and replaced it in the hidden drawer of his desk. Folding his hands in his sleeves, he left his chamber in The Keep and wandered to his favourite place of contemplation, pondering the plural all the way.

Worlds... not world.

He sat on the bench beside the yew tree's massive, sturdy trunk and leaned into the cool stone behind him. None knew the tree's true age. Only on its death could they count the year rings. He reached out and ran his fingers over the rough bark of the branch overhanging his seat and a sweet, woody aroma greeted his nostrils. Thick solid branches twisted away from the house of worship, growing in search of stronger light. Deep shade resided here, and in its closest aspect to the wall, mere dim sunlight reached most of the year, and none in winter. Dark green needle leaves canopied Eifion's position.

He closed his eyes and gave in to his meditations. His reflections went to Arlan and his journey to the border. The lad always drew him.

No, I should contemplate another.

He picked a sprig of yew and ran his touch along the needles' smooth lengths, their ends spiky against his fingers.

No other thoughts came, only those of Arlan, and strong now. Eifion leaned against the tree, relaxed his body further—and let go.

His spirit flew to the east, past mountains and rivers, forests and villages. Darkness hovered over a hamlet near the border.

Not darkness. Black.

The shell of a wee village smouldered and the souls of those lost rose and wept.

Eifion steadied himself with a deep inhalation and pushed across the border. He sensed the end of a storm. Not of wind, nor of rain, but of a battle. He stretched his vision.

Amongst trees—a forest camp with bodies slain. A few rode further east. Fleeing. Escaping.

None pursuing.

He set his spirit to look back at the camp. Those milling there were no strangers. Bàn cradled the empty body of the warrior, Erin. Her spirit gazed at Bàn, arms extended and fingers stroking his blond curls as she passed him and rose through the air. Arlan's troop examined their surroundings, securing the battle-site, and Angus peered beneath his crumpled brow at hoof tracks in the dirt.

Where is Arlan?

Morrigan crouched near a fallen figure with a bloodied head. The rest of Arlan's troop gathered to hover over the injured man. Eifion poked his sight past their shoulders.

Prince Kyle! He roused not and his eyes remained closed. A bloody trickle traced a path along his hairline.

Is he not at their clan lands by the sea? Their family's broch, Creagrubha?

The sturdy warrior, Adele, lifted Kyle with gentleness while the others constructed a litter in haste.

But... Arlan?

Eifion searched the scene, pushing his *seeing* harder.

There. A shimmer, slowly diminishing. He moved his spirit closer. Through the shimmer stood a forest.

Neither this wood, nor one of this world's realm.

He sent through a *willing*. A guarding. A gifting.

The shimmering slammed shut—like a swiftly closing door.

Eifion left Arlan's troop and returned to himself under the tree. Sweat trickled down the side of his face, his clammy hands clasped tight around the sprig of yew, and his eyes opened wide to a lavish dusk. The bird chatter of *beul na h-oidhche*—the dusk of evening—touched Eifion's ears and the yew's sweet aroma lingered.

He unclenched his hands, the sprig falling into his lap, and leaned his head on the sturdy tree, blinking against the traces of argent and pink hues streaking the clouds on the horizon.

A gasp passed between his lips.

It could not be.

He picked the sprig from his lap and thrust it into the folds of his robe, then rose in haste. His hip bone ground in its socket, and he flinched with each step through the fading shadows of dusk cast across the bailey yard.

He climbed the steps to the entrance of The Keep proper, then trod along the corridor that led to the library. He pushed open the heavy oak doors to the large room with a high ceiling and walls lined with tall shelves of parchments, scrolls, and books covered in animal skins and gem encrusted metals and ornamented wood. The dim light of early evening spilled quietly from high windows as young sages shuffled around with tapers lighting the candle trees spaced throughout this immense room. A hint of dry parchment and old leather hit Eifion's nose, and he drew in the welcome aromas, then sighed.

Here he was always happy.

Here was silent knowledge. Here was truth. Where the thoughts of those who had gone before were free to speak without interruption from those who would argue them as archaic.

Here and now, he would dare to seek the writings long locked away and where he would find the insight and answers to what he had encountered on his spirit's *seeing.*

For he must be sure. He *must* know.

His insides niggled, for the usual procedure would be to apply for permission from the head sage. That was Sage Cénell—an officious, suspicious stickler for protocols. *Blast!*

"May I be of assistance to ye, Lord Sage Eifion?"

Eifion turned; a young sage stood behind him. The light of the nearby candelabra bathed the young man in a glow. Along from him, sages sat at desks, poring over unrolled scrolls and parchments. White goose quills quivered and danced across pages accompanied by the loud scratching of senior sages taking notes. One paused, mouth pinched, and flicked his gaze up to Eifion through wild salt-and-pepper brows. Sage Cénell.

Double blast!

"I wish to review a topic in your reference area." Eifion folded his hands in his robe sleeves. This young one was his best hope. Perhaps Cénell's authoritarian legalism had not yet tainted him.

The young sage pivoted on his heel and Eifion followed as he headed to the far corner of the library from where three doors allowed exit from the main hall of the grand library. The young man paused and took up a lighted candlestick, looking Eifion in the eye.

"Your oldest texts," Eifion said in a quiet voice, though in the library 'twas like a shout.

He led Eifion through the far exit on the right and along a narrow passage that ended with a locked door.

"I have nae opened this one ever, lord sage." The keys jangled as he selected the correct key one-handed. "Ah, would ye mind?" He held out the candlestick to Eifion.

Eifion took it as an almost silent slap of leather sandal on the stone floor came along the corridor behind him. He turned. No one approached.

"Here ye are, Sage Eifion." The young man nudged the door, creaking it open, and bowed slightly. "As ye would be aware, over the years, the librarians have also stored rare texts in here, which are not locked, preferring them to be kept away from general access. Would ye be looking at those, Sage Eifion?"

"Aye, but I also desire to view *The Secret Sacred Writings of the Sages.*"

The young sage's eyes widened, and he stifled a gasp.

Eifion strode past him and placed the candlestick on the dusty table in the middle of the small, round room with a ceiling so tall it disappeared in the shadows. In this room, one of the many external round towers of The Keep, bookshelves lined the curved walls, filling the height of the lighted glow. Cobwebs hung from candle brackets and shelves. On the table, stubs of three candles sat in a puddle of melted wax set hard. Eifion lit them, their wicks taking well; they would have a good hour in them. Their weak light gleamed off the chains hanging through the locks on the lower shelves that, bar the doorway, encircled the room.

"The keys for the locked shelves, young man." Eifion held out his hand.

The sage clasped the keys to his chest. "Ah, ye'll have tae seek permission from the head sage."

Eifion leaned close to the lad, whispering conspiratorially. "Of this I am aware, but I have not the time to wait for a committee to decide if I am a suitable reader of these texts or no."

The young sage's mouth quivered as he leaned slightly away from Eifion.

"My task—" Eifion began.

"Sage Eifion." The hard voice of Sage Cénell came from the doorway. "Do you pressure this young sage?"

Eifion braced against his shoulders stiffening then took a step away from the lad. "Nae, this helpful young man has directed me to the rare texts as I requested. May I have access to the locked books?"

"You may *apply* for access, though that has rarely been granted, and for certain, not in your lifetime." Cénell's lips thinned so much they disappeared.

Eifion raised his eyebrows, feigning surprise. *But blast once more!*

"Your request will be reviewed and placed on our agenda for discussion when our sages meet next month." Cénell smiled smugly.

The young sage's eyes darted from him to Eifion and back again.

Eifion suppressed the grunt that would echo in the tall room and returned a tight grin. "I shall submit my request and content myself with what is available now."

"Hmph. Very well." Cénell hovered.

Eifion reached for a book of Dál Cruinne lore on the shelf above the locked books and scrolls. He wiped the dust off the table with a fold of his sleeve and placed the book in the light spilling from the candles. He opened the book, its pages stiff and threatening to crack beneath his fingers. Cénell grunted.

"I shall be careful." Eifion assured him. "I know how to care for aged parchment."

Eifion turned the pages written in ink now browned and in an older form of the tongue, such as spoken by the past's learned people. Cénell lingered by the door.

"I assure you I am quite capable of protecting ancient texts, Cénell."

Cénell's face hardened. "And what would you be looking for in the *Secret Sacred Writings of the Sages*, Eifion Iubhar?" Accusation poked its pointing fingers through his words.

Eifion's neck prickled. "I am a lover of history and the thoughts of the ancients. That is all, Cénell." He kept his face as calm as he was able.

The pinched-browed sage gave a slight nod, then slowly turned, his sandaled steps ringing back into the round room as he departed. The young sage chewed his lip.

"Shall I get ye more candles, Sage Eifion? It seems ye shall be a while, aye?"

"Oh, that would be so kind. And, I wonder, as it is chilly in here for my old bones, would ye go to my rooms and fetch me my cloak and a rug?"

"Ah, aye. 'Twill take me a wee while, though."

"That is fine, lad." Eifion gave as fatherly a smile as he could. "Just as you can."

The young sage's mouth flickered in a grin, then he left.

Eifion spun and turned to the locked shelves.

Running his fingers along the bars that withheld these ancient texts from the world, he found the oldest in appearance on the third locked shelf. He closed his eyes and grasped the padlock in his hands and sensed minerals and ores from deep in Dál Cruinne's ground. He withdrew the yew sprig hidden in his sleeve and concentrated. His spirit drew strength from the living plant, but it was not enough. He placed his hand on the wooden frame of the shelves. Aged-life lingered in the wood fibres and power trickled through.

He sought more, from close shelving, then from the table in the centre of the room, until a power gusted through him like a strong breeze and the lock sprung open.

He sped his gaze across the spines of leather-bound books and ribboned tags of scrolls. One title caught his eye.

The Book of the Fae.

"Aye, that would be one."

Many a story of travellers to another place, the Land of the Faerie, had mentioned a door or a gateway to their world. All folk lore, or so it was said.

"Could it be what I saw?" he whispered. "That which slammed in my face?"

He took it to the table, shoved the already opened book aside and placed *The Book of the Fae* down. Its faded cover had nicks and scars in the leather, and a musty scent emanated from it. He opened it; its leaves were a smooth vellum, as soft as kid skin beneath his fingers, as if they had not aged. Written at the bottom of the title page...

Year from Dragon Wars One Hundred and Twenty.

Eifion's breath caught. *Could this be so old?* He turned to the middle of the book and placed his hands on the pages.

But where to start?

The vellum tingled against his palms. He jolted back.

"Nae." He could not keep the wonder from his voice. "Ye wish to assist me?"

He placed his hands back on the pages.

Gateway. Door. Portal?

The page under his right hand grew warm. He turned the sheets of vellum forward until one released such heat it compelled him to stop, then read:

Many a traveller has returned from the Other World with stories
of a journey and lessons learned. Though some have gone
missing from known sites, returning not. Travellers
describe various worlds, indicating perhaps there be more
than one Land of the Fae. But all report they were gone for
a time differing in length from their absence in Dál Cruinne.

Prickles crawled beneath the skin on Eifion's arms.

"But how does Arlan return?" He turned the page.

Illustrations filled this section: a henge of standing stones, a forest, a circle of toad-stools, and a still pond, all intricately drawn.

Hmm. Eifion's brow tightened. "Most definitely a forest in Arlan's case. But which world?"

Eifion read the lines written in a slanted hand beneath the drawings.

Thwarted be, and standing still
Wishing for open portal sign
Travellers be stranded ill
Until fixed times of worlds align.

"Certain places at certain times." He gritted his teeth and spun to the shelves. "There must be a map."

He rummaged through scrolls, uncurling one and then another. No maps. He searched some more, scuffling through thick pieces of parchment and thudding books on the shelves in his efforts.

"By all that is good!" he ground out through his teeth.

Foot tread padded down the passage, echoing toward him. He started, jolting the parchment in his hands. He spun back to the table and snapped the book shut, shoved it back in its place, threaded the lock and pushed it to some semblance of closed. Then turned to the book of Dál Cruinne lore on the table.

He ran his finger along a line of text just as the young sage entered. Eifion's cloak and a rug hung over the lad's arm, and he nodded, placing them on the back of the chair. Eifion lifted his face and his eyebrows to the lad who stood staring, first at Eifion, then the book and back once more.

"If 'tis not rude of me, Sage Eifion, I would ask why ye seek knowledge amongst these texts?"

Eifion narrowed his eyes. "Who wishes to know? You or your master?"

"Pardon, lord sage." His pure voice lacked hesitation. "But I myself wish to know why ye seek knowledge from these records containing the words of a magic which we in Dál Gaedhle take no part?"

The young sage had honest eyes, and a longing rested in them.

"Let not the biases of the days in which ye live negate the experiences of those who have gone before you. Scribed not long after the Dragon Wars, the very words of the scrolls and books locked in this room ring truer than the records since of those very times, now slanted in their truths by those who penned them and the opinions and inclinations of the days in which they lived." He stepped forward and laid his hand on the young sage's shoulder. "Use your own judgement and be not blinded by the preconceptions of others." He walked past the lad, picking up his cloak and rug, and walked out of the room.

Eifion's steps rang in his ears and his research rang in his mind.

"It *was* a portal, then." His whisper echoed off the narrow walls of the passage. "And some never return."

He gasped, his heart sinking to his stomach.

"Be not lost to us, Arlan, son of my heart."

Fifteen

— • —

Protect, warrior, for this is your noblest thought.
Buckle virtue tight about your waist.
Let your words and deeds be in honour toward those not of the
warrior way.
Stay your arm at hearth; offense is for the field of battle alone.
Defend all who take shelter beneath the warrior's shield arm.

WARRIOR SAGE TAPAÌDH
(4009-4059 POST DRAGON WARS)

Our World, 2016
Abernethy, Scotland

The evening air settled around me, touching my face and hands with a chill. My teeth chattered with the lingering effects of an adrenalin surge. Fading daylight tinged the forest gold, hemming the track with pink. A hint of faecal odours hung in the air from the lad who'd grabbed me by the hair and held a knife to me.

I pinched my nostrils against the smell. He must've shat himself in fear.

There'd been no sign of him since the warrior guy had turned up and chased him down the steep side of the track, but that hadn't stopped the shivers running through me.

The Celtic-looking warrior dismounted his war horse, his boots thudding on the ground.

Where had he come from?

I stepped back, not taking my eyes off him. He bent low, wiped his sword on the fallen leaves and rubbed until the metal was clean and shiny, then spoke as he re-sheathed it. The soft snick of his sword returning to its scabbard wove through his lyrical, breathy words, an odd sort of Gaelic that was difficult to decipher.

I smiled awkwardly, my arms and legs still trembling, and my mouth dry.

He stood and stared at me. Waiting.

"Um, hi. Thank you"—my gratitude came out as a stuttering squeak— "for re-sheath-ing your sword and not murdering me," I added low under my breath, just in case he knew English.

He cocked his head and spoke a string of sounds. I caught maybe an 'Adrian' or something amongst them.

"Oh, okay... *Adrian*. Thank you, again. I'm going now." I swallowed, attempting to moisten my mouth.

Time to get out of here.

I turned and walked down the hill, the handle of my attacker's pocketknife digging into my palm, and tried to steady my breathing.

The warrior's thudding footsteps came behind me. I glanced over my shoulder. He followed me, leading that ginormous horse. It was the *only* way down this hill.

He strode, strength personified, as straight and strong as the double-edged sword now safely in its sheath at his back. Its handle stood above his right shoulder and his shield hung on the saddle. His horse remained jittery, tossing its head, chewing its bit, a constant jangling accompanying each snort and movement. The warrior, Adrian, spoke to it in the gentle, sing-song modulation of his language.

I continued walking down the hill to my cottage, thighs shaking, and concentrating hard on my footing on the rough path.

This enormous man and his gigantic horse had scared that young guy off, but my attacker's hate-filled words rang in my head, and I wrapped my arms around myself.

The lad had called me *slut*. I rubbed my upper arms to scrub away the dirty feelings.

But what about Adrian? He might have just saved me from a fate worse than death. Would I be safe with *this* man?

And what if this warrior-guy hadn't turned up? Would I have fought off my attacker? I'd disarmed the lad... almost... and was still to get away from him...

A shiver coursed through me, and I held my arms tighter around myself.

Adrian spoke again behind me, not to his horse but to me, his tone softer and without the command in his voice like he had so far, but with... Was he concerned about me? I turned.

He'd picked up another handful of dry fallen leaves and was wiping his face. Most of the blue body paint—probably woad—came off, but some still clung to his full, neat beard. And the stink! Like rotting fruit fermenting. He paused, dry leaves in his hand, waiting for me to answer.

"I... I'm okay." I faced the path downhill again and continued at a brisk pace, trying to stretch the distance between me and him with that ginormous horse. I glanced over my shoulder.

Yep. Still a scary war horse.

I reached the lane that led from the track to my cottage and marched past the field of sheep. They bleated as I passed, then scattered when Adrian did.

So, he still followed me.

Didn't he have somewhere to go?

Like home?

It grew darker with the sun fully set and the evening's glow dimming at the edges of the world. And his horse's hoofbeats now clip-clopped on the bitumen road toward my cottage.

Right behind me.

I ran the last few meters to my cottage, dragging my keys from my jacket. He called out something which could have been a 'Hey wait' in Gaelic, but I didn't stop and when finally home, let myself in, slammed the door, then locked it.

My cottage was dark, so I switched on the lights, shucked off my jacket and threw it on the couch, then ran the short distance to my kitchen window.

He'd walked the horse down my path and stood peering at the closed door, scratching his head.

Hovering.

I switched on my outside light, and his horse nickered.

I leaned over my sink to get a better view of him. He reached for the doorknob and my front door rattled.

"Oh, please go away." My voice bounced back to me from the window.

He faced my direction and walked over.

"What?" I said low into the pane. "You heard that?" My face warmed.

He now stood directly in front of me, outside my kitchen window, the exterior light shining right on him, and he looked straight at me.

And smiled.

Oooh! What a smile! He was quite an attractive man with his very long black hair and deep blue eyes.

His horse nudged him. He looked away from me then walked to the corner of the cottage. He and his horse went out of sight.

What did he think he was doing? "Where are you going?" I skittered to the window that faced the back meadow.

Adrian walked through the overgrown field, heading for the old rickety animal shelter. His black horse trailed behind him, flattening the long grass with its large hooves and grabbing mouthfuls with its big horse teeth. He led it to the shelter and walked it in, shutting the rickety gate. It looked like he removed the saddle, but I found it hard to tell now that it was almost totally dark outside. His shadowed figure returned to the house, then he resumed his position outside my kitchen window.

Smiling, all friendly like.

Hmm. My brow tightened with a frown.

What *does* this guy want?

He was a big man and fit, underneath all that blue woad-looking stuff. He could have forced his way in after me. But here he was, grinning at my kitchen window and speaking again in that tongue-twisting version of... some kind of Gaelic.

He pointed at the door, as though asking to come in. It even seemed like a *please* was in there somewhere.

Did he need to phone someone to come and pick up him and his animal?

"What about your mobile? Is your battery dead?" I shouted at the window.

His brows drew together and he shook his head.

"Do you need to make a call?" I mimicked a phone at my ear with my fingers. He seemed like an honest person—weapons aside. "Do you want to use my phone?"

He screwed up his face and shrugged, as if he didn't understand me.

Does he really *not* speak English? Perhaps I was wrong about him speaking Gaelic, and he was a Scandinavian. Maybe from Norway? Norwegian sort of sounds Gaelic-like at times. But... they all speak English there.

He could be a LARP-er. Re-enactment people were all really nice, even if a bit nerdy about the whole dressing up and fighting with era correct weapons. 'Cos that's what he looked like. One of those re-enactment buffs. Like the people at that Celtic Festival I'd attended with George.

Hmm. Maybe he *was* a LARP-er, and I'd not seen him go *up* the hill, just met him on his way down.

But the sword had looked real. Like, *really* real. And he'd not used it on me.

I shrugged and pointed aside to my door. He nodded and walked that way. I still held the pocketknife. It was heavy in my hand, so I pulled open a drawer and took out a zip-lock bag. Careful not to rub the prints from the knife, as I would report my attack to the police, I placed the pocketknife behind the toaster.

Adrian now stood at my door, so I hurried to it and grasped the handle. Here goes nothing.

Unlocking the door, I opened it up to face Adrian, my eyes at his chest height—his very sculptured chest. I stifled a gasp and pointed to the sword handle sticking above his shoulder, then down to the umbrella stand sitting beside the backdoor.

He took off the sword belt from over his shoulder and I stepped back a touch. The guy needed room. He placed the sheathed blade near the umbrella stand. No way would it fit inside. He removed the short sword from his belt and placed that in the umbrella stand with his shield beside it.

Familiar metal knotwork decorated each item. They were masterpieces, like those on display in a museum. I let a silent *wow* escape.

He leaned down and removed a dagger from the top of each boot.

I cringed at the number of blades on him. "Are you done now?"

I was used to weapons from martial art classes—blunt, hardened rubber ones—but these *were* real and had shiny-sharp edges. And he'd put them safely away at my request.

He removed a miniature battle axe from the back of his belt, then grinned, presenting his empty hands.

Hmm. I gestured for him to enter and allowed him to walk past me. Man, the guy was muscled. He went as far as the kitchen where I indicated for him to stay.

"My name's Rhiannon, by the way," I said as I walked to the kitchen table.

Adrian stepped around my tiny kitchenette and ran his hands over the smooth front of the fridge, tapped the glass on the microwave door then pressed the dials of the stove.

Huh?

Adrian finished examining the electric appliances and looked right at me with wide eyes and said something, pointing at each item. He waited open-mouthed for an answer while I chewed my lower lip and shrugged.

This language barrier wasn't getting any easier.

"I'll just get my phone," I said, and walked into the living room where I'd dumped my jacket... keeping one eye on him.

He followed me, his gaze resting on the couch and the small wooden coffee table. I pointed to the couch and he nodded and sat while I got my phone out of my jacket pocket then handed it to him.

He held it in his huge hand, squinting at it, a line forming above the bridge of his nose.

I placed some wood on the coals of the open fire and wafted a newspaper over it, letting him make his call with some sort of privacy. The coals glowed into life and flames erupted, then I replaced the fire screen. He sat in silence behind me, and it was as though the weight of his stare pressed upon my neck. I turned to face him, and his eyes darted from me to my phone still sitting in his palm.

"You can't remember the number?" I asked.

He gave an uncomfortable smile and shrugged.

The woad had caked where it remained on his face and the rest of his body. This, plus the spatters of... I peered closer—dark, dried blood... were rubbing off onto the couch. *Ewe.* A stench like soured-rotten fruit hung around him. It would leave a scent in the fabric of the landlady's drab couch.

"Ah... you'd better wash the muck off. Here, I'll show you where the bathroom is." I crooked my finger, and he rose from the couch, handing me back my phone.

What?

I led him into the bathroom, where I gave him fresh towels and waved my hand at the sink. He looked at me with a blank expression.

"To wash the blue gunk off." I enunciated every word, mimicking wiping my face and arms. "So my landlady won't complain." I nodded and left him to it, stepping back into my living room.

He was quiet in the bathroom, except for some *ahhs* and *ers*, so I walked into the kitchen and switched on the kettle. I desperately needed a cuppa. It boiled and clicked off when Adrian came into the kitchen holding the towels covered in blue, honking grime. He was free of the woad, almost.

"Why didn't you—?"

He cocked his head.

"Never mind." I shook my head at him.

Through the remaining blue smear, his sleeve of tattoos caught my eye. Celtic artwork covered his entire left arm up to and including his shoulder. It looked so familiar. Lines that never broke wove in and out and back upon themselves. The Endless Knot traced a path like a band around his mid-upper arm. The triskele swirled its way high near his shoulder with the Celtic Trinity knot prominent on his forearm. Swirls surrounded them all, plus more intricate weavings in ink.

I whistled out slowly, unable to take my eyes off the patterns.

They're beautiful.

He grunted, and I raised my eyes to his. He'd lifted an eyebrow, his lips curving up at one side. I now stood the closest I'd been to Adrian.

His eyes! They were sky blue irises with flecks of navy, edged in a navy circle. My heart rate went up a notch.

I'd... seen something like them before. *Wait a minute.* My pulse rose to my temples. *I've seen someone like* him *before.*

Now that he'd cleaned his face, I looked closely at his left eyebrow but there was no scar there like on the guy at the Celtic Festival.

He chuckled then walked around the room as I shut my gaping mouth.

No? I screwed my mouth to the side.

He picked up random objects—my petrified wood bookends then my miniature ceramic ornament of Edinburgh Castle—and gasped at them as he held them close for examination. At the taller bookshelf, my illustrated books on Celtic art caught his eye. He pulled one out and flipped its pages, then strode to me, babbling in his language, animated and speaking so fast. I stared at his lips, picking up the musical sounds, the breathy consonants, the trilling 'r's. My mouth pulled tight in a grin at his lilt, and I could feel my eyes widen. It was great to hear a few full sentences strung together, a lot of it still not making *any* sense. He stopped speaking, looking directly at me.

I blinked in the now quiet room. The open book rested in his hand and with his other he pointed to a page covered in Celtic knot patterns. The picture had larger outlines inlaid in smaller intricate swirls and lines, painted in gold, with a fine brush or quill. Each decoration, in each section of the inlay, a Celtic knot of endless design, or a miniature of a saint or an animal, or a triskelion. His finger rested on a photograph.

My heart skipped a beat. The illuminated pages from *The Book of Kells* always had that effect on me.

His face was a question, eyes large, and he nodded as though he wanted me to respond.

"Um... aye. Celtic art." I said it more like a question. How much *did* he understand?

"Aye. Celtic." His head bobbed vigorously.

He'd got it? So, we had two words in common.

"Aye. You know 'aye'? As in, yes?"

"Aye," he said, nodding again.

"And you know Celtic? Like my ancestors from a long time ago?"

"Aye. Celtic." He pointed a massive finger to his just as massive chest.

"What?" *Yeah!* The Celtic Festival. It was the same guy! "No!" I clamped my hand over my mouth to stifle a loud exclamation. *Not possible. Get a grip, girl.*

His black brows dipped, and he riveted his gaze on me.

Yeah, you're right, big guy. Stupid idea.

Just like the man at the festival, though, up close, Adrian wasn't fierce and scary anymore. He was actually quite nice and even friendly.

I frowned. He was so much like him.

You're being ridiculous, Rhiannon.

My brain dulled like it did when I needed food, and Adrian just stood there, his mouth now lifting to a smile while my stomach growled so loudly, he looked at my midriff and laughed.

I laughed back. But he should be getting home now, surely? I went to the door, indicating for him to leave. He followed me, dragging his feet and shoulders slumping, then stood by the door with a forlorn look on his face.

Maybe he didn't have anywhere to go. Was he lost?

"Oh, okay then." My tone came out like a wary question. "Do you want to stay for some food?"

He raised his eyebrows and nodded.

I squinted an eye. *Food.* Men always understood that.

I led him back to the couch.

"Please sit down." I broke away from his stare. "I'll prepare something. I know you don't understand everything I'm saying, but I feel better talking."

I stepped back to my kitchenette and searched for something to make into a meal. My stomach grumbled again as I poked around in the cupboard and found cans of baked beans. I had bread. It would have to do.

After cooking baked beans on toast, I beckoned him into the kitchen where we sat. Adrian raised his eyebrows and gawked at the food and the fork. I started eating, and after watching me intently, he picked up his fork in a clumsy big hand and ate enthusiastically.

When I'd finished my meal, and so had he, he looked at me with his fork still in his right hand. So, I found another tin of baked beans and opened it with the electric can opener. His loud exclamations filled the kitchen. I put the bowl of beans in the microwave oven and started the timer. He jumped up from the table and stood over the microwave, watching the bowl of baked beans go round and around. It *pinged*, and he flinched.

What? So he'd never seen a microwave before?

I nudged him aside, then got the hot beans out and placed them on his plate and returned it to the table. He sat down and ate slower this time, making appreciative noises around each forkful.

Leaning against the sink, I twirled a lock of hair around my finger while he ate his second dinner. He'd pointed to himself when I'd said Celtic. He had fair skin and long, thick black hair. The Celts were generally fairer... Silver rings with intricate designs held his hair away from his face at the sides. Similar designs to those on his weapons ornamented his leather belt, which was embossed with a long strip of knotwork. It sat on his hips below a six-pack like no other.

Yep, he was good looking. I shook my head to get back to my line of reasoning.

He seemed a nobleman-warrior-type with a code of conduct, so to speak—like most LARP-ers.

I scrunched my lips together. It grew late, and he seemed to not be making any moves to go anywhere.

"Do you have someone to pick you up?"

He looked at me, a crease flickering across his forehead, shrugged, then forked in another mouthful of beans.

"How do you usually get you and your horse home after an event?"

Surely, he'd have a float or something nearby.

He'd focused on my mouth while I spoke. Now he tilted his head and rubbed the beard at his throat, the rasping sound now lingering in my quiet kitchen.

Nothing? Perhaps he was stuck or his friends had abandoned him.

It *was* possible I'd be safe with him in my house overnight. He'd regarded me in a friendly way all the time he'd been here, and so far, he appeared to be a normal person—underneath all the woad.

Hmm. I'd let him stay but bar the bedroom door—and take that pocketknife with me. Tomorrow would be another day, and a good night's sleep might help me know what to do with him.

He finished the second helpings, and I took his plate to the sink. Passing the toaster, I slipped the pocketknife wrapped in its bag into my jeans pocket. I indicated for him to stay at the table and went to my bedroom, where I got a blanket and a pillow from the only item of furniture I possessed, the trunk at the end of my bed. I returned to the living room and beckoned him to the couch and, once he'd sat, placed the blanket and pillow beside him.

"*Oidhche mhath.*" An attempt at *goodnight* in my limited Gaelic might get the message across.

He bowed. "*Oidhche mhath.*"

"Oh!" It worked.

He stood by the couch as I stepped to my bedroom. I pulled the door until it was open only a crack. He'd watched me, his lips forming a pleasant grin. I shut the door the rest of the way, then shoved the dressing table behind it, screeching it into place.

Today had been weird. He still gave me the impression of being the very same man as the one who'd kissed me at the Celtic Festival. But *that* man had seemed to know me whereas this one clearly didn't. The Celtic Festival guy spoke English too. And this one didn't have a scar on his left eyebrow. That warrior had come from a forest, like this one had too...

I leaned against my rearranged dresser and huffed.

He was *so* much like that other warrior.

But modern gadgets intrigued him... like he'd never come across an electric can opener.

Or a mobile phone!

Struggling to make sense of it, I crossed the room to my bed and slipped under my duvet, snuggling deep, and kept one ear open just in case I'd misjudged this man's character—totally misled by those mesmerising blue eyes.

Sixteen

Step outside yourself,
Leave all you know.
Lose your world to another
Only to find it.

VISIONS AND SAYINGS OF THE BLIND LADY SAGE

Abernethy, Scotland

Arlan stared at Rhiannon's closed door. Scraping came from behind it, as though she dragged furniture across. Arlan's chest bubbled, and a chuckle escaped. She would be foolish to not be cautious with a stranger in her dwelling. Verra admirable, but if only Rhiannon knew she had his protection.

What a day! Arlan slumped onto the wide, well-cushioned seat and gazed into the fire.

He gulped. He'd charged at a foe with hate-filled eyes, then passed through white light and searing sound to find a young woman fighting off a bandit at knifepoint. He shook his head, blinking. An old sage tale told of a man who'd stepped into another realm from a forest. Perhaps it was only a story to stop children from wandering into dangerous places.

I've left my troop in a dangerous place!

Bàn!

Images of his sword-brother flew at him like Muir's spear, *Sleaghach*.

Arlan buried his face in his hands, his mind filling with a picture of Bàn holding Erin close, covered in her blood. How had his troop fared? Did they think he'd abandoned them, as Kyle said he would?

"Surely no'!" His cry muffled into his hands.

He ran his fingers through his hair and held tight, the flames in the hearth glowing brightly. But he'd trained them well. He let go of his hair and nodded curtly to the flames. They'd fight as a team and overcome the bandits.

And wait for him.

But how to return? His attempts to retrace his steps on that track had led to nothing. He *must* find the way home. But his traverse to here... how, by all that is good, did he get here in the first place? He lifted his shoulders. Harsh sound battering him, not only his ears, but his whole body vibrating with it, was his only recollection of the journey. And on turning and spying along the track to which he'd come... not a thing. Nae door, nor bridge...

For he surely was no longer in Dál Gaedhle, nor even in his world of Dál Cruinne. This was clear the moment she'd brought him to her abode. He'd asked her to take him to the chieftain's hall. He glanced around the chamber at the usual and unusual objects.

Not a chieftain's hall.

He must discover the purpose of the grey rectangular glazing hanging from the wall.

The fire flickered and sparked, sending warm scents of burning apple wood his way. He flung himself back in the seat and tilted his face to the ceiling of this modest abode, his chest hollow and thoughts whirling. A tiny orb dangling from a thin black rope had a light of its own. He blinked at it.

There were such unusual objects in this world.

A *bump* echoed from behind the bedroom door. So, she called herself Rhiannon—the horse goddess who some worshipped. *Strange.* She behaved like she had nae idea about horses, for she had regarded Mengus warily.

Nae, not warily—with fear.

But what a beauty! Warmth had filled his chest when she'd peered at him like a stallion at market. He'd smiled at her and, thankfully, she'd not interpreted it as a leer and refused him the rest of her hospitality. His centre tingled again. Perhaps she approved of what she saw.

He'd appraised her as well—tall, slender and fit-looking, with long, thick amber hair, eyes the colour of heather in flower and skin like cinnamon-dusted milk, and her perfume was that of a warm summer. And she was brave. She had recovered well from her ordeal with the bandit, then let himself into her home, after taking proper precautions. He chuckled. She must think she had hidden the small knife from him.

He wandered his vision over the shelves filled with books. And she was learned, gauging from her small library. And fascinated by his language. Her expression had erupted, wide-eyed and mouth agape, when they'd discovered their words in common. The tightness in his shoulders had eased then, for there was a chance they would grow to understand each other.

She'd listened with delight upon her face as he'd explained about the similarities between the picture in that book and his own decorations. His brow tightened. *Celtic* wouldn't be the word he would use for his own people, but from what he'd understood from her books, it came the nearest to describing the art and design in his own culture. If Rhiannon was anything to go by, the people in this world were essentially similar, though their social structure was a little different—nae chieftain nearby.

Hmm. The Celts. He must find out more about these people.

Her books would hold this knowledge.

It was a start.

And she called him *Adrian*. He scratched at his beard.

Aye, language was a difficulty. He must learn hers, although it was a curious tongue and like none he'd ever encountered.

He lay on the couch. It was too short, so he spread the blanket on the rug-covered floor and let sleep come.

An intriguing golden light fell through the glazing. This world's sun had risen. Arlan walked outside to relieve himself and check on Mengus. He tested the fences of the small field and found them to be sturdy enough to keep a horse in. He let Mengus out to feed on the lush green of this unkempt meadow. It hadn't seen an animal's grazing for some time. Mengus nickered as he trotted out and, patting his withers and rump, Arlan took in a lungful of the familiar scent of horse. He needed *familiar* in a somewhat strange land.

Nae, a strange world.

He grunted, rubbed his beard with a hard hand, and let his shoulders fall.

Arlan strode to the small *cottage*, as Rhiannon called it. He would give Mengus a good rub down later. He picked up his weapons on his way in, for he'd spent a night under her roof and she would trust him now, and they needed cleaning and sharpening. He passed through the food preparation and eating room. *What extraordinary objects cook their food!* Not a flame in sight. *How does it work?* Rhiannon would be awake soon, and he'd watch with care while she prepared food for breaking their fast. His stomach grumbled.

Horses whinnied, and drums beat. I opened my eyes to bright daylight and shut my mind to the dream. I always had weird dreams if I slept late. It'd taken forever to go to sleep last night after all the mind-spins.

But I'd come to only one conclusion.

He was the *same* guy.

So why didn't he know me? Perhaps he had some memory loss. That could explain why he couldn't go home last evening, because he'd forgotten where he lived. But it didn't explain why my kitchen—and a mobile phone—seemed so foreign to him.

And what about the scar on his eyebrow that was there on the Celtic Festival Day ... but not now?

It was as though for him, now was *before* that day. He looked a wee bit younger now than on the festival day... when he'd kissed me.

A flash of warmth crossed my lips, like when he'd touched his to mine.

I screwed my eyes shut, then opened them, focusing again.

Concentrate girl!

And this morning, I still felt that he was the same individual. All throughout my contemplations as I tried to nut it out—and go to sleep—I kept thinking of the way he'd spoken to me at the Celtic Festival. He'd called me *the love of his heart*. Didn't that mean we were a *thing*.

Him and I... together—in his eyes, anyway. Sometime in his future.

A clunk came from outside my bedroom door, and voices, deep and loud, were getting louder. Someone pleaded for their life.

I got out of bed, fighting the prickles crawling up my spine, put on jeans and a top, then got my back up to the dresser I'd used to barricade the door, and heaved. It scraped away with a screech. I pulled the door open a crack. A wall of back muscle filled my view. Adrian stood in front of me, and he waved around that huge double-edged sword, speaking threats to someone in his Gaelic-type language. A man answered in something similar, his tones softer then he raised his pitch and his voice quavered.

Oh, no! George planned to come up for the weekend. The prickles ran from my neck down my arms. I'd forgotten all about him!

I opened the door fully and stepped out beside Adrian. George cowered on the floor against the far wall, extending his arms in front of himself like he begged for mercy, and his eyes peered wide from behind his glasses. He saw me, but he didn't relax. Adrian spoke to me, his voice gruff and forehead bunched in furrows. I walked over to George and Adrian grunted and kept scowling, not lowering his sword.

"This is George." I placed my hand under George's arm and helped him off the floor. "He's my friend." I lifted my chin and locked gazes with the warrior.

Sweat cooled my brow, and George's arm trembled beneath my grasp. Adrian's shoulders eased, and he spoke again in a questioning tone. I shrugged. His comment made no sense to me.

"Who is he?" George asked.

I guided George to the couch and made him sit.

"How does he speak Goidelic? That's a specialised subject and very few scholars know it. Why's he in your living room brandishing a broadsword?" George's questions tumbled out. "What does he mean by calling me a sneaky dishonourable coward?"

"What? You can understand him?"

"Yes, mostly." George pushed his glasses up the bridge of his nose. "It's quite similar to middle ancient Gaelic. Why? Can't you?"

"No." I couldn't stop the sigh coming out in my tone. "You know how slow I am with languages. I haven't been able to communicate well at all. But I think his name is Adrian." I stood between George on the couch and Adrian, who'd remained in front of my bedroom door watching everything.

"I walked the hill last evening, like I usually do, and he appeared." I couldn't face talking about the attack. Not yet. I inwardly shook my head.

Leave *that* one.

"He just appeared?" George peered at me over the top of his glasses, which had slipped down his nose again.

"Yes, covered in woad and riding a ginormous horse." I grabbed him by the arm, dragged him off the couch, and marched him to the window in search of the black horse. It was there, trotting around the field, flicking its tail up behind. "Look! One very large war horse. We don't make them like that here." I turned to the warrior and pointed. "Nor ones like him either, for that matter. But we used to."

Should I voice what my mind-spins had settled on? My fantastical conclusion that Adrian and Celtic Festival guy were one and the same... but at different times in his life.

Maybe I'd been watching too many Sci-Fi movies.

George had been jealous of that warrior at the festival and perhaps he'd be antagonistic toward him now if I revealed my theory. I wouldn't have George spoiling it, not when there was any possibility that Adrian could truly be *that* guy.

I had an alternative I could present to George that totally avoided revealing who I thought Adrian really was but still provided a plausible explanation... if suggesting that Adrian had somehow been transported through time could ever be considered plausible... or sane.

I took a deep breath. "That's why I suspect we have a Celtic time traveller." Well, it wasn't a big lie.

"Don't be ridiculous." George crossed his arms and *hmphed*. "Is this a joke?"

"I'm serious, George." I widened my eyes at him. "Where *would* I get a guy who speaks Goidelic and is willing to dress as a half-naked Celtic warrior?"

"Time travel does not happen. Just ask any physicist."

"Maybe science can't explain everything." I put my hands on my hips. "What then?" I flicked a hand in the warrior's direction.

Adrian stared at us, a gentle smile on his face. I'd glimpsed him observing me during my rant to George. He re-sheathed his sword; the long, smooth scrape of metal was loud in the quiet living room, but he remained silent.

George bit a fingernail, I chewed my lip, and Adrian's smile got broader.

"I'm still trying to work out—if I'm not crazy—which period of history he could be from." I'd waved my hands in the air and they ended up on my head.

"I could understand most of what he hollered at me." George glanced furtively at Adrian, who'd folded his arms over his chest.

I lowered my hands, smoothing down my hair that had got to its usual wild state. "So, ask him where he's from. Because *I* think he's a time traveller!" My insides thrummed.

George's nostrils flared. "This is ludicrous," he said, then stood in silence for a moment while he stared at Adrian and chewed on another fingernail. "But he doesn't speak English... at all," he said at last. "And I know just about everyone who speaks ancient Gaelic." George's eyes narrowed in thought. "I... I can't think of any other explanation, so the seemingly impossible could be plausible." He glanced at the floor. "From what I can gather, he thinks you are his to protect. I wasn't going to argue with him. Once I recognised the language, I tried to tell him I am your friend. And please

88

don't hurt me," he added in a much quieter voice, then his brows drew together and he looked up at me. "Why do you call him *Adrian?*"

"That's how he introduced himself."

George laughed, soft and amused, shaking his head. No longer the terrified person he'd been moments ago.

"You, with your broken Gaelic. Look at him." George pointed to Adrian. "What, or who, does he look like to you?"

I focused fully on Adrian now. He'd listened to my conversation with George, his eyes never seeming to leave me. He stood ramrod tall and alert. A brave man, no doubt about that. From his respect for books, I gathered he was also intelligent. Eloquent, from what George had said. And regal looking, just like at the Celtic Festival.

"What are you telling me, George?"

"When he shouted at me, he said he was the son of the àrd rìgh."

"Yes, *Adri—*"

"Think again, Rhiannon."

Bells of recognition rang in the recesses of my consciousness. Not from my limited Gaelic lessons, but from a novel I'd once read based on Brian Boru's story. Brian Boru, the High King of Ireland. The *àrd rìgh.*

"What's his actual name?" I couldn't take my eyes off *Adrian.*

George then spoke to him in the ancient Gaelic. The two men had an intense conversation. I crossed my arms after a while, tapping a finger on my elbow. Still the men talked. My foot began tapping of its own volition.

The exchange became one sided and George listened to *Adrian,* who spoke at length. My living room filled with his lyrical, breathy speech. It danced off the walls and filled the air with images of tall grey mountains soaring above deep, blue lochs, and white-crested waves crashing against the dark, rocky shores of green, windswept islands.

I blinked and shook myself away from the impressions.

Wow! That hadn't happened in a long time.

A vision...

George now rocked his head from side to side, in what seemed like slow-motion. "He's just described himself to me." He shook his head more vigorously. "His explanation seems absurd. But... he's not a madman. Quite intelligently sane, actually. And I can't..." He huffed. "I can't believe I'm saying this, but his explanation is the only thing that makes sense with his dress and language and weapons... and a silver sun..." George pushed his glasses up the bridge of his nose with his index finger.

"A silver—?"

"He's not a time traveller." George's words were rapid.

"No?" The room filled with a hush, and I concentrated on the warrior standing in front of me. "What then?"

"This is Arlan Finnbar MacEnoicht," George announced, "second son of Donnach MacEnoicht, the Àrd Rìgh of Dál Gaedhle, and he claims he's from another world—entirely."

89

SEVENTEEN

— • —

Do not rely on that which you think you know.
Reach for the unexpected.
Open yourself to the impossible.

VISIONS AND SAYINGS OF THE BLIND LADY SAGE

Abernethy, Scotland

I took a step closer to Arlan, and ran my vision over his long hair, thick beard, bare torso, and leather trousers. A sizeable man, bigger in every way than the men of this world. Without taking my eyes off him, I addressed George.

"You'd better start on the ancient Gaelic lessons, then. And Arlan Finnbar MacEnoicht is in need of a shirt."

Arlan returned my gaze. His mouth held a soft curve, and his expression crinkled the corners of his eyes.

I pulled out my phone. "I'll check about his horse staying in that shed."

I had to negotiate a price, but I reached an agreement with my landlady. Arlan stared at me as I spoke on my mobile and wandered around the living room. His eyes grew wider at my landlady's voice coming from it. I hung up and placed the phone on the coffee table, then Arlan picked it up and spoke into it.

George translated. "She will not speak to me. Where has she gone? Is this how one barters here?"

"Ah, yes." I smiled, catching my lower lip in my teeth. "And not just bartering." I sent a pleading look to George, who translated again.

George showed Arlan around the cottage and pointed out objects, stating their names in both English and ancient Gaelic, where he could. Flat screen television seemed to be *TV*, no matter the language. I tried to follow George's lesson, but he spoke so fast, the conversation absorbing the attention of both men.

Hmph. Left out again.

"Look, guys." I glanced at Arlan, then directed my statement to George. "I'm short of food, so I'm going shopping. While I'm out I'll find a large enough T-shirt, too. Okay?"

"Okay," George said.

"Okay." Arlan smiled.

Oh, that smile again.

My knees softened and couldn't hold me up for a moment.

"Bye." My voice came out small and I turned on my heel—now that my knees had resumed their ability to hold my weight—and walked out to my car.

Returning home, I placed the groceries on the kitchen table and blew the hair off my forehead. It'd taken longer than I'd expected to give the police an account of the attack on the hill without mentioning a warrior from another world.

The cottage was still and empty of men. A whinny came from outside. I leaned closer to the window that faced the field out the back. George and Arlan stood near the war horse. The black animal swished its tail as it munched on the long grass. Arlan gestured wildly and George inclined his head to him. I walked out to them, their voices getting clearer with each step.

"What's going on?" I asked.

George turned, and Arlan looked across at me.

"He's amazing!" George said with a laugh. "I can hardly believe it but this guy's a linguist. He's picking up English already. I think teaching him English will be much easier than teaching you ancient Gaelic, no offence."

"Hello, Rhiannon. How are you this day? Nae, *today*?" Arlan lilted.

That stopped me mid-stride. His deep voice was quite sexy in English.

No, not *quite*.

Extremely.

My meeting him at the Celtic Festival came to mind when he'd pulled me close to himself and his melodic voice vibrated through my body. I put a hand to my mouth. The remembered touch of his lips on mine sent my heart hammering into my ribs all over again.

"See what I mean? Don't stress yourself." George's eyes glinted.

I dropped my hand from my mouth. I wouldn't give George a hint of the real cause of my reaction.

"I'll take some time off work," George continued. "I'm due holidays anyway. You don't mind if I stay and teach him, do you? I'd enjoy it."

I couldn't say no. Arlan spoke English in his future, as he'd spoken it at the Celtic Festival—in my past. I needed to discuss that with him.

Sometime.

George hadn't mentioned the similarity between the two men—the tall man in the tartan kilt of muted tones and this just as tall man here in leather trousers and not much else. George had only seen him for a few moments at the festival. But Arlan seemed very different. Apart from speaking English fluently on that day, he wasn't as relaxed in his manner with me.

And he'd made no advances—like that kiss.

I'd choked a sigh into a cough, and now both men stared at me.

"I've bought a T-shirt that I hope fits him." My words rushed out. "We need to get him looking normal, then we'll shop for more clothes." I screwed up my nose. "I don't know what to do about getting him home to wherever he comes from."

"Dál Gaedhle." Arlan's rich voice rang out as he stood straighter.

I closed my gaping mouth. He'd followed the conversation.

Wow, he was really clever.

I walked back to the cottage through the long grass and the men followed a pace or two behind me.

"Have you got permission for that animal?" The gruff tone belonged to the neighbour in the semi-detached. He stood at his rubbish bin by the fence, his gut hanging over his belt and a greasy stubble covering his chin.

"I have permission from the landlady." My tone came out sharp, but I was powerless to soften it when it came to *that* guy. His wife was another matter. Man, did I feel sorry for *her*!

Arlan ran to me, and my neighbour's back stiffened.

"It better keep clear of my kids. It's a stallion. They're vicious. Don't want it bitin' ma bairns. Okay?"

"Unless your children go into that field and play with it, they should be safe, shouldn't they?" My hands curled into fists.

All I needed was for this guy to give me trouble and point out Arlan to everyone.

"My stallion is okay. You child stay away, if you please." Arlan spoke in his High-land-sounding lilt.

My neighbour peered up at Arlan, a thin snarl on his lips. "You've not got boarders, now have you, miss? These two men not stayin' here with you?"

"They're on holiday. No business of yours, anyway!" *Unbelievable!*

Arlan's warm, large hand pressed on my forearm. I turned to him; he shook his head a fraction. He was right. My nasty neighbour wasn't worth getting all upset over. We strode past him into the house.

"And good day to you, sir," George threw over his shoulder as he passed the scruffy man.

Once inside, I unpacked the groceries and started dinner. Arlan got up from the table where he and George had sat and stood beside me, watching while I cooked.

"How does this go, Rhiannon?" Arlan pointed to the microwave oven.

"Go? Oh, you mean work?"

"Aye."

"I just put the food in, press the timer and start. Do you want to know exactly how?"

92

Arlan tilted his head, one eye squinting, like he waited for more explanation.

"George?" He was the *linguist*, after all.

George explained in ancient Gaelic interspersed with English, as it must've been hard to find the right words in the language for *microwave* and other concepts in physics. Arlan nodded and exclaimed as George demonstrated all the items in my electric appliance dominated kitchen.

I put the chicken in a pan to fry and peeled potatoes and carrots, letting the language settle in my ears. I should learn his language too. It would help me understand Arlan better.

Arlan and George moved to the living room, and I added more oil to the frying chicken. George switched on the large flat screen television, then Arlan hollered like a Highland warrior sending shudders through me.

"What's happening?" I forced down the instinct to flee and instead ran into the living room.

Arlan continued yelling, grabbing his sword he'd rested by the couch and unsheathing it. On the wall, the television displayed a wildlife programme featuring lions.

"*Felid!*" Arlan raced to it with his sword lifted high.

"No, Arlan!" I screamed. "It's not real." I grasped at his arm, my oily hands slipping off his biceps. I snuck under his upraised arm and flattened my hands on his chest. His heart pounded through it. "No Arlan! It's not real. We're okay."

He looked down at me, the tension in his body easing.

"The lions can't get us," I explained. "They're pictures. Moving pictures with sound."

Arlan dropped his arms, lowering his sword, so I stepped away from him. He frowned deeply and moved closer to the television. He poked it with his finger and stared at it for a while, then grinned.

"This channel has 'plays' where people are acting stories." George's speech flowed behind me as I returned to the kitchen, nudged on by Arlan's and George's laughter.

"This channel has moving pictures which are drawings, usually for children. This channel shows sports. That's boxing—you may be familiar with that. This one is a person telling us what's happened around the world today. It will have moving pictures. This isn't acting, but real. And I rarely watch it for long because it's all bad news." George clicked the remote again and the commentary on lions returned.

Saving the TV from a death by broadsword—just an ordinary day.

Maybe my days would never be *ordinary* ever again.

EIGHTEEN

— · —

Damn it, Diary, I knew it!

She's fallen for the Big Man. Yes, he's smart, polite, well-educated and tall. He's got the looks that women always go for. And he's big.

I didn't think Rhiannon would succumb.

I'm trying to be reasonable. Scientific. Speaking of which, there's been a chemistry between those two from the start. She stopped him from going at me with his sword.

I'm pushing against the green-eyed monster who wishes to invade me. But I just have to go work on my thesis, so I have a future to offer her if when she gets over this guy.

Did I mention he's big?

FROM THE JOURNAL OF GEORGE WILSON
PhD CANDIDATE ANCIENT CELTIC LANGUAGES, OXFORD

Abernethy, Scotland

"Well, that was a quick and fascinating two weeks. Pity you had to work almost every day, Rhiannon. We didn't see much of you." George shrugged, striding ahead of me to the taxi parked at the kerb in front of my cottage.

"Arlan's mastered English almost as if by magic." My step lightened.

"But he won't need it for long." George reached the taxi and turned to me. "English, that is. He'll find that place on the hill where he first appeared, and be gone soon, yes?"

"I'm sure he will." I flicked a glance at the kitchen window where Arlan stood inside. He must've felt George and I needed a private goodbye.

George had made no comment about the similarities between Arlan and the Celtic Festival guy. He'd been so engrossed in teaching Arlan English and so delighted at conversing with an ancient Gaelic speaker that perhaps he'd not connected the dots between the two men who were the one person. In my experience with George, academia *was* his main strength, leaving social skills and the ability to read relational cues way down on the list of his talents.

94

I chewed the corner of my mouth, flinching at the pinch there. There'd been some awkwardness over the past fortnight. George had been clingy at times and maybe he'd stayed to ensure Arlan wouldn't act any further on his belief that I was *his to protect*.

But there was nothing between me and George, and George needed to know that for sure.

"If you get stuck, phone me." George put his bag in the taxi. "Arlan's command of English over such a short period *is* astounding. You should have little trouble. He can always watch the Gaelic shows." He laughed and leaned toward me, spreading his arms wide.

I stepped back, out of the circle of his arms. "First thing we're doing is clothes shopping."

George dropped his hands.

I folded my arms over my chest and leaned against the taxi. "Even wearing a T-shirt, Arlan stands out. He looks like a mean biker." I spoke in a low voice, my heart stuttering. I couldn't keep it from George any longer. "You don't recognise him, do you?" I clamped my mouth tight after I'd said it.

"Recognise him? Rhiannon, he's from another world!" George snorted. "How could I recognise him?"

"The Celtic Festival." I let it out under my breath.

"The Celtic Festival?" George frowned, then his eyes opened wide. "He's the one who kissed you?"

"Shush! He'll hear you!"

"But he doesn't recognise *you*." George's pitch raised two notches.

"I know." I put a hand to my face and dragged my fingers across my forehead. "That means *now* is before *then* for him."

"He kissed you," George sputtered. "That means you and him..."

"Perhaps, but not yet."

"When then?" His tone was sharp.

"I don't know. Maybe never." I dropped my hand from my forehead, and a stiffness passed across my shoulders. "This could change it all. Him being here now, I mean."

"Do you want it to?" George's voice held an edge, and he stood there looking like he expected an answer to that one.

Really?

I moved away from the vehicle, my insides heating. "That's not any of your business, George." I sniffed.

"No?"

"No. Thank you for your lessons. Goodbye." I spoke harshly, but George needed to quit the interrogation.

"Make sure he finds his way home." George's brow furrowed and his cheeks turned dusky as he plonked down on the back seat of the taxi.

Arlan walked from the cottage. "Goodbye." Arlan stepped toward the taxi, extending his hand to George. "We will see you soon?"

"Possibly." George shut the taxi door and, through the open window, slid his narrowed gaze to Arlan, who slowly lowered his hand and stood with a frown. George turned his glare to me. "I'll phone."

I gave a sharp wave, and the taxi drove off. My shoulders sank, and I lifted my vision to the clouds, regretting how that'd ended. I'd hurt George... unintentionally. And he hadn't deserved it.

"You will miss your friend?" Arlan said into my ear. Another unspoken question hung through his words.

"We're going shopping." I avoided his eyes, and his question—not altogether sure how to answer it. "You need to look like a modern Scotsman, not someone out of Braveheart."

NINETEEN

— • —

A king is a shield to his people
The vanguard in battle.
He protects the people he rules
With his might,
With his own body,
With his very self.

WISDOM WRITINGS ON KINGSHIP
SAGE GLIOCAS
(2870-2962 POST DRAGON WARS)

A Shopping Centre, Scotland

Bright lights and shiny objects sat behind walls of clear glazing. Some market stalls, or *shops*, contained racks and racks of garments. Arlan walked behind Rhiannon in this place she called a *shopping centre*. Stone of some sort, smooth and shiny, paved the floor—not a cobbled stone anywhere. Arlan lifted his eyes to the lofty ceiling, almost as high as that of the Great Hall in The Keep. They passed a shop that sold food and had row upon row of shelves filled with produce. This world was wealthy and well provided—that was a certainty.

He must return to his own world. And his troop. But how?

My passage here is still a mystery.

His traverse had the feel of the Fae to it. Tales told by bards came to his mind. Stories in song of those who'd gone to the Faerie realm but returned moments later, aged and reporting wild, vivid experiences.

He shook himself at the thought.

He had made forays along the hilly path to the mound at the summit where once stood a defensive fort. He'd ridden this almost every day, in between English lessons with George and learning more of this world. The exercise had proved fruitless and unenlightening.

He sighed, a twinge tugging at his conscience. In all truth, the break from Kyle's constant derision had been a welcome reprieve. For at this moment, the prospect of spending his life under Kyle's authority once he became chief of clan MacEnoicht, did *not* press upon his own shoulders like the weight of a standing stone!

Striding ahead, Rhiannon turned to him, her long, wavy hair swaying as she did so. Her eyes bore into him as if she were examining the depths of his very soul, as they had from that first moment she'd shown her face to him on the hill.

"Come on, keep up." She resumed her brisk pace.

He followed, tugging at the breeches Rhiannon called *jeans.* She'd insisted he wear them along with the top she called a *T-shirt.* She said people would stare at him if he didn't.

They still stared at him.

Youths lolled around in a group, leaning on a rail beside a staircase that moved. The young lads' eyes followed him, and a couple pointed as he walked by, passing comments amongst themselves. One crossed his arms over his chest and locked gazes with him. Arlan squinted an eye at the whelp.

The pup should spend a day in the practice yard. That would knock the arrogance out of him.

He doubled his step to catch up with Rhiannon, and a little girl tilted her head back as her mother steered her out of his path. People were so much shorter here.

Except for Rhiannon. She was much like the women of his own world, tall and graceful—beautiful, though she seemed to know it not. But of greater importance, a woman with a natural goodness and generosity, and now she bought him clothes from her own purse. She also had courage, courage enough to take a chance and provide hospitality to him when he found himself stranded in this strange world.

He carried *plastic* bags—shiny and smooth but with a noisy crinkling all the time—containing more jeans, shirts, and a woollen *jumper,* but of poor quality compared to the garments of home.

Rhiannon had searched for a big man's store. There Rhiannon had insisted he go into a tiny room, put on the clothes she chose, then parade before her. Other men perused this store, partaking of the trader's wares. Large men, not healthy-large, but... well, they had eaten too many feasts. In fact, many people in this world had eaten too many feasts and not worked hard in the fields. All the men covered their bodies as if they were cold. Or ashamed. He'd covered his body with a shirt and Rhiannon had appraised him, her gaze sending a warmth to his belly.

"You're coping with this rather well, Arlan Finnbar MacEnoicht." She gazed at him from the corner of her eye as they left the shop.

"I have been to a market before. Not one indoors, as such."

Rhiannon smiled again, and her shoulders weren't so stiff. She'd held herself so around George and had avoided that man's touch. He'd returned to his hometown, to the place where oxen crossed the river—or such George and Rhiannon had named it—and now she fairly skipped along ahead of him as though happy George had left them. His heart danced, for he would spend his days in her company alone. The tightness of his brow eased. Aye, there was so much he wished to know of her.

He followed Rhiannon through the masses. There were so many people, such as at The Keep on a day the clan chieftains gathered to petition Father. They had to forge through in single file. People bumped into Rhiannon, who walked ahead, brushing shoulders with them as they barged past, then they looked up at him, eyes wide, and side-stepped around.

Rhiannon turned into a quieter shop-lined corridor, leaving the bustle of the main mall behind them. Here, the shops were smaller and less crowded.

"There's a bookshop I like to look in whenever I'm here." She gave a half smile, and her cheeks tinged a rosy hue. "You don't mind, do you?"

"Nae, you go peruse. I'll wait here."

Rhiannon left him and entered the shop. He stepped closer to the clear glazed frontage and peered in. Bookshelves lined the walls, and it looked more like a library. Footsteps clumped behind him, a disorderly clatter of feet on the smooth flooring. The back of his neck tingled.

Arlan turned to the male-voiced murmurs. The group of youths he'd passed by the moving staircase now milled around a doorway near the entrance to this quieter section of the shopping centre. The youth who'd pierced Arlan with a defiant stare ran his gaze over the empty passage behind himself and the other boys, but not along this shop-lined corridor to where Arlan stood in front of the bookshop. Arlan kept his eye on them. The lad rattled the door handle. It opened and the older boys surrounding him sniggered. Then he and his companions barged through the door. The door slammed shut on their laughter.

Arlan's gut niggled.

He turned back to the bookshop. Rhiannon stood at a shelf, a book in her hands, engrossed in reading its cover.

Hmm. Perhaps she would be some time.

Arlan strode back toward the door, its broken handle dangling. The label on this door read *Staff Only*. He pushed and stepped through to a plain, narrow passage. Tubes ran along the ceiling above him. A hum filled the air, and the lighting glowed dimmer. Whispered laughter echoed from ahead—youthful laughter and footsteps.

He followed their sniggers, which stayed ahead of him. The passage took some turns, curving as if he were walking in a circle. The corridor had doors equally spaced apart. He read the sign on the first—*CINEMA ONE*.

The tone of the lads' voices travelling along to him was now sharper. Some hissed as others urged. Whispered, giddy laughter echoed along the corridor. Arlan followed the curve, and the group came into view, gathered around a door. A collective yell of delight tinged with fear rose from the gang.

The hair on Arlan's arms rose.

"What are ye doing?" He spoke in the deep commanding tone he would use on his warriors if in need of a reprimand.

The door slammed and the lads ran ahead in the opposite direction to Arlan, leaving the narrow corridor now empty bar the thunder of retreating boots.

Arlan ground his teeth. These young ones needed some good focus for their energy. Again, his mind went to a practice yard.

A slap or two with a hard wooden sword would soon redirect their inclinations to useful purpose.

He turned and walked a fair way back to the broken door. He stepped into the corridor with shops where Rhiannon stood, turning her head in every direction before spying him.

"There you are!" The *v* between her brows disappeared. "I thought I'd lost you." She made a come here gesture with her hand.

He closed the distance between them, and she put her hand in the crook of his arm, sending warm tingles up his neck to his scalp. She tugged him along, travelling half the length of this narrower corridor, then stood still, nose turned upward, sniffing. A sharp scent of smoke tickled Arlan's nostrils.

A door slammed ahead, and a middle-aged man stood, struggling into his coat. "Don't you smell it!" The man asked him and Rhiannon. "There's a fire!"

A loud ear-piercing noise filled the air, shrieking—an entity in itself—insisting and urging.

"That's the fire alarm." Rhiannon's eyes went wide. "We need to find the nearest exit."

"*Eggs it?*" His forehead tightened, and he clamped his hands over his ears to stop the pain.

"The way out." Rhiannon's voice muffled behind his palms.

She led him further down the narrow corridor. Other doors opened into it and many people ran out and into the hallway behind them, their voices loud. Rhiannon said something—muffled again by his hands—so he removed them from his ears. The painful shriek stabbed his head again—worse than the squeal of a wild boar plunged with a spear.

"Oh, it's the cinemas. They'd be full today 'cos it's school holidays." She bit her lower lip and her eyebrows met in a crease.

Cinemas? What have those lads done!

In front of Arlan was the *eggs-it* she aimed for. Way, way in front of him. High-pitched voices of children mingled with deeper adult commands flowed out through the doors. Rhiannon looked past him, her mouth agape. Arlan turned in the direction of Rhiannon's wide-eyed stare.

A mass of people surged toward them like a river in flood, lined across the hall, scraping and lapping the walls like a headwater tearing along, almost upon himself and Rhiannon, and they would soon scoop them up in their wake.

People tumbled, and others trampled on them in their urgency to leave this market. Smoke touched Arlan's nostrils, and a cloud rose, swirling above the mass of panicked people. Like the breath of a dragon, the smoke held a heat and thrummed with a red flashing light. Burning scents swirled along, hitting Arlan's nose with full force.

Rhiannon held her bag close to her, her knuckles white. Arlan searched for an alcove to tuck her in for safety while the panicked crowd rushed past. *There!* A narrow inset beside a pillar-like structure. Right next to the wall on his left. He grabbed Rhiannon and she yelped. He pushed her into the shallow inset, her back against the wall, and pressed himself to her as the wave reached them.

Voices shrieked with an urgency. Adults dragged children behind them. Some wee ones ran on their own, their cries and screams filling the narrow hallway. Sharp elbows stabbed, digging points into his back. Bodies poured past and slammed against him, jolting him closer to the inset.

A large man bolted into Arlan. He banged Arlan's back and cracked Arlan's forehead against the hard corner of the pillar. Now Arlan's head thudded, but he held on to the wall and extended his hands high above Rhiannon. He spread his feet and braced himself to keep in place and bounce back against the jostling throng, his eyebrow stinging.

The flood pressed him into Rhiannon and tried to shove him along with it, all at the same time. Rhiannon grabbed his T-shirt and screwed it into her fist. The crowd pushed him closer into her, making his own body a threat to crush Rhiannon's smaller frame. He held himself back for, any closer, and he'd squeeze the air from her lungs. But he would stand between her and the deadly waves of panicked people in flight, threatening to drown them both.

Engulfed by the throng that continued to batter and kick him, he held on, arm muscles heating. His head throbbed above his eye. His kidneys ached, and the burning in his thighs increased. His tugged hair stung his scalp at the roots.

Rhiannon pulled at his scrunched T-shirt, her rounded eyes fixing on his and her lips parting. She spoke, but he couldn't make out what she said. Her gaze flicked to her right, so he turned in that direction. Still they came, but the headwaters were becoming a stream, then a trickle.

The smoke descended and the shrieking noise still engulfed them, with the red glow continuing its flashing. Light now came from the other end of this narrow corridor—the way out. Arlan leaned away from Rhiannon's shaking body and wiped his moist eye. His hand came away bloodied, a tacky trickle ran down his face and seeped into his beard.

"You've cut your head." Rhiannon leaned closer, her voice soft, and peered at his forehead.

"It's nothing. Are you well, Rhiannon? We must go. We must escape this market."

Rhiannon nodded and stepped out of the small alcove, then halted and gasped. He followed her gaze to a young child, a girl, who lay motionless beside the opposite wall. He reached the wee girl before Rhiannon and scooped her up in his arms. She was so light and moved not.

"Come, we must leave." He ran to the *eggs it*, glancing behind to ensure Rhiannon followed. A deep fog of smoke, dark and descending, chased them to the doors.

Arlan blinked at the daylight outside. A large cart on wheels, like Rhiannon's car, but oh-so-much bigger, came toward them at a pace, and the fumes these carts release wafted up his nostrils. It also shrieked with a noise of warning and a light flashed on its roof. People wearing brightly coloured bulky clothing jumped out, and some grabbed a long tube. Others attended to the crowd, moving people away from the doors that he and Rhiannon had just left.

Arlan's heart pounded as if he'd been in the ring, in a contest that had tested his mettle. His opponent was the flame and the flood—and his concern for Rhiannon's safety. He glanced down at her. She was unharmed and peered with a crinkled brow at this small, injured child.

The people who'd pushed past them in that narrow corridor now milled around this place Rhiannon called a *car park*. People standing in groups or resting themselves on the ground covered its dark, smooth surface. Some carried others who were also motionless.

"My Julie!" a woman screamed at him. "Oh, you found her. Is she okay?"

Arlan lowered the child to the woman. The young girl stirred in his arms and whimpered but did not open her eyes.

"Julie! Wake up, darlin'." The woman's voice choked.

"She's not rousing. Look, here's an ambulance. Take her to it, Arlan." Rhiannon tugged at his arm and led him toward yet another large noisy cart with flickering lights on a bar on its roof. A woman in a uniform jumped out and strode toward them, looking at the child.

"Bring her around to the stretcher, please." She directed Arlan to the back of this wagon-like cart and pointed to a narrow bed, so he placed the child on it.

"Oh, thank you," the child's mother said over her shoulder.

"Ye are welcome," Arlan replied, but the woman's attention had returned to her child.

"Excuse me." A man in uniform pulled Arlan to one side. "Let me clean that. A plaster-strip will hold it together." The man dabbed Arlan's eyebrow with a cold liquid. A sting seared above his left eye, then the man placed tiny white strips on Arlan's wound, and they stuck there.

"Thank you." Arlan touched the strips, which were stiff along his eyebrow.

"Let's go home." Rhiannon slipped her arm through his and tugged him to stand.

Arlan glanced down at his T-shirt covered in red drips, and the bags still slipped over his wrist.

"You saved me *and* the shopping." She held her mouth in a smile, but her voice wavered. "Well done, Mr MacEnoicht."

Arlan's chest heated as an unbidden flame grew, a blaze threatening to burn him.

TWENTY

—•—

The peoples roar like an ocean.
The waves toss to and fro.
A king would reign in peace,
A chieftain rule with a gentle hand.
But the waters will not still with a command.
The man of peace wields a double-edged sword.

WISDOM WRITINGS ON KINGSHIP
SAGE GLIOCAS
(2870-2962 POST DRAGON WARS)

Perth, Scotland

Work had come around all too soon. I tidied shelves in the quiet shop and now my hand lay on a book about Celtic culture. I'd wandered to this section of the shop again—the third time in an hour.

My weekend shopping with Arlan had been eventful, but at least the man looked like he belonged here now.

I stared at the immaculately clean shelf I'd already dusted—it was just a blur.

News reports had stated many people had sustained serious injuries in the panicked mob fleeing from the cinema fire at the shopping centre. I shut my eyes and grasped the memory of Arlan's body pressed against mine, a wall shielding me from the mob. He'd taken it all on his back—he'd come out in bruises already. His arms had shaken with the tension in his muscles and his body heat had blown into my face while the crowd surged past.

He'd cut his eyebrow in a bash against the wall—the left eyebrow, and it would leave a scar. I'd seen it before—on the Arlan at the Celtic Festival. But he'd laughed it off, saying he'd suffered worse in the back street fighting pits in the village below The Keep.

"Rhiannon," Mr Watson's voice startled me out of my reverie. "Why don't you order a copy for yourself?"

103

I opened my eyes. "Pardon?"

"You've gone to that book on the Celts three times in the last hour. They're a favourite of yours, aren't they?" His balding head gleamed in the shop's lighting.

"Oh, yes, I suppose I should."

"Rhiannon, business is slow today, and well, with the ordeal you went through this weekend"—he inclined his kind face toward me— "how about you go home early? I won't dock your pay. It's just that you are a wee bit distracted."

"Oh, sorry. Yes, I'm finding it difficult to focus today." I grimaced.

"No, it's alright. Go home, Rhiannon."

I parked my car out the front of the cottage and gripped the steering wheel.

Arlan was a warrior, and warriors are trained to protect.

I didn't mind that.

Having attended martial art classes for only a short time, I didn't pretend to be an expert. I *did* have limitations and, realistically, a woman was usually no match for a man strength-wise—unless you were a female bodybuilder.

I most certainly was *not* a bodybuilder.

Learning locks, holds and manoeuvres, I'd come to realise they required little strength, but sometimes a lot of luck.

Just like the attack on the hill. A shudder passed through me.

No, I didn't object to Arlan's protection—not at all.

From what I'd learned so far about Arlan, I'd feel sorry for anyone who crossed him.

"Hmm." I twisted my grip around the steering wheel. "I should be braver." A note of self-reprimand snuck out in my tone.

And I needed to find out more about him.

I glanced into the field—now empty of that large, and still scary horse—got out of my car and walked to the cottage. All was quiet inside and the fire had burned down in the grate. *Unusual.* Arlan had taken up the duty of tending the fire and replenishing the woodpile.

I stepped back out the front door and scoured the hill, the autumn sunshine barely warming my shoulders. The deciduous trees were almost bare of their foliage. No sign of a man on horseback on those slopes. Perhaps he'd gone right up near the Iron Age Fort. I had to see, so I changed out of my work clothes into my jeans. But running out the door, a nagging caught my insides. I turned away from the path up the hill and headed into the small village instead.

I walked down the main road toward the local shops, passing a row of houses interspersed with garden plots. The clop of horse's hooves echoed off a high stone wall in the quiet street. It was Mengus, and Arlan sat relaxed on the black beast. Arlan didn't look so scary in jeans and a T-shirt. I gave an appreciative chuckle. He looked... *striking.*

Just as well it was a quiet village with little traffic. What would that animal do if it saw a car? Or a lorry? Arlan didn't wear a hard hat. What if he injured himself?

Arlan kicked Mengus to a canter and covered the rest of the distance to me. He pulled Mengus to a halt and grinned as he leaned down, extending his hand.

I blinked. "I can't ride."

His hand remained outstretched. "Then it's about time ye learned, lass," Arlan replied in his sing-song version of English.

He directed me to place my foot on his in the stirrup, and pulled me up to sit behind him. The horse nickered and jostled its head, prancing, and I grabbed Arlan around the waist and held tight.

"The first thing ye need to do is to relax. For Mengus here is a sensitive soul, despite what people think. His fearsome appearance belies a somewhat nervous trait, which can mix with meanness. These are important characteristics for a war horse. But he can sense your fear and that makes him nervous, and I don't want you thrown from a horse today. Not any day."

I took some deep breaths to loosen the muscles in my arms and legs. It seemed to work and the tension in my thighs eased. Arlan nudged Mengus to a walk, then turned the animal around to the way they'd come. Arlan's body warmed my arms as I held on.

"Where are we going?" I asked, peering round the side of him.

"Ye'll see."

The rocking gait of the stallion and the clinking *clip-clop* of shod hooves on the road mesmerised me, like the clatter of railway tracks when travelling by a train. Sitting on top of a horse wasn't that bad really. Maybe I'd even get the hang of riding if I had some lessons.

We passed more houses and headed nearer to the narrow burn that crossed the village.

"You're taking me to the park, aren't you?"

"Hmm. Aye."

Fallen leaves skittered along the road and we soon arrived at the small park. Arlan jumped off and raised his arms to help me down. I reached out, holding on as I swung my leg over, and he lowered me to the ground.

"Ye need to sit in the sunshine for a wee bit." Arlan still held me, his hands warm where he touched my waist. "Ye work too hard, Rhiannon. How do you say it? Ye need to chillax."

I laughed. "Okay."

Arlan let go of me and led Mengus onto the grass, letting him nibble. He pointed to a seat, and we both sat.

There was little traffic today, only one car had passed us so far, and no one had come out of the houses on the narrow street near the park to complain about an enormous horse eating the grass.

Arlan lifted his face to the sun and closed his eyes. His chest rose with deep inhalations as he sat beside me. The breeze stirred what remained of the leaves on the silver birch behind us. In the companionable quiet, I shuffled in my seat. What was this all about? Possibly him finding a way back home—a home he'd hardly spoken of. I knew so little about him, really.

"Do you have any brothers or sisters?" I asked.

He jolted slightly, then opened his eyes and faced me.

"It's just that I was an only child, and I was wondering..." My words trailed off at his expression.

He ran his teeth over his bottom lip, like something stressed him, then he looked down at the grass at our feet.

"Aye, I had a wee sister who died at birth"—his voice thickened— "along with my mother."

"Oh, I'm so sorry." The memory of a shiny black coffin sitting in an open grave as I stood at my own mother's funeral flashed through my mind.

"And I have a brother"—he clasped his hands in front of him as he leaned forward, resting his arms on his thighs— "although at times I wish I had not."

"Why?" I would've loved to have a big brother.

"He, Kyle, belittled me. Beat me as a child." He shook his head and tutted. "Nae, he derides me still."

"Oh, that's horrible. And he still bullies you? Surely that's not possible. Wait. He's bigger than you?"

"Nae, he is not. But his mouth can be mean, and his will bent to demean me at every turn." Arlan's clasped hands tightened, and his voice held an edge of hurt. "Even in front of my troop. The warriors I command. It seemed like the larger I grew—the more I towered over him—the more intense his derisive comments became. As though he wished to knock me down with his words and keep me the child, and he the superior elder brother." Arlan grunted. "He will be clan chief. What more does he want?"

He sucked air in between his teeth and turned slightly away from me. "Many a time I have asked myself why Father couldn't see it. He was so caught up in grief over losing Mother. Then he threw himself into his duties as high king." He lifted a hand and rubbed his mouth. "I tell you the truth, I relish this time away from Kyle. From the constant battering. Excuse me. I vent my anger in your presence. I should—"

"No, no, it's okay." My heart twinged. He'd had it from his brother *all* his life. Yes, a break from the bullying was always bliss.

Like school half terms and summer holidays.

My school years came back to me in a flood. Feeling small. Stupid. Awkward. Different.

I put my hand over Arlan's white knuckles.

"It hurts, doesn't it? There seems no way of stopping them. If you respond similarly, then *you're* the bad one—the person being cruel. And *you* get the punishment for bad words."

Detention, where I was the only student in the classroom after school because I'd commented on Michelle Stone's eyes—calling her pop-eyed—after she'd picked on my weird purple irises. But she'd complained to our form teacher about me, when I'd just sucked up her taunting comment.

"You know of these things, Rhiannon? But who would dare be so mean to you?"

"Ha. The same kind of person who would bully you as a little boy and keep it up when you're the size you are now." I squeezed his hand. Then I blinked at what I'd just implied about his own brother. "I'm sorry. I probably shouldn't speak so badly of ... Kyle, is it?"

"Aye, Kyle is my elder brother and as such will lead others. It is not my place to reprimand him." He opened his hands to mine and held it gently.

"But you must not let the derogatory things said about you affect how you feel about yourself." Who was I speaking to—Arlan or me? "You're... impressive and brave. Thank you again for keeping me safe in that crush."

He smiled. "Ye are welcome, Rhiannon. I would do that any time." His fingers curled around mine.

Mengus nickered and crunched on more grass, his bridle clanking with his jaw action. Arlan still held my hand as we sat in the quiet. I turned to him as he gazed thoughtfully at the ground in front of us. We'd just shared deep hurts that had lasting effects, and my whole body warmed, despite the autumn breeze, with the thought that we'd connected on a deeper level somehow.

I couldn't deny the pain that returned to my chest whenever I recalled school. Yes, often all I thought of were the times my classmates had upset me. If only it had been different. But it wasn't.

Arlan knew what it meant. He'd been there too.

Children from the small local school, now free of classes for the day, wandered past the park in a gaggle, pointing and exclaiming at Mengus.

I nudged Arlan. "We'd better go."

We remounted Mengus and Arlan walked him back to the road. I put my arms around Arlan and pressed my face against his back. His body heat radiated through his T-shirt and warmed my cheek.

I reflected on the time since George had left. Arlan continued to behave like a perfect gentleman—with it being just the two of us, and no George around acting as self-appointed chaperone. Arlan should be finding a way to return to his own world, but he didn't seem to be in a hurry.

"Arlan?"

"Aye, lass." His deep voice rumbled against my cheek.

"Do you like it here? Earth is different from your world, isn't it?"

"You have plenty here. Your lives are easier. There is abundant food in shops and work to do, with time for leisure and no threat of war."

"But we have wars and, thankfully, they are nowhere near close to Scotland. And you experienced for yourself it's not always safe."

The gentle *clip-clopping* of Mengus' hooves continued for some moments. Arlan's head tilted to his left. "Where are the wars?" His long hair falling down his back tickled my face.

"George didn't let you watch the news, did he?" I asked.

"News? Ah, the real acting."

"The *real acting*? Oh, yes. You should watch it."

Arlan walked Mengus through the field by the cottage and up to the animal shelter. He flung his right leg over the horse's neck and jumped down in one fluid motion, then reached up and helped me to dismount. His breath caught the wisps of hair beside my cheek, and his firm grip around my waist sent a tingle through me. I stood back from the horse as he loosened the girth straps and removed the saddle.

Arlan picked up some straw from an abandoned bale and rubbed his stallion's coat with it until it shone. Sun beams angled into the shed, and the tiny silver clasps decorated with intricate swirls that held aside the small side-plaits keeping Arlan's hair out of his eyes, glinted in his jet-black hair.

I tore my eyes from their glint and wrung my hands. I *had* to say it.

"Arlan, you can't ride around the streets on your horse. What if you fell off and injured yourself on the hard road?"

Arlan stopped grooming Mengus and faced me, his eyebrows raised and head tilted.

"It is said you should never say *never*, but I have never fallen off Mengus and I don't intend on doing so." The stallion turned his head to Arlan and nickered.

"Do you have bitumen roads in Dal... Dal G... wherever you come from? They're hard, and bones break easily, no matter how tough you are."

"I can't say that we have *bitumen* roads in Dál Gaedhle, but the stone-paved ones we have are even harder, I would imagine." His left eye twitched, then he resumed grooming the beast.

"Anyway, please stick to the paths in the forest." I rolled my eyes. "It's not as if you can ride by unnoticed. It's bad enough Mr Grumpy-gut from next door knows about you. If I had to take you to a hospital, how would I explain you? A cousin from the Isles? You don't even have any ID."

Arlan gripped the wad of hay he used to curry Mengus and kept his back to me.

Damn. I'd just spoiled our wonderful time together. Why can't I just shut up and leave things?

Arlan's hand rested on the stallion's rump. "Then I shall look for a way home."

My breath stopped in my mouth, and I couldn't answer.

Get a grip, girl!

I had to be realistic. He must return to his own world. I wasn't too sure what the Celtic Festival kiss was all about, but he needed to go back. A warrior like him must be important where he comes from. And he stood out in this world. Larger than life, very intelligent, brave, so healthy and strong and...

I squinted my eyes and gulped.

Couldn't he just ride up the hill to the Iron Age Fortifications and disappear? Something had been stopping him. The silence stretched, and the air between us held a tension.

Are we arguing?

Rain pattered on the corrugated iron roof of the animal shelter and a tightness pulled between my shoulder blades. "I'll start dinner." I spun away, not waiting for a reply, and walked to the house through the rain.

Sausages were sizzling in the pan, and potatoes boiling in a pot, while I peeled carrots. Arlan stepped through the backdoor, silent as he washed his hands—having finally got the idea of taps and toilets—then walked into the living room and turned on the television. Audio of a sports-like commentary, with thuds and slaps belonging to what seemed to be a martial art, grunted into the kitchen. The news came on, and I let the journalists' reports float by me unheeded while I continued preparing dinner. It had been difficult to feed this man all the protein he required and quite a drain on my bank account. Buying the sword and shield at the Celtic Festival—the day I'd met him almost two months ago—hadn't helped the bank balance either...

But he'd finally hinted at returning to his own world and my bank balance would slowly grow again.

A chill sat at the back of my neck. He *would* leave...

I pulled myself up sharp—*I just have to get over it.*

I dished up dinner and took his meal to him. He sat forward on the couch, mouth part-open, blinking often. He took the plate and placed it on his lap like he'd not even noticed he'd done it. The newsfeed showed the Syrian War with the usual bombings and devastation on the ground. Film of refugees spilling across the borders filled the screen. I sat next to him on the couch with my meal.

Arlan hadn't touched his food. I nudged his arm, and he turned. A deep crease sat between his brows. I pointed to the plate on his lap. He glanced down, picked up the fork I'd shoved in the mashed tatties, and scooped some into his mouth. His vision never left the large flat screen while the fork went between his plate and his mouth and back again.

The drumming rain pelted the windows as the weather forecast blared from the television and Arlan ate the last of his meal in silence. An Là came on next, and while he listened to the news of the world in the Gaelic, his usually broad shoulders slowly hunched. A documentary on World War I commenced, with black and white footage showing piles of bodies and exploding bombs spraying dirt in the fields of the Somme. Arlan chewed his lip and frowned, focusing on nothing.

He hadn't spoken for a while. He usually sparked the conversation between us. In fact, he looked flat and stressed watching the news. Our conversation in the shed still echoed in my mind.

Conversation or an argument?

Maybe I knew him well enough to ask if something was wrong, but that could be too nosey. My being ached, not just my chest, but deeper. He'd never been like this. He was always bright and cheerful, but now just so... distant.

I had to do it. Had to ask.

He could only tell me to shut up and mind my own business.

A gust of wind stabbed the rain against the window.

"What's wrong, Arlan?"

He swallowed, and glanced down at the empty plate in his hands, then put it on the coffee table and gave a harsh sigh.

"Where I come from, Dál Gaedhle in the land of Dál Cruinne." He spoke his world's name with tenderness, with love even. "We are warlike and fierce, but we have lived in peace for many years. Although I love a good fight, I don't wish to be violent any longer. There's much in this world that is vicious. Much that isn't good. I wish to no longer cause harm where there should be none." He nodded, the crease now a furrow on his brow, then he sat straighter. "I will be what you would call a *pacifist*. I shall strive to seek resolutions to conflict with discussion, not weapons."

"Okay." The word stretched as it came out of my mouth.

Huh? He was powerfully built, and his world had trained him to fight with that sword. *And* all the other weapons he carried.

"But can you be that in your world? Aren't you a king's son? Our queen's sons and grandsons have all served in the armed forces."

Arlan's nostrils flared, and he shook his head in small, rapid shakes.

"I... I... will not do that. I'll no longer partake in warlike activity. There are other ways to be the son of a clan chief. Or I can deny my birth right and... och! You dinnae need to ken all of this, Rhiannon. It's my struggle, not yours." He stood and stormed outside.

My body wouldn't move.

"That was intense." I puffed, blowing the loose hair from my face.

What would he do once back in his own world?

"A pacifist in a world of swords? Ha! That's *not* going to work!" I took the empty plates to the kitchen and clattered them into the sink.

Through the misted kitchen window, I followed Arlan's progress as he stomped the last few paces to the shed. A moment later, he led his stallion into the darkening night, mounted bareback, and rode to the hill, the wind blowing his hair wildly around him.

I ran to the door but stopped myself—his broadsword rested beside the umbrella stand.

TWENTY-ONE

For portals are a sentient magic. They perceive. If the desire to pass is absent, they will deny the traveller access. On occasion, a traveller may even be called—though this is rare. For intentions and desires are the key to traversing between worlds.

SECRET SACRED WRITINGS OF THE SAGES
LOCKED SCROLL 34
BROCH OF THE ANCIENTS

Abernethy, Scotland

I walked out of my bedroom to sunlight spilling through the living room window. The blanket and pillow lay untouched on the couch where I'd put them out for Arlan's return the previous evening. I sat on the couch beside them and picked up his pillow, placing it against my cheek and inhaling his scent—musky male.

Cold swirled around in my stomach. He would've found some shelter overnight. He was a warrior, a soldier, and therefore used to harsh conditions. *Right?*

I pushed the pillow away and stowed the unused bedding, then dressed, all the time keeping one ear out for Arlan's return. I prepared to leave for work, the cottage watching me in silence. I walked to the backdoor and stopped. His big mean-looking sword still sat by the umbrella stand, its pommel a round, intricate knot. I rested my hand on it, then curling my fingers around its grip, I lifted. His prolonged grasp had smoothed the leather-bound handle. I withdrew it from the scabbard, and it sung. The sword weighed heavy in my hand, with faint scratches on the blade but no dints along the edges.

I held it to the morning light, and it gleamed in a ripple pattern, its edges shiny sharp, revealing markings along the flat of the blade. It looked like Ogham script and the words ran along the thickest section of the blade.

My breath brushed past my hand. "Wonder what that says."

A chill sat in Arlan's muscles after a night on cold, hard ground. Very much a change from Rhiannon's warm cottage. He patted Mengus' neck and his stallion flicked his head as he did when annoyed. Arlan peered round the side of the wide tree trunk he hid behind, cool settling on his brow.

Rhiannon stopped at her backdoor and handled his sword, looking intently at the inscription on the fuller. She put it back, then walked to her car chewing her lip. She drove off.

He mounted Mengus and rode the short way to her cottage, a heaviness sitting between his shoulders. He'd thought long and hard throughout the rainy night, but the pain remained in his heart.

He was compelled to find his way home and aid his troop's defence, pacifist or no'.

He knew nothing of how travelling between worlds functioned, but surely he would enter where and when he left his world. For if he recalled correctly, in the tales told by bards and sages of people lost in the Faerie Realm, on their return moments later at the same Faerie mound, they would describe varying amounts of time away from home. *Some even away for years.* He swallowed.

Although the bandits had been scattering and most fleeing, one had been charging toward Arlan himself when his world had gone white. So, he must be prepared to continue the fight where he left off. It would be foolish—even deadly—to return ambling as if on a summer's day's ride when that skirmish meant the *droch dhuine's* blade would be at his neck the very moment he reappeared back in his own world.

Arlan heaved a sigh, then groaned at his own unwillingness. He wished not to live beneath Kyle's scorn, and to go home meant he must return to it. In truth, it was as though the rod, which beat his back continually, had ceased its stinging thuds since his arrival here.

Neither did he desire to be bound to a life in which he had no say. Whatever role designated to him as a second son of a clan chief, he would make his *own* choices about his future!

Nor did he wish to leave just yet the woman who now drove down the road away from him.

He shook his head and grunted, then retrieved his weapons from her backdoor.

"Well, my friend," he said to Mengus, "we shall try." He lifted himself into the saddle. "If we must." He kicked his war horse to the track leading up the hill and rode to the top.

A worn earth works sat at its peak. A mound of rubble lay in a pile to one side, and the grass covered ground on the other side led to a steep drop. He turned to the view. A wide river ran along the base of this hill, through the village and a broad green valley. In its day, this fortification would have been a place of protection for the original villagers below and a grand place for a lookout. Aye, one could see for miles and the enemy had nae chance of cover. Those who manned this fortification would spy a war boat rowing up this river in time to prepare.

But that was this world, and he must get to his own.

He breathed out through his nostrils and slumped his shoulders.

"Aye, I shall try, once more." He spoke loudly, then winced at the reluctance in his tone.

Mengus nickered. He steered his stallion around and walked him to a familiar-looking spot. Perhaps *this* was the place. He'd ridden this track almost every day since his arrival, peering at every section for a tree or branch or dip in the track, trying to sense the very place he'd entered. His entry had occurred so fast—he in the midst of a charge, and then pursuing the one who held a knife to Rhiannon—that his recollections were unclear. With autumn's leaf fall and the light of this world's sun, the trees seemed to change their appearance daily. It was as though this wood was a living creature, such as a slithering serpent changing its curves as it moved along the ground.

Hmph!

He nudged Mengus on through a narrow section. The foliage grew thinner, and here he stopped. Today he would try a new tactic. He would recall what he'd been feeling when he had... *come through.*

Anger had filled him. With battle lust upon him. He'd felt murderous.

He screwed his mouth to one side.

He felt far from that today.

"Must I stir myself to a rage?"

The trees didn't answer. He shrugged, kicking Mengus to a trot, then a canter. He lifted his shield, raised his sword, and yelled. His voice rang through the wood and Mengus' hooves thudded against the heavy track.

He reached almost the end of the track but remained here.

Again, he did the same.

Yet another time.

He turned his mount and nudged again, yelling, waving his sword at the trees and the sky.

Nothing. He remained in this world.

Easing Mengus back, a chortle rippled through his chest. He took a breath and released a throaty laugh.

"This is ridiculous!" His shoulders shook, mirth stifling his voice, and heat filling his cheeks.

He wiped tears from his eyes and coughed until he composed himself.

"Och. I owe it to Bàn. I owe it to my warriors. I owe it to all!" His words sobered him. But to himself...?

He swallowed, then pressed his lips together.

It would mean leaving Rhiannon.

He shook his head. By all that is good, there was *something* about her. He wouldn't leave this world without answers to the questions that nagged at the back of his mind and had come to the fore while he'd tried to sleep in the cold, dark forest.

But how and what would he ask Rhiannon? Nae, he could not ask a thing until the niggling thoughts had substance... proof he could present to her to support his case.

Arlan urged Mengus down the hill. He flew past the neighbour's house. The man stood out front, his scowl on his woman, who placed rubbish bags in the large bin that sat by the fence they shared with Rhiannon. The scruffy man lifted his glare to Arlan, but Arlan kicked Mengus on and into the field behind the cottage. He jumped off, removed the saddle, and let Mengus graze. He'd rub him down later.

But first he had something to do. He strode to the backdoor, which was out of view of the neighbour who peered around probably in search of him. Rhiannon had locked the door, so he pressed his shoulder into it. It budged and snapped open.

Och, he must implore Rhiannon to secure her doors more effectively.

The door opened to the passage that led to her bedroom. He paused at the entrance to her room, pulse drumming in his ears. He curled his hand into a fist.

Rhiannon would not like it, but he must discover more about her.

He stepped through. Her perfume, that unique scent that spoke of her, flooded him, filling him with a heady floral bouquet. He stood and sniffed deeper.

The sparsely furnished room contained a dressing table, a wardrobe, and a trunk sitting at the foot of her narrow bed. Sunlight streamed through her window, illuminating the wood grain of the trunk. He stepped closer and ran his hand over the lid. Nicks and scratches bobbled beneath his fingertips, and the wood had dire need of polishing or painting over.

He grasped the lid then grunted a nod. *Aye, I must do it. For her sake and my own.*

He lifted the lid. A shield decorated with horses sat on top of garments, a book entitled *Photo Album,* and a long object wrapped in a cloth, its shape familiar. He lifted it and unwrapped.

A sword. He chuckled. A reasonable weapon. But for Rhiannon?

He re-wrapped it and went to return it to its place. His hand froze as his heart seized mid-beat.

Beneath his hand lay a maroon tartan plaid.

TWENTY-TWO

— • —

A king seeks truth in all matters.
A treasure sought above riches.
Of greater worth than lands and fortresses.
As priceless as the loyal sword arms of a thousand warriors.

WISDOM WRITINGS ON KINGSHIP
SAGE GLIOCAS
(2870-2962 POST DRAGON WARS)

Abernethy, Scotland

Driving home from work that afternoon after another quiet day in the small bookshop, the fields beside the motorway flashed by the edges of my sight. Many times today I'd had to force my concentration back to the job, and push away the emptiness that kept creeping in.

And I had to do it again.

Arlan may not be at the cottage.

I let the air go out of my lungs and drag the heaviness with it.

I'd grown used to him. The way he stocked the woodpile and kept the fire going. How he sat honing that gruesome-looking sword, running the whet stone along both sides, then smoothing it with a soft cloth. He said that sharpened the edge somehow. My giggle echoed back to me from the windscreen. Any rational person would say I should be scared, but all I felt was safe. I'd even miss his mean-looking black beast of a horse, only because he loved it so much.

My thoughts returned to Arlan's hair flying wildly in the wind as he galloped Mengus through the rainy night. Boy, he was a man conflicted. For someone who wanted to be a pacifist, a battle raged inside him.

I parked my car in its usual place.

No horse in the field. *He's gone.*

I wrapped my arms around myself, hugging away the ache, and leaned my head on the hard steering wheel. It pressed into my forehead as my eyes stung with tears.

"Oh, don't be *so* silly!"

Arlan would leave. He must. He had to go home to *Dál G... G.*

"Damn!" *I'd never learned how to pronounce it.* "Doesn't matter now."

I wiped the damp off my cheeks, got out of the car and marched into the cottage. At the door, his shield and broadsword rested beside the umbrella stand as usual, their knotwork glinting in the sunlight.

Arlan sat at the kitchen table wearing his leather breeches, his bare chest rising with an inhalation and his expression a tempest of emotions barely held in check.

"Hello." His deep voice lilted his Stornoway-type accent.

"Hi." My voice sounded husky, so I coughed to clear my throat. "I thought you might've gone home."

"Did you?" He raised his eyebrows, then dropped them again and slumped back in the chair. He fiddled with the dagger in his hand, twirling its handle, his face dark. "I tried everything I could think of up there on that hill. But as you see, I remain here."

So, he would have gone without saying goodbye.

That hurts in an unexpected way.

A pressure began in my lungs, and I had difficulty dragging air in. I dropped my bag on the kitchen floor and leaned on the chair opposite him, catching my breath.

"I may never get home." He continued twiddling the dagger.

"But you do return!" I clamped my hand over my mouth—*too late.*

"What are ye telling me, lass?" Arlan stood up, towering over me. "Ye know for a fact that I go home?"

I went to walk past him, but he caught my arm, causing me to halt mid stride.

"You need to explain, if ye would nae mind." He lowered his face to see mine.

I swallowed, but I locked my gaze with his sky blue irises, the navy flecks seeming to glitter. "I've met you before."

He blinked, thick black lashes covering the blue for a second. "When and where?"

So intense.

He glanced down at his hand surrounding my upper arm, and the tight band of his grip loosened.

"Two months ago, at a Celtic Festival." My heart banged against my ribs.

Arlan shook his head, not understanding, and loose jet-black hair, free of its silver clasps, fell forward over his shoulders, a wisp catching on the whiskers of his cheek. He was big, and... sturdy, and *beautiful*, in a manly sort of way. And so near, his chest brushed against me, his warmth radiating to touch the exposed skin at my neck. His closeness almost overpowered me. I had to look away. I stared down at his arm and the triskelion in ink stared back.

No way will I tell him about that kiss.

"Where people dress up as Celts and have mock battles." I held my breathing steady.

"Did I speak to ye?"

"Yes, but it seemed like you already knew me." I fought to keep my voice level.

Arlan tilted his head to the left. I'd discovered he did this while thinking. He double blinked. "So, I know how to move between your world and mine?"

I nodded. I also wouldn't tell him he'd called me *a ghràidh chridhe*, the love of his heart.

Well, maybe I will, but not today.

"What else did I say to you?"

"Nothing." My face heated.

"Nothing?" His eyebrow rose, tugging the healing scar. "Then why are ye going red?"

I bit my lip so hard I tasted metal. My determination to not reveal more couldn't withstand his insistence. I gulped. "You came from the forest on the grounds of the Highland Estate." I paused, and now all my resolve fizzled to nothing. "You kissed me."

The start of a grin curled the corners of Arlan's mouth, but his stare intensified.

"It surprised you that I didn't know you," I continued, "and you said something about coming through too early."

He tilted his head to the left once more. "So, I have come at another time." He spoke to himself, his gaze drifting, and he squinted one eye.

I stepped back from him. His body heat and closeness had finally overwhelmed me.

"What were ye wearing, Rhiannon, on this Celtic Day? Were ye dressed as a Celt?"

"Yes." I pressed my lips together, clasping my hands in front of my body.

"Do ye still have what you wore that day?"

"Aye."

"Go put it on, then." His voice held a softness. "Let me see what sort of Celt ye make."

He stood there; his mouth turned up in a half grin, his eyes slowly crinkling.

He wanted to know what I looked like in my outfit? *Hmm.*

Perhaps he wanted to see me in garb similar to his world... if my makeshift costume grab of whatever I'd found in my wardrobe that day could even achieve it.

Still, I walked to my room, my insides jumping—I was about to show him me as a warrior. I opened the trunk at the end of my bed and raked through it, then dressed in the same costume I had worn the day I'd first met him, except for the fake tattoo. I tied the plaid around my waist with trembling fingers.

What will he make of it this time?

I grasped the handle of the shield covered in horses with my left hand, and the sword with the intricately carved handle in my right, its steel cold to my grip and heavy in my grasp.

I walked out of my room to where Arlan sat on the couch, waiting. He rose, his gaze travelling from my head to my feet and up again. His Adam's apple bobbed a few times.

"Ye look like one of my warriors." His voice came out husky.

"Oh, great! So, I look like a man!"

"No." His grin held pride. "I have women warriors in my war band. They are just as brave as my men, if not braver."

His gaze rested on my sword, and he pressed his mouth tight, repressing a smile.

"What?" The heat rose to my cheeks. The sword *was* large and heavy, and I held it awkwardly.

117

"Come here, Rhiannon." He held out his hand. "Show me that weapon of yours."

I stepped closer and handed him the broadsword. He examined it, turning it over, then hefted it in his hand. He held it out horizontally and placed the blade on his outstretched index finger near the handle. It balanced. He pursed his lips and nodded, then peered at the metalwork on the handle.

"Nice blade." He held the weapon as if ready to fight. "Good balance. Very blunt. Pretty handle. But tell me, what will ye do with a double-edged broadsword made for a man my size?" His mouth broke into a grin. "Come with me." He took my hand and tugged, walking me outside to the small patch of grass at the front of the cottage by the bird bath.

"Stand here, if ye would." Arlan stood back, then moved the blade around his body in swings and arcs of various angles. It floated through the air, an extension of his arm, and of his body. He flowed with it, danced with it, fully in control, giving it a life of its own. He moved like music, and if his actions were a melody, it would be a sonata for the sword.

My face tightened in an irrepressible grin as the blade whooshed past me with each stroke, the wake from close strokes lifting the stray hairs beside my face. Perhaps this display would've been dangerous in anyone else's hands, but Arlan mastered this sword. The blade's arcs came near, and my ears caught its whistling slice through the air. My heart ran wild, and I had to force my feet to be still beneath me.

"Wow, that's awesome," I yelled when he finished his routine.

"As are you. And an exceedingly beautiful warrior you make." Emotion vibrated through his tone.

He took the shield from my hand and placed it with my sword on the grass, then stepped closer, his hands coming to rest on my hips. His tender grip sent a shiver through me, kicking up my pulse rate. I lifted my head, noting every line of muscle and every dark hair on his body within my line of vision as my eyes travelled to his face. My hands found their own way to his arms, still radiating heat from his work with the blade. He was so alive, and so real.

A jet-black beard surrounded his lips. He lowered his face to mine, closed his eyes, and brushed my mouth with his. For a big man, he was gentle. His lips covered mine in warm softness as he kissed me deeply, then rested for a moment on my lower lip.

I swallowed on a gasp.

Emotions swirled inside me. Like... a need... to be with him, and only him, and never anyone else. With a man from another world, no less.

How could I feel like this?

But I savoured it as his scent surrounded me and the skin of his arms felt soft beneath my fingertips. He was all strength and hardness to the world, but just now, tenderness itself.

Arlan pulled away, his ribcage rising with an intake of air, and he let go of me, his expression wide-eyed as his throat worked. I had to stop myself from holding onto him. Holding on to his touch that reached my heart, my very soul. And right there, deep within my being, a certainty came.

He really will go home.

TWENTY-THREE

—·—

It beckons ye hame,
The land which birthed ye.
Earth, sky, and sea
Ken ye by name,
Know your heart,
And guide your feet to whence ye came.

VISIONS AND SAYINGS OF THE BLIND LADY SAGE

Abernethy, Scotland

Arlan shut the bathroom door behind him with a clunk and leaned back into the firm wood. Driving rain had started, forcing him and Rhiannon to run inside. It now turned to sleet on this bitter night, preventing him from riding out on Mengus such as he had the previous evening.

For at this moment, he needed to remove himself from her. From Rhiannon.

I cannot feel what I do for her.

But it'd swirled inside him and built until he could contain it no longer. He groaned.

Rhiannon had trembled and her warm hands had reached for him as their lips met. Rhiannon had returned the kiss and the emotion and would have kept her lips to his...

What am I thinking?

Who was he trying to fool? Himself—but it would not work.

He grabbed his head with his hands and groaned again, the small bathing room echoed his distress back to him. He dropped his hands and rested his head on the hard door. In the large looking glass ahead of him, he faced a Dál Gaedhle warrior. A man out of place in this other world. A world so wealthy, yet so violent. One that appeared to supply a life of ease, yet danger and death came from everywhere, even in a place of leisure and fun.

Being a pacifist was a noble notion. No war involvement. No fighting as a warrior. No hurt.

Just peaceful measures to solve my world's problems.

Many warriors in this world only used their skills in sport. He could do the same in Dál Gaedhle. He could enter sword-master contests, or even fight in the backstreet pits and earn a decent living. There was such a thing as free will. Every day people lived out their choices and that *must* be an option for him. In this world *and* in Dál Gaedhle.

If I go back.

Rhiannon maintained he did, but it could all change.

Rhiannon... So much about this woman he didn't know. He scratched his bearded chin, then rubbed it hard, for his actions of this day while Rhiannon worked would upset her. But his discovery demanded many answers.

I must broach the subject.

He stared hard at the reflective surface of the mirror. He looked scruffy and unkempt. Time to bathe. He turned to the tiny cupboard with the rain in it. Warm rain. He would *shower* once more.

I went to my room and changed back into jeans and a jumper. The shower ran in the bathroom, sending scents of apricot shampoo and goat's milk soap down the hallway. I sat on the couch, my finger tracing my lips where his own had touched them.

Arlan's kiss had been wonderful, nicer even than the first one, and shivers of warmth ran down my spine, then deeper.

But he'd pulled away, stopping himself. What was *that* about? Was he confused?

Well, I am.

He will go back and then what will I do?

I swallowed. We were together in the future, according to the Arlan who had kissed me at the Celtic Festival. My future, and his too. I'd discovered this in my past, a past he knew nothing of because it belonged to his future, which hadn't happened for him yet. I shook my head. My emotions confused me enough without trying to figure *that* one out.

The water had stopped running and moments passed. A grunt of exasperation came through the bathroom door. Then another. I walked to the door and stood.

"Ow, ahh," muffled through the door.

"Arlan?" I placed my hands flat on the door. "Are you okay?"

The door swung open, leaving my hands in mid-air, so I snatched them down. Arlan stood there, wearing only a towel wrapped around his waist, his hair dripping, and my manicure scissors dangling from the section of his bushy beard where they sat entangled.

"What are—?"

Arlan raised his index finger. "One moment." He closed the door and a soft thud came from behind it. Then he opened the door, now wearing his jeans and the scissors still attached to his beard.

"Would you help me please, Rhiannon? I wished to neaten myself but have only caused pain and maybe a bald patch." The corners of his mouth turned down, mirroring his shoulders. Drops of water ran down his bare torso from his scraggly, wet hair.

I tore my eyes from his chest. "May I come in?"

Arlan stepped aside to allow me to pass. My shoulder brushed his bare skin in the narrow space of the bathroom, spiking my pulse rate.

"You'd better dry your hair." I grabbed the spare towel off the rack and passed it to him, avoiding his gaze.

Steeling myself, I then faced him and reached up to his beard. His facial hair had grown long in the time he'd been here. I untangled the whiskers jammed in the scissors near the screw and right against his skin.

"Ahh...thank you."

"You're welcome. Want me to trim your beard?"

"Ye can do that?"

"Yes. My mother was a hairdresser. I have her kit." I gave a tight smile and raised a shoulder, then let it drop.

"Very well then, make me neater." His eyes warmed with a smile. "I'd never keep myself in such a poor state in my own world."

I opened the vanity cupboard, my fingers trembling as I dug around to the back where I kept the box containing Mum's hair scissors, comb, and a shaver. I turned and placed the small stool in front of the mirror and indicated for Arlan to sit.

Arlan sat, and I took Mum's scissors and comb out from their box while he towel dried his thick bushy beard. I inched closer as he rubbed the ends of his long black locks of thick, healthy hair. When he'd finished, I placed the comb in his wiry facial hair. I stood so close to him, the air whispered as it passed through his nose, and the scent of spiced apricots surrounded me. I blinked to regain my focus and tried to steady my trembling hands.

I *had* to break the silence. "I used to trim Dad's beard," I murmured. "My mum, God rest her soul, taught me. And how to cut my hair, which you can see I don't do often." *I'm rambling.*

The short dark hairs of Arlan's sculptured torso caught my peripheral vision. I suppressed a moan—*he is a very masculine man.*

"I'm sorry to hear your mother passed away. Where is your father?"

"Both my parents died a while ago. They were old when they adopted me." The snip of the scissors echoed in the tiny bathroom.

"They must have loved you very much. I'm sorry your parents are no longer with us." Arlan adjusted his knees as I moved the comb and scissors across his face, allowing my legs to navigate his as he sat on the low stool.

"Me, too. Yeah, they loved me." My voice had softened. "But they just didn't get me." I sighed heavily. "I suppose all teenagers feel like that about their parents. Don't they?"

Arlan didn't answer. I flicked my gaze from my work on his beard to his eyes. He stared straight ahead, his focus at middle distance, with a crinkle to his brow. I finished trimming his beard and turned to the sink to clean the comb and scissors. Arlan stood up behind me, placing his large hands on my shoulders.

"Rhiannon." His warm breath caressed my ear. "What do you see in your looking-glass?"

I stood straighter to peer in the mirror, leaning back against his warmth.

Distracting.

Arlan was intense, like he had a point to make. Heat rose to my cheeks at his inspection. I had to get this conversation off *me*.

"I see you! A warrior."

He continued looking in the mirror at me, his hands growing hot on my shoulders.

"And in front of him?" He remained patient. Unrelenting.

That didn't work.

I pressed my lips tight. Sensations tugged at my focus—the heat of his hands on my shoulders, his voice in my ear, his attention on me. I couldn't speak.

"*I* see a tall woman with a passion for the history of a people known as the Celts." Arlan's stare, reflected in the mirror, remained on me. "Who also has enthusiasm, but not the skill, for the Gaelic language." He mimicked a pained expression.

"It's bad, isn't it? Sorry." My chest vibrated with a giggle and my cheeks heated.

His warm laughter spilled over me, joining with mine.

"Aye, but you'll pick it up, Rhiannon." His hands gently shook my shoulders, and he smiled. "What do you know of your origins, Rhiannon?"

"Nothing. I was an abandoned baby." I stumbled over my words, my throat tightening around my lifelong unanswered question. *Why did my biological mother not want me?* "My parents found me in a wood. They had to get a solicitor involved, but they won adoption rights." My voice came out like a croak, so I coughed to clear it. "But you mean where were my true parents from, don't you?"

Arlan had dropped his gaze, all laughter gone. "I am sorry ye were left, Rhiannon, as a babe... I sense that you have felt you never fitted in." He lifted his head, locking his gaze with mine in the mirror again, his expression serious. "You state your parents didn't understand you and I have witnessed ye are shy and self-conscious at times." Arlan pointed at me in the mirror. "But *I* see a beauty who, like the Celts from this world's past, has the love of art, nature, and knowledge that is a trait of these people." He spoke with a husky voice. "One who is intelligent, and has the curiosity and creativity, the bravery and tenacity common to people of those origins." He nodded and smiled. "Aye, I have read while ye were working."

My reflection scowled back at me as Arlan continued his steady gaze.

"You said you're not Celtic, only like them."

"Aye, their designs are the closest I can say." He scrunched his lip then his expression cleared, and he set his mouth, like he'd decided on something. "Come with me, Rhiannon." He took my hand and led me toward my bedroom.

At the doorway, I pulled my hand from his and stopped in my tracks, grabbing the hard door jamb. Arlan didn't waver but strode into my room and stood at the foot of my bed. I held my breath. He stood in *my* room, right next to *my* trunk, like it was familiar to him.

"I have something to confess." His dark brows dipped.

I stayed by the door, numbness preventing further steps, but indicated for him to continue.

"Today, when ye worked, I looked through your room." His mouth twisted to one side and his broad shoulders hunched in a slight cringe. "I desired to know more of you, Rhiannon." He raised his hand, palm outward, as though he expected a verbal outrage from me.

I bit my tongue and rubbed my arm, my breathing speeding up.

"I apologise for this, Rhiannon. I recognise this is what you would call 'an invasion of privacy', but I needed to discover who you are." He stood tall and his teeth played with his lips as his eyes searched mine. "Your features are familiar to me. You look like a woman from my world."

What?

"In this trunk at the foot of your bed, I found this." The lid creaked open.

I gasped. He'd seen my private things, the sentimental objects from my life, and raked through them without my consent. My stomach lurched. Arlan brought out a pure wool rug of a rich maroon colour in a tartan pattern.

"That's my baby rug." My voice held an edge and I stepped forward a pace. "I know that's weird." I gave a sharp shrug. "Most baby rugs have cute bunnies or stuff like that on them. But it's all I have from *my* babyhood."

Arlan took his gaze from me and carefully unfolded the rug, revealing a crest. "I know this tartan, and this crest is dear to my heart."

"Why?" *An eagle in flight superimposed over a castle on an island*—an emblem indelibly printed in my memory.

The hairs on the back of my neck stood on end.

This is getting weird.

"It's the clan crest of my mother's family. This is their tartan. The noble house of Gallawain." Arlan's stare bore into me from the end of my bed. "How did your parents come by it?" There was a hint of sharpness in his tone.

I closed the space between us and grabbed my baby rug from his hands, then pressed it to myself, clutching it to connect the entire front of my body with its aged-softened material. The pure wool fibres accepted my body heat and warmed against my skin.

"I don't know." How dare he ruin my childhood memories! How dare he rummage through my past and accuse my parents!

Of what?

I held the intricately woven tartan to my face and sniffed deeply, inhaling a perfume blend of wool wash, Mum's lilac perfume and the distinct fragrance of *baby*. Mum's face was so clear in my mind's eye I could almost reach up and stroke it.

Tears spilled, despite my efforts to hold them back. Arlan's warm arms surrounded me, enfolding me in an embrace.

"Rhiannon." He spoke gently. "I don't wish to upset you. I only seek answers."

"Well, I don't have any!" I sniffed and wiped my face with the back of my hand. "What's your theory? You seem to have one."

Arlan didn't speak for some moments, and I relished the rise and fall of my head against him with each one of his breaths.

"There's a portal between our worlds. Maybe more than one. You tell me I have come to and fro. Although, I haven't yet found a way back."

Because you are not trying hard enough, Arlan Finnbar MacEnoicht.

"I'm fast concluding this is true and that you may have made that journey as a babe. I believe you are a daughter of Dál Gaedhle."

I pulled away from him. "How?"

"You have my mother's clan crest and tartan in your possession. How else would you have such a *baby rug*, as you name it?"

I raked my fingers through my hair, clutching the rug to myself with my other hand.

"If it were true—and I'm still not sure how I came to be here—it would mean we're related. You could be my brother!" I gulped.

That would make my feelings for you very *unhealthy.*

"No, not my sister. A distant kinswoman." His lips curved.

"My having this rug doesn't actually prove what you're claiming."

"What if it could, Rhiannon?"

"But even if it could, it doesn't answer how I got here," I said with a shrug, then I took a deep breath. I had so much to consider. "But it sure explains a lot. Why I've never belonged. Why I'm nothing like my parents. Why my whole focus seems to be in an entirely different place than everyone else's."

Arlan nodded throughout all I said.

"But what if you're wrong?" My shoulders slumped. "What if I *am* odd and this seems a reasonable fantasy to hold on to? Then I'm just sad."

"Och, Rhiannon." His expression turned earnest. "If by sad, ye mean pitiful? You are never that." He pressed his lips tight as if to stop himself from saying more.

The wind blew outside as the sleet-filled night continued, and Arlan remained quiet.

I put my baby rug to my nose and inhaled the perfume of my childhood once more. A million memories flew at me, pounding me for individual recollection, like each drop of frozen rain pelting on the window outside. Followed by a million questions.

"So, if I'm from the same place as you, we'd better find the way home, hey?"

Twenty-Four

— · —

It was discovered to be so—only those mage masters adept in the control of the wilful beast, such as the felid, the wild boar, or the stag, were successful in the mastery of the larger animal known as the dragon.

DRAGON SCROLLS
INNESSFARNE
DATE OF TEXT UNKNOWN

World of Dál Cruinne
Post Dragon Wars Year 6083
Eastern Clanlands of Dál Gallain
Drostan's Workroom, Lord Ciarán's Tower

"Water," Bram said.

Ahh, yes. Drostan grunted softly to himself. It fitted perfectly. The young man's long cascading hair, graceful gait, and the ease at which he had flowed into the rhythm of life at this caisteal and assimilated alongside himself as master, all pointed to the yielding nature of his power conduit.

"That is grand, for we shall use the divination bowl fashioned from solid stone filled with your *source*," Drostan said.

"We shall search together, my master?"

"Aye, for we have much to accomplish. As you have observed, our lord is exacting in his demands. Portals *and* dragons."

Drostan sent a *staying* to the bolt on the door and ordered Bram to do the same. They would have no intrusions.

"Come closer and place your hands in your source." Drostan moved to the far side of the large divination bowl and settled his hands on the polished rim, soothed by the smooth coolness under his palms.

Bram stepped up to the bowl, stood opposite Drostan, and immersed his fingers in the clear water of the dish.

"In the Central Meadhan Mountain Range, you say?"

"Aye, my master. Just east of the main group of elevations, or so it is recorded. In the dense forest that skirts the grand mountain range resting in the heart of our land."

"And they have seen it?" Drostan shook his head slightly, still unable to restrain his disbelief. Dragons were animals of legend—not of actuality—having died out millennia ago. Incredulous to him that the master mages of the learned isle had seen them in their visions and travels across the landmass of Dál Cruinne.

He recalled from his recent reading of the ancient writings that to control a dragon was a difficult thing. They had an inherent self-protection, which mages of the past had found challenging to break through. The writings maintained only a master mage-sorcerer could gain success in wresting control of these beasts. And dragons, being such powerful beasts, had crushed the minds of the weakest of even the most skilled mages. This ushered in the time of recognition for mages who successfully commanded dragons. An opinion popular with the clan chiefs of that age.

The age that led to the chaos of the Dragon Wars of so long ago. He released his breath through his teeth.

"Shall I meet you there?"

"Nae, Bram. Travel with me."

Drostan focused on the stone under his fingertips. It tingled, joining the hum emanating from the sandstone walls of the round tower. His soul reached out and caught the power, then left his body. He met Bram's soul there, in that unseen space—the place in between.

They both dropped into the vision in the bowl.

They soared together over the land and traced the great river to its origin in the mountains that sat in the centre of the landmass. Snow blanketed high summits as grey crags stabbed through ice, and not a creature stirred. He willed to Bram, sending his intentions, and they travelled over rocky snow-dusted peaks and descended to the snow line where wind-blown heather and flattened grass spread for leagues below it, and patchy forest grew on the lower reaches.

Here and there, enormous boulders, the size of a keep, protruded through the forest like natural brochs. A clump of three close together broke into Drostan's view, and Bram indicated he had seen it also.

They dived.

Three tall, wide boulders jutted out from a triangular base. Drostan soared closer. At the base of these enormous tower-like boulders, stone masoned walls joined each one, forming a fortification with a gateway. The wooden gate, rotted and hanging ajar on rusted hinges, led to an empty bailey yard, adding to the evidence of abandonment of many years. Now uninhabited by people, but with a life force present.

A sizeable life force.

Drostan hovered with Bram beside him. A cave opening stood in the largest broch-sized boulder to their left and inside was solid dark. The cave emitted a grating noise, like that of hauling logs over gravel, plus an undeniable sense of a living being.

Agreement came from Bram's soul and they both slid into the black.

An animal stirred, now leaving the cave. Drostan clung to the rock walls while the great scaly creature passed by. Shiny scales reflected the light from the cave entrance—an armoured hide with skin covered wings tucking into the animal's side. Drostan slid his gaze up from the beast where Bram danced around it, as if fearless, his spirit's eyes large as he watched the magnificent reptile trudge with an arched neck out of the cave.

In the courtyard, it stood on hind limbs and opened its wings wide, flapping and stretching like a cormorant on a pier pole, turning its head about, searching.

For them.

Drostan held back and hovered by the cave mouth. The dragon was no pet. Not domesticated, though the ancient texts had stated it was possible to tame some sub-species of dragon, but this one, so long away from human contact, emanated a natural wildness.

His recent research revealed there were many breeds. The smallest being the size of a large snake. The largest grew to be massive, and black in colour, possessing fangs which sprayed a caustic substance, melting the flesh off the bones of the victim on contact. Other texts spoke of fire flowing forth from the mouths of these larger animals.

He had scoffed at the notion but now facing a live dragon, a cold settled in his guts, alerting him to the fact that his body by the divination bowl in his chambers was reacting to his spirit's response, and innate instincts for self-preservation were now taking effect. This beast now alert to them, tested its environment with twitching ears, flicking tongue, and vertically-slitted pupils.

In the daylight of the ancient bailey yard, the scales of this reptile shone a deep blue and sat flat against its hide except for the ridge along its spine. Its feet had claws, and so did the wingtips. The dragon lumbered to the stone cut wall, as tall as the average bailey wall, stretched to its own full height and looked over the top with ease. The animal was roughly twenty-four cubits and not black, so not the smallest of these creatures.

Drostan sought Bram, for he had not sensed the lad as he examined the dragon. He searched the courtyard, then sent his inner vision back into the cave.

No Bram.

Grunts and whines echoed off the wall of the abandoned fortress. Drostan returned his sight to the beast. Bram floated around the animal, lingering near its back, and drifting to its immense head. The dragon twisted, its large snout and broad nostrils whipping by Bram who floated closer and, resting his spirit on the back of the beast at the base of its skull, stretched his arms and hugged tight.

Bram! Take care!

The animal bucked like a steed unbroken, twisting and cavorting, stomping around the inner bailey, snapping its lengthy tail, flapping wings, and shaking its head, as if a physical animal fastened to it.

Release your hold! Drostan threw the command.

Bram released his grip and rose above the animal. It turned and sought him, as if seeing his spirit. Bram ascended, chased by open jaws and pursued by saws of teeth.

Flee! Drostan sent a spirit voice of compelling.

Bram accelerated his ascent. Jaws snapped the air at his spirit's feet. The animal spread its wings and ran a pace, preparing for flight. Its cumbersome form on the ground, now lifted by powerful wings, rose majestic in pursuit of Bram's spirit.

With me! Now!

Slithering through the air, Bram diverged and flew to Drostan, the dragon at his heels.

Drostan grabbed Bram and held tight. He drew power from the stone dish to which his physical body clung, dragged his source from the caisteal stonewalls, and sought the energy in the massive natural broch mountains where their spirits floated.

He sped away, the dragon's roar diminishing the further they fled.

Drostan looked back. The animal had not pursued—no doubt due to the sense of their presence leaving—and had settled back to its lair.

They soared overland back to the tower and exited the divination bowl. Drostan clung with his soul to his energy—but he must release it. His apprentice required a reprimand.

He returned to his body, and with the cool smooth stone beneath his fingertips once more, he opened his eyes. Bram stood opposite; his hands still immersed in his source.

"What were you doing?" Drostan growled as he leaned into his acolyte.

"My master, I sought an entry to the beast."

"Pardon?" Tension's strong fingers gripped Drostan's shoulders, adding an edge to his tone.

Deep brown eyes bore into Drostan. "Why did we seek such an animal? Either to use, or to not. But if to seek for control was your wish, why, when found, would we not seek use of the creature? For our art has a stream whereby we master great beasts and bend their wills to ours, does it not, my master?" Bram bowed his head. "Pardon if I speak above my station."

With the lad's intense stare now off him, Drostan exhaled through pursed lips. There was logic in Bram's comments.

His apprentice was correct.

His own disbelief had not prepared him for encountering a dragon and the superb animal had absorbed his attention, occupied his being with awe, the importance and purpose of such a find flying from him. He shook his head.

Even so, the lad acted without care, causing danger to us both.

"You were reckless," he snapped. "We would have planned how to tackle this beast on a further occasion. We are still yet unpractised in even smaller beasts."

"We were *there*, my master." A hint of defiance edged his voice.

"You could have been lost!" He leaned so close now, Bram's hair blew back with his speech. "Too impulsive! If one's spirit dies, all is gone." He eased back from the young mage. "Once you have ascended to the next level of your training, when you have performed Urrainn and met your *spirit* power... then you—*we* shall endeavour further to manage such an animal."

"Forgive me, my master Drostan." Bram held the floor with his gaze. Then his brows relaxed, and a curve touched the corners of his mouth. "But I have found the way in."

Twenty-Five

—·—

A chieftain's life is not his own,
It is forfeit to his people.
All wishes and desires set aside for the nobler cause:
The welfare of his clan.

WISDOM WRITINGS ON KINGSHIP
SAGE GLIOCAS
(2870-2962 POST DRAGON WARS)

Our World, 2016
Abernethy, Scotland

Dim light filtered through my windows. I sat at the kitchen table, hitting the keys of my laptop and blinking grittiness from my eyes. Sleep hadn't come, and all night my mind had flown with the possible ways of travelling to other worlds.

If Dál Gaedhle was my home—my true home—I'd be going.

There's nothing for me in this world. It's never made me feel welcome.

"What are you doing?" Arlan spoke over my shoulder.

A map of Britain's Ley lines filled my laptop's screen.

"Do you have anything like a time machine, or similar contraption, in Dál Gaedhle?" I turned to Arlan, whose brows met in the middle. "Thought not. Portals it is then. Good old Google."

"Who is he? Where have the pictures come from?" Arlan's questions came in rapid fire, and he reached over my shoulder to touch the keys. "Now the picture has disappeared. Where did it go?" I swatted away his hand. "What is this appliance?"

"I usually do it on my phone. I forgot you've not seen a computer. It's how we find out things. Like a library, but bigger."

130

"This looks very much smaller than the library of our sages. Most libraries, in fact. Especially the one they say is contained in the Broch of the Ancients. Where does it hold so many words and pictures?"

"I'll let George explain that one." I continued typing my next question into Google. A few seconds later, I had the pertinent page on the screen. "It suggests standing stone circles, tors, cairns, burial mounds, and natural phenomena such as Ley lines and Uluru are associated with folklore and myths regarding portals to other worlds. So, we could try those. But not Uluru. That's in Australia. Too far away, sorry." I swivelled in the chair and grinned up at Arlan.

He frowned. "Why are ye doing this?"

"To get you home."

Arlan's mouth thinned, and his eyes narrowed.

I stood, and that place between my shoulders was as tight as his now clenching fists. "Arlan, you must return and take me with you."

"What!" He stepped back. "No, lass. It will be too dangerous for ye."

"We need to go *home*. You said it's my home, too."

"Aye, but there are things in this world that are not in mine. I have noted them as I have watched the Tee Vee. Things ye may not have considered. For example, although we have wise healer sages, we have nae such things as the potions that kill the wee beasties." His eyes widened. "Have ye thought o' that?"

"Wee *beasties?*"

"The ones that poison the blood. Ye give a *medicine* for that, aye?"

I blinked. "Oh. Antibiotics?"

"Aye, nor the sleep potion that enables your healers to cut a person without them flinching."

"A general anaesthetic? Arlan I... I don't care. I want to go home. I'll take those risks."

"Well, *I* am not ready to return." Arlan straightened his shoulders. "And naught worked when I tried yesterday."

"Arlan. You go. This is a fact." I held my voice firm, but my mind spun in confusion. "Why don't you want to return? What's so bad?" Apart from no anaesthetics, antibiotics... and probably no contraceptive pill. I forced down a cringe.

"Nothing is bad. It's a beautiful place." He stood tall. "Much like your pictures of the Scottish Highlands on the Tee Vee."

"Why not, then?"

"Because I'm a clan warrior-prince and will be clan war chief one day, whether I wish to be or no'." He spoke rapidly, his face hard.

"Warrior-prince... War chief..." *Oh, that makes so much sense.*

His bearing. How he handled that sword. How he'd startled me with his air of command at times. The mounted warrior that burst into my life.

"Wait a minute. You don't want to be a warrior-prince? You *are*. Everything about you is *warrior*."

"But I have nae choice."

"That's it?" My eyes strained with their gaping. "Because they're *making* you? Forcing you to be who you are?" I put a hand on my hip. "You're having a hissy-fit 'cos you have no choice about it? Arlan, I can't believe you." My neck hurt from shaking my head. "That's *so* selfish."

Arlan's jaw muscle bunched, and his eyes narrowed, but he didn't say a word.

"You know our queen's sons—"

"Aye, ye have told me about your queen's sons!" His loud voice filled the room. "I give not a care what the children of the queen of *this* world do. *I* will not be forced." Arlan's nostrils flared.

"Arlan, I really don't understand. You're a natural leader, and from what I saw of you with that sword the other day, you must be an awesome fighter. You'd be a brilliant war chief."

"Och, ye sound like Bàn!" He flung his hands in the air.

"Who's Bàn?"

"My sword-brother."

"Your *sword-brother*? Wow!" I breathed out the words. "That sounds so cool."

"Och, I ken *cool* can mean the weather or something impressive in this world, but the role of a warrior is a serious matter, Rhiannon. I am skilled at killing people. I train and lead other warriors to do the same. Does that no' scare you?"

"No."

"Well"—he thrust his face into mine— "it should."

"It doesn't scare me because *you* don't scare me. You're a man of honour. Yes, you can fight, but you don't go around murdering people. Please take me with you when you go back. I want to go home."

"No, lass." Arlan spoke deep and low, and he leaned in close again. "When I return—if I return—I will enter a skirmish where bandits are raping women and slaughtering warriors. I'll no' put you in the midst o' that." He stood back a pace, his eyes flicking around the room, focused internally.

Thinking of what he'd left, no doubt.

"That must've been scary. No, you wouldn't be scared. You're brave. You... you were fighting the people who were... hurting the women?"

"Aye, my warriors and I were freeing women and girls from bandits. Evil men." He narrowed his gaze. "We have bad people in our world, too. And I thought I saw..." His shoulders slowly lowered. "We'd lost Erin."

"A warrior woman?"

"Aye." His voice softened as he looked at nothing, but his nostrils flared.

"I'm sorry," I said. "That must be hard."

"Aye." He blinked. "Bàn was fond of her."

I shoved my hands in my pockets. "Did you... free the women?"

Arlan tilted his head. "I'm unsure. For I left"—he lifted a shoulder— "in the midst of it all. And there I will return."

"They'll need you," I said.

His gaze darted to mine.

I held firm. "Or does you now claiming to be a pacifist negate any warrior status you once had?"

He started at my comment, then his look quickly turned to a glower. "We require more wood for the fire." He turned away from me. "I shall cut some."

TWENTY-SIX

—.—

My love holds my heart
Though I dare not hold hers.
A love as strong as death can kill.
Shame cover the man to cause such a wrong:
To hold a love in his heart yet have not the right to fulfil it.

POETRY OF THE WARRIOR
WARRIOR SAGE TAPAÌDH
(4009-4059 POST DRAGON WARS)

Abernethy, Scotland

The percussive thud of the axe on wood rang in Arlan's ears.

Thwack. No one would compel him into any role.

Thwack. None would rush him to return.

Thwack. The more he lived beside Rhiannon, the harder to leave her.

Thwack. Powerless to suppress his feelings for her.

Thwack. The most beautiful woman, in every way.

Thwack. Impossible that she could ever be the love of my heart.

Slam. The chunk of wood split and crashed into the growing pile.

He shouldn't have kissed her. He gritted his teeth.

It must not happen again.

He picked up the freshly cut wood for Rhiannon's fire and stacked the pieces neatly to one side, a warmth growing in his heart as he returned his grasp to the axe handle.

Och, she was not afraid to challenge him. Speak her mind. Point out his faults... his inconsistencies. His claim to be a warrior and yet a pacifist.

She had not mocked, and her raised eyebrow and piercing stare were embedded in his mind.

Aye, she would keep him in check. Make him question his own thoughts.

Didn't that mean Rhiannon was good for him?

The neighbour's backdoor opened, and he ambled out, wearing a dressing gown and, as in his usual manner, presented himself unkempt and unshaven.

"Do ya ken what time it is? It's Saturday mornin' and the sun is nae even up yet!" He moved along his path, his voice husky with sleep. "There're laws against making a noise early in tha morn'."

Arlan thunked the axe into the woodblock, squared his shoulders, and strode toward the fence. The neighbour took three steps backward. Arlan stood by the fence, clenching his jaw, and holding himself back from this irritating person.

"Aye. And there are sure to be laws in this world against a husband hurtin' his own wife and his child." Arlan spoke in a low growl, for the ears of this *droch dhuine* only.

"What're you accusing me of?" The neighbour bristled.

"Ye shud be disgusted with yoursel'. Ye are the man. Ye are the one who should protect them from harm, not abuse them."

The scruffy man thrust his chin forward and his voice went as low as Arlan's. "Have you ever seen me abuse them?"

"I have heard ye—"

"Sorry, Mr Beasley." Rhiannon stepped beside Arlan and shrugged an apology. "The house is cold, and I asked Arlan to stoke the fire for me, but we didn't have any wood."

Arlan stepped back, turning at her voice having not sensed her approach—*I'm slipping and getting soft in this world.*

The neighbour grunted and returned to his door but half in, he faced them. "You're dangerous. I've seen yoo with that sword." He stabbed a finger at Arlan. "There are laws against that too, ye ken?" He scuttled in and slammed his door behind him.

Arlan drifted his gaze past Rhiannon and gathered the chocks of wood. Rhiannon stood with her arms crossed as she remained by the fence.

"Let's have some breakfast." Her voice wavered. "I'll cook you what they call an English Breakfast, but we also eat it here in Scotland."

Perhaps she'd heard his accusations to the poor example of manhood in the next dwelling. She would have gathered his intent, but she uttered not a comment as they walked inside together. Rhiannon placed a cast iron pan on her stove, then got long strips of bacon, eggs, mushrooms, tomatoes and sausage from the fridge. The bacon sizzled and popped, filling the kitchen with a smoky, salty aroma.

A car pulled up outside the neighbour's house, and Arlan glanced out the kitchen window. Rhiannon stepped next to him and looked out. The car had a row of lights on its roof, like ones that flashed, but these sat dull and unlit. A man and a woman in a black uniform got out of the car and walked to the neighbour's front door.

"What are the police doing at that horrible man's house?" Rhiannon stepped back to her stove and turned the bacon. "Maybe someone has complained about him yelling at his wife." Rhiannon snorted a laugh.

A sharp blade of alarm sliced through Arlan's insides. "Ah, lass... I may have said some things to upset your neighbour."

Rhiannon spun from the stove, her eyes round. "He wouldn't call the police for that, surely?"

Two figures caught the corner of Arlan's vision. The police officers now entered Rhiannon's path and came toward her door.

Rhiannon gasped. "Quick! Hide."

"Hide?"

"Yes, they mustn't see you. You have no ID." Rhiannon pushed against him, directing him into the living room.

Arlan planted his feet. "I'll no' run and hide," he said against Rhiannon's failed attempts to budge him.

"Argh!" Rhiannon scowled at him.

Those in uniform knocked, and Rhiannon's shoving ceased abruptly.

"Answer it, Rhiannon."

"Don't say a word." She pointed her index finger in his face. "I'll do the talking, okay?" He nodded.

She crept to the door, squared her shoulders, then opened it.

"Good morning. I'm Sergeant Findlay and this is Officer Ross, and we are from Scotland Police." The tall, thick-set man of middle-age indicated to the younger woman beside him, his tone official but friendly.

"What can I do for you, officers?" Rhiannon's shoulders remained tense, but her voice was forced-calm.

"Your neighbour has complained about the man who lives here," Sergeant Findlay said.

"That is I, sir." Arlan stepped forward, ignoring the sharp glare Rhiannon sent his way. "What is his accusation?"

"He states you have a weapon. A sword, I believe," Sergeant Findlay said. "Now there are no laws against possessing such a weapon, but I'd like to see it, please."

"Aye, sir. One moment." Arlan glanced at Rhiannon who'd turned to him with a warning in her eyes, then he strode to the living room where he'd placed his weapons by the couch since sharpening them earlier.

"So, there's no law against having a sword?" Rhiannon spoke a touch too loud.

"No, madam, if it's in a collection, or used in martial art classes, or for a re-enactment." Findlay spoke matter-of-factly, his voice drifting into the living room. "Medieval days and the like. You must transport them safely, though. Sheathed and in a locked container."

"We attend Celtic re-enactment days," Rhiannon said as Arlan handed Findlay his weapon.

Well, she did not lie.

"Nice sword." Findlay examined it, focusing on the handle's decorations, then returned it to Arlan. "Your neighbour is a little heated about it. Just keep it out of his view. I'm only here to inform you he's complained and perhaps be a wee bit more discrete with it. Aye?"

"Aye." Arlan's heart warmed to the officer.

"He yells at his wife," Rhiannon blurted.

Findlay's eyes darted to hers. "We're aware, but we need more than that. Let us know, aye?" He gave a brief nod.

Findlay and the other officer said farewell, and Arlan stood by the open door, following their return to the car.

Rhiannon released a lengthy sigh. "We need a day off. Let's go out after breakfast."

"No' to a shopping centre, if you dinnae mind."

That brought a genuine smile to her eyes. *So beautiful. And so oblivious to it.*

"I need to do some things in Edinburgh. You should see Edinburgh Castle. We could make a day of it and go to a pub for dinner."

"A caisteal and a tavern. Did ye choose those especially for me?" He chuckled. "It sounds grand, Rhiannon. How should I dress?"

Arlan sat in the passenger seat beside Rhiannon. The jeans he wore rubbed coarse against his legs, but the leather jacket, which Rhiannon had obtained for him from her phone with some kind of *net*, felt soft beneath his fingers just like his leather breeches. Rhiannon drove her car on the wide road she named a *motorway* much faster than any horse could gallop. Enormous, loud wagons rolled beside them. He resisted grasping the dashboard.

Never show your fear.

Rhiannon found a car park on the high side of the city, on the hill opposite the caisteal. They walked through the city's streets, where many people stepped beside, behind, and past them. Arlan kept alert in all directions, but Rhiannon marched through without a care.

"Ye are used to this? So many people?"

"Aye, yes, I haven't been to Edinburgh for a while, but I used to work here." A slight frown tinged her brow.

"Do you miss it?"

"Ah..." She blinked, seeming to collect her thoughts. "No, I don't miss the city. I... I loved my job in the university library. Cost cutting, you know?"

He screwed up his mouth, her phrase making little sense to him.

"Not enough money to pay me." She shrugged.

"Ye charged them too much?" A passer-by bumped into his arm and kept walking without apology.

They crossed the road obeying the coloured lights and a pedestrian knocked Rhiannon without acknowledging.

"Where are people's manners?" *Do physical hurts mean naught in this world?*

"We can cut through Princes Street Gardens to get to the castle," she said. "That way won't be so busy."

Rhiannon led him through the public gardens then along the street and up a steep flight of stone steps to the esplanade leading to the moat and drawbridge. Music floated toward him, stirring his soul. The skirling notes and the haunting, airy quality of the music of the pipes brought to him visions of grey peaked mountains, barren and wild, and gentle, rolling green hills split with the rush of a brisk burn spraying over the rocks as its water fell. The piper's tune changed, and in Arlan's mind's eye a row of clansmen warriors beat their swords against their shields, facing a dark enemy army. They raised their swords and spears, their roar echoing across a moor. It was Dál Gaedhle—his land. Ache churned in the centre of his being where a knot formed, the one that tied him to *home*.

He drew closer. A lone piper stood and played these melodies while people threw money into a hat set on the ground at his feet. Was this man's lot so poor he would beg? Did they not need him in their battles?

This caisteal was unusual, for Rhiannon paid to enter. Their warriors wore kilts, as he would have for ceremony. He moved through the gateway and Rhiannon looked up, cringing at the spikes of the portcullis, then surveyed the ground.

"I've never really understood why they arrange the cobblestones like this." She pointed to a narrow section of close-packed stones in the centre of the winding cobblestones that lay in a horizontal pattern snaking their way up the hill of the inner bailey leading to the other sections of this fortress.

"Och, you know nothing of horses, do ye, lass?"

"Horses?" Rhiannon glanced at the stones again.

"With the stone arranged thus, they can grip with their hooves and get up this hill." He flicked an eyebrow as comprehension dawned in her expression.

Other visitors ambled past: women with children, and a crowd of students with their teacher, her Scottish lilt so much like his own version of English, all gazing up at the walls of the inner bailey and the buildings within. Groups of young people chatted as they tramped past in plastic coats holding umbrellas above their heads against the autumnal rains. Their voices rang in different tongues, none known to him, but yet with a familiarity.

"Who are they?" He nudged Rhiannon's attention to the group nearby.

"Foreign students from Europe. A lot of them come here to learn English. They're French." She indicated to the group walking past on their way out, having finished their tour of the impressive fortress. "That group over there are Italian, and I have heard some German too."

"They all come to your grand city to learn English. What about the Gaelic?"

"You have to go to the Highlands and Isles for that."

A soldier marched past, looking directly at Arlan, the recognition of a fellow warrior in his eyes. Arlan returned a nod of respect.

"Please don't, Arlan. I can't afford for you to attract attention. Hmm. Maybe not the wisest of ideas to bring you here. You look military enough as it is without getting friendly." She glanced up to him and focused on his head. "Apart from your hair. What would you say if they asked where you served?'

138

"In the Highlands and the Isles," he answered.

Rhiannon slapped his belly, leaving a sting, and a half-smile flicked out the corner of her mouth.

The cobbled path followed the wall leading them up to a platform where solid black tube-like structures sat on four wheels, all made of metal, pointing outward over the castle walls. Arlan came to a stop; unable to move—there was warlike intention to these objects. A woman walking behind knocked into him and tutted as she brushed past.

"They are weapons." His vision remained locked on the sleek black tubes as Rhiannon backtracked to him.

"Yes. They're cannon. You don't have them in Dál Gaedhle?"

He struggled to release his gaze from the *cannon* as Rhiannon's warm hand tapped his arm. "Arlan?"

"How do they work?" His heart skipped a beat. "You must show me."

"I can't. They've sealed them up and they're not usable. And... I think people will get suspicious if you keep asking as intensely as you are, so please just chill a bit, Arlan." She widened her eyes at him.

He hastened to the nearest one and ran his hands over its black smoothness. The end pointed past the outer wall overlooking the park and the city below. The tube of metal was solid and heavy.

"What do you mean, *sealed*? What would take place if they were *open*?" His hand lay affectionately on the dark tube as he spoke to Rhiannon, who stood at the end.

"They put the cannonball in the open end and fire it out." She pointed behind him to where the tube aimed out of the wall.

"Fire it? What flame do they use? And... a ball?"

"Ah, not fire. Gunpowder. The cannonballs are made of lead."

"Lead... Gunpowder." His mind flew through the many possibilities, then skidded to a halt.

A pacifist would not be so intent upon a weapon.

He shook himself, then grabbed Rhiannon's hand. "Come, show me the rest of this magnificent fortress which your ancestors built to show their power and protect their people."

Rhiannon led the way and took him to a building-lined square.

"There are the Royal Apartments." She pointed to the building facing them. "But nobody lives here."

"Where does your queen live?" He squinted, partly from the sun now peeking through the watery sky, and partly from confusion as to this world's royalty.

"The queen has a few palaces, but her official residence is Buckingham Palace in London, which is in England. Scotland doesn't have its own monarch exclusively anymore. Just read the history." She placed her palm on his chest. It was small and warm where she touched him. "Way too much to go through to explain *that* one." She turned him around. "You must see the Scottish crown jewels. They're not the fake replicas for the tourists like at the Tower of London, but the real thing. From when we had a monarchy of our own."

Rhiannon took him through a small doorway with thickened doors and two grim-looking guards. A sceptre, a sword and a bejewelled hat lay in a display case of thick, clear glazing in the centre of the room.

"The hat is the crown?" He pointed past the ceremonial sword—too ornate to be a proper weapon—to the pearl-encrusted gold headpiece.

"You don't know what a crown looks like?" Her brows knit.

"My father, the àrd rìgh, wears a torc of silver around his neck." His voice rang in the small chamber, deep and clear.

The guards glared at him. Rhiannon grabbed his hand and dragged him out.

The caisteal's Great Hall sat next to this building. At the far end of this great hall, the keepers of this caisteal had set a red rope across the width of the room in front of four outfits of shiny silver-coloured metal. This must be a body protection of some kind. As well as breast plates, this metal covered arms and legs. The tough metal gleamed where the light from the high windows fell upon it. On one display, a strange-looking garment sat beneath the shiny plates.

"Of what is the grey tunic made?"

Rhiannon squinted, repeating his words to herself. "Oh, you mean the chain maille?"

He raised his brows. "It is knitted metal?"

"It's small rings of metal made into a suit. Stops swords from getting through."

"Ahh, this should be a simple task for our metal craftsmen."

Against a side wall, mounted on a stand in front of an array of swords and daggers, rested a long double-edged broadsword, the handle bound with leather and the edges dull.

"Are all weapons in this world blunt?" Arlan huffed, then moved back to the entry. He spent some time examining the pieces of armour just inside the Great Hall where the rope cordoning them off stood closer to the suits of armour on display.

"Please, don't touch," ordered a woman in uniform standing nearby.

Arlan's index finger remained poised, about to connect with the shiny metal. The woman's badge read, *security guard.*

"Your pardon, madam, but of what is it made?"

"Steel, sir."

"Such as my sword is fashioned?" He cocked his head. "But it would be so heavy—"

Rhiannon nudged him in the ribs.

"We dress up," she said to the security guard. "It's a fake." She pulled his arm and he let her drag him away from the guard's stern expression.

"Don't. Just don't." Rhiannon shook her head at him and directed him from the hall.

They walked out of this courtyard and on to another battlement. Arlan stood before a massive cannon, greatly larger than the black sleek beauties on the circular battery below. He gasped and his legs wouldn't move.

"You'd better close your mouth. You're drooling, battle chief," Rhiannon whispered, standing close.

"This one is massive. How does one move it?"

"If you read the info about Mons Meg, you'll see it was too big, and it eventually blew itself up." The warmth of her hand on his arm seeped through. "Arlan, it's no use to you without gunpowder. Do you have gunpowder in your world?" Her quiet whisper came to his ears, batting away his imagination's visions of the damage such a weapon could do.

An excessive amount of damage.

"Nae. I have not heard the sages speak of it." He shook his head.

"Stop dreaming then."

"I wasn't dreaming." He straightened as a group of people with greying hair ambled past.

"You were. Don't deny it." Rhiannon's hand went to her hip. "Pacifists do not contemplate"—she waved her other hand at the massive weapon, including the boulders that were its cannonballs sitting beside it— "weapons of mass destruction." She squinted at him.

He steadied his breathing. "Perhaps such a weapon could deter a conflict. Persuade an enemy to discussion and negotiation."

"You can't help yourself, can you?" she whispered, her words just audible. "You can't stop thinking like a warrior—*a general.*" She shook her head and led him away from the *beast* that was an instrument of war.

"My feet are killing me." Rhiannon walked by Arlan's side as they strode under the portcullis, and out across the esplanade where, on either side, workmen removed seats on massive stairs. "The Tattoo's over."

Just being with Rhiannon coursed strength through Arlan and he stood taller. A group of men entering the caisteal sent lengthy glances in her direction as they passed. She seemed not to notice but continued her explanation. "They're removing the grandstands and won't reassemble them till next year's Edinburgh Military Tattoo season."

Arlan squared his shoulders and stared down a man who'd kept his gaze on her until the man's eyes darted away. Arlan stayed close to Rhiannon while they wandered to the gardens in Princes Street. She bought coffee, and they sat on a park bench and drank, watching the squirrels cavorting in the trees.

"Aren't you homesick after walking through that castle?" Rhiannon cupped the warm paper coffee mug in both hands. "Is it anything like your home?"

"It's similar to The Keep and other caisteals of our land, but we live in ours." His mouth tugged at the corners for a moment. "Our Keep is beautiful. My mother, Lady Alana, designed the gardens and ensured they would be in flower for most of our spring and summer. They are a living memorial to her."

His soul twinged at her name spoken out loud.

"You must miss her," Rhiannon said.

A simple statement, but the twinge grew with her comment.

"Aye, I do." His words caught at the edges, and he blinked at the emotion in his voice.

"Oh, Arlan. I'm so sorry." Rhiannon sat quietly for some moments. "You've barely spoken of your family or Dál Gaedhle. Did I say it correctly?"

"Aye." He chuckled at Rhiannon's face lighting up in triumph, and his belly rocked with a laugh he couldn't contain.

"So, your dad's the àrd rìgh. And you're war chief of your clan?"

"Nae, not as yet. But I will be when my father deems me ready."

"Who will be the next àrd rìgh then?"

"Our traditions hold that the high kingship is transferred to whoever wins *Tòireadh*, the Quest, ye would name it. That is, once the serving àrd rìgh has passed away."

"Oh." Rhiannon looked down, searching the ground at her feet. "A quest. How exciting. You mean it's not automatically passed on to his son? *You* have to contest for it?" She faced him, her eyes glinting above her rosy cheeks.

"No, Kyle as eldest and heir to our clan lands, has the privilege of competing in *Tòireadh*." He grimaced at the thought of Kyle left behind in that skirmish.

And the brother of his heart, Bàn. Arlan bowed his head. He'd given them little thought these past few days, so intent on this world and the incredible woman who sat beside him.

Rhiannon's lowered head came into his view. Her face, tight about her mouth and eyes, turned up at him. "What's wrong, Arlan?"

"Nothing." He shook himself, lifted his head and cast his gaze over the crowd now gathered in the green of this parkland. An elderly gentleman stood on a raised platform and spoke to a crowd who milled around him. "Let's hear the orator. This sage may give me an important insight into this world."

"I know you're trying to change the subject, Arlan MacEnoicht." She sat taller and half smiled. "He's on his soapbox about something."

"*Soap box*?"

"Okay, let's hear him." She stood and held out her hand.

Arlan took it and threaded his fingers with hers, and they walked toward the crowd. Some of those gathered jeered at the speaker, who read from a piece of paper. His cap shook with emphasis at each point of his speech.

"Valour is contagious..." Arlan drew closer, and the man's words became clearer, but the comments of the crowd often drowned out his speech. "When a brave man makes a stand... others find their courage." The man looked up from his paper and, facing out toward his audience, set his gaze firmly on Arlan.

"As Edmund Burke is famously quoted as saying, 'All that is necessary for the triumph of evil is that good men do nothing'."

Arlan stopped mid-stride, as if a sword had torn through his chest, dead centre.

Rhiannon strode ahead a pace, their entwined fingers stretching their arms. "Arlan?" She stepped back.

The crowd cheered as the man left his platform, then they all dispersed, but the world around Arlan had stilled.

That was he—a good man doing nothing.

Nae, not doing nothing—refusing to do good.

Refusing to take his place in his world and fulfil his role—the task of leading good men to fight against evil, so it would *not* win.

He let out a deep sigh, and angled toward Rhiannon's anxious face. She'd said it already and her arrow had hit the bullseye.

I am being selfish.

And his selfishness would lead him to seeking the use of his fighting talents for his own ends without a care for his world or his people, while he played at being a pacifist.

"Arlan?" Rhiannon's expression was one big question.

"Ah..." The thudding of his heart became as great as the sudden shame that filled him. He dropped his gaze to the pavement, unable to meet her eyes. He couldn't face her. What if she knew the whole truth of the predicament of his world? She'd already shown her disapproval of his reluctance regarding the role he should play in its protection. The role his world's customs ordained him to assume.

The role he was having a *hissy-fit* over.

"Let's go to that tavern?" He clasped her hand tighter and strode out from the parklands, leaving the chatter of people and squirrels behind while the words of the wise sage of this world stabbed at his soul with every pulsation of his beating heart.

TWENTY-SEVEN

— • —

I roar a battle rage.
I cut my foes before me.
They scatter; they flee.
I wipe their gore from my blade; it stains the ground red.
I return to my hearth with my weapon sheathed.
Here, I love in tenderness.
In the security I have wrought for myself.

POETRY OF THE WARRIOR
WARRIOR SAGE TAPAÌDH
(4009-4059 POST DRAGON WARS)

Edinburgh, Scotland

Grey stone walls glowed soft amber in the streetlights. Distant traffic noise funnelled down the narrow lanes, sending their indistinct murmur into Arlan's ears as he walked beside Rhiannon out of the tavern and down the Edinburgh city street. The meal had been a feast of tastes with a robust ale, and sufficient distraction to ward off the discomfort he'd experienced in the park earlier. The voices of noisy restaurant patrons, the aroma of roasted meats with rich gravies, and the fruitiness of good ale alternated with the cool night air as they passed each establishment along their way to where Rhiannon had parked her car.

He reached out to Rhiannon, and she placed her small hand in his. She trembled. A flame ignited in Arlan's centre, reflecting the amber-warmth of the streetlight's glow.

"It's great to walk the street at night and be safe." She looked up to him, her russet curls cascading down her back, like a burn's waterfall after a snowmelt... Arlan swallowed hard.

"You don't always feel safe?"

"I'm learning to defend myself, but I wish I didn't have to. I know it was pure luck that I fought off that guy with the knife. You could teach me heaps. I only just started weapon lessons in self-defence classes, and I'd love to use my sword."

He didn't answer, letting her enthusiasm hang in the air between them.

Aye, her world was not a safe place. If only he could stay here, he would protect her. But he wouldn't be around, for his guilt-ridden soul could stand it no longer, despite his attempt to ignore it. The words of the wise sage of this world had touched his inner-self and spoken directly to his conscience.

He would find a way to return to his own world... *and then I will leave her.*

Shouts from many agitated voices floated their way, and Arlan turned in that direction.

"Oh, that's right. There's going to be a demonstration about the Refugee Act, or something." Rhiannon did her half smile. "It may be in the square where I parked. That was silly of me."

"A demonstration?" Arlan raised his eyebrows and tilted his head to the left. "About refugees. Why then are they yelling?"

A man's voice, speaking unnaturally loudly, came through the side streets and a crowd shouted in reply. Arlan lifted his hand to his sword hilt—and touched air.

Dragon's teeth! Rhiannon had insisted he leave it at home, speaking of security and metal detectors.

"It's okay. The guy's loud 'cos he's speaking through a mega-phone." They walked beneath the streetlight and Rhiannon took his hand again. No tremble this time. She flashed her gaze up to him, her eyes their usual mauve, and his mind went to a mountainside in summer, where the heather flowered. The distant shouting grew harsher and more raucous, with an edge to it, snapping him back to the present.

Around a corner, a bright light illuminated a man speaking into a trumpet-like object standing on a platform at the front of a grassed square, the crowd spilling onto the road. The sea of people stood between himself and Rhiannon, and Rhiannon's parked car on the other side of the road.

Arlan stopped and surveyed the crowd. Men shouted, holding fists high. Some milled about, and at the front of the large group, people scuffled, and the orator shouted louder. This wasn't the jeering audience of the afternoon in the Princes Street Gardens. He'd seen it before. Now he sensed it again—the tension in the air. The restlessness.

"What?" Rhiannon tugged, trying to move him forward. "It's probably the neo-Nazis counter protesting. We need to get to my car."

Arlan's feet wouldn't move.

"I've been to demos. Never had any trouble." She raised her eyebrows and lifted her chin in her car's direction. "We should be okay. Just keep your head down."

"I don't like it." He shook his head and stood firm, preventing Rhiannon's progress, searching for the path of least resistance. "I suggest we take the long way around by the rear of this horde."

"My car is right *there*." She pointed directly ahead through the middle of the throng.

Arlan tightened his grip on her hand. The air held a sharpness, honed with stress, an acrid scent etched on his memory.

Do not engage. Ensure Rhiannon's safety.

Rhiannon had dropped her pointing hand and now cast her gaze across the crowd. Scuffles rose in a wave throughout, and shrieks and curses rippled along it. The mob seethed and shifted like a rough sea.

Rhiannon faced him, her lips pressed together and the confident expression of moments before now replaced with tight lines about her eyes.

"You're rubbing off on me." She let out a tight sigh. "You're right, *general*, it would be stupid to go through that."

He nodded, then headed along the side of the crowd with Rhiannon staying close by his side. Yelling voices blared at him, and Rhiannon grasped his hand tighter.

He took a few more paces, reaching halfway along the length of the crowd. Thuds came from his right as people threw punches. Then a tussle of bodies, fists and kicking boots burst through the crowd and onto the footpath in front of him. He dodged the commotion and pressed Rhiannon close to the fence edging the churning crowd, then picked up his pace.

"They're taking oor jobs! Scots should get first preference! Aye!" a woman shrieked and cursed into his face, then swore at Rhiannon behind him.

He manoeuvred Rhiannon ahead into the narrow track between the crowd and the wrought-iron fence.

"Not far now, and we can skirt the back of this throng." He gritted his teeth.

He pressed her forward, his shoulder shielding her from elbows and signs attached to the sticks people waved around to make their point known. He reached the back of the demonstration, shoulders easing a little at the gap running along behind the crowd. He forged ahead.

"Straight across now." Rhiannon had to shout up to him over the rants and cries as they passed behind a bald man with tattoos of a type of cross. "My car's about—"

The man stepped back and caught Rhiannon's foot with his heel.

"Oops, sorry." Rhiannon's voice was tight.

The man turned and yelled, his face a snarl. He raised his fist at Rhiannon and Arlan lifted his arm to block the blow. The man connected with his forearm and Arlan's own arm shuddered with the impact. The man stared up at Arlan. Filled with hate, the man's glare equalled that of the bandit who had sought to slay him in the skirmish he'd left on his entry to this world.

"You will leave her alone." Arlan used a tone his warriors would obey without question. "It was an accident."

The man hesitated. Half a dozen or so people near him turned to Arlan and looked him up and down. The man glanced aside to those drawing near and, nodding to them, lunged for Arlan, pitching his shoulder into Arlan's midsection. Arlan tightened his midriff and stepped back to keep his balance as another man swung a fist at him. Arlan blocked that blow, then with knuckles bared, crunched the face of the man who had thrown the punch. His lips were soft and his teeth sharp against Arlan's knuckles. Blood soon poured from the man's mouth.

Three other men had grabbed Rhiannon and were dragging her toward the far edge of the crowd.

"Let me go!" Rhiannon's heated words rang from his left.

Arlan flung away the man who still held him, his assailant landing hard on the road with a winded grunt. Others turned from the crowd and yelled at Arlan, ropey veins in tattooed necks standing out above white T-shirts. One protester held a metal pole and raised it to strike. Arlan stepped in under the arc of the man's blow and grabbed his hands, then twisted them. With a sturdy kick, Arlan removed the man's feet from the ground, the sword-length pole coming out of the man's grasp and his body slamming onto the ground.

Not a broadsword, but it would do.

Arlan sprinted toward Rhiannon's yells, thrusting aside any protesters in his way. The men had hauled her through the crowd, two holding her wrists tight. Another pulled at her long, thick hair. She kicked her legs out at the men and twisted her wrists around, trying to loosen their grasps. Rhiannon's shrieks alternated with cries and grunts gnashing out through her gritted teeth. Near the footpath at the other side, they threw her on the road right next to her car. Her attackers had their backs to him, holding her down, intent on causing harm.

Easy targets.

A swift overhand arc landed the pole to the one on the left. He dropped with a grunt. A sideways swipe to the one on the right caught him in the ribs, crippling him and he crumbled to the ground, moaning. Gripping the pole tighter, Arlan planted a downward cut on the man leaning over Rhiannon. That one landed face down right beside Rhiannon, who now lay in between groaning, semi-conscious men. She was panting, and Arlan helped her to stand.

"Are ye harmed?" Her arm shook beneath his grip. Her blouse lacked most of its buttons, and scratches left red welts on the curve of her breasts above her undergarment.

She fumbled for her keys.

"We must leave." He held the pole out in defence, for they'd caught the attention of others in the crowd. He grabbed the keys from her shaking hand, *clicked* the car open and pushed her in. He threw the pole at an approaching growling man, then jumped in behind her. "Are ye able to drive?" He *clicked* the doors locked.

Rhiannon nodded, sucking in a shaky breath, and he handed her the keys. They rattled in her grasp. Another shout rose from behind them, and a thump echoed on the car's roof, hollow and metallic. Rhiannon flinched and gasped but quickly recovered, starting the car and edging through the people standing around.

"Ye are doing well, lass. They cannae touch us in this car. Keep driving." He forced a gentle voice to calm the atmosphere inside the car—and Rhiannon. She drove, the cries of the shouting crowd diminishing behind them. Police cars, their lights flashing, roared past them, heading to the demonstration, followed by men on horseback.

"Mounted police." Rhiannon said, her voice rough. "They'll push the horses through the crowd to disperse them." She had both hands on the steering wheel, fingers and thumbs trembling, and stared straight ahead at the road, tears sliding down her face.

Giant's steps! If only I could drive this car.

Five full minutes later, and well away from the clamour, he touched her shoulder, her muscles hard beneath his fingertips.

"Stop here, lass. Ye need to gather yourself."

Rhiannon pulled over as large tear drops fell from her face. She parked the car and turned off the engine. He reached over, undid her seatbelt, lifted her toward himself, and sat her on his lap. She turned her face into his shoulder and cried. He held her shaking body and rested his cheek on her soft hair. Warmth swelled within him, for unused to fighting—real fighting—Rhiannon had shown extraordinary self-possession under attack and outnumbered by her foes.

The silence ricocheted inside the car, and Arlan slowly shook his head.

My resolve to be a pacifist has lasted as long as a mist blown off a loch.

But nothing would stop him from preventing harm to Rhiannon.

"I thought they were going to... to..." Rhiannon's words came through shuddering breaths.

"Ye are alright now." He kissed the top of her head. "They won't get you."

"Thank you." Rhiannon pulled her blouse tighter, covering her scratched breasts and exposed underwear. "I was so scared." She heaved a shaky sigh. "If I wasn't so upset, I'd tell you how awesome you were with that sign-post." Her gaze slid out of the corner of her eye, and she blinked away her tears.

"You were brave, Rhiannon. Like a warrior."

"*Pfft.* They were too strong. I couldn't free myself from their grip. I was so afraid, I was useless..." Her words ran out and she buried her head in his neck.

He pulled her close, holding tight. "Och, no. Ye were nae useless. Rhiannon, you were brave and fighting. Overwhelmed but still fightin'. I'm so proud of you." He kissed her hair again.

But how will she take my decision?

No. Now wasn't the time to tell her he *must* go—and go without her.

Twenty-Eight

— • —

For what is in the heart of a man?
Only his own soul holds that knowledge.

SAGE GLIOCAS
(2870-2962 POST DRAGON WARS)

World of Dál Cruinne
Eastern Clanlands of Dál Gallain
Lord Ciarán's Tower

The best vervain grew in the hottest and driest section of the herb garden on the west side of the tower. Bram bent down, the hood of his mage robe falling over his head, blocking his view of the low bushes of vervain. Although the work of gathering the herb could be a repetitive and mindless task, it could be a meditation of sorts. Drostan gathered along the next row, meditating in his own way, most likely.

Time with his new master had seemed like a lifespan. This sorcerer-mage was an exceptional teacher and a generous master. Drostan had revealed to him mysteries of the art to which only an acolyte of a higher level should have access. He had accelerated Bram's learning, speaking often of Bram's gifting, and how Bram reminded him of himself. He absorbed all that he could from this sorcerer-mage. For, although the man made no claims to such, such he was. Warmth settled in the centre of his being.

"Any attempt at gratitude would seem feeble," he whispered, tugging at the stalks.

From his master's workshop, combining their energies at the stone-carved divination bowl, they had practiced the art of entering and controlling a beast. Now they had found a dragon, Drostan insisted Bram himself be expert at the skill before attempting to control one of the great creatures. Bram hummed to himself. The feline was the most enjoyable subject, for the sleek animal could slip in and out of human gatherings unnoticed and provide observation and collect information—when awake. Horses were too flighty, too bored, or too mean. His mouth pulled to the side and his humming

149

ceased. The dog, always by the master's side, was an invaluable tracker. But all these beasts were far too small for the experience required, even the war horse.

Exasperating.

Sweat stuck his robe to his back. It was an honour to wear the black of a mage, but not on this warm early spring day. He tugged at his undershirt and lifted the sodden material from his skin. But they couldn't stop yet. They required a harvest. The dried stems, leaves and flowers were essential for infusions to enhance their visions.

A clamour arose in the tower's courtyard with the clatter of shod hooves as Lord Ciarán returned from a late morning ride. The lord's loud voice, vibrating around the edges, echoed from the flagstones and across to Bram.

Drostan slowly rose from his task, placed his handful of plants into the basket, and turned to Bram.

"I think we should attend." Drostan's tone matched his serious expression.

The pitch of Lord Ciarán's voice, raised even further, set the creases on Drostan's brow, now mingling with beads of sweat.

Bram followed Drostan the short way to the courtyard. A young stable hand stood with head bowed and hands clasped before him, his face hidden by a long fringe of hair. Lord Ciarán faced the lad, his back to Bram, his tall dark stallion pawing the flagstones. He stood beside the beast, keeping his grasp on the reins, his words now subdued, a mere rumble from his throat, but his voice held a malevolence.

Lord Ciarán threw the reins over his steed's back and issued a command. Bram strained to hear it. The lord spoke words of the old tongue. Drostan quickened his pace and Bram ran to keep up with him. The war horse shrieked a whinny and reared on its hind legs. The lad raised his head, his hair flying back, his eyes rounded and panicked. He lifted his arms, shielding his face, and staggered away from the war horse. But the massive beast trod closer.

"No, my Lord—" Drostan shouted.

Lord Ciarán raised a sharp hand, silencing Drostan, not breaking his stride on his way to the tower entrance. Behind him, the dark horse clumped his hooves on the lad. The crunch of bones rang throughout the courtyard as the boy crumpled to the ground. Lord Ciarán reached the doorway, and without turning, spoke once more in the ancient tongue. The metallic ring of the horse's stomp on stone paving mingled with dull thuds as heavy, shod hooves pounded human flesh. Lord Ciarán continued his exit from the courtyard.

Drostan snapped his fingers by his side. "Stay with me," he whispered to Bram, and followed the lord up the stone stairway. Bram obeyed, trailing close to his master, mouth drying.

"My Lord," Drostan called up the stairs. "Please—"

"*Please what?*" Lord Ciarán spun on the steps, three above where Drostan stood. "The lad is already dead. My stallion will not cease until he senses the life has completely left him." He glared at Drostan. "Let that be a lesson to those who wish to defy me." The lord's statement echoed in the narrow stairwell.

Drostan stood motionless and mute before his master.

"How fares your pursuit of dragons, mage?" Lord Ciarán bent toward Drostan; his eyes kept a hint of fire as his bared teeth shone in the half light.

"We work diligently, my lord. You have assigned us no simple task."

"Bah!" Lord Ciarán raised a fist. His body shook, then he spun on the stair and ran up two at a time, the door to his library slamming shut above them.

Drostan slowly exhaled, and Bram rose to the step beside him. Sweat trickled down Drostan's face.

"It is a secret between us," Drostan whispered so quietly his breath barely stirred the air. "That thankless lord need not know until *we* desire to inform him of our discovery. We are safe, for he regards us as a valuable resource. But we must be as cunning as he, for the man is sharp."

"But why the stable boy?" Bram's voice rasped as he gaped at Drostan.

Drostan shook his head almost imperceptibly.

"It need not be much, I fear." Drostan continued his whisper. "The wrong horse blanket. The stirrups a fraction too long. The wrong day for *that* poor lad."

The door to the lord's library squeaked open above them and Lord Ciarán raced down the stairs.

"Are you still here?" His hair flew about him. "Mage, I would have you attend me in the Great Hall. Now!" He stormed past them. "And bring that scroll I had you prepare for the assassin, Vygeas."

"Aye, lord," Drostan answered, then turned to Bram. "Return to the herb garden. Do your work there, for I must attend to the lord." His gaze followed Lord Ciarán's journey down the stairs. "Lord Ciarán seeks a distraction from his perceived lack of progress in certain matters." Drostan's mouth became a leer. "He would begin a game with an old foe of mine." His eyes brightened. "I go to start the unfortunate soul on a course."

Bram descended the stairs, hurried to the herb garden and stood by the basket of vervain. Voices drifted across from the courtyard, but his master was not in sight. The lord's man strode across the yard, his clumping gait now a strut of sorts as he disappeared through the entrance to the dungeon. Days earlier he had shoved into its dim depths a handful of prisoners, deserters from Lord Ciarán's army after a recent battle. Bram repressed a shudder. He could only imagine the deprivations the lord's man delighted in inflicting upon the prisoners below.

Bram returned to plucking plants, but kept his ear directed at the dungeon's entrance. Moments passed, then a clanking of chains crossed the courtyard. He straightened up and stepped the few paces closer to get a better view. A tall warrior staggered from the entrance to the dungeon, the lord's man pushing him from behind. The warrior raised chained hands, squinting through matted hair at the bright sunlight, adjusting eyes after days of incarceration. His long, grey-hooded cloak wore a hem of stain from the slops on the dungeon floor. He was young, though his scarred face told of many clashes with a blade.

"Move on." The lord's man thrust a fist into his back and the prisoner trudged to the door of the Great Hall where Lord Ciarán performed his lordly obligations.

Bram moved to return to his task but halted as Drostan exited the tower and strode across the courtyard to the Great Hall with a scroll in his hand and his chin held high beneath a tight smile. Not long after, the young warrior left. The lord's man handed him his weapons and pointed to the stables, then shoved him toward the smithy's forge. To free him of his bonds, no doubt.

A strange day. One liberated and one killed.

What fates and fortunes lie ahead for us?

All at the whim of that one Lord Ciarán.

Drostan joined Bram in the herb garden, slapping him on the shoulder, his mouth a half grin. "Vengeance is a thing of beauty, my young acolyte."

"My master?"

"I have used the lord as he has used me. Lord Ciarán plays with souls like pieces on a board and delights in watching the game unfold. He shall use me to do so, but in this instance, *I* shall find the pleasure."

Bram squinted. In all truth, he had spent so little time with his master that Drostan had not yet revealed many an aspect of his character. Was this a vengeful bent in him? They stepped up to the workroom and hung the herbs to dry on the rack near the small fireplace.

"That warrior owes me all." Drostan turned from the last of the hanging herbs with a gleam in his eye. "When I was younger, before I gained access to study on the learned isle, I practiced my magic from a cave just outside of the village where that warrior grew up. All said I could grant each their heart's desire." Drostan leaned over to Bram, dropping his voice in a conspiratorial manner. "And that I could, for I had learned much. I... had already met my true master." He stood straighter. "Of more you shall learn in time."

Bram blinked. True master? He opened his mouth to ask and shut it just as quickly.

Drostan would only reveal what he wished when he wished it.

"Ye know him? The prisoner?"

"Aye. Vygeas. Lord Ciarán's sell-sword-come-assassin." Drostan's eyes focused mid-distance, as if the man dragged thoughts from the past. "He came from peasant stock but wished to be a warrior." Drostan regained his focus and pierced Bram with his gaze. "Vygeas sought magical gifting to that end. As you well know, magic comes at a cost. I enticed Vygeas, worked on his insecurities, offered a magic gift of heightened senses and exceptional prowess in the martial arts. He relinquished the one he loved to have the skills he wished." Drostan narrowed his eyes. "A warrior can do much with the anger arising from a broken heart. It fuels the motives, drives the darkest instincts, keeps the edge on hate. And hate leaves a fighter not content without a kill."

"Why do you hate this Vygeas so?" Bram could contain the question no longer. "If you pardon my boldness, my master."

"Vygeas took my only chance at love." Drostan's tone was thoughtful, wistful, then he jolted and stood tall. "But love means naught to me now."

"Then why your hatred still, my master? When as a mage dedicated to magic... love is not for us?"

Drostan's face grew dark. "Because he took away that chance without a thought for me."

Drostan ordered Bram to assist in tracking the progress of the warrior, Vygeas, now that a day had passed. Bram placed a staying on the door while Drostan stood at the divination bowl and *sought*. He grew tall and glowed, his plain features sharpening to more youthful, softer lines. His face tilted upward, his neck arched, mouth parting in a gentle smile and his eyes loosely closed, then his hands clenched the divination bowl—the very moment his master's spirit left his body. Bram would guard him for this vulnerable time, holding a *staying* on the door plus a *shielding* on his master's body.

The splash of sunlight through the slit of window had barely shifted in its course along the bare floorboards of the workroom when Bram sensed his master's return. Drostan's soul lingered in the power on entering his physical form, for this was the sorcerer's habit. He straightened and sighed, then brushed past Bram and hastened to the lord's chamber. Bram lowered the hanging rack, then busied himself with storing the herbs already dried. Soon Drostan burst back into the workroom.

"The old methods are always the best." Drostan rubbed his hands together. "Divide and conquer."

"My master?" Bram's brow tightened.

"Mayhap I can distract the assassin enough to miss his mark—lose his freedom and his life." Drostan sneered. "I go on a journey, my young mage. You must hold vigil until my return." He grabbed a leather satchel. "I will have to stay close to my conduit, but standing stones will be strewn along my way. The peoples of the past worshipped with henges. And, like those who also worshipped trees and fire and such elements, they knew nothing of the true power they contain. Nor did they comprehend how to wield it. Or the genuine sources of power in this world." He rummaged through a pile of stones sitting in a wide-necked clay pot, each one the size of a man's fist. "I head for the nearest standing stone."

TWENTY-NINE

— • —

For this is an edict of the universe:
There is an order to the powers of this world and time.
Only one reigns supreme
But many would vie for the place.
The game is long, the patience great, the conflict inevitable.
The mage's choice
The master's gain.
Make wise your decision, for it is binding.

MAGE MASTER FÀISTINNAECH
(3310-3380 POST DRAGON WARS)

Eastern Clanlands of Dál Gallain
Lord Ciarán's Tower

Bram awoke to a pounding on his chamber door. He threw on his robe and pulled the door open. The tall figure of Lord Ciarán filled the doorway.

"Where is he? Why is it taking the mage so long? It has been three days!"

Bram had never stood so close to the man. His shirt sleeves pulled taut on his muscled upper arms and a natural energy vibrated from him. He had tied back his greying hair and the scent of beeswax hung around his freshly cleaned leather armour.

He tapped his foot. "Go look in your bowl."

Bram lowered his gaze and scurried past into the workroom opposite, where weak morning light shone through the narrow window.

"Lord Ciarán, my master has set the times for communicating to be late after noon."

"I care not." Lord Ciarán stomped behind him. "I wish to know now." He halted by the pedestal.

Bram placed his hands on the divination bowl's rim, preparing to receive any communication his master may send this early in the day, then ground his teeth. He should

154

have acted quicker and shut the door and placed a *staying* on it. Now Lord Ciarán breathed down Bram's neck and peered into the instrument of his craft.

Bram tightened his grip on the bowl, he must not let Lord Ciarán distract him. For if per chance Drostan sought communication at this early time of day, his master would fill his palm-sized hollowed stone—a miniature divination bowl—with water and speak with him thus. Bram glanced aside at the lord, who scowled severely as he loomed beside him.

The water in the divination bowl stirred with energy. Bram took his focus from Lord Ciarán and placed it in his conduit.

"Master?"

The face of Drostan peered up at him. "Aye, Bram. Fortuitous that you stand beside the divination font. For my quarry hasten on, and I know not what this day will bring."

"Lord Ciarán is asking of your progress."

"Has he found them?" Lord Ciarán said close to Bram.

Bram spoke into the bowl, blocking out the blustering man beside him, who understood not the mechanisms of a divination bowl. "He wishes to know if you have—"

"Tell that mage there is no time to waste!" Lord Ciarán shouted in his ear.

Bram retracted his focus from Drostan. "My Lord Ciarán, sir, he cannot hear you. Only a mage drawing from their source can—"

"Spare me the mage-mumble. What does he say?"

"Tell me, my apprentice." Drostan's voice brought Bram back to the bowl. "Are you alone?"

"No, master." Bram's neck heated. "Lord Ciarán insisted I seek you."

"Tell him to remove himself from my chambers!" Drostan's image loomed closer, the veins in his forehead bulging with congestion.

"My master, he is Lord Ciarán, your benefactor. I cannot order him."

"What is going on!" Lord Ciarán grabbed Bram's robe at the collar and shook him.

Bram lost connection with Drostan. He closed his eyes to shut out the ranting mouth next to his ear, focused once more on his conduit, and reached out to Drostan. Lord Ciarán's grip held, his voice like gravel, and his spoken orders slipping through to Bram's hearing.

Bram sensed his master in the divination bowl.

"Tell me," Drostan demanded, "why the one who constantly derides our magic, seeks once more to avail himself of its services!"

Thank the elemental energies the lord who now grasped his robe could not hear Drostan.

He would tear through the workshop in a rage.

"Your lord and master says"—Bram began to repeat Lord Ciarán's orders to Drostan, then withdrawing his energy from the bowl, faced the lord beside him— "I dare not say that, my lord."

Bram straightened, steeling himself, for the expression on Lord Ciarán's face told him there would be serious consequences if he did not relay the message from lord to mage. Bram returned his attention and his inner energies to the divination bowl.

155

"My master, your lord wishes me to say that you will complete your task, or you will have no benefactor, no post, no prospects."

Bram swallowed, the ripples in the bowl obliterating his view of Drostan.

Bram placed the fresh-picked herbs on the long bench in his master's workshop, the cool, moist leaves soft beneath his fingertips. The scent of rosemary and lavender, overpowering yarrow and plantain, permeated the room.

Two days had passed without communication from Drostan.

Bram held his shoulders tight, and his stomach burned with acid. This was something he'd not experienced since leaving his homeland and kin, and travelling across what had seemed like the world, to the island of Innesfarne to study under the master mages. And now he must find how his own master fared. He would try to not disturb his activities but seek his location and observe.

Bram slid the bolt further along the door's lock, ensuring none could enter his master's chamber where the stone-carved divination bowl resided. Bram trusted the *staying* he placed on the door's bolt to hold.

I will have no intrusions from that impatient man they call lord.

The man was too bold and discourteous, held no respect for the magic arts, and treated Drostan like a servant.

"Does he know not the power the sorcerer wields?" Bram's deep voice echoed in the quiet chamber.

No, Lord Ciarán does not.

Bram paused with the acknowledgement.

He stood by the dish, its surface as still as a loch on a tranquil day, and just as reflective. The image in his mind of his home in the high mountains of Dál Gaedhle brought a tightness to his chest. He breathed it away. No time for sentimentality. Drostan, his master and teacher, had not yet reported in and once again the day grew late.

Bram stilled his body, set aside all reminiscences of home, calmed his mind, and directed his inner vision into the bowl.

Sensing a churning disruption, he opened his eyes to a troubled, roiling surface where once was a glassy sheen. He placed his hands on either side of the dish to steady himself and see with clarity. Stone, as cold as the deep ground, cooled his palms resting on the rim. He slid his hands into the water and willed his soul to dive in.

His true self flew through the darkening night, beneath thunderous clouds and over rain-lashed fields, skirting wave dashed shore and broad pebbled beach. Bram dived to the ground and, drawn by the emission of power, slid through a slit in a rocky cave opening.

He entered the cave, a roar filling the confined space now surrounding him in rock. A sharp shining stalactite dropped from the ceiling into the roiling, boiling waters of a massive subterranean pond directly beneath. The spray flew through Bram's spirit, leaving an impression of heavy minerals.

A plexus of energy drew Bram's soul and he turned to where the energy focused on a dark-robed form. Two sandaled feet extended from an outcropping of rock now washed by waves from the miniature ocean crashing over the side of the subterranean pool.

Bram drew closer, following the line of the legs of the person so familiar.

It *was* his master's form.

Drostan lay behind a natural lectern where no doubt he had orated his spell. The effects of this magic still energised the cave around him with a surging sea swelling the pond's water. The wind and waves were declining by the moment.

He called to Drostan, his spirit reaching out.

Drostan moved not.

Bram drew even closer. If only he could move beyond spirit and a give a physical touch! Shake Drostan's shoulder. Roll him over to look him in the eye.

But not a movement. Not a breath. Not a stirring of life.

No sense of his master's soul emanated from his inert body.

No! Drostan, my tutor and mentor, is gone.

Empty ache threatened to overtake him, overwhelm him, and give a desire to return to his own body by the divination bowl.

But I will stay here! There was more he must discover.

If he were in his physical form, he would gather the man in his arms. Tell him he admired him above all others. Then the last words Drostan heard would be Bram's own, promising to carry on the work where he had left off.

Traces of power filled the cave even as the storm in the miniature sea abated, the energy drawing away from Drostan's body.

Bram hovered over his master. It was like he slept, such as the times when sedated for days after using his magic, as if passed out with too much herb, leaving Bram to attend to his master's chores himself. Bram shook his head as other instances of Drostan's over imbibing had left the sorcerer invigorated, and Bram would run to keep up with him.

But his master's inert body told a more serious tale.

Drostan has taken in too much power.

The mages of Innesfarne warned against excessive magic. It clasped on to a mage tighter and tighter if imbibed too often. *You must master the power*, they said, *or it would master you.*

Drostan now lay stilled, evidence of the truth his mage instructors espoused.

Bram sighed and gazed at his mentor's lifeless form and pushed away what he would feel.

He would not give in to these emotions until his soul re-joined his body. Then and only then would he allow the ache to fill him and spill from his eyes in his body's own salt water.

The energy had hovered in the far corner of the cave and now surged, directed at him.

It was familiar... not Drostan. But an essence *in* his master. He had sensed it when they met in that space *in between*.

Bram held his soul tight, straining to discern the source of this living power. It filled the cave, yet it focused on the body of his tutor. Bram hovered over the black-robed form as the torch's glow dimmed by the moment, yet the intense spiritual sensation that surrounded him increased.

The eyeless sentient energy inspected Bram, then beckoned him. Bram's spirit tingled with recognition of its call, his master's source now offering itself to him. He moved closer and stretched out his soul to embrace it. The power flew to him, and he shuddered as the primordial force filled his soul and his world.

Now this was his very existence—all else an insignificant, bland, soundless blur.

Bram awoke in his body. The hard wooden floor seeped cool into his cheek, and his arms folded in an embrace of the pedestal holding the stone divination bowl. An owl's call flitted through the narrow window of the tower chamber. The pale light of a half moon shone, casting its gleam into his eyes. He blinked and let go of the pedestal, patted his coarse robe, rubbed his stubbled chin and ran his fingers through his long hair.

He was the same, but not. In his inner being, he was anew.

I have my master's power.

And must do my master's work.

Bram rapped on the heavy oak door to Lord Ciarán's room in the round tower and straightened his shoulders.

I will stand before this lord and never flinch, no matter the disdain thrown at me.

"Yes?" His master's lord dragged out the word behind the closed door. "Come in, then!"

Bram breathed deep, turned the handle, and pushed open the door.

Lord Ciarán sat at his desk and peered at a piece of parchment in front of him, a bronze statuette of a dragon keeping one edge firmly on the desktop. The sides of the scroll fought against the beast's effigy and strained to return to their original curled position and prevent further inspection by the grey-haired lord who held the other end of the scroll down with a fist. He lifted his attention from his parchment and placed his scrutiny upon Bram.

"What do you want?" Lord Ciarán's eyes retained their squint.

"My lord, my master Drostan will not be returning."

The fire crackled in the hearth, and Lord Ciarán's eyes narrowed. "You know this how?"

"I have seen it. He has... left this world." Bram swallowed and pushed against the prickling behind his eyes.

Lord Ciarán stood, lifting his fist from the parchment. It snapped shut, reverting with speed to its rolled state, and the dragon statuette skidded off the desk and *thunked* onto the floor.

"Are you speaking of his death? Have you seen it?" Lord Ciarán's voice rose, and he moved from his chair. "So, he will not bring me the prize nor any satisfaction with the demise of that young assassin, Vygeas?" He stepped around the desk, knocking the dragon sculpture with his slippered foot so it skidded along the wooden floor and crashed against the fire hearth. *"Dragon's breath!"* He limped to the window. "And I am now without a mage." Lord Ciarán spun, grey eyes raking Bram from top to toe. "He's taught you enough. You'll do." He nodded and muttered, "Where would I get another from? Those tight-fisted—"

"I am your mage now, my lord." A statement, not a question.

I will let this lord know I am no servant.

"Yes, well, your first task is to aid my search for dragons." Lord Ciarán rubbed his chin, the rasp of his hand running over stubble was the only sound in the room for some moments. "I have armies to acquire, and battles lie ahead." His grey eyes bore into Bram's. "Your predecessor investigated the existence of the great beasts, although none have sighted one since the Dragon Wars of millennia past." He huffed. "He has taught you of them?"

Bram nodded in reply with an ache in his heart at this lord's omission of condolence—a non-acknowledgement of the greatness of the sorcerer who now passed from this life.

"I need one. Go look in your pot." Lord Ciarán flicked his hand at Bram and returned to the curled parchment on top of his desk. "You can leave this caisteal without problems, yes? Not tied to stone, or any other element, are you?"

Bram's nails dug into his palms as he conquered the burning within.

I will endure this man. Lord Ciarán was Drostan's lord, but he will never be mine.

Bram's master—his new master—was one more powerful than this lordling human who stood there, arrogance personified.

He would use Lord Ciarán as he could, but he would answer to no man.

His one true ruler, the spirit he had met in the cave, had shown him greater realms. Bram would serve him, and him only.

THIRTY

— • —

Eternity stretches behind and before.
A life in time—a hand's span.
The actions of each touch another and more.
All connect, all vibrate, all expand.
Each decision we make, each instalment of time
Has its place in the grand master plan.

SAGE GLIOCAS
(2870-2962 POST DRAGON WARS)

Eastern Clanlands of Dál Gallain
The Great Hall, Lord Ciarán's Tower

The lofty ceilings of the Great Hall echoed with the rhythmic connections between its stone floor and Ciarán's right boot.

It had not gone well. The young lord warriors standing by his hearth appeared to be reasonable men, yet they brought a report they assumed would please him.

But it did not.

Encountering the troop of warriors from the west, they fought, injuring two of them, one severely, killed another two, including the leader.

Or so they declared.

Bram had informed him otherwise. The dish the mage had inherited from his predecessor revealed the aftermath. Ciarán's own warriors, these lords who were sons of lesser nobles of the east, had abandoned their duties at the first sign of trouble and run, after a brief skirmish, leaving the troop from the west to lick their wounds. They had reported deaths, but Bram indicated most were of Ciarán's own warriors.

Bram now stood beside him by the large hearth of the Great Hall. The young mage had flowed seamlessly into Drostan's role and had done well, if not better, than that mage. Losing Drostan had not been an impediment after all.

160

And Bram had sensed a portal in that vicinity, but these lordlings stated no evidence of such.

Ciarán flared his nostrils. They had delivered their report with cagy glances, one to the other, the tall one restless on his feet. He would believe Bram over them. He slitted his eyes, wishing he could slit the throats of these young men. But he needed arms and warriors for his grander scheme. Killing the sons of lesser lords who would join their armies to his own did not make for a good strategy.

As to raiding the villages of the border, that had not been as bounteous as expected.

"My Lord Ciarán?" The stocky, dark-haired one expected a response. And a reward.

Sunlight flooded through the narrow windows of the main hall of his tower, these thin vertical apertures indicative of its function as a fortress for defence. He protected these lesser lords, and yet here their sons stood, begging for payment.

Who do they think they are? They owe me everything!

"I give you thanks for your services and assure you of my continued protection." He used a tone to indicate his deafness to their request. "Please inform your lord fathers of my appreciation and expectation of your further services."

Both young lords stiffened, surprise at going unrewarded blatant on their faces. If they were wise—an imperative for their sakes—they would bow and leave.

They hesitated, hands resting on sword hilts at their belts.

Ciarán dragged deeply on the chill air of the hall.

"My lords, let me escort you out." Bram stepped briskly from his side and hastened to the warriors and, with a gesture, directed them out of the Great Hall.

The young mage was wise and had learned to anticipate the progression of his moods. The junior lords would come to recognise the prudence of retreat in this instance, and many others.

Thank Cernunnos the mage expiated their exit.

Ciarán marched from the Great Hall and took the stairs two steps at a time, and on reaching his landing, ran into his library, slamming the door behind him. He strode to his desk and, snatching up the scroll that lay on his seat, threw himself into the chair.

How I abhor failure!

He raked his fingers through his hair, then thudded his hands on the arms of his chair. A gentle tapping came through the door. He rolled his eyes, flung his head back, and examined the ceiling.

Maybe if I ignore it, it will go away.

Another *tap, tap*. A little firmer this time.

No. It is not to be.

He flung the scroll onto the desk. It tousled with the other parchments scattered there. He cracked his knuckles, preventing himself from grabbing the scroll and tearing it apart.

"What!" *Why does the mage press me so?*

The door opened, and Bram entered with the same condescending expression as his predecessor.

Has he inherited that also?

161

"My lord, do you wish me to search further to ascertain the survivors of the foray involving these warriors? I may discover how goes the welfare of one in particular. The young Dál Gaedhle warrior with grey eyes—"

"No!" Ciarán roared.

The mage barely flinched, but Ciarán gave not a care. His forays to the east had not provoked the response he had wished, nor unsettled the person to whom he had directed his activities. Displaying that *fannlag's* true nature of weakness.

Ciarán gritted his teeth. Subjugating the clan chiefs here in the east had required more resources than he had anticipated. While he struggled to fulfil his own designs for Dál Gallain, Donnach MacEnoicht remained in the west, sitting snugly on the throne of the Àrd Rìgh of Dál Gaedhle!

Ciarán burned within.

"What I want—no—*order* you to do, is go find me a dragon and send it northwest to destroy Donnach Finnbar MacEnoicht!"

The deep brown eyes of the mage blinked but once. "Are you certain, my lord?"

"Yes!" The library resounded with his hissing answer.

"I shall leave you to your ruminations and go search." Bram turned and left, shutting the door behind him.

Birds chattered outside the window of the workroom as Bram crushed the leaves of wood anemone between his fingers and rubbed it on his temples.

The man gave him a headache.

The task Lord Ciarán now demanded would be arduous. First, Bram would seek permission. It was no insignificant matter to gain control of a beast such as a dragon—a task he had never performed.

But to set it on a man... and a king—an àrd rìgh—no less...

Aye, his assignment to Drostan as acolyte apprentice had been a privilege, and taking on the role of Lord Ciarán's mage a natural progression. But could the mage masters of Innesfarne free him? Reassign him?

Lord Ciarán, so intent on his course of action, would deny them for certain. Hold him a prisoner, most likely.

No, submission was the logical course. Moreover, his new master's compelling, received on his first encounter, was strongly to stay here.

Bram lit a candle to dispel the dark of the room and placed it beside the stone-carved divination bowl. The touch of the cold stone provoked fond memories of his mentor. He sighed, recalling the day of the man's death, and the spirit he had encountered in the cave. At that time, grief had mixed with anticipation.

He now sought to enquire of that same spirit of power. To ask if the task assigned to him was permissible... Acceptable... In accord with the master plan.

He pushed against the tremor rising within him. He may not be strong enough to even succeed. And if he did, controlling the dragon may eventually extinguish his soul and take his life.

He had not encountered his master's spirit of power since submitting to it in that cave. Nor had he ever performed the act of *summoning*.

Bram placed his hands in the bowl of silkiness and took a settling breath, filling his lungs with the scent of approaching rain on the wind.

Water—the most beautiful element of the universe.

A soothing sensation ran through his body from the bowl.

Hmm. The sky blesses us with it in soft cool moisture, small baubles of rock-hard ice, or floating frozen flakes. It lies still in a loch until stirred by the wind. It flows in power coursing along a burn.

Joy rose within him as he filled with the energy from his source.

Water, so giving in its form, yet able to wear away the solidity of rock.

Aye, yielding yet so powerful.

He sent out a *seeking*, a question.

He waited, headache abating, calm ensuing.

An outside presence came within, shadowing his chamber, smothering the flickering light. He grew cold, yet it warmed him. His neck prickled, yet it stilled him. The air thickened, clamping his limbs and pressing down, immobilising him.

A dragon to subdue. A man to kill. What is the will of my new master?

In the chamber's quiet, from the stillness within him, he sensed the unseen, and heard the unspoken.

THIRTY-ONE

—·—

For the heart to be true
Every fear is ignored
And selfish desires relinquished.
All must embrace their part.
Order comes from destiny's course.
Chaos when the brave lack courage.

WISDOM WRITINGS ON KINGSHIP
SAGE GLIOCAS
(2870-2962 POST DRAGON WARS)

Abernethy, Scotland
Our World, 2016

I don't know how I drove home, but somehow, I managed. Now my hand shook, my house keys rattling at the backdoor lock. Arlan reached past me, taking the keys from my trembling fingers, then opened my cottage door, switching the light on as we walked in. I blinked against the glare and went straight to the bathroom.

Yep, just as I thought. Bloodshot, red-rimmed eyes looked back at me.

"Are ye okay?" Arlan's rumbling voice came from the doorway. A soft rumble. He was being so kind.

"Ah, yes. I guess."

"Come here." He leaned into the bathroom and took hold of my hand. "Ye are feeling the aftereffects of battle. Och, you are still shaking."

Arlan led me to the couch and shook out a blanket from his neatly piled bedding. He looked at me for a moment, then sat down, drawing me with him and landing me in his lap.

I didn't protest.

He swirled the blanket around me, encompassing us both. I leaned against his firm chest, warmth surrounding me and chasing away the silent tremors that rose from my middle every couple of seconds. The rise and fall of Arlan's rib cage rocked me gently with every one of his breaths.

"How can you be so calm?"

"I am used to combat. And... men seem to recover quicker than women. I know not why. But I'm sure your scientists could tell me." He chuckled, shaking my head as I leaned against his chest.

A dog barked, echoing in the distance, and a night bird chirped. The blanket was rough against my cheek and the leather jacket Arlan wore filled my nostrils with an earthy scent. I sank deeper into him, my shivers gone, and drifted...

His arms clamped tight around me, and I jolted awake. Moonlight streaming through my kitchen window poked a beam into the living room.

"Och, ye are awake. I think, for a better sleep, ye should go lie down on your own bed." Arlan's mouth curved up on one side. "Not that I don't want to hold you here all night, but ye will curse me for the crick in your neck in tha morn." The other side of his mouth curved too.

What, and leave this lovely warm cocoon of your warmth? And you?

"Ah, I guess you're right." I slipped the blanket off and stood up, my legs stiff from being curled up close to him. "Goodnight." I managed to keep the reluctance from my tone.

"Goodnight." His voice was husky. He coughed, clearing it. "Ye rest as long as you need, Rhiannon." He scrunched the blanket over himself, and I turned, forcing my feet to walk me to the bedroom.

I crashed onto my bed. The lines of scratches on my breasts stung, and a vision of sneering faces full of hate came unrequested. I shivered and pulled the duvet around my ears, the feather-down stuffing crinkling and snapping delicately.

I stared at the ceiling. Light crept around the edges of my bedroom curtains, so I turned and faced the wall. *Maybe I'll get a little more sleep.*

Something weighed on Arlan's mind, and not the riot at the demonstration, or the guys who attacked me. He'd been distant since hearing the man in the Princes Street Gardens. The words of the street preacher had hit him, but he'd not spoken of it during our meal and... well, then *other* things had prevented further conversation.

He'd fought, defended like he was trained to do. But he'd done it for *me*.

My heart glowed, and I couldn't stop the slow shake of my head. He'd wounded those guys to get them away from me. Wielded that pole like a sword. He was magnificent. There was no other word for him.

He must be something special in his world.

His world.

He said he wouldn't take me back because it wasn't safe when he'd left.

Well, it isn't safe here!

But no, it was probably because we could never be together. He'd end up with some beautiful noblewoman—a clan princess! Dál Gaedhle sounded so traditional, there was sure to be some rule about clan chief's sons—*high king's* sons—only marrying for resources and inheritance. And children of noble landowners joining to form alliances and make bigger armies and the like. And I had no idea if I was one of them.

I sank even deeper into my duvet.

That's the real reason.

Brave as Arlan was, he didn't have the guts to tell me. His father, the àrd rìgh, would want a noble woman for his son, not a nobody from another world all together!

I opened my eyes again. Now bright sunlight beamed through the gap in the curtains. I must've drifted off to sleep. A whinny came from outside. Arlan would be with Mengus. He hadn't had the chance to ride his horse yesterday, and he usually groomed and rode the stallion every day. I got out of bed and stumbled to the window, my eyes gritty as I peered through half-asleep lids.

The fearsome warrior on the war horse painted in woad looked different from the man in jeans now trotting his black horse around my field. But he was the same man. The same Dál Gaedhle warrior. And, by the set of his shoulders, something bothered him. He cantered Mengus out the gate and up to the hill with the ruins of the Iron Age Fort at its peak.

I dressed and spent the morning cleaning the cottage in silence, flicking dust off my bookshelves, and pummelling the cushions on my couch. I clattered yesterday's dirty dishes into the sink, then leaned heavily on the bench, my breath catching.

What if he found the way home and disappeared?

Shouts drifted over from my neighbour's home. Honestly, the man was a pain but at least his wife shouted back today. Near lunchtime, the clop of horse's hooves caught my ear, and I ran out the backdoor. Arlan trotted Mengus past and into the field, his face tight. Our eyes met but he didn't smile. I followed him to the makeshift stable with an ache, like an empty place, sitting in my ribcage. I hugged myself.

Arlan slipped off the enormous black horse, landing lightly on the ground, then led the stallion into the animal shelter. He removed the saddle and the bridle, then placed a halter that he'd made from a rope over the stallion's head and tied the lead to a hook on the wall. He leaned down and grabbed a handful of clean hay from the diminished pile and curried in large sweeping strokes across the horse's flank.

"Hi." One of us had to break the silence that was as sharp as the sword on his back.

His currying strokes sped up, but he didn't respond.

"Have I done something wrong?"

His shoulders drooped and the grooming stopped, all in one motion.

"No, lass." He turned, his eyes moist.

Ice cold spread through me like a flash of lightning. "What's wrong, Arlan?"

"I must go," he said simply.

"I know." My voice thinned to nothing.

"I must confess to you and let you know the kind of man I truly am. You think me... what word did ye use? *Awesome*. You've also called me selfish. The latter is the most accurate. You and the sage-orator in the park have brought me to my senses."

"Wow, you make it sound so serious, Arlan. You're not—"

166

"Oh, but it *is* serious, Rhiannon." His shoulders rose and fell as the silence stretched between us, his expression a storm of emotions.

"Tell me, then." My guts clenched.

The telling won't change the going, and the fact he doesn't want to take me with him.

"This world is in turmoil. I see it in the news, and I've known it for myself..." His eyes flickered, as though he pursued his thoughts. "You have so many good things. Great things. Equipment to make your life easy. Food a plenty. The knowledge your world possesses far outreaches anything our sages could imagine. Any who have the means of acquiring it can know it with a tap of their fingers." He shook his head slowly. "But there's evil and suffering everywhere. Danger." His voice grew husky. "Ye are well? From yesterday?" He held me with his eyes.

"Yes, I'm fine." *Don't stop now you've started.*

Mengus snorted, so Arlan reached around and led him out. He patted his stallion on the rump, and the animal trotted out into the field.

"From what I've seen, your world was as beautiful as mine," he continued. "There are memories of this original perfection in nature, such as the untouched parts of your world. Exquisite, like Dál Cruinne when *Tobraichean na Beatha* formed it." He paused and looked at me.

My forehead tightened, the meaning of the Gaelic words eluding me.

"These words translate to the *Source of all Spirit,* the being that we believe made all. The lives of men and women reflect its innate goodness and through their personalities they show the love and kindness of this *Source.*" Arlan paused. "Are ye following what I say, Rhiannon?"

"Yes, except I don't see that in my neighbour."

He cocked his head to the left, and the corner of his mouth lifted.

"There's a badness in the world, Rhiannon. Most likely coming from dissatisfaction, selfishness, and greed. It has escalated to pure evil, affecting the natural world that now turns on humankind. Your floods and earthquakes. Global warming." He raised a shoulder, then let it fall.

I stood silent, not daring to move in case he became quiet again.

"My world, Dál Cruinne, is on the brink of the same." He glanced down at his hands fiddling with the clump of straw he still held. "There is a badness creeping in, and we must crush it in its genesis." Arlan raised his eyes to mine. "My father, the high king, hasn't seen *this* world, but he has the wisdom to know what the same kind of evil could do to ours."

Arlan's gaze dropped to the floor and his shoulders rose with a heaviness, like he was in pain but needing to speak. I willed my feet to stay put so I wouldn't run over and wrap my arms around him.

"To my shame, I stalled action. I should have put my support behind the move to march on the enemy to the east, to fight this evil." Arlan's jaw clenched, and he gouged a hole in the dirt floor with his boot heel. "But given the evidence"—he lifted his head and his gaze pierced me— "I denied its importance. I couldn't believe the reports from the southeast. Our life in the west of Dál Cruinne was idyllic. I didn't want it disrupted. That was before I came face to face with that very evil. Then, amid my first fight against it, I was somehow, and by some means I know not, transported to this world. A seemingly idyllic world also, I believed, until I experienced the dangers and evils personally. And with you."

"So, you'll go soon," I said, the words coming out harder than I meant.

He nodded. "My world will become like yours if I don't return to fulfil my duty. I must not sit by while our distant cousins in the east suffer. We are aiding the refugees." His brows lifted a fraction. "Aye, we have displaced persons also. I'm now determined that we must mount an offensive and push this evil back."

He stepped toward me and gently held my upper arms, his look set, and his forehead hard lines.

"Rhiannon, you are so right. I have been a selfish and too comfortable fool. I don't deserve the role for which my father prepared me. I've soaked up my position and privileges, enjoyed my life, and resented any notions of obligation." His voice cracked around his words and his face pinked. "My *hissy-fit*, as you called it, is over. I only wanted freedom to choose my destiny. We all are who we are. It's what you make of your destiny that truly matters."

I kept quiet, his hands hot on my arms.

"Your world has wealth, medicine, technology, scientific advances that make it possible for you to send machines you called rockets to other planets! But you remain brutish and violent. Your wars involve weapons that could obliterate it all. My world is not so advanced, but we share the inability to avoid violence. If it must be so, I'll use what I know to combat that evil. Bàn, the brother of my heart, believes I should be war chief. And, it seems"—he tilted his head— "you agree." His intense gaze, as blue as the clearest sky, bore into me. "And I now *choose* to take up my role as warrior-prince of my clan, ready to be war chief when my father deems me ready."

My cheek tugged for a second. A flickering smile at his self-discovery, and his resolve. The empty space in my chest I'd hugged away, now slowly expanded, but I tried not to let it. Arlan's choices were bigger, more crucial, than any need I had for him.

"If war is what it costs to wipe out the badness in my world," he continued, "then war I will make. I now understand I must fight to change it. We either stand against the evil, or we are overcome by it."

I wavered on my feet, needing his strong hands to hold me up, and my thudding pulse echoing in every corner of my body. Arlan meant to go, but he would leave for a rightful cause. This man had understood me and around him I felt *normal*—exceptional even. I swallowed the lump in my throat.

Anything good is always too good to be true.

"Are you okay, Rhiannon?" His large hands held tighter.

"Yes, I'm fine. A lot to think about, that's all."

Arlan frowned and tucked me into his side, then we walked back to the cottage. I had to take extra-long steps to keep pace with him. Everything about him was larger than life.

That empty place inside me crept past its borders.

He must go. I'd be the selfish one having a *hissy-fit* if I argued against him leaving.

"I must go back and apologise to my father." His deep voice broke into my inner turmoil. "For being so self-centred." His glance was tight. "I need to return to my warriors and my brother. They'll need my help."

"How will you go?" My words came out strained. We'd reached the door of the cottage and I pointed to the hill ahead of us. "Where *is* that portal up there?"

He sighed. "I've spent all morning trying to find it. I rode through all the wooded areas in search of it. Again."

We entered the house and, after Arlan left his weapons by the door, he went straight to stoke the fire. I dropped onto the couch and the scent of wood smoke hit my nose as a numbness threatened to envelope my toes and fingers. He stood staring at the flames with his back to me, his shoulders bunched.

Something thudded in me, like I'd *truly* seen Arlan for the first time. He was a leader, a fighter, a defender. A man with gifts, talents and skills that led to responsibilities. Born into a position where obligation was unavoidable—a demand.

A warmth, undeniable and inescapable, swelled within me, filling the empty place. This man was impressive.

My focus zoned out, and the room faded away.

Surf pounds on rocky, grey islands. Mists cover moors. Steep snow-capped mountains sit beside still lochs mirroring clear blue skies—a beautiful, pristine world.

I gasped and sat straighter.

Arlan dances with his sword in a battle, where he is the victor. An evil man and his army are his conquest. Muscled men and women dressed in leather armour and brandishing sharp blades fight beside him or guard his back. My limbs tense with every sword clash. Deep throated shouts of victory surround Arlan, and my body vibrates with the rumble of their cries. They embrace Arlan in bearhugs, their fierceness and loyalty to him as strong as death itself.

And as real in the room as the air I inhaled.

The vision faded, and the young man in front of me remained gripping the mantlepiece. I clutched my cushion as tight as I would hold my own sword. My pulse pounded my temples, and I panted as if I'd just fought in that battle beside him.

Arlan had bared his soul—faults and failings laid out on the table. I'd witnessed the war. Not the war he spoke of—the one he would now go to fight—but the war that had occurred in his soul. The most important battle a person could win—the war against selfish complacency. Against denying the realities of the state of the world. The war against fear. One that makes a person either sit back on the couch and watch television while the world goes to hell or pick up their weapons and run out the door and into the battlefield.

Wherever and whatever that may be.

It may be a battle or two on the eastern borders of Arlan's country, or it could become an all-out war. But he also spoke of an evil. A shiver passed through me. Arlan would be heavily involved in it. I'd glimpsed the natural and gifted general in him, and the convictions he'd just expressed would compel him to lead his warriors in an assault.

Could I be in a world like that—one at war with evil? And involve myself so closely with a warrior who would go into battle? My feet tapped rapidly, hardly remaining on the rug.

Oh, hell yeah.

I'd follow Arlan onto the field. I would be Boadicea in her chariot right there with him!

I thrust the cushion down onto the seat.

"I'm coming too." My statement echoed over the crackling logs.

Arlan braced his hands on the mantelpiece, his knuckles threatening white, and shook his head. He exhaled loudly. "No, Rhiannon." The edges of his words frayed.

I jumped off the couch and strode to him at the fireplace, but stopped short of flinging my arms around him. I couldn't be like that with him. Not when I had no idea of my real heritage.

And there's most likely no possibility of the kind of love I desire between us.

"I want to be in Dál Gaedhle, if it's as great as you say. I don't want it going to shite like this world has. I want to be part of what you'll do."

Even if we can't… be together.

Arlan's breathing staggered, and I pulled back from my impulse to hold him. Maybe I'd said too much. Overstepped the mark.

That doesn't matter now. I don't care anymore.

I'll do all I can to be with him wherever he is—despite the terms.

"You say I can't come with you now, but you came *back* for me." My shoulders sagged. "But I didn't know you then, so I've missed that boat." My veins filled with numbness and poured their contents back into my heart, negating the burgeoning warmth.

He let go of the mantelpiece and, for a short while, the crackling of the fire dominated the room, then he turned.

"Nae, not now. That is yet to be. In my future. So"—he lifted a shoulder— "be ready."

I gasped. "I can go to Dál Gaedhle? You'll let *me*"—my mouth twitched as my brain searched for the right term— "an other worlder?" Warmth resurged and pushed away the cold empty numbness that sought to invade my resolve to fight beside him, no matter what.

"Rhiannon, you are no *other worlder*. I'm convinced there's a reason your dear mother gave you that plaid you call a *baby rug*. Ye *are* from Dál Gaedhle, and I promise to discover the truth."

Thirty-Two

— · —

It is the time between times.
Neither dark nor light,
Nor day, nor night.
At dawn and dusk it occurs.

SECRET SACRED WRITINGS OF THE SAGES
LOCKED SCROLL 36
BROCH OF THE ANCIENTS

Abernethy, Scotland

Arlan's vision slowly blurred. He'd stared at the glowing screen for an age. Like a span of time as long as a lecture from Sage Cénell. Rhiannon's warmth brushed his leg as she sat beside him on the couch. She'd *googled* once more, enquiring of portals. Ley lines featured again, and pictures of monuments ancient to this world filled the screen.

"Hell—oo!" Rhiannon waved her hand in front of his face, disrupting his connection with the screen of the laptop sitting on the coffee table. He broke away from the glamour in which it held him.

"Are we near any of these?" he asked.

"Yes, the Iron Age Fort on the hill could fit into this category. We were over halfway to it when you came through."

Arlan shook his head. "Nae, trees are the common thing. A forest covers the hill, and I was in a forest in my world—"

"When I first met you"—Rhiannon's eyes widened— "you'd walked out from the forest on that Highland estate."

"Hmm. That would be in my future and your past. When it's safe for you to come, I must return to just after this time now." He pointed to the floor.

"What if you don't come back for years? Our timelines may not even be parallel. You know, like the Mobius Strip?"

"The who?" he asked.

"What if you return and I'm an eighty-year-old woman?"

He had no answer to her question. "Eifion, my father's sage adviser, would say our two worlds are as the lines of the endless knot." He sighed. "Eifion. Oh, how I wish for him now. He would surely know."

Rhiannon peered at him, shifting in her seat a wee bit. "You call it the endless knot too?"

"Aye. Our worlds cross over and under each other." With his forefinger he tapped the armband of deep blue interlacing lines inked on his upper arm. "They never touch but yet live close beside one another. At some point, and in certain conditions, they connect. What we are naming a *portal*, is it no'?" He lifted his gaze to her mauve eyes peering out beneath her fine brows—portals themselves, stirring in him a desire to step through. He cleared his throat. "But as to the different times involved..."

"Wait a minute. Maybe you came back at the Celtic Festival *because* I didn't go with you."

He blinked. *What?*

"Look, we could've changed things already. Who knows?" She leaned forward on the couch, reached out, and grasped his hands. "This part of it may not be written in stone. I can return with you, and you won't have to work out how to come back to this *now*."

"No—"

A car pulled up outside, a door clunked shut, then the vehicle drove away. Mengus whinnied in the field. Footsteps approached the door, then someone knocked and opened it. Arlan sprung from the couch and sped through to the kitchen as George walked in. Arlan skidded to a halt.

"Hi." George's smile was broad but uneasy. George's gaze flicked from Arlan to Rhiannon, who'd hurried behind him to the kitchen. "I decided to surprise you guys with a visit. I'm ahead on my thesis work and, well, I needed a break. And phone calls and texting only do so much." His gaze rested on Rhiannon as his glasses slid down his nose. "I thought I'd see for myself what you both were up to."

Rhiannon stepped beside Arlan, and for a heartbeat, silence surrounded them.

"We're so pleased to see you, old friend." Arlan clasped George's hand tight and tugged him into a hug, slapping him between the shoulder blades.

George coughed. "Nice to see you too, Arlan." George's words echoed with the thuds on his back.

"So Arlan, you're still here? That's good," George stuttered. "We'll be able to talk more. Believe it or not, I can always do with practicing my Goidelic." He scratched his head. "Though I find it difficult to understand that you haven't yet found your way back."

"We've been figuring out how," Rhiannon said. "Arlan will keep trying the woods on the hill because a forest was the common factor."

"Perhaps you like it too much here." George's voice was tight, and Arlan shifted on his feet.

"He had stuff to figure out, George." Rhiannon widened her eyes at him. "He's travelled between worlds, remember?"

George's shoulders were like a steel board.

"You haven't come up with any brilliant ideas, Mr Celtic Expert," she added.

"Language expert," George retorted, keeping a scowl on Arlan.

Perhaps something was wrong with his friend, George.

"You are well, George?" Arlan asked. "Ye can stay a while?"

"I'm fine, thank you." George waved a hand casually. "I could stay for the weekend, if that's okay with Rhiannon."

"Yes." Rhiannon dragged the word and set a soft frown on George.

George looked through his spectacles from Rhiannon to Arlan and back again, his mouth twitching.

Och, is the man jealous?

Perhaps George could see how Rhiannon and he were... closer than when he last saw them.

But Arlan must endeavour to return Rhiannon to his world eventually. *Her* world also. He was convinced of it, though it must be safe to do so. She had much to learn to be proficient in Dál Cruinne, and George could assist.

"George, I would ask a great favour of you." Arlan took a step closer to his friend.

George's mouth dropped open, loosening his tight expression. He glanced aside to Rhiannon, who shrugged.

"Rhiannon and I have discussed this. When we have discovered the way to access the portal, I will leave, and Rhiannon will wait until I return to take her through to Dál Gaedhle—"

"What!" George's arms stiffened by his sides and his mouth stayed open.

"I want to go," Rhiannon said in a gentle tone. "I belong there."

George blinked twice. "Rhiannon, what are you saying?"

"I'm going. I... I can't tell you why I must. But I will go."

George glared at Arlan. "What do you wish me to do? Don't expect me to be party to this... this... *This* is ridiculous!" George, now red-faced, spoke directly to Rhiannon, and pointed at Arlan with his thumb. "You want to go and be with *him*?"

Rhiannon tensed, then rubbed her neck, the silence stretching. It seemed she couldn't say it. Neither could Arlan.

To voice what I really feel for Rhiannon will make my leaving her all the harder.

George's neck matched his tomato-red cheeks.

"I want to be in Dál Gaedhle," Rhiannon said, allowing no contradiction, "where life's beautiful and there's a world worth fighting for."

George screwed up his face. "Rhiannon, how can you—"

"George," Arlan interrupted, "I understand how difficult it will be for you to see your friend Rhiannon go." He took a breath, for he must leave her for a time as well and what a crevasse it will cause in his own life. "Until I return, would you please assist Rhiannon to improve her Gaelic?"

George raised his eyebrows at him, his lips parted but he didn't answer.

"Before I leave," Arlan continued, "I must obtain gunpowder."

"Wait. What!" Now George spoke. "Why?"

"Cannon." Rhiannon's eyes sparkled. "You're going to make a cannon." Rhiannon's lips curved. "I knew you would, *general.* But how?"

"If I return with some black powder, the sages will determine its ingredients and make it."

"You know it's very volatile?" George's flush had diminished to pink. "People have died making their own. Why do you need to take some with you?" George stared at Arlan with an expression of genuine curiosity. Then his eyes focused inward, appearing as though his mind worked, dragging forth information on the subject. His skin returned to its normal pale colour as he turned his energy to this problem to solve. "Just find out the ingredients. And a formula."

The tension in Arlan's shoulders eased, and Rhiannon blew out a puff of air, her fringe flying up with the gust. George took his laptop from his bag and opened it and soon he had pictures of cannon on his screen.

"Gunpowder is seventy-five per cent potassium nitrate, fifteen per cent charcoal, and ten per cent sulphur. Take a list with you"—he placed his index finger on the bridge of his glasses and pushed them up his nose— "when you go."

"Of those substances, I only know charcoal and sulphur," Arlan said. "We have hot spring caves on our far west coast where we mine sulphur. But potassium nitrate?"

"Bird poo," Rhiannon said. "I read it in a novel once."

"Yes, but you'll require a huge amount. Do you husband fowl in Dál Gaedhle?" George asked. "They would be an easy source. It's also called saltpetre. Wouldn't know the translation for that. Odds are, if your world is so like ours, you have the same substance but a different name for it."

"The sages will solve this for me. It *is* possible. Very good." Arlan took the notepad from the coffee table and wrote all he could regarding this topic.

"Sage means *wise*, but are they scientists?" George asked. "They'll have to experiment with this. I hope they don't blow themselves up in the process. Like I said, it's very volatile."

"Och, I've enquired of the right learned man. Please record this for me." Arlan handed him the notepad covered in scrawling in his own language.

"Wow." George examined Arlan's writing, then made notes of his own.

"And I'll endeavour to explain to our smiths the garment of looped metal, which ye named *chain maille.*" He gave a slight nod. "It will be a protection."

Rhiannon ran to her room and moments later returned holding a silvery cloth. "This is fake chain maille—made with metallic thread. They make real mail from interlinked metal rings. But this should be enough of a hint for your smiths." She handed it to him, then stood back. "As you'll try to leave again, and possibly succeed, we should have a farewell meal for you, Arlan." Rhiannon's tight smile didn't reach her moist eyes.

"That would be grand, lass." Arlan spoke gently to her and forced a smile he didn't feel, so stiff it may have come across as a grimace.

Rhiannon went to the kitchen and soon the clanking of pots and the *snap* of a knife on a wooden block came from that direction. Ten minutes later, she walked from the kitchen.

"I've put on a roast." She leaned against the door jamb.

"So, if you're using this in a cannon, your balls need to be perfectly spherical." George didn't look up at Rhiannon but continued his instructions to Arlan. "You must use a mould. They used to roll them in barrels to smooth them out."

"How do you know all this?" Rhiannon wiped her hands on a towel.

"I enjoy history." George's mouth turned up in a half-grimace. "Medieval warfare is fascinating. Although from what Arlan says, Dál Gaedhle seems a little less advanced. No offence."

"I shall collect my possessions." Arlan stepped to the umbrella stand at the door.

"You mean your weapons and your horse. You only came with the clothes you wore. And that wasn't much." George added his last comment under his breath.

Arlan retrieved his weapons from the doorway and walked to the living room, holding his sword.

"Aye, I would be lost without *Camhanaich.*" He pulled his sword from its sheath, the familiar soft snick a comfort to his soul, for emotions swirled within him, confusing his desire to return home, and painting it with a sadness.

"*Camhanaich?*" George asked. "You named your sword *twilight?*"

"Aye." Arlan stood tall and set a stance, ready to cut through a foe. "For she will send my enemies into the darkness or into the light. Either way, they are gone from this life."

"Whoa." George gulped, his eyes fixed on the shiny sword point.

Rhiannon's gaze locked with Arlan's, her cheeks flushed, and a beautiful smile covered her full lips. Arlan's mouth tugged at the corners. He would share this moment with her. She scrunched the towel in her trembling hands, her lips parting.

"Please don't, Rhiannon." He gave it as a gentle command for her not to comment, but the tightness in his throat added an unwanted hoarseness to his voice.

Her shoulders drooped slightly, but her features hardened. "I'll put the vegies on." She turned to the kitchen.

Arlan sheathed *Camhanaich.* The hiss of the sword returning to her home sent his mind to his warriors. Erin had lain dead in Bàn's arms, and who knew how Kyle had fared after bolting past Morrigan.

His heart stilled for a moment. Aye, he *must* find the way home to his troop.

And take up *his* role in *his* world.

The aroma of roasting boar wafted through the small cottage. George finished his notes and handed the pages to Arlan, then walked to his bag in the kitchen.

"I brought us something special." George drew a bottle from his gear. "A single malt from the Highlands. Very appropriate now Arlan is definitely planning to leave."

The meal was soon ready, and Rhiannon dished up the vegetables while Arlan cut the meat, the carving knife sliding through the succulent, roasted hog. He served the portions, then sat cramped beside Rhiannon with George opposite him at the tiny kitchen table. They all ate, none speaking between mouthfuls. George had relaxed, his hard words and glances as sharp as daggers had eased with Arlan's talk of his determination to return to his own realm. This man he called a friend, but was also an opponent regarding Rhiannon's affections.

Arlan swallowed hard on a mouthful of meat.

What am I thinking?

Slim were the chances of him returning to Rhiannon. Coming back in her lifetime would only happen if he could work a portal. If *working* was even the correct way of managing one. Even if he found it... was traversing it a safe endeavour? Perhaps only by sheer luck he'd survived the transport between worlds. All the more reason to leave Rhiannon behind.

Or perhaps by a mage's devices he'd come through to this land. Or the portal could be a natural phenomenon, such as the Ley lines Rhiannon had found on Google. And how would he direct himself to this place at the desired moment? Would he even return to Dál Cruinne?

And be with Rhiannon again, in either world—

George scooted out his chair. The scraping screeched through Arlan, breaking into his thoughts and grating on his nerves. George rose from the table and put his plate in the sink.

"You're very quiet, Arlan." Rhiannon's soft fingers brushed his hand resting on the table.

Warmth shivered up his arm, the hairs rising at her touch, and he stifled the longing it evoked. He lifted his gaze to hers, his throat so thick he couldn't answer.

I will leave her and trust she will wait and not allow George to cause her to forget me.

Rhiannon and Arlan cleared the table and washed the dishes, then joined George by the fire. He'd retrieved the single malt from his bag and held three glasses, and now poured a generous dram into each glass, the pleasing glug of whisky leaving the bottle filling the quiet. He handed the drinks to Arlan and Rhiannon.

"*Slàinte mhor!*" George raised his glass in salute.

"*Slàinte mhor!*" Arlan replied with Rhiannon.

Arlan sipped. It was a braw *uisge-beatha.*

Och, no. This scotch is magnificent.

Rich to the tongue, warm in the throat and glowing in the belly. The smoky vapour lingered in Arlan's nostrils and left the memory of peat on his palate.

Rhiannon's face glowed in the firelight and her russet hair gleamed deep red. George stood on the hearthstone, facing Arlan and Rhiannon on the couch.

"When the ancient Celts celebrated, they told stories and sang songs." George took a sip of the amber spirit, then voiced a throaty *hmm*. "So Arlan, as the guest and honorary Celt, I wish you to be the bard and tell us a story, if Rhiannon doesn't mind."

Rhiannon dipped her head in agreement, then she and George raised their glasses.

Arlan grinned and snorted a short laugh. "I'm no bard." He rose. "But I shall try my best, friends."

He stepped to the hearth, running his fingers through his beard, then drained his glass of *uisge beatha.* Perhaps the deep golden liquid would do its task and loosen his tongue.

If only Douglas were here with his ready jokes and riddles.

176

His fingers fumbled as he placed the glass on the mantle, his troop's faces flashing through his mind in a blink of an eye—Bàn's blond features lingering. He'd see them soon.

Maybe.

"Once upon a time—"

Rhiannon raised her palm toward him. "You're not starting with *once upon a time.*"

"Is that no' how you begin stories here?"

"That's how you begin a fairy tale."

"Yes, we don't want a children's story." George moved to sit beside Rhiannon, giving Arlan centre stage on the hearth. "Give us a good old bard's tale."

"It won't rhyme, if that's what ye wish." Arlan's face heated at his lack of skill in such things. "But it will be adult. And from the lore of Dál Cruinne."

George indicated for Arlan to begin, so Arlan cleared his throat.

"The Ancients say the sun is the silvery hair of a goddess who wears a blue robe, giving the sky its colour."

Rhiannon put up her hand.

"Aye, lass, ye have a question? But I've scarcely begun."

"The sun is *really* silver?"

"Aye."

"Please continue, Arlan." George glared out of the corner of his eye at Rhiannon.

"This goddess comes out at daybreak and spends all the day spreading her volumi-nous skirts across the sky."

Rhiannon raised her hand again.

"Rhiannon!" George faced her, scowling.

"But what if it's cloudy?"

"The clouds are her underskirts," Arlan explained, then continued the tale. "The moon is the shining head of her husband, and the dark of night is his cloak."

Rhiannon opened her mouth and the look on her face told him she readied another question.

"No." George and Arlan spoke in unison.

"The *stars* are the jewels in his cloak," Arlan continued, "for he is a king."

Rhiannon tapped her foot.

"What, lass?" Arlan asked.

"It's a valid question." She glanced aside at George, who frowned at her. "What about when it's a half moon or a crescent moon? What's going on then?"

"At these times he is half turned away, going about his kingly business."

Rhiannon squinted. "Are you making this up as you go along?"

"Rhiannon," George hissed.

"No, I am not, for I have not the talent for such," Arlan protested. "This is truly a story the sages tell us. Now, if I may continue?"

Rhiannon bowed her head, her cheeks pinking.

"It is only possible for them to meet at dawn and dusk," Arlan went on. "These are the moments in which they make love."

Rhiannon and George both stared at Arlan from the couch, their faces a vague blur to him as his thoughts shouted for his attention.

Arlan gasped. "*Beul an latha* and *beul na h-oidhche.*"

"The dawn of the day and the dusk of evening," George translated.

"The *time between times*. Our ancient traditions say natural magic would happen at these moments of the day. I know not more than this"—Arlan focused on Rhiannon, her expression reflecting her dawning understanding— "but it may be my way home."

THIRTY-THREE

— · —

There is beauty in the sky,
Ages in the rocks.
Wisdom in the trees.
Provision in the sun and the rain.
Love in the warmth.
Strength in the cold.
And it is home.

SAGE GLIOCAS
(2870-2962 POST DRAGON WARS)

Abernethy, Scotland

George's snores in the living room reached me in the kitchen.

"He brought us a grand Scotch." Arlan stood at the open backdoor, tilted his head and downed the last of his dram.

"Well, he enjoyed most of it." I glanced over at the couch where George lay sprawled. "He'll be out for a while."

Arlan stepped out into the night. I followed, the cool, crisp air caressing my face, and my vision unable to leave Arlan's shadowed form. His tall, broad figure, though shaded subtly in the moonlight, drew me like a beacon.

Thank you, George, for falling asleep.

Now I had Arlan to myself. It was like an instinct—that desire for exclusivity. Wanting just to be with him...

Arlan stood on the grass beside the birdbath, and I joined him. The birdbath was empty; the lichen growing in it had dried, and now was a grey crust in the night's light. We both turned our faces to the not-quite-full moon, which shone clear in between wispy clouds passing its silvery orb.

I looked to the horizon, from where the sun would come. That ball in the sky which, when it decided to show its face, cheered me with its warmth and light.

179

Don't rise today. Please. Because that would mean he goes.

Beside me, his warmth radiated, touching my bare skin—neck, face and forearms. I turned to him. He now stood closer. So much closer.

When did he move?

"You're a silent one. Used to sneaking up on your enemies—*general?*" My tone came out cheeky as I tried to hide the other emotions that plagued me tonight. My guts were churning.

Well, it's better than showing how nervous I am.

A shiver started in my centre. From the cold? *No.* From Arlan so near me.

Moonlight cast a gleam on him, softening his features. Curves of muscle, strands of long black hair. The scar on his eyebrow was still pink but fading above navy pupils... deep pools in the night.

Eyes on me.

He looked at me like he was memorising every feature.

Just as I did for him.

The surrounding silence lifted to the night and ricocheted back.

"Rhiannon, I cannot leave without... There's something you must know..."

Is he stumbling over his words?

"I know not what it will mean..." he continued, "the implications of what I'm about to say."

He swallowed, the soft *gulp* coming over to me. He stood so near I saw the artery in his neck, right next to that throat muscle, pulsating in time with his heartbeat.

"I love you." His voice trembled.

My heart did it again, just like the first time he spoke to me... skipped a beat.

Say it girl. This is your chance.

"I love you back. A million-fold. Take me with—"

I was within his arms, pressed to his chest, his lips devouring mine—savouring me.

I kissed him in return, running my hands into that black mane, his skin hot, his breath faltering.

He kissed me more and my knees no longer held me up. He lifted me so I could wrap my legs around him, and he hugged me closer. Chest to chest—his heart bounding like Mengus at a gallop.

He broke away, leaving me gasping for air.

"I love you... I can't stop myself." Apology slipped through his words, and his lips pressed together, drowning in that black beard... like I was.

"I knew you did." I finally found my voice. "Well, that you *would.* 'Cos, like I said, when I met you at the Celtic Festival... it seemed like we were together."

He grazed his teeth over his lower lip, then rubbed the back of his neck with one hand, supporting my weight with his other.

"Our love will *be?*" I asked, but he didn't answer. *Wait!* "You mean it's possible it couldn't? Because you're determined to go without me? Or because nobility is a prerequisite?"

My heart was now in a turmoil, tightening by the moment.

180

"You're betrothed to a princess." I cringed. I'd thought with my mouth—again. *Well, it was out. Too late to retrieve it.*

He gave his head a brief shake. "No."

"Well, you're a king's son. You're bound to be."

So why did he kiss me? And tell me he loves me?

"No." Understanding dawned in his expression. "I am not betrothed to any woman. I would never betray such a promise."

I squinted at him. "So, you get to choose your wife?"

"Aye." His answer held a silent, *of course.*

"Must she be a clan noblewoman?" I pursued.

"Aye, it's a necessity." He swallowed. "For resources, alliances and joining warbands."

"So, I may not qualify? Probably don't even come near to it."

He shrugged, then kissed me again, playing with my lips as though he was tasting me. A soft, nervous chuckle rose from his throat.

"Don't leave," I said. I pleaded.

"I must return."

"No. I mean, don't leave *without* me."

Rain pattered on my head and Arlan looked skyward. Clouds had thickened, covering the night, and he blinked against the drops on his lids.

I slid from hugging his waist with my legs and we ran inside, leaving the rain to fill the birdbath and wash away the unspoken words of our conversation.

Rain fell steadily, its gentle patter on the roof and windows keeping George asleep on my living room couch. I now stood by the kitchen window, its chill touching my face, and my vision on the dark night outside. I shifted focus from the raindrops travelling down the windowpane to the reflection that bounced off the glass.

Arlan sat at the kitchen table, where we'd spent the rest of the night. If he were correct, I didn't have much longer to be with him, and I'd spend every remaining second beside Arlan Finnbar MacEnoicht, the man who was once a stranger and now the one I loved.

He'd told me of the beauty of Dál Gaedhle. His words of his world were almost poetic and voiced with love. He spoke of his warriors and his sword-brother Bàn with affection. But not so much his actual brother, who, as the eldest, would become a clan chief. He'd told of their broch, the round tower castle of his clan lands. It sounded like the brochs around Scotland, all ruins now, and the most intact way out on the Orkney Islands.

"Ye should learn to ride"—his soft voice drew me from my thoughts— "practice the Gaelic, and keep attending self-defence classes, for they'll be good preparation."

I faced him, putting conviction into my voice. "I'll be okay. I'll keep out of the way."

"What?"

"When we ride through."

Arlan rose from the table and grasped my upper arms in a warm, firm grip, tightening with the corresponding widening of his eyes. "Ye have nae idea of what I speak. I was in the midst of a charge! Ye saw me." His volume increased with every word, threatening to wake George. "I'll most likely return to that charge and kill my opponent. Or he'll slay me. And then you—after raping you." His faced loomed closer. "You are not returning with me. And that is final."

"But I *can* fight. *You* saw me with that guy on the hill—"

"Self-defence classes do not make a Dál Gaedhle warrior!" His voice surrounded me.

I stepped back, disengaging my arms from his massive hands. The man standing in front of me was Arlan Finnbar MacEnoicht the war chief, issuing commands. My gut niggled. I'd always relied on myself and had managed that way since Mum and Dad died. I could see his point, though. The niggle dissolved a touch... he cared enough about me to be concerned.

No. Not just *concerned*. He *loved* me. I returned to that moment, reinforcing the memory. The inflection of his voice, the closeness of his breath, the intensity in his eyes darkened by the moonlight. And I'd summoned enough guts to respond with how I truly felt.

His tall form standing in front of me brought me back to now. His firm stare held as he took a step closer. I stood my ground but drew in deeply, filling my lungs with his musky male scent.

If only I didn't have to be without him.

George stirred, the couch creaking not far from us in my tiny cottage. "What's all the yelling about?" Sleep slurred his waking voice.

Arlan let go of me and faced George, crossing his arms. I stood taller, lifting my chin and holding it there.

Neither of us answered George.

George's eyes flicked from me to Arlan and back again, then he glanced at his watch. "We need to get up the hill if you've got to be there for sunrise."

"Aye, I'll saddle Mengus." Arlan collected his weapons and strode outside to the makeshift stable. I leaned close to the window, my exhalation misting on the cold glass and obscuring my view of Arlan traipsing through the rain-dimmed pre-dawn.

"It's great he's figured out the way back, yes?" George sounded the cheeriest he'd ever been.

I remained staring out, my fists chilling against the cold windowpane, and my breath hitching as Arlan brought his war horse from the shed. George and I put on our coats and stepped outside to join him.

The sky lightened with grey rain clouds hugging the hill, bleeding into the forest, their edges undefined in what remained of the night. The Iron Age Fortification earthworks were lost in the rain. We trudged up the hill in silence, our raincoats slowly drenching. Rainwater dripped down Arlan's bare shoulders and his long black hair, today in a single plait, fell down his back, wet and heavy, like the tail of a despondent horse. The rain pattered on the bare branches of the deciduous trees and the pine needles glistened and sagged with the weight of collected water drops. The path was slushy, and I slipped often. Arlan reached out to grab my arm and stay a fall more than once.

Mengus snorted and nickered, and swished his tail. I could have sworn that war horse knew what was about to happen.

Arlan's face was stony. No doubt preparing himself to re-enter a battle. I couldn't speak; my lungs were so tight I could hardly breathe.

"I've just checked." George looked up from his smartwatch. "Sunrise is at 06:17. We'd better hurry. It's 06:09."

He was the only one with a voice.

We were soon at the spot where Arlan had arrived, as far as I could tell.

"Farewell, friend." He extended his hand to George. "I'm indebted to you for teaching me your tongue."

George's grin almost split his face. "You're welcome. *Slàn leat.*"

Arlan turned to me, his face tight, black brows dipping over navy-blue flecked eyes. My gut clenched.

I will not let him go without me!

"I'm coming." I grabbed the sword belt across his chest with both fists. "I *can* do this."

"What?" George's tone came out almost as a snarl.

"No. Rhiannon. Ye are not." The knotty muscles of Arlan's arms stood out.

The rain pattered on the branches and dripped from the sparce leaves, like the trees themselves cried. Arlan's glare didn't falter. His massive hands covered mine, releasing my grip from the leather and clasping them firmly between us. They were rough on my skin but filled with the warmth of life.

"I know ye are brave." Gentleness tempered his voice. "But you need to find the courage to allow me to leave without you."

He has *returned. He* will *go.*

My throat was so tight I couldn't answer. He pulled me into a hug and pressed my face against his chest, where his heart beat strong and loud against my ear.

If only I could stay here, surrounded by his body heat, inhaling his spicy scent.

My eyes pricked where tears would force themselves out. I should be going home too, but there was truth in what he'd said. My insides softened a fraction. He just wanted to protect me.

"*Slàn leat.*" His voice muffled through his chest, then he pressed a kiss into my hair. Releasing me, he nudged me away.

I still couldn't reply. Couldn't say farewell. I savoured the heat on my cheek—left from him. My tears escaped, their warmth cooling as they trickled over the traces of his touch.

Arlan mounted Mengus as the wind whipped the trees, stirring the branches and showering me with heavy drops. He slid his arm into his shield straps, the leather grips creaking in protest, and unsheathed his sword.

"How shall I tell if the sun rises? The clouds cover the sky." Arlan scanned the horizon, with Mengus curvetting beneath him.

George shrugged. "You don't have long, it's almost 06:17."

183

Arlan turned his horse tightly, his eyes never leaving mine.

I may never see him again.

Ever.

My insides tore.

Arlan kicked Mengus to a canter and travelled ten metres down the track to the small open space beneath the trees that had witnessed his arrival. I gripped my hands and wrung them together, my vision glued to my warrior's back.

My warrior! I groaned and sprang to a run.

"Rhiannon!" George caught my arm, his grasp firm and fingers digging in. "You'll get trampled. Stay here." He tugged me back to his side; my feet skidded on the damp track.

"I want to go." My protest did nothing to ease George's grip on my arm.

For a second, I caught a flash in George's expression. It was as if he didn't want to risk that I *would* go.

I turned to Mengus' heavy hoof tread as Arlan continued his ride along the forest track.

He didn't disappear.

"What?" George checked his watch in the dim light.

I scanned the horizon, where the sky's edge glowed with a stronger light. Arlan had turned and now rode toward where we stood, his gaze fixed on me. I wrenched my arm free from George's grip.

"Arlan, I *have* to come with you." My words vibrated at the edges. "I deserve to find my roots! You can't deny me that!"

He slowed Mengus and re-sheathed his sword in its leather baldric, not turning his animal. "Och no! Ye are nae listening." His loud voice was sharp, like the dagger at his belt. "It is *not* safe."

"But I—"

"It's for your *protection*," Arlan growled and Mengus skittered sideways.

I stopped sharp, heat exploding in my chest at the unfairness of it all.

So, he thinks I'm pathetic!

"You're a *chauvinist!*" My voice cracked.

"Och, I ken not what that is!" Arlan's mouth tightened. He walked his horse right up to me, leaned over in the saddle and, grabbing my jacket, pulled me to him. His warm mouth covered mine, pressed hard and with longing, my tears mingling with our kiss. Mengus stirred and jostled us.

Behind me, George grunted a loud but unintelligible protest.

Arlan pulled his lips from mine. "I'll learn the ways of a portal, then I *will* come back for ye." Arlan spoke close to my face, out of focus, so I only felt his words against my mouth, in the softest whisper. So soft, I was sure George never heard.

"You'd better." I spoke just as quietly into his bearded face.

Arlan released his hold on me, turned his war horse and kicked his sides. Mengus broke into a gallop.

The sun peeked over the horizon and blazed through the strip of the clear sky between land and the dense cloud mass above, turning the water vapour a brilliant magenta. Sunlight hit Arlan, a golden touch on bare back muscle covered by a sword's leather sheath. Mengus shrieked a whinny and Arlan unsheathed his sword again, roaring a battle cry like the Highlanders of old. Shivers charged down my spine, joining the tingles left by his kiss.

He was gone.

The dirt from Mengus' hooves fell to the ground on the empty track.

Thirty-Four

A band of brothers may your warriors be.
Able, faithful, daring.
They your shield, your spear, your strong arm.
Weapons forged in conflict.
Tempered in adversity.
May your hall echo with their tales.
Your rafters ring with their laughter.

ADVICE TO WAR CHIEFS
WARRIOR SAGE TAPAÌDH
(4009-4059 POST DRAGON WARS)

World of Dál Cruinne
Post Dragon Wars Year 6083
The Border Between Dál Gaedhle and Dál Gallain

Bright glare for a fraction of a breath silenced Arlan's war cry in an enveloping white. His voice returned, piercing his ears, rocking the trees, vibrating the ground and searing his throat. Arlan grasped his sword tight and drew his shield closer to his body as Mengus reared and shrieked a whinny, landing with his front hooves stirring the dust.

Arlan pulled his stallion round, scanning the scene.

Dead bandits lay where they fell, their weapons pillaged, and useful items confiscated. The campfire's hearth sat dark and cold, as though extinguished for days. Makeshift shelters stood ripped and torn. Not a warrior, horse, hostage, nor bandit within his range of sight.

"Argh!" He lifted his face to the sky as his body rocked and his mind reeled. "*Not* like the Fae, then?"

I could have brought Rhiannon with me.

His nostrils flared. "Dragon's *damainte* breath!"

His chest and shoulders heaved.

"At least I'm in the right place in the right world!" he shouted, kicking Mengus to a canter and heading to the exact place of his re-entry.

He rode through. *Nothing.* No white light enclosing him in a silence.

He did it again.

Naught.

"Too late!" he roared, his lungs searing.

Mengus side-stepped and skittered, nickering uncomfortably. The taste of dust sat on Arlan's tongue. He leaned forward in the saddle, resting his head on his sword-arm, and gritted his teeth, a burning ache filling him.

He could wait till sunrise and try again. But where—no, *when*—would he return to?

"Nae"—he lifted his head— "I must learn more of this portal." He faced the horizon's glow, the silver sun of his home world now gone to her rest till morning. "Wait for me, Rhiannon," he whispered.

Eifion would know. Or if not, the wise sage would discover the truths of the portal's mechanism for him. But now he was home, and his life called. Aye, Rhiannon had challenged his attitudes and stirred him on to take up his responsibilities.

And that he would now do.

The soft glow of twilight faded, and darkness was falling. He searched for tracks in the diminishing light. A cluster of hoof prints churned the ground at the far end of the camp and led away to the east.

That would be the bandits' tracks.

He trotted Mengus back to the campsite. By the far firepit many footprints over-lapped each other, which led to two sets of hoofprints with drag lines travelling away and to the north.

Arlan followed the trail. A full moon rose, shedding its light on his path, causing deep shadows that allowed him to track the ruts in the night.

I must be grateful for that.

He rode on, at times guessing where the ruts led, losing them for a distance, then picking them up once more through dead leaf matter or loose soil. One set of drag-lines would be a litter for Erin's body, and Bàn would treat her with the respect a fallen warrior deserved. And the other?

Och, they had wounded.

Arlan's mind whirled, and his whole body jittered. He would soon be with Bàn, who knew and loved him well. Bàn would grieve Erin's loss and wait in a safe place for Arlan's return. His brother Kyle would be ready with condemnation for his irresponsible action of deserting.

"How do I explain my absence?" Arlan shrugged, patting Mengus' neck. His stallion gave a soft nicker. "Ye are right, Mengus. I'll tell the truth, for naught else will suffice."

The night stretched on, and the trail continued through another forest and along the base of the mountain range. His troop would wait for him somewhere. Bàn would not forsake him. Yet he had no idea of how much time had passed for them.

He rode on, blinking back sleep over some leagues. Light twinkled in a shadow of a copse, so he kicked Mengus to a canter.

He drew closer to the light and slowed to a walk. A campfire's glowing coals spilled its orange light on sleepers resting beside it. A capercaillie, not a night bird, drummed its distinctive warning—a familiar signal-call.

Arlan halted near a clump of rowan. "Bàn?"

The branches close by rustled and the soft crunch of footsteps on loose dirt approached, and Bàn's golden head gleamed in the moonlight. Arlan slid off Mengus, and Bàn embraced him in brawny arms. By the campfire, the dogs stirred, and sleepers shuffled in their plaids, awaking.

"Where have you been, Arlan?" Bàn's question was husky as he released his hold.

"I have been—och, ye will scarcely believe it—to the other world." There, he'd said it and, so far, didn't feel foolish for having done so.

"The other—?" Bàn paused, a soft gulp coming from him. "You will tell me all, sword-brother. But you disappeared from us, Arlan." Bàn shook his head, the moonlight casting shadows across a bewildered expression. "I held Erin... Your war cry ceased. I looked to see if the bandit so intent upon you had injured you... overcome ye. But you... weren't there. Ye were nowhere." Bàn bowed his head and sighed.

Arlan placed his hand on Bàn's arm. His knotty muscles were tighter than usual.

"I trusted ye would lead the warband well. I saw Erin's loss. I ken ye cared for her. She was a worthy fighter. Brave. True."

A sob escaped Bàn's lips, then he pressed them tight and cleared his throat. "They pursued us not. The bandits fled. Erin wasn't our only casualty, my Lord Arlan."

"Take me to my troop." He led Mengus behind Bàn, steeling himself for what Bàn would show him of how his warriors had fared.

They approached the campfire which had burned down to coals and Arlan counted the sleeping bodies. Only one warrior was missing. People stirred, and the dogs whined. Angus jumped from where he lay, his sword part way out of its sheath.

"Lord Arlan!" He bowed, re-sheathing his blade. "Oh, you cannae know how relieved we are—"

"Golden barrels of *uisge beatha*!" Douglas rose to his feet. "Lord Arlan, ye are restored to us."

Adele strode to him and enveloped him in a hug. "Pardon, lord." She released him from her burly embrace. "It's so good to see you. We thought you lost."

"Some of us believed you lost." Leigh held back the hound by his side. "Others knew it to be impossible."

A groan of effort came from Arlan's left. Muir rose stiffly, gingerly holding his heavily bandaged arm, his wrinkles cutting deep lines in his face. Kyle's man assisted Muir to stand, but the warrior shook him off. Muir stared silently at Arlan and he gave a nod in reply.

A slight form wrapped in a blanket lay under a tree a fair way from the fire's heat. Half a dozen women, those rescued from the bandits, huddled close beside the fire, and they stirred wide-eyed at his approach. He smiled a grave greeting to them, and their hunched shoulders eased.

"What's the tally of the injured?" Arlan ran his gaze over his troop, searching for signs of bandaged injury.

"Muir received a deep scrape. The others the usual bruises." Bàn pointed to the fresh scar on Arlan's eyebrow. "Ye were injured also?"

"Aye, but not here," Arlan replied.

A frown flickered across Bàn's brow, then he continued. "Your brother, my Lord Arlan..."

"What of Kyle? He sleeps, for if awake," Arlan whispered, "I'm sure to have a battering from his tongue."

"Your brother Kyle sleeps for certain. He received a blow to his head. We've bandaged him, but sleep is all he does."

A sharp cold blade sliced Arlan's insides. "Take me to him."

"My Lord Arlan." Morrigan crouched beside a quiet form at the edge of the camp.

Arlan stepped closer to Kyle, who lay on a litter. So, one set of drag marks belonged to Kyle! Now detached from his horse, the litter became his stretcher. He lay still, his head tightly bandaged, his ribcage slowly rising and falling. With his eyelids closed, Kyle slumbered like a helpless child.

"What happened?" Arlan could hardly muster a whisper.

If only he'd received the berating. *I would welcome it so much more than this.*

"The bandit who charged you, my lord." Morrigan lifted her head, her eyes glistening. "When you disappeared from sight... in front of all of us... he headed straight for Prince Kyle."

"Aye, lord." Angus picked up the recounting. "It was as though he ignored us."

"Blades and bows! But the *bassa* was after ye both." Douglas let an expletive fly. "Pardon, ladies."

"On his first swing at Lord Kyle, his blade missed," Muir reported with a gravelly voice and the eye of a seasoned warrior. "He turned his steed and battered down with the pommel of his sword. My Lord Arlan, I heard the crack."

Arlan closed his eyes and cringed, choking down bile.

"A fatal wound for certain, my lord prince," Muir continued, "but one that takes its cruel time in the killing."

"I've seen men recover from such a wounding," Leigh interjected. "A horse kicked my cousin. Left a dent in his skull for the rest of his life, but months after the blow he awoke."

"Aye, but was he ever the same?" Angus asked.

"Shh!" echoed through the gathered group.

Morrigan knelt on one knee, her head bowed. "Forgive me, lord. I tried, but Lord Kyle ignored me. The only way to stop him following you was to draw my weapon. And I couldn't do that to a prince... If only I had—"

"Hush now, Lady Morrigan." Arlan's sigh whistled past his teeth. "I know my brother. If he was determined, nothing could have prevented him. Berate yourself not."

"There are healer sages skilled in tending to such wounds to the skull." Morrigan moved back to the sleeping Kyle and tucked his plaid closer to his chin. "We should

JENN LEES

seek them out as we journey home, for maybe we will travel past a sage hold where some reside."

"Aye, we should enquire." Bàn placed his warm grip on Arlan's shoulder. "My lord, ye have a lot to bear. And you're weary-worn. Rest now. We can do naught until we commence our journey home, which we shall now we are reunited with our battle chief."

"Aye!" The shout of approval resounded around the group.

Arlan remained by Kyle's inert form, his own heart almost as immobile from a numbness. Beside the fire, faces glowed in the light of the hot coals. Warriors gazed at him with adoring eyes and smiles of relief.

"I'm grateful ye waited for me, my friends." Arlan said, blinking at the emotion in his voice. "I thought perhaps my brother's words had rung true in your minds, and you had believed I'd run and abandoned you all."

"Never, lord," Angus said with a vehemence. Grunts of agreement travelled around the fire.

Arlan's throat threatened to close as a silence settled amongst his troop.

"But where were ye, lord?" Angus enquired, bold as ever.

Arlan rubbed his thigh. "I have... travelled to a far place." He held up his hand at their gasps.

"To the Fae?" Angus said, ignoring his upraised hand.

"I'll explain further, but first I wish to speak with Lord Bàn."

"Leigh," Bàn ordered, snapping all out of their hush. "Your watch."

Leigh called the hounds to heel and walked to the lookout point where Bàn had met Arlan.

Arlan tugged Bàn aside. "I can't sleep, my friend. Not until I tell you where I've been, for I surely have a tale to relay." Arlan's tongue was thick around words in his own language, as if a lifetime had passed since he had spoken so many together.

Arlan walked with Bàn, who'd begun a trek to a place not far from the group where they could speak in private.

"How long have I been away?" Arlan asked.

"Away?" Bàn blinked. "Our skirmish was but yesterday."

"Yesterday?" Arlan's voice rose.

Bàn gripped his arm and pulled him further from the troop settling back to sleep. They came upon a clearing where a standing stone stood tall and solitary in a level place. Swirls of circular pattern were engraved on the top half and runes spoke their words beneath. Moonlight illuminated it like an electric sign from Rhiannon's world. Arlan took a breath, stifling an ache in his chest.

Rhiannon, I may never see you again.

"I've lived in another world for two turns of the moon."

Bàn started. "So, ye *have* been with the Fae. You're fortunate to have returned."

"Och, no. Not the world of the Fae, but a land like ours. Well, parts o' it anyway. I've learned much, which shall take days in the recounting. But I must return and bring a woman—"

"I thought so." Bàn grinned. "Ye had that look about you."

"Och, no. She is from here. She also travelled to the other world when but a bairn. She must come home, for she doesn't fit in that world. Rhiannon is too gifted, too clever, too smart, too beautiful—"

"And ye are too besotted, brother."

"She is a noblewoman from a noble clan, I'm certain. I wish to investigate. But tell none, I beg you. This must stay secret, for if I cannot find her origins..." How much should he even relay to his closest friend? *I may never find a way back.* "I shall search for a portal. Perhaps there may be another one, maybe even near my home clan lands on the coast. Or near The Keep." By all that is good, he wished to not return to this one in enemy lands. "But I *must* find one." He blinked at the desperation in his tone.

"Portal?" The word shot out from Bàn. "Ye sound like an ancient sage."

Arlan shook his head. "The portal that returned me didn't work when I tried to go back for her... for Rhiannon." His breath caught at her name. But now his responsibilities would hold him here. *My own wishes will have to wait.* "We must find a healer for our wounded." He placed a hand on his friend's arm. "Bàn, I must go to my father and beg his forgiveness." He stared at the ground.

"Why, Arlan? None account you with any blame for your brother's injury. He disobeyed your orders and followed us into a skirmish that he should have never entered."

"My father asked me to observe only. To not engage. I angrily rushed in."

"You protected people. A warrior's duty." Bàn straightened, his tone filled with a conviction at the rightness of the act. "At your command, we saved these women. The sole survivors of a massacre that we will report to the àrd rìgh. Arlan, don't berate yourself so. The àrd rìgh will understand. I support your decisions, so do we all."

"You are faithful, Bàn, and I'm grateful for you. But I require forgiveness for much more. I have been self-seeking." He faced Bàn. "You were right, my truest friend and sword-brother. When I protested that my father and, indeed, social traditions, forced a vocation upon me, with my own will regarding the matter ignored, you said we all have a predestined role to fulfil. My time in the other world has shown me I do have a choice to make. And I choose for my land and my people. I will be clan war-chief, and I'm okay with it." He finished with a slight nod.

"O... kay...?" In the moonlight, Bàn's face screwed to crinkles.

THIRTY-FIVE

— • —

It streams along unrelenting.
An irresistible current in an ever-flowing burn.
I see all.
Behind and afore.
What has been; what is now; what will be.

VISIONS AND SAYINGS OF THE BLIND LADY SAGE

The Border Between Dál Gaedhle and Dál Gallain

"Our diversion to ensure our paths didn't cross with the bandits has caused us to be further north than on our outward journey, Lord Arlan." Bàn threw the last dregs of tea from breaking fast on the campfire sending a hiss of thin smoke swirling in Arlan's eyes.

Arlan blinked away the sting. Dogs whined and horses snorted as warriors saddled their mounts and loaded the gear.

"We must find the nearest village and seek a healer." Bàn leaned closer to Arlan and lowered his voice. "Muir slept poorly. Morrigan reports he has a fever. We may have two warriors succumbing to their injuries if we don't soon receive the ministrations of a healer sage."

Arlan rested his hands on his belt and took in their surroundings under a crisp-blue sky. To their right sat a curious mountain group, broch-like in formation. Three tall mounds of rock sat together with the top of their dome-like rock towers visible in the near distance. Further along, and northeast of these, rose the Central Meadhan Mountain Range. Tall and majestic, they guarded the middle of Dál Cruinne and fed the fast-flowing rivers that coursed their way to the seas.

"As we move from these lesser mountains," Arlan ordered, pointing to the broch-like group, "we shall keep the Central Meadhan Mountain Range to our right and head for the point of the sun's emergence on the horizon. This will surely head us northwest and to The Keep." He mounted Mengus and nudged him to a walk.

192

Kyle lay silent on his litter dragged behind his horse led by Adele, and Morrigan rode behind, keeping a watchful eye on the casualty. Erin's horse pulled the litter carrying her body. Douglas assisted Muir onto his horse and rode close beside him as Muir leaned heavily into the saddle. All, except for Muir, rode with one of the rescued women behind.

The nearest habitation was a small hamlet half a day's ride, comprising a dozen wattle-and-daube dwellings and no tavern. An elderly man sitting on his front step greeted them. They were fortunate, he reported, for a sage hold hugged the base of the Central Meadhan Mountains, not a day's ride from this village. Healers lived there, he assured Arlan. Arlan thanked him, and the party headed in the direction the man had indicated.

The sun had neared its journey to the horizon when Arlan led his troop through vineyards that went on for leagues. Finally, the high wooden walls of the sage hold came into view. A forest grew on the hill behind it and animals grazed in meadows to the far side. A high outer wall of vertical wooden poles surrounded the high mound. The gate opened and a lone sage in a green robe stepped toward them. Behind him in the near distance, stood another wooden fence, the equivalent of an inner bailey wall.

"Greetings, friend," Arlan said. "We require the aid of a sage skilled in the healing arts. Will you help us?"

The sage wore a welcoming smile, his tanned and leather-beaten skin, crinkling at the outer corners of his eyes, hinted at many hours spent outside. "Ye are welcome to our hold, for we observe ye carry an injured man, and another who barely sits ahorse. Please enter."

Arlan released a huge sigh, and they rode their horses in through the tall wooden gate. Rows of crops, then fruit trees, skirted the path they followed, with a kitchen garden planted closer to the inner structure's outer buildings. They walked their mounts to a round wooden building surrounded by many other constructions of slatted wood. Here chickens scurried out of their path and other sages shooed goats aside. A sage walked from the main building, stooped and slow in pace, also wearing the green robe, the apparent uniform of this hold.

"Welcome, friends. I am Bayrd." The sage had a strong, deep voice. "If you please, follow Sage Jakodi to the infirmary where we will tend to your injured." He spoke with authority and the younger sage who had welcomed them scurried to Morrigan, who led Kyle's horse and guided her to a far building. Kyle's man dismounted and followed.

Another young man led Erin's horse, his head bowing in respect for the bundle on the litter.

Muir fell forward, collapsing over his horse's neck and Angus jumped off his mount, hastening across to steady him. Douglas dismounted also and assisted Angus in bringing Muir off his animal, supporting him between them.

"Come with me, my lord," Bayrd said. "My fellow sages will attend."

Two sages hurried to assist the three warriors and headed for a building off to the side, most likely the infirmary. Adele led the women who travelled with them, some also requiring the ministrations of the sages.

Arlan dismounted and followed Bayrd, the rest of his troop doing the same except for Leigh, who took the horses to a stable at the direction of yet another sage, the dogs staying close by him.

Bayrd led them into the large hall where trestle tables lined the sides with bench seats running along each of them. A fire burned in a deep fire pit in the centre. Sages moved about this hall, setting the tables for an evening meal.

"You must join us, lord warrior." Bayrd regarded Arlan, raising his brows.

"Your pardon, Sage Bayrd, for I've not introduced myself. I'm Arlan MacEnoicht, son of Donnach Finnbar MacEnoicht."

Bayrd stood still, his lined face crinkling slightly, and examined Arlan's features. "We are honoured to give hospitality to the son of the Àrd Rìgh of Dál Gaedhle." He gave a slight bow.

"The man who doesn't rouse is my elder brother, Kyle MacEnoicht." Arlan lowered his voice.

"We shall do our best for him, Lord Arlan. I await the assessment of his condition from the chief healer sage. In the meantime, please sit and enjoy some food. Ye all look travel and battle worn." Bayrd left them and walked out the door they'd entered.

Arlan sat, joined by Bàn and Adele, and the others soon trickled into the hall, which quickly filled with robed sages.

"They're learned in the healing arts, my lord." Morrigan sat across the table from Arlan, and Leigh sat on the other side of Adele. "The healers appear to know what they both require."

Arlan leaned his elbows on the long wooden table and rested his face in his hands, the place between his shoulders easing some of its tightness.

The aroma of freshly baked bread blew in from the adjoining room and Arlan lifted his head. The warm yeasty smell swirled around the sages who brought in platters of cheeses and cold preserved meats. A door swished open, revealing a kitchen the size of the one in The Keep that fed the full accompaniment of its workers and serving men and women. A quick head count showed Arlan this sage hold comprised a similar number of souls. The aroma of a hearty broth wafted behind the smell of bread and Arlan's stomach grumbled.

Soon the other seats filled with the sages who'd brought in the food, and the rest of Arlan's troop, except for Kyle and Muir, and the women who had travelled with them. Sage Bayrd returned and sat beside him.

"Your warrior has a festering arm." He leaned into Arlan. "We have applied a poultice." His lips tightened. "Your brother, my lord, requires more attention. We shall use our skill as best we can."

"Thank you, Sage Bayrd," Arlan said. "I'm indebted to you."

The door to the eating hall slid open and the sage who sat opposite Arlan cast her gaze over those who entered. "Lord Arlan, I wish to make you aware that here we tend to those troubled in mind as well as in body. The poor souls who now join us for repast are such. Please do not mind them, my lord."

A small group of people approached the table, their clothes clean but not all dressed neatly. A young man stood against the wall, hunched into himself in self-comfort, barely lifting his head to those seated at the table. A sage who entered with this group stepped to the table and took a hunk of bread from a serving board and handed it to the youth who then ate, his full focus on his food, not lifting his eyes to those around him. An older man found an empty seat beside Leigh and placed himself there. Another stood behind Adele and moaned. A sage approached him and encouraged him to move along the table to sit.

"We've disturbed their routine," Arlan said. "My apologies, Sage Bayrd."

"It is well, my lord." Bayrd shook his head. "Nae need to apologise."

The man behind Adele followed his keeper, leaving an elderly woman standing directly behind Arlan. Arlan returned to his meal, taking the advice of his host, and minding not those who milled around and ate in a different fashion. Whisky infused the preserved meats, the cheese was soft and creamy in texture, and the crusty bread still warm. Arlan broke a chunk of bread off for himself and placed a pat of churned butter on it. It soon melted, running in golden rivulets and pooling on his wooden platter.

"Come, Giorsal." A sage spoke behind Arlan, urging the old woman to move along.

Arlan sipped the wine poured into his mug by his host. Behind him, the cajoling motions of the sage continued.

"Nae," the old woman croaked, and her reply rose over the dinner conversations.

Bayrd paused in serving wine to Leigh and twisted, looking behind, and examined the situation.

"She will not move, Master Bayrd." The sage spoke in rueful tones.

"It's well, my friend, she's no bother." Arlan indicated to the elderly woman with a flick of his head, both hands now busy—one gripping a spiced meat, and the other holding warm bread drenched in melted butter. "They'll not offend us."

"Behold!" The voice from the old woman grew strong, vibrating through him. "Your warrior king!" Her statement rang out in the hall, her loud tones reaching the high rafters.

Chatter ceased, along with the clank of cups on wooden boards, and the bustling emitted from the cooking area.

All faces in the hall turned to Arlan.

Angus lifted his eyes from his meal, his jaw dropping open and a chunk of dark bread in his hand now hovering halfway to his mouth. Leigh turned to Arlan, one eyebrow slowly rising. Across the table from Arlan, Bàn stared at the woman, his mouth firming and his serious gaze drifted from her to Arlan. He nodded slowly in silent affirmation.

Behind Arlan, the woman's clothing swished loudly in the now silenced hall. The weight of people's stares clamped on his shoulders. Face heating, Arlan placed his unfinished bread on his platter and turned. The woman stood tall, her arm outstretched, with a commanding set to her shoulders. She flicked her head to the side, tossing her long greying red hair behind her. Her bony index finger pointed at him.

Arlan ceased his chewing and swallowed his mouthful with a gulp.

The old but regal woman's finger jabbed at his very soul. He blinked, as deep within him a wisp of acknowledgement rose to meet her touch.

Whispers susurrated throughout the hall, but the rising thunder of the pulse in his ears drowned them out.

"Take Giorsal back to her room," Bayrd ordered the sage attending her.

Two other sages stepped to the woman and assisted her keeper to direct her out of the hall. She complied and allowed them to usher her away from Arlan, her expression serene, and her clouded eyes locked with his.

"I beg your pardon, lord prince," Bayrd said beside him.

Arlan dragged his gaze from the doorway where the elderly woman had now exited and turned to Bayrd, whose face blistered red.

"The woman is mad and thinks herself a seer," Bayrd blustered. "Some even believe what she says. They call her the Blind Lady Sage."

Arlan had barely finished his broth when Jakodi came from the infirmary with a message of summons from the chief healer, Sage Phelan. He rose and, accompanied by Bàn, followed the brisk step of the young sage to one of the lesser rooms of the infirmary. A fire crackled in the hearth and many candles burned on candelabra set around the bed where Kyle lay. Rushes covered the floor and the half dozen sages present spoke in hushed tones.

The elderly healer sage had a head of shaggy grey hair and a calm demeanour. He stood beside a low table spread with various implements, most similar in appearance to tools found in a carpenter's workshop.

"Your brother's condition worsens, my Lord Arlan." Healer Sage Phelan looked Arlan straight in the eye. "Do I have your permission to perform a trepanning?"

Arlan glanced at Bàn, whose brow creased many-fold. Arlan searched for a meaning to the word but found none.

"Please, Lord Sage, I know not of what you speak."

"Your brother has bleeding inside his skull. If we do not release it, the increasing pressure of the blood on his brain will crush it within his skull. In short, he will die."

Bàn placed a steadying hand on Arlan's shoulder.

"What will you do?" Flashes of medical shows on the *Tee Vee* in Rhiannon's world returned to Arlan's mind. *Surgery*, they called it. And *infection* marked as a considerable risk. Much like the festering occurring in Muir's arm. "He's the heir to my father's clan lands. His life is precious, more so for he's my only living sibling." Arlan blinked at the waver in his voice.

"My Lord, your brother inherits naught if we do not proceed, that is for certain. The outcome of this"—he waved his hand over an instrument similar to a ratcheting drill— "is still uncertain, but I have had much success in prior situations of the same nature."

Kyle moaned and his limbs stiffened.

"Lord Arlan, it grows dire." Sage Phelan glanced at Kyle. His attendants leaned over Kyle with concerned expressions. "Do I have your permission?"

"Aye." Arlan turned to go. "I'll not watch." He strode out, not able to look back.

He would leave his brother—and his trust—in the skill of the healer sage.

Arlan went to the room provided for him by the sage hold and lay on his cot, wide awake. Turning his thoughts from Kyle—for he could do nothing but wait and pray—he focussed on the next step. The sages had welcomed the women rescued from the bandits, who now had nowhere to live for their village lay decimated. He must report to Father and his council the news of the attack on the village, and the increased activity of the bandits of the east as soon as possible. In short, he couldn't afford such a delay, for it may be days before Kyle would be well enough to journey.

Kyle...

Arlan's stomach cooled, and icy fingers wrapped around his insides, then grasped tight. This drilling into Kyle's skull to relieve the pressure there may be unsuccessful. And if so, Arlan himself would have to step into his place as the next in line to be chief of clan MacEnoicht until Kyle was restored to health.

Only then, in an unpredictable future, could he be any sort of king... as the blind old woman had announced.

And what of her? Her clouded stare had touched him. Madness came in many forms and Sage Byard had dismissed her comments, angry at her behaviour. But some here believed the words this old woman uttered. A knot of pain rested in the centre of Arlan's forehead, then moved to his heart. Kyle would have to succumb to his injuries for such a statement to be fulfilled. A prophecy, some in the dining hall had named it in whispered tones. He stifled that line of thought...

Arlan sighed and rolled over, staring into the night while the sage hold around him slumbered. Sleep came eventually.

Quiet voices and the stirrings of animals joined the early morning light coming through the open window of his room. Arlan arose from his bed and strode to the infirmary, accompanied by Bàn. He approached the room where Sage Phelan and the other healer sages had performed Kyle's surgery the previous evening. A young sage granted him entry.

Kyle lay still in his bed, with a fresh bandage wrapped around his head. A junior sage tended to him, bathing his arms and chest. The table was bare of implements, and fresh herbs and rushes were spread on the floor. Arlan stepped closer, the sharp aroma of thyme hitting his nostrils with each step.

The door closed with a gentle thud. Sage Phelan had entered, his wrinkled features more lined, and weariness hung about his shoulders.

"My lord sage, how is he?" Arlan spoke low.

"The trepanning went well, and I believe we drained all the clotted blood. But only time can tell if the bleeding has ceased and if your brother will survive. He needs rest."

"How long will it take?"

"If you are asking, can he travel?" Sage Phelan shot Arlan a grave look. "Nae, he should not."

Arlan bowed his head. His boot had crushed the tiny flowers on the thyme twigs, a pale pink against their green stalks and leaves.

"In the next room sleeps your injured warrior," Phelan said. "The junior sage tending him reports his fever broke overnight. Always a fortuitous sign. He is a stoic man, but he requires rest. It will be a few days before he is ready to travel." Sage Phelan gave a curt nod and left the room.

The junior sage finished washing Kyle, covered him with a rug of fox fur, then gathered her basin and cloths. She placed a chair beside the bed, then paused by the door.

"Ye may speak to him, if ye wish. He can hear you, Lord Arlan." Her soft voice mingled with the creak of the opening door.

"I shall be outside, sword-brother," Bàn said, shutting the door quietly behind himself and the sage.

The fire snapped and cracked, and a stream of sunlight caught the ash motes floating in the air. Arlan swallowed and stepped closer to the bed.

Kyle lay immobile. Not a muscle twitched. The rise and fall of his chest was the only sign that his soul remained in his body.

Speak to him. What to say? Kyle, now the captive audience, couldn't interrupt, nor chide... nor shush him to silence.

"Brother." Arlan flinched, his voice loud like a ram's horn calling warriors to battle in the quiet room.

He leaned closer. Kyle's hand lay on top of the fur where the sage had placed it. He reached out and grasped it; his brother's skin felt damp and cool to his touch. Arlan cleared his throat.

"Kyle... I know not if ye will awaken again, but I am assured ye can hear me. There are some things I wish to say..." Arlan dropped into the chair by the bed and buried his face in the fox fur.

"Why did you beat me?" His voice was muffled in the soft pelt. "Why do you continually belittle me?"

Why do you not love me as you did when we were boys?

"What happened?" He lifted his head. "When did you start to hate me?" Arlan spoke low. There was no one else in the room, but what shame it would cause if any overheard.

The soft regular passage of air through Kyle's nostrils was the only reply. Arlan buried his face in the fur and scoured his childhood memories. The last one of Mother came to mind. Tall and slim, with a protruding belly full with child. Their baby sister. The one lost. And their beloved mother with her.

He was five and Kyle was ten. A slow montage played in Arlan's mind.

Och, no. Kyle—a weeping, red-faced boy slapping hard. Over and over. The stinging on Arlan's bare legs now as fresh as the day he'd received the blows.

"Kyle, I can't make up for the love of our mother, but I'll love you, my brother, always." He gripped more firmly around Kyle's limp hand. "I'll serve you, my clan chief. One day you will be king, and I shall lead your warriors to defend you, our lands, and our people." Arlan's husky words echoed in the quiet room. "Know this," he whispered into the fur, "I forgive you."

Bàn had waited outside and the sage who guarded the door led Arlan and Bàn to a nearby room, similar to Kyle's, but no fire burned in the hearth.

Morrigan sat by Muir's bed. Muir lay with eyes closed and a thickly wadded bandage wrapped his upper arm.

"He sleeps, lord." Morrigan rose. "It will delay our journey home by many days—"

"Nae, it will not." Muir opened one eye and flinched, rose to a half sit, then he moaned and lay back again.

"Don't exert yourself, Muir," Arlan admonished.

"Do not wait for me, Lord Arlan. The àrd rìgh must learn of our report of villages near our border ravaged by those who know no mercy and come from Dál Gallain. We must station troops to guard our border forts." Muir's voice held a note of gravity.

"Aye." Arlan inhaled the air in the room, pine and vinegar's sharpness hitting his nose.

"Therefore, ye must not delay." Muir took a breath, his speech tiring him. "Begging your pardon, my lord, I'll no' tell you your duty, for I ken ye know it well."

"We'll come back for you." Arlan stepped forward and gripped Muir's good arm.

"Nae, Lord Arlan, I shall stay with your brother and once he is well, *I* will return with him. I trust it will be in time to go with you into battle, for these old warrior bones of mine tell me this awaits us."

THIRTY-SIX

— • —

Who dares to awaken the sleeping behemoth?

DRAGON SCROLLS
INNESFARNE
DATE OF TEXT UNKNOWN

Eastern Clanlands of Dál Gallain
At the base of the Central Meadhan Mountains

Passing through the gates of the sage hold, Arlan glanced at the cloud filled sky then at his warriors, their numbers depleted by three. He held a glow in his chest at their efficiency in commencing their journey, for he'd given them short notice. He'd thanked the sages with a heavy heart. Only time would tell of Kyle's recovery, but leaving Muir and his man with him had eased the icy churn of Arlan's guts somewhat.

"The sages advise it will take a whole day to traverse the mountain pass that will lead us to the moors of Dál Gaedhle." Bàn's eyes drew away from Erin's corpse. It lay stiffly wrapped and secured to her saddled horse that trailed behind him. "The sages have embalmed and bound Erin's... body." Bàn's throat worked. "I shall take her to her clan home in the north."

Arlan placed a gentle hand on Bàn's shoulder. "Aye, ye do that, brother. But first we face a week's long ride home." Arlan kicked Mengus to a canter, and the pounding of hooves followed him.

They rode to the snow line, where grey granite covered by low growing heather and grass met in sharp contrast to pristine white only broken by knuckles of rock. Cold emanated from it and here the rock-strewn track narrowed.

"We must dismount." Arlan wrapped his plaid tighter.

The others followed suit and led their horses, whose misty breaths surrounded their muzzles with white. Above them, clouds shrouded the dark granite peeking through the snow.

On the other side of the pass, the land flattened out for a ways. They walked their horses through a wood on a narrow track of springy sphagnum moss which cushioned each step. Their footfall stirred the earthy scents into Arlan's nose. Many birds sang, but none showed their presence. Deer spore littered their path and Arlan sighted one or two in the distance through the forest of tall, straight trunks. The deerhounds bayed.

"Nae, hold them back," he ordered Leigh. "We have plentiful supplies thanks to the generosity of the sage hold. No time for hunting, catching, butchering, and carrying a deer."

Arlan headed them out of the shelter of the trees onto the peaty, heather-covered moor, through which a burn ran. The wind blowing cool over it brushed Arlan's face and stroked his beard with invisible hands. The heather was dead here, the ground soggy and the horses' hooves stuck often while they continued to walk them, the horses dragging their legs and heads drooping from the hard day's trek.

At the edge of the moor, a forest grew near a mound of moss-covered boulders as high as a bailey wall. "We'll camp here this night," Arlan announced. "Tomorrow we traverse the burn."

They ate a meal of dried venison. The fire kept at bay the chilly mist rising from the nearby bog, and the mossy ground, not so damp here, would provide a soft bed for the night.

"I'll climb those boulders for a view of our passage tomorrow." Arlan pointed to the moss-covered rocks they camped nearby. "I hope to see any obstacles ahead."

"Aye, lord," Angus said. "The journey home seems to take an age." He pouted and slumped over his meal.

The dogs stirred, still unsettled from their trek through the woods filled with the scent of deer, and Leigh tethered them near the horses. Angus and Bàn accompanied Arlan to the rocks, a jumbled rocky wall littered with scraggly plants. Arlan trod with care, choosing each foothold, and grasping the raspy granite or tufts of vegetation, and lifted himself up its stony face. At the top of the natural configuration, the view was wide but hidden by some mist.

"Perhaps we should try again in the morning, once the sun has burned off this fog." Angus stood staring into the outlook blanketed in water vapour rising from the bog.

"We'll be gone long afore then." Bàn stepped near the edge and peered down at their camp.

Arlan clambered over the top of the rock formation, the others following, and reached its furthest side. He stood at the edge, on a natural platform between vegetation daring to grow in such a harsh place. Arlan peered over to a deep glen. Below him on the cliff face, a large section of dark shadow indicated a split in the rock on this side.

"If I'm not mistaken, there's a cave below me." Arlan crouched.

The hounds at the camp barked, and Leigh shushed them just as loudly.

"What's set them off?" Bàn scanned the dimming horizon.

"Do you see anything, lord?" Angus asked.

Arlan stood silently with his companions. The friendly banter of the warriors remaining in the camp and tending to their gear interspersed with the hounds' unsettled whines and barks followed by Leigh's reprimands. Now the horses stirred.

Beneath Arlan, the ground vibrated. "Did you feel that?"

Angus and Bàn shook their heads.

A grating shudder rumbled beneath Arlan's feet, and he unsheathed his sword. At this, Bàn and Angus drew their own swords.

"I see nothing, lord." Bàn stepped closer.

The grating, deep below them, grumbled louder.

"We *are* above a cave." Angus' voice ruffled at the edges. "And we've disturbed its occupant."

The ground continued to vibrate under Arlan. A roar arose from the drop beside him; it shook his body, and he couldn't name the animal from whence it came. The grating of rocks over gravel echoed into the small glen below him. He spread his feet, steadying himself and gripped his sword tighter as his heart rate quickened and sent a rhythmic thudding into his temples. He faced the direction of the noise, for perhaps he would spy the creature who owned the wild cry.

A gushing wind, like an enormous bird lifting in flight, came from below Arlan as he stood at the edge of the rock. A massive head rose, black scale-covered and owning small slits for ears and a large snout. The nostrils flared, sniffing him. Large, red eyes had cat-like pupils, and vertical slits that appeared to jump as the reptilian second lids blinked.

"Och!" Arlan's brow cooled, and he wiped away the sweat that dribbled into his eyes, all the while never taking his vision off the beast's red glare.

The dragon—for it could be naught else—rose further and let out a roar, sending the full blast of it into Arlan. Hot breath buffeted him, but he stayed his ground. The magnificent creature ascended with another flap to its broad, skin-stretched wings that lifted a gigantic body, which dangled long-taloned claws, and a tail as thick as a tree trunk.

Arlan's limbs refused to move, and his own breath stilled as he followed the creature's movements, but his heart now rocked his chest.

"It cannot be!" Angus shouted.

The dogs in the camp barked frantically, the horses shrieked, and their companions' shouts of warning echoed across to them.

The dragon flicked its head down, its gaze running over Arlan, then sent another roar in his direction. Arlan's arms obeyed his will at last, and he lifted his sword in an iron grip, assuming a fighting stance.

"Come on then, beast. Do your worst! I'll not falter just because you look so mean." His words came out hoarse and his head thundered with the rush of blood.

A powerful grip tightened on his shoulder. "My lord, move!" Bàn shook him. "*Arlan!*"

The dragon inhaled and opened its mouth wide. Two fangs projected from the massive upper jaws, directed at him. Another pair of strong hands grabbed Arlan's other shoulder, and both men dragged him aside. Arlan landed in the short vegetation on the top of the rock formation, its sharp tufts scratching his body. Angus tumbled over him, limbs entangling in Arlan's legs, and his sword missing his shoulder by a blade-width. Arlan rolled away from the sword edge onto something warm and solid, and Bàn grunted in Arlan's ear.

Sprays of flame flew out from the fangs of the dragon and hit the ground where Arlan had stood. Smoke arose and the green moss covering the boulder now burned. The granite beneath hissed and squealed, disintegrating where the fluid flame touched.

The animal continued its ascent and flew northward into the night, its sturdy, enormous body majestic, and its flight bent on purpose.

Arlan disentangled himself from Bàn and Angus as smoke and the stench of singed rock seared his nose.

"*Dragon's breath!*" Angus stood and sheathed his sword.

"Aye, exactly." Bàn punched Arlan's shoulder, the hard thump leaving a knob of pain in Arlan's muscle. "By my blade!" Bàn yelled. "What were you thinking?" His deep voice echoed through the glen behind the rocks. "Ye cannae fight such a beast."

Arlan sheathed his sword.

"I... I sensed it wanted to kill." Arlan screwed his face. "The animal emitted such an intention."

"But it did nae get you, Lord Arlan." Angus' eyes widened.

"Thankfully." Bàn's glare remained on Arlan.

"The beast is awake. We may yet need to know how to fight one." Arlan studied the charred, partially melted rock at his feet. "Although I know not how, for a blade is useless against fire. But... I have something I must discuss with the sages that, possibly, could assist us."

THIRTY-SEVEN

— · —

In flight, as graceful as a swan.
Legs of iron; hide a shield.
Razor-ridge backed, and talons spiked.
Who commands this one and orders like a bridled steed?
None the fires can contain.
He who tries so
Puts his pride to shame.

DRAGON SCROLLS
INNESFARNE
DATE OF TEXT UNKNOWN

Western Sovereignty of Dál Gaedhle
The Keep

Eifion sighed, his chamber in The Keep still in the darkness of night. He shifted back the covers, then reached to his nightstand and lit a fresh candle with the stub of the old.

Wisdom comes with age, but so does a lack of sleep.

This night, it was not his body depriving him of rest, but his soul. Something seemed amiss, and he grasped at fleeting images.

He took the candlestick and stepped to the broad window and pulled aside the heavy curtain. Below him, and over the outer bailey wall of The Keep, moonlight softened the gentle rolling fields that sat beside the River Ruairidh. Crickets chirped and the soft croak of frogs lifted from where they lived in the quieter section of the Ruairidh as it wended its way past the caisteal. The road leaving the town at the base of The Keep and leading to the east over the narrow stone bridge sat empty.

Although night remained, it neared time for *beul an latha,* the dawn of day, and a pale light rimmed the horizon.

Eifion sat on the cushioned seat of his window and turned his focus into himself.

The unease lingered.

Was it Arlan?

He pushed his thoughts out, seeking. He had done this frequently since viewing the *shimmer* up close, for Arlan had certainly ridden through it. On every occasion, he had come against a barrier. A blank. No sense of Arlan, his spirit, nor the essence of him.

But this time, something stirred. A vague watery image tinged with Arlan's presence. *And a darkness.*

How he longed to inform Arlan's father of this knowledge. But he could not, for it risked revealing the secret he had held for almost a lifetime.

That there exist mages of good intent.

But millennia of belief that all magic is bad and all mages evil, stood between himself and telling Donnach the truth of what he really was. He'd served the high king of the sovereignty of Dál Gaedhle here in the west for over thirty years, and the man was biased indeed. If Donnach MacEnoicht ever discovered his head adviser sage was actually a mage...

I would be lucky to escape with only banishment.

Hurried footsteps approached his chamber door and gloved knuckles rapped with force.

"Sage Eifion," a gruff female voice yelled through the door. "My lord?"

Eifion hastened to his door and opened it. A warrior stood there, middle-aged and slim, clothed in breeches and a linen tunic with a sheathed sword hanging from her belt.

"The àrd rìgh is awake, lord sage, and..."

"Aye?"

"Och, he's behaving oddly." The warrior looked to the floor and scuffed her boot. "He says he's dreamed, and he orders his armed bodyguard to attend him while he rides out."

"When it is still night?"

"Aye, my lord sage." She leaned into him and raised her brow. "*Oddly.*"

Eifion dressed in his day robe and followed the warrior through the dim corridors of The Keep. Loud voices came from the floor where the àrd rìgh's chambers were situated. Eifion peered through the opening arches facing the inner bailey as he passed. Hastily lit torches flamed to life, doors banged, and the hustle of waking men and the clang of gathered weapons blared through each opening. Horses whinnied their displeasure at stable hands stirring them in the dark, while stable boys saddled the mounts of the àrd rìgh and his bodyguard, and warriors issued orders.

The warrior led him through the open door of the àrd rìgh's chambers.

"Eifion!" Donnach stood dressed in breeches and boots; leather sword straps crossed his chest and the handles of these long weapons stood high above his shoulders. Although greying, and his face showing his years in wrinkles, he remained a commanding figure—a warrior through and through.

Beside him, Leuchars, the war chief, scowled. His scars were now accentuated beneath ginger hair glowing in the torchlight, and his bulky muscled arms crossed his chest.

"I must go to my sons." Donnach spoke with an intensity. "They are in danger."

"My lord king, you do not know where they are." Eifion grasped tight to calm, not allowing Donnach's words to stir his own rising concern.

"Aye, my àrd rìgh." Leuchars' scowl lessened. "The sage is right. Listen to his counsel, I beg you."

"I will head east." Donnach paused in tightening the belt that held his dirk, apparently oblivious to the statements of both men present. "I have dreamed, Eifion." His eyes widened as he strode closer to Eifion. "A dragon seeks them."

Eifion's back stiffened, and a drifting image stirred—one that had haunted his sleep.

"But there is no longer such an animal, my lord king."

"Och, no." Donnach grabbed Eifion's shoulders. Eifion flinched against the strength of the grip and the ache it shot through his spine. "I have seen it in my dream. *It is real.* It seeks to destroy my lads. My precious sons who hold the future of my clan lands. The next rulers. The future àrd rìgh. It desires to take the kingship from them." Donnach screwed his face as if willing Eifion to comprehend. The silver torc around his neck gleamed in the flickering candlelight. "It hates them and wants the kingship for itself."

"A dragon, my king?" Eifion's incredulity escaped through his words, but he quickly tempered it with a concerned expression.

"Aye, Eifion." Deep crinkles surrounded Donnach's eyes, and his mouth pulled taut as if in pain. "I must protect them from this beast."

"Nae, ye must not, my lord king!" Leuchars' usual hard tone now quavered at the edges.

Hmm. Leuchars was always the calm, stoic warrior.

"Can you not send a troop to investig—" Eifion began.

"No, sage," Donnach commanded. "It is *I* who need go."

"Then I shall accompany you." Eifion and Leuchars spoke in unison.

"Och, no! I need wise heads here in my absence."

"My lord, I beg you, *this* is not wise." Eifion gathered his robe and slipped out of Donnach's grasp.

"I will go. That is final." Donnach set his glare on Eifion, then Leuchars, then spun and left the room. "Let my warriors know I am on my way. Is my horse ready?" His voice trailed through from the corridor.

"I will attend the àrd rìgh," Leuchars said simply.

"No, Lord War Chief," Eifion said. "What if the danger encroaches on The Keep?"

"What danger?" Leuchars' tone held scorn.

"Aye, there you have it. The àrd rìgh requires a counsellor more than a warrior." Eifion rested a hand on the lord warrior's solid forearm. "I fear our king is unwell. To think there is such a creature about, and even to fight one... I shall follow him, Lord Leuchars, and when he is come to his senses, I shall bring him home."

Eifion turned to the warrior beside him. "Let me pack a few things and—"

She nodded. "I'll meet you in the stables with a saddled horse, wise sage."

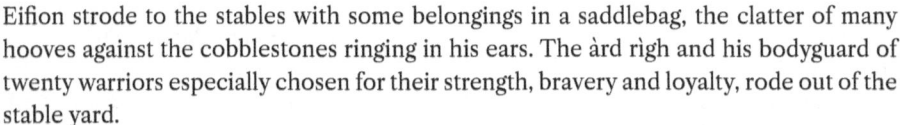

Eifion strode to the stables with some belongings in a saddlebag, the clatter of many hooves against the cobblestones ringing in his ears. The àrd rìgh and his bodyguard of twenty warriors especially chosen for their strength, bravery and loyalty, rode out of the stable yard.

The warrior had held good, and she awaited with a placid-looking mare ready saddled.

"We shall keep our distance. I defy my king if I ride from here." Eifion took the reins from the warrior and mounted. "But I must."

Donnach rode between a double row of warriors out through the high gated tower, the empty market square, then out of the town, passing the closely-packed dwellings of those who worked the fields. Within, souls stirred, readying for another day's work. Lights flickered as townsfolk, disturbed by the drumming of horses' hooves, opened their doors, and with lit candles in hand, peered at the passing warriors.

The àrd rìgh and his escort had soon crossed the narrow bridge over the river and passed the fields and meadows closest to town. Eifion followed at a distance. He must not attract the àrd rìgh's attention, but with Donnach MacEnoicht so intent on his task, there was small chance he would look back. A warrior in the rear guard glanced briefly at Eifion but faced ahead without a remark, seemingly unperturbed by the àrd rìgh's adviser-sage following.

Daylight tinged the western sky, giving light to the fields spread out ahead of them and dispelling the eerie tones of night. Yellows, greens and browns glowed in the dawn's welcome. Birds sang their morning song, a fox retreated to the far edge of the fields, and sleepy cattle woke and nibbled at the meadow's grass, their long shaggy coats stirring in the breeze. Far ahead in the east a forest began, thick rich growth darkened its interior, the morning's sunlight unable to penetrate.

A flock of birds fled from this forest, shaking the trees, as thick and numerous as a murmuration. The birds flew to the west behind the travellers, squawking their alarm. Their shadow passed over Donnach and his warriors, then briefly darkened the sky above Eifion and his warrior companion. A roar echoed from behind the forest and to the southeast. It appeared to shake the early light, silencing the dawn cacophony.

Another roar rent the air.

Ahead of Eifion, Donnach and his entourage halted. A figure stirred within the group, hurriedly dismounted and ran into the field next to them. *Donnach!* His bodyguard flew off their horses and followed their king into the field.

Eifion dismounted. "Stay here," he said to his companion, and strode to the drystone wall enclosing the meadow.

A roar, now much closer, came from the forest to the east. Rising above light-tinged foliage, a flying beast headed toward the meadow where Donnach stood. Broad, black-skinned wings stretched over bony, finger-like segments, bat-like in design, spread wide as the beast glided toward the field. Its horned head, spear-like talons hanging beneath a solid body, and a long tail ending in a barbed tip, sharpened in definition as the beast soared closer. The great animal emitted another roar and Eifion's feet vibrated with the ground beneath him.

A firm hand grabbed Eifion's shoulder. "Stay here, my lord sage. Please." The warrior spoke into his ear.

The animal's facial features grew clearer in the growing daylight. Dark red orbs, with slits for pupils as black as the depths of hell, directed their stare at the àrd rìgh.

Eifion's mind almost seared. The reality before his eyes fought with his reasoning as he battled for comprehension.

It cannot be.

"Dragons are a myth. The tales of the ancient sages! The subjects of bard songs."

The stomping of horses' hooves and the acrid scent of terrified beasts surrounded him. The vibration of tramping hooves vied for dominance above the dragon's roar rocking the air, the ground, and through Eifion himself. He leaned on the grey stones topping the wall and strained to hear what Donnach said to his men.

"My king!" Donnach's chief bodyguard pleaded. "We are exposed here. Let us take cover."

"This is the animal. I have seen it. The very same black beast of my dream." Donnach stepped a pace further into the field. "It will find me wherever I am."

The head bodyguard signalled to his warriors who then surrounded the àrd rìgh. Shoulder to shield, they encircled Donnach.

The ground vibrated with another roar of the approaching dragon.

"I shall stand my ground and defy this evil that seeks my sons," Donnach yelled. "It would take the kingship from them. It shall take me first, if it dares, and if it must. Warriors, stand with me!"

Donnach spoke like a madman. Yet every word rang with a truth in Eifion's mind and gelled with images from his own sleepless night.

Donnach MacEnoicht stood to his full height, towering above his guard, his torc glinting in the early dawn.

The dragon flapped skin-stretched wings above a scaled hide, completely black bar its red belly. A blast of air blew through the meadow, ruffling Eifion's robe and buffeting him as he gripped the drystone wall. The mounts of the àrd rìgh's bodyguard whinnied and scattered.

Eifion scanned the grassland of field and pasture.

"I require a tree!" he shouted. "A large one." If he could get to the ancient oak that grew on the outskirts of town, he could send a *protection*. He turned to the warrior beside him.

"Why do you need a tree?" Her eyes narrowed and the edges of her mouth grew taut. "Badness brought this beast, for our histories tell us that only by the power of a mage such an animal would seek to attack a human." They had reached their horses, but the warrior did not mount. "Why then do you seek a large tree, my lord sage? Is it by magic you wish to repel it?" Her face remained hard.

Eifion lifted himself into the saddle, but his warrior's feet remained planted on the road.

"Not all magic is evil." Eifion leaned toward her, deepening his voice with the truth it held. "Not all battles are physical."

The warrior mounted, her brow remaining crinkled. Eifion dug his heels into his mare's flank. She rose to a gallop, and he headed her toward the town's edge, his warrior following. A deafening roar engulfed the meadow and beat against his back, vibrating his eardrums and throughout his entire body.

His horse shrieked, and he pulled her up sharp, and spun. Heat flew in a wave toward them. A funnel of flame vomited out of the dragon's mouth and settled on the àrd rìgh and his shield of warriors.

"Oh, no!" Eifion covered his mouth with his hands, his mind scrambling to accept what his vision showed him. *Oh, no. Oh, no.*

The warrior beside him let out a pained cry.

The dragon kept its fire fixed on Donnach and his warriors for a breath's span of time, then shut its jaws and flapped its massive wings, lifting its body high into the sky, and flew back whence it came.

Eifion kicked his curvetting mount back to the meadow. Panicked horses fled past him in the opposite direction, battering his animal and that of his companion's. He arrived and slid from his mare and faced the field. A firm hand stayed him. The biting stench of burned flesh and hair filled the air and settled its cloying grime in the back of Eifion's throat.

"Don't go near it, my lord sage." The warrior's grip clamped on his shoulder. "See, the stone wall is molten."

Heat bathed his face and liquid rock glowed red.

Beyond, a flat scorched field met his vision—a circle of ash where once stood brave warriors and a noble àrd rìgh.

THIRTY-EIGHT

— · —

For all know magic will exact its price.
Use it wisely.
It is a blaze.
A valuable servant.
A pitiless master.

MAGE MASTER FÀISTINNEACH
(3310-3380 POST DRAGON WARS)

Eastern Clanlands of Dál Gallain
Lord Ciarán's Tower

Coarse bedding covered Bram's body, the rough touch on his naked flesh stirring him from slumber. Bram opened his eyes. His limbs were heavy and his head full of ache. The door to his narrow room stood open. The brash voice of the lord's man funnelled up the stairwell of the tower, the man's cocky demeanour unchanged. Another servant, a kitchen hand most likely, received a mouthful of invective from him. His heavy stomp up the stairway echoed into Bram's room, then a knock as he rapped on Lord Ciarán's library door below.

Someone coughed nearby. A woman, stooped and wrinkled, stepped through Bram's doorway.

"Oh, ye are awake at last, lad." Her voice croaked. "Ye hav' been asleep many days."

Bram shuffled his hands into the straw mattress to lift himself off the cot, straining muscles screaming at him.

"No, no, lad." The woman pressed him back into his bed with a wrinkled hand. "Rest, now." She leaned closer, peering at him with kind green eyes. "Regain your strength before the lord and master uses ye again for his bidding. He is a one who cares not what it costs, only that he gets his wishes. He knows not the tax paid on a body by magic."

Bram gasped, flinching at the prickle of sharpness in his side. "You are a mage, madam?"

"Ahh... A healer." She avoided his gaze. "Lord Ciarán's man summoned me when ye would not rouse. Collapsed at yer post, ye was." She straightened his bed clothes and grinned. "I have seen it afore. And ye would well ken that all sorcery has a cost. Is that no' what yer mage masters tell ye? Rest. I shall bring ye some broth." She turned and left.

Bram lay back and stared out his door. She had spoken of his magic as *sorcery*. Did the healer admire him, then? Did he have skills above others? A natural talent, as his mentor had said?

Across the landing, the door to the workshop stood ajar and the divination bowl sat proudly on its pedestal. The rants of Lord Ciarán flowed out through his library, his man receiving the brunt of the abuse.

Bram closed his eyes and his ears to the din.

Images returned. A dark sentient presence giving assent. His hands deep in the silky waters of the divination bowl. A lengthy journey in his spirit to the far reaches of this land. A black beast with a red belly. The shuddering entrance to its mind and will, like prising himself through a tight gap in solid rock and opening to an underground cavern. Wresting control and directing the creature on a long flight to the caisteal they call The Keep. A belly of flame, a mouth seared, a smoky after-taste. Bram swallowed, the charr lingering still. The brisk escape as he left the enraged animal and soared away out of the range of spiked teeth and a plume of heat. Then back to his body in Lord Ciarán's Tower, muscles heavy with exhaustion and ribs sharp with hurt.

Bram woke with a start, heart pounding, sweat drenched, and what little energy regained now diminished. He focused on the view of the pedestal through the doorway, straining to keep his mind in the present.

I have done it.

Slaughtered a king.

He shuddered.

The man had stood tall, surrounded by his warriors, staring with defiance into the eyes of the creature. Challenging. Fully knowing his fate and yet braving it.

Bram buried his face in his hands.

Honourable men destroyed for the master's will.

"Ye must not use him so." The croaky voice of the healer who had attended him replaced the roars of Lord Ciarán. Bram strained for the words as they floated up the circular stair of the tower.

"He is *my* mage." Lord Ciarán's tone remained firm. "I shall order him as I wish."

"Then ye will kill him." Her voice was now steadier, solid and holding the sound of youth. "It is far too much ye ask of the lad, my lord."

"Dragon's teeth!" Lord Ciarán followed this with a curse. "He is gifted. He is the only one who can perform the task."

Bram sunk deeper into the bedding. Aye, it had taxed him. The fatigue dragged at his limbs and his heavy head pressed into the pillow. He swallowed. There would be more. More journeys in a beast and more men to destroy. He had glimpsed the vision streaming behind the sentient presence.

Sharp talons scraped inside him and wrapped his gizzards around their points.

Had his master Drostan known of this? Had *he* been a willing accomplice?

Or like himself, a poor sod conned into the game. His affection for that same master used to recruit him. His unique gifts and talents to be employed in the dire master plan. He gripped the thin blanket, fingers white.

For contracted to its completion, I am unable to resign my post.

A strong hand rapped on Ciarán's library door as he sat at his desk, the lady mage having finally left him.

Who is it now?

"Yes," Ciarán snapped, and the door opened, revealing his servant and a stranger.

"My Lord Ciarán." His man hesitated, casting an edgy glance at the travel-worn man beside him, who wore foreign attire. "This one turns up at our gate. He says he's travelled for days. Does nae know from what town he came but says he's from... *another place*." His man gave a short cough. "He has nae weapon, mi lord."

Ciarán rose from his desk and walked toward the scruffy traveller. He appeared of middle-age but stood tall, if not weary-looking, wearing breeches, of a sort, and a dirty jacket tailored to his torso. The shirt had a pointy collar poking from the neck and its fastenings strained at the midriff. The man held his gaze, never flinching.

"Who are you?"

"My name is Rabbie Findlay. I'm from Scotland Police ." The man straightened his shoulders, his tone one of authority.

The authority of Scotland Police —whoever they might be.

Ciarán clasped his hands behind his back and leaned into Rabbie Findlay as a tingle began at the base of his skull.

"And where in this great land of Dál Cruinne is *Scotland Police*?"

"No, Lord Ciarán, sir. Not this land. You see, I followed a group of young people and have passed through to *this world* from my own."

THIRTY-NINE

— • —

Hands lie stilled
Never more a sword to grasp.
The kingly torc bereft of a noble throat.
Oh, how the brave mourn
For ne'er a worthier son of Dál Gaedhle lived
Who now resides in majestic places,
Sharing the caisteal with the great.

WISDOM WRITINGS ON KINGSHIP
SAGE GLIOCAS
(2870-2962 POST DRAGON WARS)

Western Sovereignty of Dál Gaedhle
The Field Before The Keep

Arlan had pushed them hard over the past few days. Leigh and Douglas had taken turns to rest a weary hound draped on their saddles. Now, two nights and three days later, they approached the village to the south of The Keep from a north-easterly direction, coming upon it through the forest. They reached the edge of the village, where the aromas of evening meals cooking in the dwellings hit Arlan's nostrils, and his stomach ached. So close to home, they hadn't stopped to eat since morning.

Arlan glanced at his warriors and released a heavy sigh. Bloodshot eyes stared back above dishevelled and dust-covered clothes, and the men wore their five-day-growth on their faces. The horses, covered in a lather of sweat, panted and snorted at their masters riding them so hard.

They slowed their mounts and walked them through the village. People stood at their doors watching and children ran ahead of the riders, scampering off to their respective homes, their loud calls alerting their parents to the party's return.

People stared at Arlan with solemn eyes.

"They look for their prince," Bàn said beside him.

How could they know?

A drystone wall marked the boundary of a meadow near to the bridge that spanned the River Ruairidh and led to the town below The Keep. A guard of warriors stood beside it. Another group of warriors stood in a circle in the middle of the field: sombre, stationary sentinels facing outward, their shields tucked to their chests and spears held upright, reminiscent of a stone henge.

They stood on the circumference of a large circle of grey ash.

Arlan halted his party and dismounted stiffly. Beside him, Bàn and the other members of his troop eased themselves from their war horses. Hooves clattered on the bridge as a small party crossed and approached him. Eifion headed them and on reaching Arlan, halted his mare and dismounted with slow movements, his face drawn and eyes red rimmed.

"Eifion." Arlan stepped to the sage, embraced him. "What's amiss?"

"Oh, Lord Arlan." The old man's voice muffled against Arlan's chest. "I saw you as I sat under the yew tree. Where is your brother?"

Arlan could barely discern his words. "He's injured. I've left him in the care of skilled healer sages. Those experienced in the art of tending a wound to the head."

Eifion stepped back from Arlan, nodding with tears spilling down his face. He showed no surprise and said nothing.

"Kyle may not recover." The words came out piecemeal and Arlan braced himself for what he would say next. "I must see my father the àrd rìgh at once."

A murmur travelled through the guard standing watch, the warriors by the road and the crowd of villagers slowly gathering. Gasps accompanied the hum of the crowd as people absorbed the news of Kyle's serious injury, no doubt.

"I have dire news for you, my Lord Arlan." Eifion stretched taller and tilted his crinkled face to Arlan's. "I scarce know where to begin."

The lines of Eifion's face cut deeper and his knees buckled beneath him. Arlan caught him and held him up by the elbows and a guard by the drystone wall moved to assist.

"Eifion," Arlan said, "let me get you to a seat—"

"Nae, I must tell you tragic news." Eifion shook his head, putting out a hand to refuse the guard's help. "I know not how to soften this blow, so I shall tell you plainly. Your father sleeps the last sleep."

Cries of disbelief rang in the familiar voices of his troop, and Douglas stifled a curse. Arlan blinked, his hands holding Eifion went numb.

What?

The numbness travelled up his arms and joined the forming emptiness in his chest.

"How?" Arlan forced the word passed a tightness. "When? Take me to him, please." His mind swirled blankly as his mouth asked the questions.

Eifion now stood with his own strength, and Arlan released his grip on his elbows. The sage walked toward the drystone wall, where the guards parted. Arlan followed. A section of the wall sat lower than the rest, and the stones were undefined, like the wax melt of a candlestick after a long night. Eifion led Arlan into the field next to the road where the warriors stood arranged like a henge. Footsteps behind Arlan told him Bàn had followed close.

Eifion approached the guard, and two sombre warriors parted, revealing the circle of stone-grey ash covering the charred ground they guarded.

"What is this?" Arlan's mouth dried. "Why do you bring me here?" He fought to keep a sharpness from his tone.

"Three nights ago, your father awoke from a dream in a state. His only concern was for his sons. He said a dragon sought to kill you. Sought to take the kingship from you." Eifion fought to speak, his mouth wavering around words frayed by emotion. "He ordered his bodyguard to accompany him. He left when still night, heading east to find and protect you both." Eifion lifted his gaze from the ash circle. "This is as far as his journey took him and his brave warriors." Eifion stared at Arlan. "For from the south came a great dragon."

Arlan inhaled sharply. Beside him, Bàn stifled a cry.

"Aye, my lord prince. Impossible is what I thought—"

"Nae, not impossible, for we saw a dragon three nights ago. On the boggy moor, a day's ride from the Central Meadhan Mountains. Large and black and spitting flame." Arlan forced his gaze to the ash circle. "The same one?"

"Aye, perhaps." Eifion placed a hand on his arm. "This one was a fire breather also. Pray *Tobraichean na Beatha* there is only one such as this that would enter the realms of man." He took a steadying breath. "Your father and his warriors took their stand in this field. This is all that remains."

Arlan lifted his head and closed his eyes.

So much loss in such a brief time.

His brother damaged—if he lived. His father ... the ash at his feet—a noble, gracious, strong warrior and king.

If only Rhiannon were here now...

An ache for her consumed him. She was all his soul reached for in this moment. He would hold her tight and bury his head in her breast. A warm hand rested on his shoulder—the sturdy hand of Bàn.

He let out a sob as he opened his eyes, squeezing away tears to clear his vision. Near the centre of ash an object glittered, shiny amongst the grey. He strode between the warriors and stepped to the gleam, ignoring the alarmed grunts of those near him at his desecration of this cremation site.

Arlan picked up the circular object and a shower of ash fell from it. Father's silver torc and the emblem of his kingship and rule. Arlan wiped it clean on his plaid and brought it to Eifion.

"My father's royal torc. How could it survive a dragon's blast?"

"I know not, for I now believe I fully understand nothing in this world." Eifion sighed. "It represents the very thing your father said the dragon desired to destroy."

Arlan clasped the torc to himself and hugged it. Warm wet trickled down his cheeks. He closed his eyes once more and brought Father's face to mind, holding it there for as long as he could.

No remains to inter in the tor, the burial mound of his ancestors on their lands by the sea. No sword remained to place in Father's dead grasp while he lay in his grave. No heavy slab of cut stone would be the final resting place of Father's corpse. No memorial to visit and aid his mourning, or to bring Kyle once he came home, so they could share their grief.

His shoulders shook, and his breathing stuttered. He sucked in air, so tight were his lungs.

Soft sobbing surrounded him—Eifion, Bàn, his troop, and the men and women of Dál Gaedhle who'd gathered.

"Lord Arlan," Eifion said in sombre tones. "Ye are now the heir responsible for your clan until your brother recovers."

Arlan nodded. *For that I have come home.*

But returned to this...?

A wind arose, stirring the trees of the distant forest to the east, like an ocean's roar behind them. Arlan opened his eyes to a tear-blurred view. Wiping his cheeks with the back of his hand, he turned. The roaring wind drew closer, rippling the long grass of the fields like the waves of the sea, and arrived at the circle of ash where it gathered.

Arlan stepped back from the circle. Eifion, Bàn and even the warrior sentinels joined him, buffeted and pushed by the force of the wind. It swirled around like a mini whirlwind, sucking the ashes in its wake, and lifting them, like a tornado spout, up into the air. The plume sucked all the remains from the ground, leaving it bare, and carried the ashes high into the sky, transporting the àrd rìgh and his warrior guard into the heavens.

FORTY

— • —

Deep calls to deep.
Soul calls to soul.
Worlds cannot divide.
They will find their home.

VISIONS AND SAYINGS OF THE BLIND LADY SAGE

Our World, 2016
Abernethy, Scotland

"Wow!" George's voice echoed in the cool morning air, slowly warming with the newly risen sun.

The woodland track ahead was empty, just like my heart.

Arlan was gone.

I'd never meet another man like him. Or ever have the love of a man like him... in this world. I clenched my hands into fists. I should've forced the point further and insisted. No matter what.

And just gone through behind him!

I sprang into a run, right to the very spot where Arlan had disappeared. George didn't try to stop me this time.

Maybe the portal was still open. I'd go through and face whatever was there.

I ran past the place.

Nothing.

I turned and ran through it once more.

Not even a surge of energy. Or a tingle.

Surely, I would've sensed something!

"Rhiannon?" George's voice held a hint of reproach.

Too Late! I gnashed my teeth and fisted my hands.

"Rhiannon? Are you okay?"

217

The rain started again, heavy drops pelting my head. Cold dripped down my face, threatening to wash away Arlan's kiss. I pressed my palms to my cheeks.

"Rhiannon." George stepped beside me now. "Put your hood up, you're getting drenched."

My shoulders slumped, and I dropped my hands to my sides. George was just being his usual *good friend* self—faithfully with me in my turmoil.

"George. I love him." I looked him in the eye. *There, George knows for certain now.*

George's gaze hardened a touch. "Yes, but he's gone." He shrugged. "I doubt you'll ever see him again."

I pressed my lips together, trying to prevent them trembling, and sucked in a stuttering breath.

He glanced at my mouth. "Sorry. I know that's a harsh thing to say, but it's reality, Rhiannon. How would he return?"

I spun and stormed down the hill.

"It was pure chance." George trod doggedly behind me. "And if he did return, how would he manage to come through at this exact point in time."

I couldn't stop the tremble in my lips. Hadn't he considered I'd thought through all of those issues? Argued the same point with Arlan? George didn't have to remind me!

And wait! Was George pleased Arlan had gone? I marched on, facing forward, determined not to answer him. If I did, I'd burst into tears.

"I'm only being realistic, Rhiannon."

I couldn't reply. Taking in air was difficult with my gut tightening further with each of George's comments. The rain pattered on my hood, almost drowning out what George said.

"—weird, bizarre even, to meet someone who claimed to be from another world. He was an interesting interlude in your life and—"

"Interlude?" I yelled, then stopped and pivoted into his face, fingernails digging into my palms. Didn't he care about my feelings in all of this? My throat nearly closed. *That's almost unforgivable!* "I'm going home. I'm determined to fight for Dál Gaedhle. I—"

"What do you mean, *home?*"

I sniffed. George's face loomed in front of me; his glasses covered in so many drops of rain it was a wonder he could see.

Oh, he'll find out soon enough.

"My parents adopted me. I'm originally from Dál Gaedhle." My thoughts came out staccato, matching the beat of my heart.

George raised his eyebrows. "Your parents were part of an adoption agreement between Scotland and Dál Gaedhle?"

"Don't be sarcastic, George." I narrowed my eyes. "It isn't becoming." I resumed my march, blinking away both rain and tears.

"Can you hear yourself, Rhiannon? He's brainwashed you."

What!

"So, you don't believe what you've experienced for yourself? George, you're the last person I thought would ridicule me. Or him." I glanced aside at him as we marched down the path. "You know he's real. So where he comes from is real."

"Yes, but you aren't from there."

We reached the yard, and I pushed ahead of him into the cottage. I ran straight for the bedroom, dug the tartan plaid from the trunk at the end of my bed, and stomped back to the kitchen. George was drying his spectacles with the kitchen hand towel.

"Look." I held up the tartan, crest foremost.

He gawked at it. "Where did you get that?" There was awe in his tone.

"From my mum. But Arlan says this"—I pointed to the eagle flying over a castle on an island in the middle of a loch— "is the clan crest of the noble house of Gallawain. His mother's house."

"So, he's your brother? That's sick, Rhiannon. Your brother kissed you—"

"No. Arlan said he'd know if we were related. Well, close ties anyway. I'm a distant cousin."

"And that sort of thing is okay in his world? It's regarded as incestuous here."

"George! He's the only one who's ever made me feel good about myself." Stirrings heated inside me, dispelling the cold my drenched hair trickled down my neck. "I'm not from here. That's why I'm odd." I winced. *It's not coming out right.* "Odd here, is what I mean. Oh!" I spun and strode into the living room. "I don't care how long he takes to return." I put my fists on my hips. "I'm going. I'll find a way."

"Rhiannon," George spoke in a tone you'd use on a mad person. "It may be a while. And even never. But I'll help you with your Gaelic." The rain beat on the roof. "I'm here for you, Rhiannon."

The heat in my veins cooled a little. "Thank you, George. I know you are. I'm sorry. I'm a bit..."

"It's okay, Rhiannon." George smiled in a forgiving way.

I stalked to the bathroom and grabbed a towel off the rail to dry my hair. My mind flashed back to the memory of the same action and handing a towel to a tall, muscular man with dripping wet, shiny black hair and eyes like the deep ocean, but speckled with a sharp navy-blue. I wiped the rain and tears away with the towel and faced the mirror full on, recalling Arlan's warm chest touching my back while he stated his opinion of me.

His words rang in my head. His affirming words, praising all that was *me* and most of it the reason I felt like an outsider—*in this world.*

I believe ye are a daughter of Dál Gaedhle.

Objects glinting next to the sink caught my eye. Round hair clasps, about the size of a ring and intricate in design, shone their solid silver beneath the bathroom lighting. I picked one up and turned it in my hand. Arlan wore them in his hair, warrior-style, to keep the loose strands from his eyes. I slipped it on my index finger. It fit perfectly.

I returned my vision to the mirror and into the reflection of my deep mauve eyes. My lids had narrowed slightly. I traced the lift of my shoulders as I inhaled a determined breath.

219

"I will be with you, Arlan. I *am* a woman of Dál Gaedhle, and I *will* go home."

THE END

Join Jenn Lees' newsletter group and be first to know release dates.
Join today and receive the free eBook novella, *Running with the Stags*, as a thank you gift.
https://jennleeswriter.com

Acknowledgments

This novel has been years in the making. The idea started in 1995 when, long before I took up writing, I imagined a warrior crashing into this world from one where loyalty, bravery and one's word mattered. I have written (and discarded) various drafts as I learned my craft and now I feel this story is finally ready for you all.

There are so many people to thank on this journey and I'll endeavour to list them all. Forgive me if I fail. It has been a while.

Firstly, to my editor Candida Bradford of *A Place Of Intent* Editorial Services. How can I say how much I enjoyed working with you? You picked up this manuscript, nudged and poked, and posed questions to get the best out of this writer, all with a gentle hand, and helped improve this story and its characters. Thank you, always. Love your work.

Thank you to my cover designer, Fiona Jayde Media, for great covers for this series and flexibility with the title changes.

My critique partners in Word Menders (part of Realm Makers). Karen Sweet, S L Dooley, M D Boncher, Nathan Veyon. You all made such a difference to the manuscript. I always appreciate your critical eyes and support, and that you aren't afraid to say what you think.

To my beta readers:

Gill Lister, Ileana Noble, Steve Briggs (who also told me to keep writing this story at a moment when I'd almost given up) Jill Williams, Sue Jacka and Jeni Franklin. You have all read drafts of various stages. I hope you like the finished product and thank you always for your comments.

Thank you Ink & Insights Competition judges for your comments over the three years I kept submitting this manuscript in its various forms. I'm also thankful that you never seemed to get sick of it.

To my writing buddy, Melinda Graham: thanks, wee sis, for your support, encouragement and always being there when I needed to talk about writing.

Thank you, Eifion. I am grateful for you allowing me to use your strong, beautiful Welsh Gaelic name for a most important character.

For the Gaelic, I referred to Am Faclair Beag, Scottish Gaelic Dictionary, and my memories of the language having lived close to a Gaelic speaker from the Isles. Apologies to any native speaker who hears my attempts at this beautiful tongue.

Lorraine McCluskey and Leanne Prosser. Your love of horses and comments and tips have enriched how I've presented these wonderful animals and their relationship with humans.

Thanks to our son, Frank, for fight scene tips.

Thanks to my husband, Frank, for finer points of rhyme in the old bard's song. (Even though I agree with Milton that verse doesn't need to rhyme.)

Our youngest daughter, Emma, my techno-wiz and seer. Your sharp eye and sense of story will be ever invaluable to me.

Finally, I'd like to express gratitude to my husband Frank. You love, protect and care for me as Arlan does for Rhiannon, so I hope you see elements of yourself in him, for once again, you're the inspiration for my story's hero.

RECOMMENDATION: read *MURTAIREAN: AN ASSASSIN'S TALE* prior to *OF WARRIORS AND SAGES: ARLAN'S PLEDGE BOOK TWO*

GLOSSARY of GAELIC and SCOTS WORDS

A gràidh chridhe	love of my heart
Am fuath	the fae
Àrd Ghliocas	high wisdom
Àrd Righ	high king
Bayrd	sings
Beul an latha	the dawn of the day
Beul na h-oidhche	the dusk of evening
Boireannaich	woman
Braw	Scots for good/great
Broch	round tower of iron age construction
Burn	a small watercourse, creek, brook
Cernunnos	Celtic god of beasts and wild places
Creagrubha	rocky outcropping
Cruinne	the globe/world
Cumhachd Adhar	power of the air/bad spirit
Dál	denotes belonging or ownership
Damainte	damned
Deamhan	demon/evil spirit
Dearg	to redden/draw blood
Dreich	Scots for dreary/ bleak

Droch dhuine	bad man/reprobate
Eilean	island
Fàistinnaech	wizard/prophet/diviner
Fannlag	weakling
Giorsal	grey hair
Gliocas	wisdom, prudence
Heid	Scots for head
Murtair	assassin
Muir	sea
Oidhche mhath	goodnight
Phelan	wolf-like
Ruairidh	red king
Sàsaichean	council
Sleaghach	spear
Stramash	Scots for disturbance, uproar
Tapaidh	clever smart brave heroic
Tobraichean na beatha	the fountain/source/issue of life
Tòireadh	a quest, diligent search
Trobhad	come here!
Uisge beatha	malt whisky
Weesht	Scots for *shush*

Author's Note

At the top of a steep climb up the hill behind Abernethy, Scotland, you can find the remains of Castle Law—once you have regained your breath. It is an Iron Age fortification. On the mound where once stood an earth works and stone based fort, you will find sections of a ruinous timber-laced wall (most of it covered over after a dig). The view of the River Tay and the valley through which it travels is magnificent. The information stand states that on a clear day you can see from the Trossacs to Dundee and the Tay Rail Bridge.

Whatever the reason, the exercise, the history or the view, the hike up the hill is inspiring at the most and exhausting at the least.

And it's where, since 1995, I've envisioned Arlan coming through from his world to ours. These old sites always stir my mind and emotions as I wonder what the people and their lives were like, and even if an ancestor or two of mine where among those who lived there. I love history and I love fantasy, and I find most of my inspiration for the latter comes from the former.

Of course, I have used a wee bit of poetic licence in my arrangement of Rhiannon's cottage and the hill behind it where the Iron Age Fortifications are situated. And no portal exists there... as far as I am aware.

There is an excellent museum in Abernethy itself right next to the Pictish round tower situated in the village. All very worth a look if ever you are there.

ADDITIONAL NOTE:

I (and other readers of this series) recommend reading *Murtairean: An Assassin's Tale* next as the characters and the stories overlap and intertwine at this point.

ABOUT AUTHOR

DESTINY RELATIONSHIP COURAGE

Award winning author Jenn Lees latest release, *Of High Kings and Mages: Arlan's Pledge Book Three*, reached the Semi-Finals in the OZMA Book Awards for Fantasy Fiction 2024 CIBAs (Chanticleer International Book Awards).

Of Warriors and Sages: Arlan's Pledge Book Two reached Semi-Finalist in the OZMA Book Awards for Fantasy Fiction 2023 (as the manuscript *The Quest*). Long Listed in the Realm Awards 2025 Fantasy Section. As the manuscript *The Quest* reached the Top 10 in Ink & Insights 2021.

Jenn Lees' Best Selling novel, *Of Myths And Portals: Arlan's Pledge Book One* achieved First Place Award (Gold) in The BookFest Fall 2024 Fiction-Romance-Fantasy, Second Place Award (Silver) in The BookFest fall 2024 Fiction-Fantasy-Magic, Myths and Legends, and Fiction-Christian-Fantasy

The Crossing: Arlan's Pledge Book 1, (Re-released as *Of Myths and Portals*) achieved the finals in the OZMA Book Awards for Fantasy Fiction (previous draft manuscript) CIBA 2021. *Restoring Time* (Book 4 of the *Community Chronicles Series*) reached the finals in the CYGNUS Awards for Science Fiction 2021 CIBA.

An Ink & Insights Competition judge says of *Arlan's Pledge*:

'Beautifully crafted, full of rich setting descriptions, tension that caught my attention and kept it, and characters that leapt off the page. This author is a skilled storyteller.' (Melody Quinn. Ink & Insights 2021 Competition Master Category Judge)

Retired nurse, Jenn has travelled extensively and lived on three continents. Scotland remains her source of inspiration.

Jenn loves walking through a forest and climbing a mountain to experience the view.

Her only disappointment in life is that time travel is not possible... apparently.

Find out more about Jenn Lees and her novels.

Sign up for the newsletter and receive *Running with the Stags*, a free novella in the *Arlan's Pledge Series*.

www.jennleeswriter.com

Want more of Jenn Lees?

Support Jenn Lees Fantasy Author on Patreon. https://www.patreon.com/c/jennle esfantasyauthor/members

Discover Vygeas' and Leyna's story in *Murtairean: An Assassin's Tale* , another novel by Jenn Lees set in the world of Dál Cruinne. Recommended reading prior to *Of Warriors and Sages Arlan's Pledge Book Two.*

ALSO BY JENN LEES

OF WARRIORS AND SAGES
ARLAN'S PLEDGE BOOK TWO
THE HEART QUEST MUST WIN

OF HIGH KINGS AND MAGES
ARLAN'S PLEDGE BOOK THREE
A KING MUST DIE

NOVELS IN THE WORLD OF DÀL CRUINNE

MURTAIREAN: AN ASSASSIN'S TALE
*RECOMMENDED READING PRIOR TO OF WARRIORS AND SAGES
ARLAN'S PLEDGE BOOK TWO*

AN ASSASSIN'S TWO HITS: ONE FROM THE PAST TO HAUNT HIM. ONE TO
FREE HIM

A MAGE WHO PURSUES ... AND A WARRIOR WOMAN WHO LINKS IT ALL

THE COMMUNITY CHRONICLES SERIES

THE CRASH
STOLEN TIME
SAVING TIME
RESTORING TIME

ALSO AVAILABLE IN AUDIO
(VIRTUAL VOICE)